THE
ARCANE
BARGAIN

Copyright © 2025 Kate McKinsey
All rights reserved.
ISBN: 978-1-966640-06-6 (hardcover)
ISBN: 978-1-966640-05-9 (paperback)
ISBN: 978-1-966640-04-2 (ebook)

DEDICATION

*To my readers—
Thank you for walking with me at the beginning of this journey.
There are so many more stories to tell, so many more hearts to unravel.
May your shelves overflow, and may you always find beauty in
villains who were never truly lost.*

CHAPTER 1

Zakar

She thought she could escape me.
For five years, she almost succeeded. Almost.

Zakar fastened the final strap of his gauntlet with a sharp tug, the leather creaking as it tightened against his wrist. He adjusted the black cloak draped across his shoulders, its silver trim catching the faint glow of the chamber's sconces. His reflection stared back at him from the tall mirror—formidable, unyielding, and ready. His thick black hair was tousled around his pale face, loosely falling down his back in waves, his green eyes fixed with cold clarity. This was the face of the man she had betrayed. The man she thought she could leave behind.

But no one escapes the Master of the Arcane.

His lips curved into a smug, satisfied smirk as he turned toward the desk dominating the room. A map of the kingdom lay unfurled across its surface, fine inked lines tracing roads, rivers, and the hidden paths where she had been rumored to appear over the past year.

For so long, she had been nothing more than a phantom—slipping through the dense trees of Farenvayle Forest, vanishing beneath the Hollow Mist whenever it descended, always just out of reach. But tonight, the chase was over.

Myrithia. Even thinking her name was an ache and an

accusation. She had walked into his life like a storm, unrelenting and destructive. For one fleeting moment, she had made him believe she could be something more. Something real. And then she had shattered that illusion with the cruel edge of her betrayal.

She had taken more than his trust. She had cost him his crown.

Zakar ran a gloved hand over the map, his fingers tracing the circle marking her location. He imagined her now, hiding in the depths of the enchanted forest, oblivious to how close he was. He had followed every whisper, every faint trail she had left behind, and now the charm cloaking her was failing. Even the Hollow Mist—dreaded and untamable, always shifting, always breathing—had receded, leaving her laid bare to the world.

"Myra," he said, low and aching, like the sound alone could summon her back to him.

By this time tomorrow, she would be in his grasp. She would kneel before him, and she would pay for everything she had done. He didn't just want her submission. He wanted *her*. In *every* sense of the word.

The smirk returned to his lips as he swept out of the room, his cloak billowing behind him like a shadow. Tonight, Myrithia would learn there was no escape.

CHAPTER 2

Myrithia

The scent of dried herbs hung in the air, mingling with the faint smokiness of the hearth fire as Myrithia prepared her tea. Sunlight streamed through the small window of her cottage, warming the wooden countertops where jars of leaves and blossoms sat in neatly arranged rows. Her hand trembled faintly as she reached for a small clay jar marked with a faded symbol, her fingers brushing the cool surface. Inside were the dried leaves of Valdoran sage, their potent, earthy aroma drifting upward as she unsealed the lid.

Her movements were unsteady and slow, careful not to spill as she shakily smoothed her fingertips inside the jar and emptied the last remnants of the leaves into a simple ceramic teapot. A kettle of water simmered over the flames, and she leaned down, carefully lifting it with a cloth-wrapped handle. Steam spiraled upward as she poured, the water hissing faintly as it met the leaves.

Myrithia sighed and stepped back, letting the tea steep while she inhaled deeply, the mere scent of the sage beginning to soothe her pain.

It had been happening more often lately—this creeping pain that would come as quickly as it would go —these unsettling moments of weakness. She pressed a hand to her chest, frowning at the dull ache beneath her ribs. The curse was spreading. She could feel it in her bones, a dark thread weaving itself tighter with each passing day. The only thing that helped, that granted her even a moment's reprieve, was the crushed leaves of Valdoran sage.

But her supply was gone. She had stretched it as far as she could, rationing every last leaf, but there was no delaying the inevitable. The Hollow Mist had finally retreated again, and that meant it was safe enough to go into town.

Her expression tightened.

It was never *truly* safe for her to go into town. But what choice did she have? And more pressing than the sage—more vital than anything else—was reaching the Arcane Citadel.

Master Sorien, if he didn't despise her like so many others, might take pity on her. Might hear her plea and help her. Because gods knew he was the last person left who could.

Forcing the thoughts aside, Myrithia tossed her long silver hair over her shoulder and picked up the teapot, carrying it to the small table outside. Her cottage was tucked deep within the Farenvayle Forest, hidden from the world by a charm she had woven years ago. The magic wrapped her home and the surrounding land in a protective shroud, obscuring her from even the most skilled of trackers, protecting her even from the effects of the Mist.

For five years, the Mist had shielded her from the world she had betrayed.

Where the Hollow Mist devoured all who entered-swallowed them whole with no whisper of return—she had carved out a pocket of safety. A meadow untouched by judgement. A cabin suspended between deadly reality and conjured safety. Her enchantment had woven roots into the soil, wrapped around the trees, whispered to the wind: This place is mine. And it is safe.

And for a time, it had listened.

But now, the charm frayed at the edges.

Her strength, once steady, had begun to flicker—like the final breath of a candle before the dark. It seemed even sanctuaries forgot how to shield a person when the world decided they no longer belonged. She could only hope her strength would hold on a little longer.

The forest stretched endlessly around her, a patchwork of

emerald and gold. The trees swayed gently in the breeze, their leaves catching the light and scattering it like jewels across the forest floor. Birds flitted from branch to branch, their songs a bright counterpoint to the hum of insects. A pair of deer emerged from the underbrush, their delicate movements cautious but unhurried as they grazed in the clearing.

Myrithia lowered herself into the chair by the table, cradling the teapot in one hand as she poured the amber liquid into a small porcelain cup. She let the steam rise, breathing it in before taking a tentative sip. The warmth spread through her, easing the discomfort in her limbs.

Her gentle blue eyes wandered over the peaceful scene, but her thoughts refused to stay tethered to the present.

How many more mornings like this would she have? A few months? Perhaps less? The curse was patient but unrelenting, unraveling her bit by bit. And the worst of it hadn't even started yet. She set the teacup down and folded her hands in her lap, staring at the worn fabric of her skirt.

Maybe I deserve this.

The thought whispered through her mind, unbidden but persistent. She clenched her hands together, willing it away. But it returned, stronger now, curling through her like smoke. She had made her choices. She had betrayed him.

Zakar.

His name lingered in her mind, a fresh wound that stung just as much as the day she fled. She had thought of him often in the years since—too often. The memory of his voice, his touch, his gaze haunted her like a phantom she could not banish. She had hurt him in ways that could never be undone.

Myrithia settled her stare over the trees in the distance, breathing in and out gently, letting the sunlight warm her face. The curse's slow grip felt almost merciful, a punishment she could not outrun. Maybe it was fair. Maybe it was justice.

She lifted the teacup to her lips, but before she could take another sip, something in the air wavered. The world outside the cottage remained untouched—golden light filtering through the trees, the soft rustle of wind through the leaves—but the space around her felt different. Tighter. Heavier.

Something was out there.

It wasn't the weight of the Hollow Mist—she had long since grown accustomed to its shifting gravity, learned to move with it as it ebbed and swelled over the years. No, this was different.

A pulse of energy, cold and menacing, sent a shiver racing down her spine. She wasn't imagining it. The presence remained unseen, intangible, yet she felt it closing in, pressing against her like invisible hands reaching, grasping.

Her fingers tightened around the cup. *Move*.

She pushed back from the table, rising swiftly to her feet. Her heartbeat was steady, her breath controlled, but the urgency in her movements betrayed her. She stepped inside, eyes flicking over the room with efficiency. She spied her cloak and she snatched it up, her heart beginning to race, preparing for the inevitable.

She had been careful for five years. She had been smart. But it wasn't enough.

She cast one last look around the small space, her stomach twisting as the reality settled in. This was the end of her time here. She had known it would come, but not like this—not so suddenly, not with this unseen force pressing against her chest.

Her grip on the teacup was the last thing to loosen. She exhaled in a rush and placed it on the table with quiet finality.

Then she turned to the door, her pulse hammering in her ears. She had run out of time.

CHAPTER 3

Zakar

The rain tore through the forest like a relentless drumbeat, lashing at Zakar's cloak, soaking through the heavy fabric and mingling with the earthy scent of wet leaves and decay. He stood unmoving beneath the storm, his hood drawn low over his face, as though the weight of the rain matched the weight of his thoughts. His emerald eyes burned with determination as they fixed on a faint shimmer ahead—a speck of silver so small and fleeting that only someone trained to notice such things would have seen it.

Behind him, his Sentinels waited, silent and still, half-swallowed by the stormlit gloom. They were nothing but wraiths in the darkness, their black skeletal forms shifting like smoke as they awaited his command.

Zakar reached out, his fingers brushing the silvery fleck suspended in the air. The moment he made contact, the magic unraveled, expanding outward with a low, resonant hum. An oval-shaped portal formed before him, its edges shimmering like liquid starlight. Within the portal, the same forest stretched out before him, but it was an entirely different world.

Bright sunlight poured through the canopy of trees, gilding the leaves in gold and green. Birds chirped, their songs weaving through the stillness. Squirrels darted across the ground, their small claws scratching over twigs and fallen leaves. The air seemed lighter, alive with the hum of an untouched world. It was the same place, yet it couldn't have been more different.

Zakar smirked, a faint curve of his lips that carried both triumph and amusement. "How quaint," he murmured, his voice barely audible over the rain. Without hesitation, he stepped through the portal.

The shift was immediate. The rain vanished, replaced by a warm, golden light that seeped through his cloak. The heaviness of the storm gave way to the gentle rustle of leaves and the soft crunch of earth beneath his boots. His Sentinels followed silently, their spectral forms brushing against the portal's edges as they crossed.

Zakar strode forward, his gaze keen as he scanned the forest around him. Twigs snapped beneath his steps, and dry leaves scattered in his wake. The air smelled of pine and wildflowers, fresh and unspoiled. Birds flitted from branch to branch, their wings a blur of motion. He let himself drink it in, the stark contrast to the cold, rain-soaked forest he had left behind.

It was almost poetic, he thought. Myrithia had always been like this—bright and elusive, always just out of reach. She had the uncanny ability to turn the bleakest of situations into something golden, slipping through his fingers before he could grasp her. Even now, after years of searching, she had managed to hide herself in a place that mirrored her nature so perfectly.

His eyes narrowed as the cozy silhouette of her cottage came into view. The smoke curling lazily from the chimney was the final confirmation. He had found her.

The corner of his mouth twitched upward again as he approached, his gaze sweeping over the simple structure. The weathered wood of the porch glowed faintly in the sunlight, and the windows were framed by climbing ivy. It looked peaceful, almost too peaceful for someone with a bounty as significant as hers.

Zakar climbed the steps of the porch, the wood creaking softly under his weight. His hand grazed the doorframe briefly before he pushed the door open and stepped inside.

The warmth of the cottage enveloped him, the smell of woodsmoke and herbs filled the air, mingling with the faint metallic tang of magic that clung to the walls. A fire crackled in the hearth, its glow casting flickering shadows across the modest room.

He let the door swing shut behind him, his gaze trailing over the small interior. Shelves lined the walls, crowded with jars of dried herbs and vials of unknown substances. A simple table sat in the center, and his gaze settled on the lone teacup resting on it. He stepped forward, lifting it carefully, the ceramic still faintly warm against his fingertips.

The faintest scent of Valdoran sage reached him as he breathed in, observing the scattered tea leaves at the base of the cup. His eyes narrowed as he caught sight of the soft stain on the rim—a faint, ghostly imprint of her lips, a shade of red he knew too well. His thumb brushed over it, a whisper of a touch, as a memory surfaced—her mouth curling into a knowing smile, those same lips pressing against his in the stolen moments of a past he had not yet let go of.

His jaw ticked, and with a sudden, purposeful motion, he placed the cup back down, the porcelain meeting wood with a sharper sound than intended. A silent reminder. She was not a memory. She had been here—only moments ago.

His boots thudded softly against the wooden floor as he moved deeper inside, his gaze sweeping the dim corners, scanning for even the smallest trace of her. But the room was empty, and with every passing second, his anticipation gave way to frustration.

The fire still burned, and the kettle was hot. She had been preparing tea, no doubt clinging to the rhythm of her quiet little life, as though the world wasn't hunting her.

Zakar's gaze flicked back to his Sentinels, their ghostly forms waiting in the doorway like silent sentries. "She couldn't have gone far," he said, his voice low and edged with anger. "Find her trail. Now."

The wraiths shifted, their forms dissolving into thin tendrils of smoke as they flowed back out into the forest.

His gaze fell to the desk by the window, where a stack of parchment lay haphazardly atop a small pile of books. One sheet, slightly askew, caught his attention. He picked it up, his fingers brushing against the worn edges.

It was a *wanted* notice, with Myrithia's likeness sketched

in flawless detail, her name clearly printed below it. The sum beside her name had grown—a clear indication that the crown was growing impatient. He scoffed under his breath; no one in the kingdom held true loyalty to the king, but coin had a way of turning even the faithless into eager hunters.

His fingers twitched at his side, the mere thought of Draevok, that damned usurper, seizing her sending a slow, burning fury through his chest. For all the grievances he carried against Myrithia, none compared to the seething loathing he felt for the tyrant who had taken his crown, his kingdom, and sullied everything it stood for. Draevok had reduced Valthoria to a shadow of its former glory, his reign marked by oppression, corruption, and cruelty. The man had slighted him in every conceivable way—stealing the throne that should have been his, spreading lies to discredit him, and using those closest to him as pawns in his pursuit of power.

This hatred was not just personal—it was his purpose. A duty etched into the very marrow of his being. Draevok deserved to suffer, to feel the weight of every life he had crushed under his reign. Zakar would strip him of his power, his pride, and finally, his life. And when Draevok lay broken at his feet, all of Valthoria would see that there was only one man fit to rule the kingdom. Zakar would reclaim his throne, the throne that was his birthright.

He stepped back, letting the bounty poster drop softly to the floor. He stalked out of the cottage, his boots crunching against the forest floor, the rage simmering in his chest only growing as he stepped into the warm glow of the enchanted sunlight.

The stark contrast of the idyllic scene to his own seething frustration was almost mocking. Hummingbirds flitted above his head, marmots and dormice darted playfully through the underbrush, and the breeze carried the faintest hint of wildflowers. It was perfect—too perfect. And it grated against him like iron scraping stone.

He let out a sharp breath, his lips curling in disdain. With a swift wave of his hand, his magic surged outward, colliding with the charm that enveloped the forest. The illusion cracked, splintering like delicate glass. The pieces shimmered briefly, refracting the false sunlight in a cascade of colors before falling to the ground and vanishing into the same glittering dust that was unmistakably hers.

The sunlight gave way to darkness. The rain came back hard, a punishing downpour that blurred the world around him and stung against his skin. The cheerful melody of the forest was replaced by the steady drumbeat of raindrops against leaves, the occasional groan of wind through the trees. Above him, the moon hung in the sky, obscured by thick clouds that churned like a restless sea.

The transformation was instantaneous, and the contrast left him standing there, drenched, his jaw tight with irritation. Even the animals scattered, their momentary peace replaced by the harsh reality of the storm.

Zakar's gaze shifted back to the cottage—or what was left of it. The charming, cozy structure he had entered mere moments ago was now a crumbling ruin. Its roof sagged under the weight of moss and rot, mushrooms sprouted along the walls, and trees grew through what had once been her home.

His lips twitched, half in frustration, half in reluctant admiration.

She had built this life for herself, piece by painstaking piece, hiding away from the world, from him, from the Mist—ensconced in a sanctuary woven from the very fabric of her own power.

But no spell lasted forever.

And for all her skill, for all her clever little tricks, she would not evade him. There would be no more hiding.

Not from him.

Not from his Sentinels.

He would find her.

CHAPTER 4
Myrithia

The rain needled down in icy sheets, blurring her vision and hissing through the leaves as she pushed deeper into the forest. Water streamed down her face, mixing with the sweat beading along her brow, but she barely felt it.

Her fingers flared with magic, silver specks igniting in the darkness like fleeting stars. With a sudden burst of energy, she flashed forward, her body surging fifty feet ahead.

The world blurred. Trees warped past in streaks of green and shadow.

Then—another flare. Another fifty feet.

Her breath came rough, shallow, burning with every inhalation. *Just a little more. Just keep going.*

Whatever was tracking her was moving slower than she was. If she could keep this up, she could outrun it—lose it in the storm, vanish into the night.

Lightning flickered in the distance, illuminating the twisting branches and jagged terrain. She grit her teeth, fingers sparking, and propelled herself forward again.

The burst of magic tore through her body like a lash. Too much.

Her chest heaved, every muscle burning under the strain. She was weakening.

But she couldn't stop.

The next jolt of power barely carried her. Only ten feet this time. A choked sound left her lips. She stumbled, dizzy, catching herself against the rough bark of a tree, her palm scraping against the wet, uneven surface.

She couldn't feel her pursuers anymore, but instead felt something else.

The forest had gone still.

Her vision blurred, rain streaking across her lashes, but beyond the haze—a thick, curling fog loomed just ahead.

The Hollow Mist.

Her lungs seized mid-breath.

It had receded over time, but in her frantic escape, she had somehow chased it down. It lingered before her, swirling and waiting—as if it had always been there, waiting for her.

Her pulse roared in her ears, pounding with a chaotic, erratic rhythm. But beneath that—beneath the storm, the rain, and the panic—she thought she heard something else.

It was soft. Familiar.

A whisper, calling to her.

Without thinking, she stepped forward. Then another step followed, unbidden.

Her limbs felt weightless, detached, as though they no longer belonged to her—as if they were answering to something else entirely.

She knew it was wrong—knew she should turn away. But she had never been this close before. She had lived beneath it, hidden under the safety of charms and wards, but she had never touched it.

Her heart slowed. Her breath fogged the air, soft and slow.

Her pale, trembling hand reached out—

"Stop!"

The sharp cry shattered the trance. A man's voice, distant but urgent, cutting through the hush.

Myrithia froze, the breath she hadn't realized she was holding finally releasing in a violent exhale. She turned, her vision swimming, struggling to focus.

A man was approaching—his form blurred by rain and

exhaustion, his movements slow and deliberate. The only thing she could make out clearly was the pale gleam of moonlight reflecting off his bald head.

His arms were raised slightly, his stance careful, as if he were approaching a wild animal poised to bolt.

Myrithia squinted, trying to get a better look, but the world lurched beneath her feet. She stumbled, her legs buckling.

A tree caught her fall, her trembling fingers scratching against the bark as she tried to steady herself. She let out a low exhale, the breath shaky in her throat. Then came a shift in the air—subtle, but unmistakable.

The man no longer sounded concerned.

"I don't believe this," he murmured, voice edged with intrigued disbelief.

Her breath quickened.

Slowly, her blurred vision sharpened, focusing on the glint of brass—a sword handle, sheathed at his hip.

Her heartbeat slammed against her ribs.

Not a traveler. Not some harmless stranger.

She lifted her gaze, scanning beyond him—past his broad shoulders, toward the firelight flickering in the distance.

A bonfire burned bright in the night, casting long shadows against the trees. And around it stood five men, all of them watching her. Tension coiled like a noose around her throat.

Bandits?

She didn't have time to process, didn't have time to react, because the man lunged. His fingers clamped around her arm, tight as iron, and in one violent jerk, he dragged her forward. A strangled, frightened yelp ripped from her throat, her nails clawing at his grip, at the slick mud beneath her heels as she fought against him.

Panic exploded inside her. Her power flared at her fingertips, her body acting on pure desperation. Silver sparks ignited and she vanished from his hold, but only for a heartbeat. She flickered a mere foot behind him, collapsed to her knees, her limbs boneless, useless. Her chest heaved, her fingers twitching. She tried again, but still *nothing*.

The sparks fizzled and died before they could even take form.

THE ARCANE BARGAIN

She had nothing left. She had spent everything trying to outrun her pursuers, and now she had no way to escape. Terror clawed at her throat, raw and suffocating. She scrambled, trying to summon even the weakest flicker of magic, but her body betrayed her, her power as drained as her strength.

The man above her laughed. The sound was deep, rolling, triumphant, but his voice was already fading into the distance. The world tilted, her vision darkening at the edges.

The cold earth pressed against her cheek, the rain soaking into her skin, muffling the sound of the men closing in.

Then there was nothing.

CHAPTER 5
Myrithia

Myrithia's eyes fluttered open, her senses slowly returning as the world around her sharpened into focus. The wet, earthy scent of the forest filled her nose, mingling with the faint hint of smoke from a recently extinguished fire. The full moon filtered through the dense canopy above, casting dappled patterns of moonlight across the ground. The cold bite of metal against her wrists and the unforgiving pull of a chain in front of her jolted her fully awake.

Her heart lurched violently as she fully grasped the extent of her captivity. Shackled, the heavy irons weighing down her wrists and chafing her skin. The chain connected her to the back of a worn, weathered wagon, its wheels caked in mud. The ground beneath her was damp from the rain, but mercifully the rain had ceased pouring for a while.

How long had she been unconscious?

She tilted her head, eyes searching the sky. The moon hung only slightly lower than before.

Not long. An hour, maybe. No more than that.

Around her, the camp was in movement. Five men, gruff and rugged, moved with the efficiency of seasoned travelers. Saddles were secured to horses, packs were hoisted, and the remnants of a dying campfire were kicked over, its embers smoldering weakly before fading into the wet earth.

A shadow fell over her, and she stiffened as a tall, broad-shouldered man approached. Her heart sank as she immediately recognized him—the bald man who had called out to her beside the Mist.

The rogue's presence was commanding, his posture exuding the confidence of someone who had lived his life with a blade in hand and had taken whatever he wanted without consequence.

"Now that you're awake, I suppose we can extend pleasantries." His tone was all slow confidence, a smirk playing at his lips as he crouched before her. "The name's Kierdan." He extended a hand toward her in feigned civility, then flicked his eyes toward her shackled wrists with a knowing chuckle. Clicking his tongue, he curled his fingers back into his palm. "Ah, right. Maybe later."

A sick wave of unease coiled in her gut as Kierdan's gaze dragged lazily down her cloaked form—as if the fabric wasn't even there.

His eyes lingered.

Her chest. Her waist. Her legs.

She recoiled instinctively, the cold bite of iron cutting into her wrists as she shifted against the chains.

Kierdan chuckled—a slow, indulgent sound, thick with amusement. He was savoring this.

"Can you believe my luck?" he drawled. "Here I was, minding my own business, enjoying a quiet evening, and what do I see? An old woman, walking willingly toward the Mist." His smile widened, lazy and knowing. "Thought you'd lost your wits. Thought I should stop you. Imagine my surprise when I realized who you were."

His voice was smooth, casual—but his eyes gleamed with something else.

Something darker.

"Myrithia," he mused, tilting his head. "The famed white-haired traitor to King and country, stumbling right into my camp in the dead of night." He exhaled, his gaze crawling over her once more. "And far lovelier than the Wanted notices give you credit for."

Her pulse hammered.

Kierdan leaned in, lowering his voice to something silkier, filthier.

"I can see why the Prince let you lead him to ruin. If I had a woman like you in my bed, I'd have let you ruin me too."

His grin turned wicked, a slow stretch of teeth.

"Hell," he murmured, "I have half a mind to lift your dress right now—see what all the fuss is about."

Laughter rumbled from his men a few feet away.

One of them muttered something low, something vile, and the sound of it slithered under her skin, foul and suffocating.

Nausea fluttered at the edges of her stomach. But she refused to react. She would not give them the satisfaction.

She forced herself still, locking every muscle into place, willing her face into ice—as if their words, their eyes, their filth meant nothing to her at all. She would not let them see the fear licking at the edges of her composure, even as it clawed violently in her chest.

"Why are you doing this?" she demanded, though the answer was obvious.

He knew exactly who she was.

And in a kingdom where every bounty hunter and mercenary wanted her head, that made her a prize worth taking.

Kierdan straightened, brushing a stray leaf from his tunic as though she were nothing more than a mild inconvenience. "Because of the bounty, of course." His tone was light, conversational, like they were discussing a simple business deal. "You're worth a fortune, sorceress. Enough to make me and my men very comfortable for a very long time."

Her insides pulled tight at the thought of being delivered to Draevok, but she forced herself to meet his gaze.

He chuckled lowly, his eyes still raking over her in a way that made her skin crawl. "In fact..." he mused, throwing a glance over his shoulder at his men. "Might be a shame to ride through the night when we could re-light the campfire, hmm? Get some extra rest for the journey ahead. Pass the time. Release some tension."

THE ARCANE BARGAIN

A ripple of agreement passed through the mercenaries, the meaning beneath his words making Myrithia's blood run cold. Her muscles went rigid, but she bit her tongue, refusing to react.

Kierdan smirked, clearly entertained by her discomfort. He crouched lower, his face inches from hers. "Lucky for you, my lust for gold outweighs my lust for women." His voice dropped, and before she could jerk away, his hand landed on her thigh, his fingers pressing in just enough to make her breath hitch. He gave her a slow squeeze, the touch far too familiar, far too intentional. "For now."

Revulsion slithered through her like poison.

His thumb stroked once before he withdrew, standing as if nothing had happened. "We ride now," he told her, his voice deep with authority. "But you'll be traveling in *my* lap. Perhaps I can have both my lusts sated this evening." He shot her a wink before sauntering off toward his horse, leaving her frozen in place, bile rising in her throat.

She had to get out of here. Now.

Before it was too late.

Myrithia tugged again at the chains, her frustration mounting as the irons refused to budge. She twisted her wrists, ignoring the sting of the metal digging into her skin, but it was useless.

She needed to think. She needed a plan. The Arcane Citadel was waiting, and every second in these irons dragged her further from it. Time was slipping through her grasp like sand through an open palm—wasted, irretrievable. If she didn't act now, she might never reach it at all.

Her fingers twitched as she stretched her aching hands, testing the weight of the chains. Slowly, she turned her gaze to her fingertips, wiggling them slightly—and there it was.

Soft silver sparks flickered to life. Her magic had returned. Not fully, but enough to try. She cast a quick glance toward the mercenaries. They were still preoccupied, loading supplies, tightening the straps on their saddlebags, their voices low, unconcerned. For now, they weren't watching her.

But Kierdan was moving.

She felt his gaze begin to shift—felt the moment slipping

away. Seconds. That's all she had. Desperation ignited her magic, weak but answering. It flickered hot in her chest, surging to her fingertips, seeping into the iron shackles that bound her. Silver specks shimmered, swirling like dust caught in moonlight, gathering around her hands as she focused and pushed.

The metal snapped open. Clenching her fists, she summoned what little strength remained, forcing her magic outward in a final, desperate surge. A figure materialized in front of her. It was an exact likeness of herself, standing tall, unshackled, her silver hair gleaming in the moonlight.

Kierdan froze mid-step, his keen eyes locking onto the illusion. The shock on his face lasted only a breath before twisting into fury.

He bit out a harsh curse, lunging forward.

Fake Myrithia turned her head toward him, a taunting smile curling her lips before she vanished in a blink of silver light, only to reappear behind him.

Kierdan spun around, wild-eyed, just as the illusion tapped him lightly on the shoulder. His men shouted in confusion as she disappeared again, reappearing a few feet away, looking entirely unbothered, almost playful. It was enough.

Myrithia breathed through the burning ache in her chest and bolted. The mercenaries' shouts rang behind her as the illusion continued to bait them, flickering from place to place, leading them further into the dense forest. Their curses filled the air, boots crashing through the underbrush, the chaos covering the sound of her real escape.

She stumbled toward the horses, her fingers trembling as she reached for the nearest one. The animal tensed, sensing her urgency, but she pressed a hand to its neck and whispered an incantation, her voice barely more than breath.

The horse stilled, its muscles relaxing beneath her palm.

"Good," she whispered, her fingers threading into its mane as she hoisted herself onto its back.

A final glance toward the mercenaries showed Kierdan and his men still snarling in frustration, their attention fully on the illusion that continued to flicker between the trees. She gritted her teeth and kicked the horse into motion.

THE ARCANE BARGAIN

The hooves struck the wet earth with silent force, the enchantment muffling the sound as she rode into the night. Cold air rushed past her, whipping her cloak behind her, the trees blurring as she pressed forward.

The Arcane Citadel. She had to make it before it was too late.

She didn't look back. She couldn't. Not until the fortress of magic was in sight and she was beyond reach.

CHAPTER 6

Zakar

Kierdan lay sprawled on the damp forest floor, his breath coming in ragged gasps, his body trembling under what might be his imminent demise. Around him, the corpses of his men lay still, their lifeblood soaking into the earth, steam rising faintly where warmth met the chill of the night. The scent of iron hung heavy in the air, mingling with the petrichor left behind by the rain.

A boot pressed against Kierdan's chest, pinning him down. Above him, Zakar loomed, his eyes glinting like a blade catching the moonlight.

"I'll ask you one more time," he said, voice smooth as silk but edged with something dangerous. "Where did she go?"

Kierdan swallowed hard, his pulse likely a frantic drum against his ribs. His lips parted, but no immediate answer came—only a desperate wheeze. Zakar's patience thinned. He had neither the time nor the inclination to entertain useless men.

He leaned in slightly, his magic simmering in the air around them. "If your next words aren't useful, I'll gut you like the others and step over your corpse without a second thought."

"She vanished," Kierdan finally sputtered, his voice shaking. "I swear it! One moment she was there, then she was gone—I don't know where she went, Arcane Master, I swear! Spare me, I had no idea you were also seeking her!"

Zakar scoffed, sarcasm threading through his ire. "Of course you didn't. But that hardly matters now, does it?"

The bounty had risen. And with it, the greedy and the foolish had come crawling, blind to the danger they had invited upon themselves.

How unfortunate that these particular fools had simply been camping for the night—utterly unaware that Myrithia would be the one to stumble upon them. If she continued crossing paths with mercenaries before the night's end, it would make for a bloody evening. At this rate, he'd be the one painting the forest red by dawn—one hapless fool at a time.

Zakar sighed, irritation coursing through him.

That damn silver hair of hers—she might as well be a beacon to every cutthroat desperate for coin.

In the entire kingdom, no one under eighty bore hair like hers. If she wasn't using a glamour to disguise herself, then she was either arrogant or simply being foolish.

Kierdan flinched as Zakar's fingers flexed at his side, dark energy crackling at his fingertips. "Please," Kierdan rasped. "Let me go. I'll—I'll leave the bounty alone. I won't hunt her again, I swear it!"

Zakar studied him, expression cool, calculating. He was already growing bored. There was no satisfaction in killing a man who had already surrendered to fear.

"Then you'll do something useful with your life." He leaned down slightly, lowering his voice to a measured whisper. "Deliver a message to the king."

Kierdan's breath stilled, his eyes wide.

Zakar smiled coldly. "Tell him: The woman is mine."

Kierdan barely had time to process the words before Zakar's fist collided with his temple. His body jerked once, then went still.

Zakar shaking off his hand as he turned to his Sentinels lingering just beyond the glow of the moonlight.

"Find her."

Without hesitation, the creatures dissipated into the night, their movements soundless as they melted into the trees. Zakar exhaled slowly, rolling his shoulders before stepping over the bodies of the mercenaries he had slain.

His fingers tensed at his side, still thrumming with the residual fury from the moment he had laid eyes on her in the clearing. The way she had ghosted through the air, taunting them as they shouted their obscene, lewd threats to her, moving with an almost playful grace. He had caught her, had wrapped his fingers around her delicate wrist—and then she had dissolved into a shimmer of silver dust.

An illusion.

His jaw clenched. He had been foolish to let excitement override reason. His initial thrill had turned to wrath the moment he realized he'd been tricked. The mercenaries had never stood a chance, but perhaps their end had been more brutal than necessary.

Zakar turned, his gaze sweeping the remnants of the clearing. The horses were still tethered to the trees, shifting uneasily, their breath misting in the cold night air.

Something itched at the back of his mind. Slowly, he began to count. One. Two. Three. Four. Five.

Five horses.

His gaze flicked to the dead men on the ground, the leader unconscious among them. Six.

His lips twitched, the beginnings of a smirk tugging against the remnants of his annoyance. Clever girl.

She had stolen a horse.

Zakar exhaled, rolling his wrists as a slow, knowing grin stretched across his lips.

He would catch her.

***

The dawn bled across the horizon, its soft golden hues breaking through the thick canopy of the forest, spreading fractured light upon the damp earth below. Zakar remained still atop his black steed, his emerald eyes locked on the figure moving in the distance. *Myra.*

She stood at the threshold of the Arcane Citadel—his home, his stronghold—its towering silhouette a formidable presence against the morning sky. The great fortress was carved from obsidian stone, its dark spires reaching toward the heavens like grasping talons. The walls shimmered faintly with arcane sigils, protection wards that repelled the unworthy. Only those attuned to magic could breach its barriers, could walk beyond its looming gates without being turned away by the very fabric of its defenses. And yet, there she was, taking careful, hesitant steps forward, utterly unaware that she was walking into her own entrapment.

Zakar's expression shifted, the smallest trace of satisfaction touching his mouth. Fate had an exquisite sense of irony. For years, he had scoured the land, pursuing the phantom of her existence. And now, after all this time, she had come to him. Willingly.

Had she any inkling of what she was walking into? Of the many bounties placed upon her head, did she have even the faintest notion that he was among those hunting her? He doubted it. She had no reason to suspect him. No reason to believe that the prince she had once betrayed was now the Master of the Arcane, the sovereign of the Citadel itself. Perhaps she thought it still belonged to the old mage who ruled before him, Master Sorien.

It hardly mattered.

His fingers pulled tighter around the reins as he recalled the moment he had found her, just before the break of dawn. His sentinels had tracked her through the night, guiding him through the dense woodland with a hunter's precision. There, in the clearing, he had watched as she tied her stolen horse to a tree just outside the Citadel's reach, unaware of how close she had come to meeting her fate. He had considered taking her then— swooping in like a shadow, capturing her before she could flee once more. But as he had sat back, watching, realization had dawned upon him.

She had been walking toward the Citadel of her own volition.

And the moment he had known her destination, his patience became an indulgence.

The sheer poetry of it was too delicious to ruin with premature action. Let her step willingly across that enchanted threshold. Let her believe she was seeking shelter, safety. Let her think she was making a choice. Because once she passed through those gates, she would never leave unless he willed it.

Zakar inhaled deeply, straightening his posture as he gave his horse a slight nudge forward.

It was time to prepare for his guest's arrival. He had waited five long years for this reunion. The least he could do was make sure she was comfortable... in her new prison.

CHAPTER 7

Myrithia

The Arcane Citadel loomed before Myrithia, its towering spires knifing into the gray morning sky, its stone walls veined with shifting runes that pulsed faintly, alive with enchantment. She stepped forward, her heart hammering against her ribs as she approached the massive wrought-iron gates.

The moment she neared, the doors groaned open on their own, a whisper of magic stirring in the cold air around her. Two knights clad in dark armor strode out to meet her, their presence stark, imposing. One of them, helmless with a scar cutting through his left brow, took her in with a scrutinizing glance.

"State your purpose," he said, his voice clipped.

Myrithia lowered her chin, resecuring her hood lower against her face. "I need to see the Master of the Arcane," she said, willing her voice to remain steady. "It's urgent."

The knight studied her for a moment before inclining his head. "Follow."

As she stepped past the threshold of the Citadel, something inside of her wrenched. A sudden pull in her core, as if a vital part of her had suddenly been severed. Her steps faltered, breath hitching as she reached instinctively for her power—only to find nothing.

She stopped, her fingers twitching.

The knight turned back to her, an eyebrow lifting in question.

"Why do you hesitate?"

Myrithia clenched her jaw. "There's a magic dampening spell here."

The knight chuckled. "Naturally," he said, as if it were the most obvious thing in the world. "The Master does not tolerate threats. The entire Citadel is enchanted to suppress magic. Keeps things... civil."

Civil. She scoffed inwardly at the thought. It was nothing more than a way for the Master to keep himself untouchable. A magic-nullifying spell ensured there were no battles within these walls, that no sorcerer or mage could rise against him in his own stronghold. But while it leveled the field for some, it left her at a distinct disadvantage. She was small. Slight. Without her magic, she was nothing but a lone woman in a den of wolves.

The knight watched her, as if reading her thoughts. "You can turn back, if you're having second thoughts."

Myrithia hesitated, staring at the long hall stretched before her, the dim torches lining the walls flickering in unnatural hues of blue and green. *A trap,* her instincts whispered.

But she had no choice.

If she left now, she'd be stepping straight into Draevok's clutches. And she knew with a sick certainty that he would never stop hunting her. There would be no second chances. This was her only real hope.

So she squared her shoulders, lifted her chin, and said, "No. I'll continue."

The knight smirked. "Very well." Then he turned, leading her deeper into the Citadel.

The halls swallowed them in a quiet hush, save for the occasional murmur of voices behind the doors they passed. The air smelled of ink and parchment, aged stone and something distinctly magical—a scent that was neither metallic nor earthly, but something in between.

The walls were adorned with lush, velvety drapes in deep emerald, sapphire, and crimson, shifting subtly in the still air as if caught in an unseen current. Enchanted flames flickered in gilded sconces, their glow trailing across the black marble like liquid gold.

THE ARCANE BARGAIN

Magic pulsed beneath every stone, every breath of air in this place, a quiet reminder of the power she could no longer reach. It mocked her, withheld just beyond her grasp. Yet even if she had access to her magic, she knew it would do little to protect her here. She was surrounded by those who had every reason to despise her, and no doubt, many did. She could hardly blame them.

Even the Master of this citadel, the one she had come seeking, would likely have cause to hold her in contempt. She had met him once, years ago—a fleeting encounter, yet one that lingered in her memory. He had taken an interest in her then, enough to offer her an apprenticeship. But that had never been her choice to make. Draevok had already claimed her as his servant, and his grip had never loosened.

Myrithia's eyes flickered to the figures moving through the corridors—men in robes marked with sigils of rank, murmuring amongst themselves, their gazes keen and shrewd. Others, clad in leathers or enchanted armor, strode through the halls with purpose. A sanctum for magic users. A sanctuary, in some ways.

But not all who walked these halls were allies. There were rivalries here, feuds simmering beneath polite exteriors. This was a viper's nest, and its peace was fragile, held together by the single truth that none of them could act against one another. Without magic, it was only a matter of wit and strategy that kept them alive.

She swallowed. Here, she was exposed. She had spent years avoiding places like this, places where mages gathered in clusters, measuring one another in the quiet ways of their kind. She kept her hood low, trying to appear as a mere nameless, faceless phantom in these halls.

The knight led her through the vast corridors until they reached a large waiting chamber.

It was a richly furnished room, with arched windows that let in the pale dawn light, the thick curtains drawn partially closed. A long table sat in the center, flanked by high-backed chairs upholstered in dark green velvet. Along the far wall, a stone hearth crackled softly, warming the otherwise cool space.

But she wasn't alone.

Two men sat within, their conversation halting as they turned their heads toward her. Their eyes raked over her cloaked form as she stepped inside, and she quickly lowered her hood a fraction further, obscuring more of her face.

The knight beside her didn't seem to notice—or care. He gestured toward one of the chairs. "The Master of the Arcane will see you shortly." Then, without another word, he turned and strode out, shutting the door behind him.

Myrithia exhaled, steadying herself. She had made it this far, but she was not safe yet. She sat rigid in her chair, the nervous tremor in her fingers betraying her outward calm. She wasn't sure if it was from the relentless curse threading through her veins or the sheer gravity of her predicament.

A shift of movement across the room caught her eye. The two men who had been loitering near the hearth abandoned their idle conversation and approached her. One slid into the chair opposite her, leaning back as if they were old friends settling into a casual discussion. The other moved behind her, his presence a looming weight pressing at her spine.

She tensed.

A hand grasped the hem of her hood.

"Myrithia?" The voice behind her carried a note of wicked amusement.

She snapped her head to the side, but before she could react, her hood was pulled down, her silver hair spilling free. Instinct took over, and she moved to stand, but strong hands landed on her shoulders, pressing her firmly into place.

"What are you doing here?" the man behind her murmured, voice dripping with interest. She didn't know him, but he seemed to know *her*.

Her skin crawled.

"That's none of your concern," she answered, forcing steel into her voice. "Leave me alone. I'm here on business."

The man across from her chuckled, leaning forward as he rested his elbows on the table. His smirk was slow and knowing. "Your business is our business," he said. "After all, you played a role in Draevok's rise to power, didn't you? And now, we all get to reap the consequences."

Tension roiled through her middle like a storm waiting to break. She had anticipated danger the moment she stepped foot in the Arcane Citadel, but she hadn't expected it to come so soon. Nor in this particular form.

"Let me guess," she bit out. "You're either planning to kill me, or you're hoping to drag me to Draevok like a loyal hound to fill your pockets."

The man behind her laughed softly, the sound of it grating against her ear. "Oh, I'd never hand anything of value over to him." His hands didn't tighten, didn't shake her, but his grip was firm enough that she knew it was a warning. "The only thing I want from you," he mused, "is repayment."

Her heart pounded. "Repayment?"

The man across from her tapped a finger on the wooden surface, his smirk fading into something colder. "I lost nearly everything when Draevok took the throne. My wealth, my home, my title. I want to see the man burn." His eyes darkened as he added, "And if I can't have that, well, perhaps taking your life will make me feel better."

Myrithia's pulse thundered in her ears.

"What seems to be the problem?"

The voice cut through the room like a blade.

Myrithia froze.

She knew that voice. Knew it in the depths of her bones, in the hidden corners of her memories, in the remnants of stolen touches and whispered words that no longer belonged to her.

No.

No, it couldn't be.

Her chest tightened, her breath shallow, as she turned her head, dread creeping through her limbs like ice.

And then—

Zakar.

Draped in black, his long, tousled hair spilling over the fine fabric of his tunic, his vivid green eyes holding a knowing glimmer.

He was watching her.

Watching her with the same smirk that had once left her breathless, the same smirk that now sent terror pooling deep in her gut.

Her pulse pounded in her ears, her body torn between two warring instincts—fight, flee.

Or maybe, some traitorous part of her whispered, *run into his arms like you once did.*

She silenced the thought before it could fester.

The two men stiffened immediately. One of them muttered, "Master," while the other bowed his head and murmured, "Dark One."

The words echoed in her mind, crashing through her like a tidal wave.

Master?

The Master of the Arcane.

The realization struck, cold and absolute.

Zakar was the Master of the Arcane.

The breath she'd been holding escaped in a trembling exhale.

She was trapped.

A long silence stretched between them as Zakar took a step forward, his gloved hands clasped behind his back.

His gaze flicked to the two men, his smirk deepening, edged with quiet condescension.

"Let's not be uncivil, gentlemen," he mused, the smooth cadence of his voice laced with performative courtesy. "I was under the impression that my citadel was a place of sanctuary."

The man behind her stepped away instantly. The other looked uneasy, but forced a placating smile.

"Just exchanging words, my lord."

Zakar hummed, tilting his head. "Is that so?" His green eyes flicked to hers. A single glance, peeling through her like a blade sliding through silk.

She tried to steel herself, but his scrutiny was too precise, too unnerving. There had been a time—long ago, another life ago—when those same eyes had looked at her differently. When they had held warmth. Devotion. Love. A time when she had wanted nothing more than to drown in that gaze. But now?

Now, it was hunger. It was power. It was vengeance, sharpened into something dangerous and cold.

And still—gods help her—she felt something beneath the fear.

Something dormant, buried, wretched. She wanted to look away, but she couldn't.

"Well, I do believe I require a word with the lady myself," Zakar said, his voice smooth as silk. "In private."

The men hesitated.

Zakar arched a brow, his smirk never wavering. "Do you require an invitation to stand down?"

The pressure of his authority sent both men retreating at once. They muttered apologies, bowing before stepping away.

Myrithia remained rigid in her seat, her mind racing.

She had two options. If she stayed, she would die. If she followed Zakar, she would die. And he knew it, and likely rejoiced in it.

His gloved hand extended toward her. "Come," he said smoothly. "Let's get you settled."

Myrithia stared at his offered hand as if it were a viper poised to strike. There was nowhere to run. Nowhere left to hide. She was caged, and he knew it.

Ignoring his hand, she stood stiffly, brushing past him. "Lead the way."

Zakar chuckled, utterly delighted as he turned, falling into step beside her. "Of course," he murmured, his voice dripping with satisfaction.

She stole one last glance at the men who had threatened her, knowing they were no longer her immediate concern.

No. Now, her problem was far, far worse. Because she was walking straight into the lion's den, and the lion was smirking.

CHAPTER 8

Zakar

Zakar led her through the winding corridors of the citadel, his pace unhurried, measured. He could feel the tension radiating off her in waves, though she said nothing. Good. Let her stew in silence, let her mind race with a thousand frantic thoughts. The longer she dwelled on her predicament, the deeper the realization would settle—there was no escape.

Her magic was useless here. Her wit, her cunning, all the tricks that had once ensnared him—they meant nothing now. She was entirely at his mercy, and he relished that knowledge. The satisfaction curled deep in his chest, warm and slow, as he stole a sidelong glance at her. She was flustered, her face carefully composed but betraying her distress in subtle ways—the tightening of her jaw, the slight crease between her brows. How delightful it was to be the cause of her disquiet.

His suite awaited at the end of the hall. He pushed open the heavy doors, stepping inside, and watched as she hesitated on the threshold. The moment stretched between them, her wariness palpable as she took in the lavish space with a searching glance. Still, she entered, albeit with measured caution. Zakar stepped in after her and closed the door with a quiet finality, locking it with an easy twist of the key.

Her shoulders stiffened.

Zakar said nothing, only drinking in the sight of her as she turned, her wary gaze sweeping the room. It was a grand space, worthy of its master—dark-stoned walls lined with towering bookshelves, rich velvet drapes in deep jewel tones framing the arched windows. Candles flickered in sconces, pouring golden light over the polished marble floors. But her attention inevitably landed on the table set near the hearth, a meal laid out between two waiting chairs.

She stepped toward it, tentative, trailing her fingers along the back of one chair before glancing at the goblets of wine, the plates of fine food. Then her gaze roamed further, taking in the rest of the room—the towering four-poster bed of onyx at the far end, its silken sheets the color of midnight.

Zakar's lips curved slightly as he watched her fingers tighten on the chair. Even without words, he could hear her thoughts as clearly as if she'd spoken them. Every fiber of her being was telling her to run. To flee.

"Were you expecting me?" she asked, spinning to face him, accusation lacing every syllable.

Zakar's smile didn't falter—if anything, it deepened, a slow, knowing expression that undoubtedly made her pulse hammer in warning. He closed the distance with quiet control, relishing the way she instinctively edged back a half-step.

"Yes," he murmured, his voice smooth as silk. He reached past her, grasping the back of the chair, the movement purposeful, calculated. She stiffened at the sudden nearness, her breath catching ever so slightly as he pulled the seat back with a soft scrape against the stone floor. His lips flicked upward in amusement. So easy.

"Please," he urged, his tone deceptively polite. "Have a seat."

A muscle in her jaw clenched, defiance and fear warring behind those striking blue eyes. For a moment, he thought she might refuse outright—might spit some venomous retort and attempt to run. But then, after a taut beat of silence, she lowered her chin and sank onto the chair, her movements controlled, but reluctant.

With an air of leisure, he circled the table, taking his time as he settled into his own chair. He lifted his goblet, tilting it toward her in mock salute. "To a long-awaited reunion," he mused, the rich red wine swirling lazily before he took a slow, indulgent sip. He held her gaze over the rim, watching the way her throat bobbed ever so slightly.

She sat rigid, every muscle in her body taut, her hands resting in her lap rather than reaching for the goblet before her.

"If you're going to kill me," she snapped, her voice tight, riding the edge of desperation, "then get it over with."

His smile deepened, laced with something unsettling.

He leaned forward, setting his goblet down with an intentional, weighted clink against the table. "Kill you?" he echoed, tilting his head as if the very notion amused him. "Now, Myra, where would be the fun in that?"

Her name rolled off his tongue like a lazy caress, and he didn't miss the way her fingers tightened subtly against her skirts. Ah. That reaction alone was enough to make his blood hum.

"So please," he continued, gesturing to the spread of food between them, the flickering candlelight painting warm golds against the glossy fruit and gleaming silverware. "Eat. Drink. I insist."

She stared at the meal, her resolve flickering for the briefest of moments. And then, as if on cue, the softest, betraying growl rose from her stomach. A flush of mortified pink crept up her throat.

Zakar exhaled a quiet laugh, deep and satisfied. Of course she's starving. The chase had been long. She had run from him all night, foolishly expending what little strength she had left. It was almost cruel, the way she forced herself to deny even the simplest of comforts in some desperate attempt to maintain control.

He picked up a single grape from the tray and rolled it between his fingers, watching her closely before popping it between his teeth, the skin breaking with a satisfying snap. The taste bloomed on his tongue, sweet and full. He sighed, tilting his head slightly as he let the moment stretch.

She wasn't going to last. Not against him. Not here. This was just the beginning, and he intended to savor every moment as he shattered every last wall she had left.

She looked down at the food, her fingers fidgeting slightly in her lap, seemingly weighing her options. But even as she lingered, hesitation flickering across her face, she was already making her decision.

Abruptly, she stood. "This was a mistake," she murmured, the tremor in her voice betraying her fear. She swallowed hard, the sound loud in the heavy silence, and turned away from him. "I will take my leave."

Zakar didn't move. He merely watched as she strode toward the door, her steps too swift, too unsteady to be mistaken for confidence. She reached for the lock and turned it. It didn't budge. Her shoulders slackened subtly, her fingers pressing against the door, hesitating, before she glanced over her shoulder.

"Would you open the door?" she asked. Her voice was softer now, almost innocent—like she truly believed he might let her go.

He chuckled, setting his goblet down like he had all the time in the world. Then, in a whisper of darkness, he was in front of her.

She gasped, stumbling back against the door, her fingers gripping the handle as if it might still offer her salvation.

"Your magic works here?" she asked, her voice laced with disbelief, horror creeping into her expression.

"Of course it does." His tone was smooth, undeterred. "I am the one who enforces the charms within my fortress. They do not bind me."

Her breath stilled, realization dawning over her in slow, painful increments. Her power had been stripped the moment she stepped inside. But his? His was untouched. She had walked straight into his dominion, where every rule bent to his will. And now she was looking at him—really looking—understanding, perhaps for the first time, just how completely outmatched she was.

She sucked in a quick breath as she pulled herself away from the door, creating distance between them, as if that could somehow weaken his hold on her. "Will you..." She cleared her throat, lifting her chin, though the movement was forced. "Will you let me leave?"

His slow-spreading smirk was answer enough.

Her body stiffened, and she cursed under her breath. She turned her head, perhaps scanning the room for an escape, for something—anything—that might offer her a way out. But there was no exit, no weapon, no hope.

THE ARCANE BARGAIN

Zakar had seen that look before. Desperate, frantic, futile defiance. He had seen it on so many faces. But never had it tasted so sweet as it did now, etched into hers.

CHAPTER 9

Myrithia

Panic clawed at her throat, a suffocating weight that wrapped around her lungs and squeezed tight. Every muscle in her body screamed for her to flee, but there was nowhere to go—no open doors, no shadows deep enough to slip into. The walls of his fortress trapped her just as surely as the calculating gleam in his eyes. And *him*—he was too close, standing there with a patience that unsettled her more than any act of violence could.

Memories of him assaulted her, vicious and unrelenting—flickering images of another time, another life.

Warm laughter shared in secret halls. His hands on her skin—careful, reverent, full of weight. And that look in his eyes, so close to love it still hurt to remember.

Love. A vicious ache bloomed in her chest. And the way he was looking at her now... Was it the same? Or was she only imagining it, desperate to find some glimmer of advantage in this twisted reunion? She swallowed hard, gaze flicking toward the table.

The intimate glow of candlelight. The food laid out between two chairs. Beneath the taunting amusement, beneath his satisfaction, was there something more? Did he still harbor feelings for her? Could she—

No.

She crushed the thought before it could form. She was not here to play games. She was not here to repeat old sins.

There had been a time when she had known how to get what she wanted from him. When a well-placed touch, a lingering gaze, a soft sigh in the right moment could bend his unyielding will into something pliant, indulgent, willing. She had used that knowledge.

Used *him*.

She had played him like a fool, coaxing him into love while keeping a blade poised for his back. And she had never forgiven herself for it. She would never do that to him again, even if it meant her own destruction. Even if giving in was the only way to survive. She would never hurt him that way again. A wave of self-loathing threatened to rise, but she shoved it down, pressing a hand against her stomach, willing herself to focus.

Focus on what?

There was no way out. If she ran, she would die. If she fought, she would die. She knew she should surrender. She deserved this.

She should roll over, accept her fate, take whatever punishment he saw fit to give her. But she wasn't ready to relent. Not yet. Not while there was still a sliver of hope left. Even if she had no idea what that hope was.

Her throat tightened, dry with fear, as she took a single, hesitant step forward.

Zakar watched her, waiting, knowing. His smirk deepened, his green eyes glinting like he could see straight through her.

She felt exposed beneath that gaze. Like he was peeling her apart, piece by piece, uncovering every shameful thought she'd ever had, every flicker of fear, every fragile moment of regret.

She hated him for it. And she hated herself more for having no plan, no control, no path forward now that *he* was the Master of the Arcane.

She had come here prepared to bargain for the Syltharic Tome. But now, trapped in his fortress, she realized that there could not possibly be anything he wanted now more than her own death.

Think. Think, damn you.

What do you do? What do you say?

Breathing in slow, measured draws, she moved past him, forcing herself not to flinch as she brushed too near.

She reached the table, lowering herself onto the cushioned seat. A single breath passed before she grabbed for the wine, fingers curling tight around the stem of the goblet.

The rich scent filled her senses, and she hesitated only for a moment before tilting it back, draining it in one swift, desperate motion.

A deep chuckle rumbled from behind her.

His footsteps sounded behind her, steady as they closed the distance, followed by the drag of his chair as he returned to his place.

"Have you decided to eat now, Myra?" His voice dripped with amusement, low and velvety, taunting.

Myrithia didn't answer.

She set the goblet down and tried to steady her nerves. She needed to think—to find some thread of control in this twisted game. The scent of roasted meat and seasoned greens hung in the air, rich and tempting, a cruel reminder of how long it had been since she'd tasted anything truly indulgent.

Against her better judgment, she began to eat—small, cautious bites, each one harder to resist than the last.

Eat. Stay sharp. Find an opening.

Zakar didn't seem to share her urgency.

While she ate, he only picked at his food, never truly indulging, never breaking his unwavering focus from her. She had no doubt he was enjoying himself. Perhaps watching her was enough to sustain him.

"How is it?" he asked after a while, tilting his head slightly.

She swallowed, forcing her voice to be measured, polite. "Delicious." It was the truth. There was no point in lying, not about anything so trivial. She was entirely at his mercy, and she had to move carefully now.

The wine was already weaving its way through her system, leaving her limbs warm, her mind sluggish. By the time she finished her meal, she felt lighter—just enough to grasp onto the courage she needed.

She parted her lips, ready to speak, ready to begin whatever dangerous game she would have to play to get through this.

But before she could utter a word, Zakar leaned forward

slightly and asked, "Would you like a bath?"

The question took her off guard. She hesitated, her fingers tensing around the edge of the table.

He gestured vaguely toward her travel-worn state, the dirt and exhaustion clinging to her like a second skin. "You've had a long night, haven't you?"

His voice was smooth, casual, but she wasn't fooled.

"A bath might make you feel better."

Myrithia stiffened.

Her first instinct was to refuse, but she hesitated. She was filthy and exhausted. And the thought of warm water easing the ache from her weary body was almost enough to make her tremble.

She knew better than to trust him, but she was also too tired to keep resisting for the sake of resistance alone. Still, wariness coiled tight in her gut.

She lifted her chin slightly. "Why are you doing this?" The question slipped from her lips before she could stop it, the thought that had been lingering in her mind since he led her away to his suite. "Why feed me? Why offer me comfort?" Then, softer but no less sharp, she asked, "Why be kind?"

Zakar laughed, a deep, rich sound, one that sent a slow chill up her spine.

"Kind?" He echoed the word as if it were a joke, an absurdity he hadn't considered before. He pushed to his feet with languid grace, his movements fluid and precise.

Myrithia's breath snagged in her throat like a snare as he prowled around the table. She stiffened when he stopped before her, the space between them suffocatingly small.

Instinct whispered for her to rise, not wanting to be caught in a vulnerable position while he loomed over her.

So she did. She pushed herself to stand, only to feel a fresh stab of dismay when he still towered over her.

He was broader than she remembered, more commanding, his presence pressing against hers like a shadow she could never quite escape.

The scent of him—dark spice and fragrant cedarwood—filled her senses, threatening to unravel her carefully constructed walls.

A memory struck her without warning.

Kissing him, her fingers pressed against his chest, his body warm beneath her hands as he breathed her name into her skin.

Her heart slammed against her ribs, her body betraying her even as she fought to stay composed.

No. That was another life. Another her. She refused to let nostalgia weaken her. Not now. Not when his stare weighed heavy on her, assessing, unwavering.

"I want you comfortable," he murmured, his voice like silk laced with steel. "That is all."

His tone was soft, almost gentle, but she wasn't foolish enough to believe it. This was not kindness. It was control. And he was exercising it with a deftness that sent unease through her stomach.

"You've had a trying night," he continued, tilting his head slightly, watching her the way a cat might watch a trapped bird. "I'd be a poor host if I let you sit here in your filth while you plead your case."

A flicker of impatience crossed her face. "I have no intention of staying long," she bit out, forcing steel into her tone. "So let's discuss my business, and I'll be on my way."

Even as she said it, she knew it was a lie. A poor, desperate lie that neither of them believed.

His lips curled at the edges, amusement flickering in his green eyes.

"Business can wait until you've rested." He gestured lazily toward the grand, obsidian-framed bed at the far side of the chamber, his voice maddeningly smooth. "If you're too tired for a bath, you're welcome to sleep first."

Her gaze betrayed her thoughts as it flicked—traitorously—to the bed. Another memory surfaced. Another bed just as luxurious. His hands tangling in her hair. His lips trailing along her throat.

Her fingers twitched, pressing slightly into the fabric of her sleeves. She tore her gaze away, forcing herself to breathe evenly.

"A bath," she said at last, her voice quieter now.

If he refused to speak of business until she rested, then she would play along.

Just a little longer.

He studied her for a moment, then, evidently pleased, gestured toward an adjoining door.

"This way." Without waiting, he turned and strode toward it.

Myrithia hesitated, then followed. She trailed behind him into the adjoining chamber, her body tense, her mind racing.

The moment she stepped inside, warmth washed over her, thick with steam and the rich scent of milled oats and lavender. Candles lined the polished stone walls, their glow flickering over the surface of a sunken bath, deep and filled to the brim with heated water.

The entire space felt soothing, almost welcoming. But she knew better. This was not comfort. It was calculated. Another move in his game that she still hadn't figured out.

Her eyes flicked toward him. Zakar stood just inside the threshold, arms folded, watching her. He hadn't left.

Myrithia locked her shoulders, suppressing any visible reaction, unwilling to let him know how much he unnerved her.

"Are you going to stay and watch?" The words came out sharper than she intended, edged with the lingering effects of wine and exhaustion.

His smirk widened, dark amusement flickering in his emerald eyes. "I wouldn't mind."

Her pulse spiked, her breath catching for half a second too long. He was toying with her. That much was obvious.

She lifted her chin, steadying her voice. "And if I prefer otherwise?"

His gaze gleamed with wicked delight. "Do you truly think I care for your preferences, Myra?"

Her fingers tightened around the fabric of her sleeves. No, of course not. He had made that abundantly clear.

She turned away from him, exhaling slowly, trying to recenter herself. She reached for the clasp of her cloak and unfastened it, letting the fabric slide from her shoulders, pooling to the floor.

Then, as if in response to her disrobing, she heard his footsteps retreat—the door creaking open, then clicking shut behind him.

She exhaled, a fleeting sense of relief washing over her. A small mercy.

But of course, he could afford small mercies, couldn't he?

After all, she was his prisoner now.

And there was no use in pretending otherwise.

CHAPTER 10

Zakar

Zakar lounged against the headboard, exhaling a contented sigh as he trailed his fingers along the silken sheets. The night had unfolded far better than he anticipated. Not only had Myrithia walked straight into his domain, but now she was bathing in his chambers, bound to his will in more ways than she yet realized.

He had wanted to watch.

Wanted to see her strip away every last piece of clothing, to watch her step into the water, her skin glistening as she lathered herself beneath the flickering candlelight.

He had wanted to savor it.

But there would be time for that later. Tearing down her modesty all at once would be a waste—where was the fun in that? Not when she was exhausted. Not when the wine had softened her edges, leaving her pliant but unaware.

No, not yet. He had far more patience than that.

Soon, she would emerge from that adjoining room, freshly scrubbed and pink-cheeked, undoubtedly flustered by the gown he had so generously provided. He had taken the liberty of having the servants remove her garments. The dress she had arrived in was ruined—soaked in rain, stained with mud, a tattered remnant of her desperate flight through the night. She needed something cleaner. Something new. And he had always preferred her in red.

It suited her—so rich in color against her pale skin, striking against the silver waves of her hair. She would have an entire wardrobe brought in by that same evening. She may be his captive, but he would savor every moment of her presence, and that included the pleasure of dressing her exactly how he pleased.

The door creaked, and he lifted his gaze lazily as she stepped hesitantly into the room.

Ah. There it was. The unmistakable discomfort tightening her posture, the rigid way she held her arms over herself, attempting to obscure the view of her breasts.

She looked breathtaking.

The sheer, rose-colored gown cascaded over her frame like mist, whispering over every curve, every soft slope of her body. The delicate fabric did little to conceal the shape of her, and the flickering candlelight only deepened its translucence.

He let his gaze drag over her, slow and indulgent, watching as one of her hands slowly lowered to shield her sex from his view. She knew precisely how little the garment concealed, and her awareness of it only made the moment sweeter.

"Is there another gown?" she asked carefully, her voice threaded with quiet hesitation, the stiffness in her tone barely concealing her unease.

He smirked, reclining back against the pillows, purposefully at ease. "If you don't like it, you're free to wear what you brought."

Her brows drew together, a flicker of uncertainty passing over her features. "You had my clothes taken."

"I did." He nodded, as if that settled the matter.

Her fingers curled tighter around the fabric at her chest, but she swallowed whatever response she might have had and instead moved toward the bed, wariness clinging to her every step. She paused at the edge of it, glancing back at him with a reluctant glare.

"Where am I expected to sleep?"

Zakar arched a brow at her. "Here."

She blinked, as if she had misheard him. "And where will you sleep?"

"Here as well."

Her lips parted slightly before pressing into a thin line, her resistance wavering beneath something far more fragile. "I'm not tired."

He chuckled at that, shaking his head in amusement. "You spent the entire night running through the forest, being hunted like an animal. If you don't sleep soon, you'll regret it."

"I can sleep on the floor."

Zakar hummed as he stood, moving with calm precision, his presence growing heavier with every step as he prowled toward her. She stiffened, watching his every step, but he only tilted his head in amusement as he stopped just before her.

"You can get into the bed willingly," he murmured, voice deceptively soft. "Or I can tuck you in myself—kicking and thrashing as you may be. Your choice."

Her breath caught, and for a moment, he thought she might defy him out of sheer stubbornness. And he would've liked that too, feeling her warm body against his own as he would hoist her to the bed and keep her there. Gods, he *wanted* to. Her attempts to cover her nakedness were futile, her body practically on display for him. His fingers ached with the desire to touch her, to feel every curve of her.

But at last, her shoulders sagged just slightly, and she stepped past him, her movements stiff with humiliation as she climbed into his bed.

She tucked herself beneath the covers, drawing them high over her body, as if the thick fabric might shield her from his view as well as his demands. He watched, arms crossed over his chest, debating the merits of slipping beneath those same blankets and unraveling the fragile composure she clung to so desperately.

But she was exhausted. And while the idea of keeping her awake for entirely selfish reasons was tempting, he was playing a much longer, far more satisfying game.

For now, he would let her rest.

"I'll return in a few hours to wake you," he said simply, turning toward the door.

"Thank you," she murmured softly.

He scoffed, pausing only briefly before stepping out.

She was grateful now. That, too, was part of the game.

And however she perceived his kindness, it was only because he had crafted it that way.

CHAPTER 11

Myrithia

Myrithia's eyes studied the door long after it had shut behind him, her breath slow and steady as she waited. Was he really gone? Or was he just beyond the threshold, listening, testing her, seeing what she would do the moment she was alone?

But as the silence stretched on, unbroken, she exhaled and shifted. Her limbs felt leaden, her muscles aching with the exhaustion of her journey, but there was no time to dwell on it. Not when she needed to act.

Cautiously, she eased the blankets off her body and swung her legs over the edge of the bed, bare feet pressing against the cool floor. She moved slowly, wary of how much sound she might make. The thin nightgown did little to warm her as she padded toward the tall window, the golden glow of the morning sun spilling across the polished floor. The brightness startled her, momentarily disorienting after the long hours of running through the darkness.

The sight beyond made her chest tighten.

The forest stretched for miles, an untamed labyrinth of thick, endless foliage. Somewhere out there lay the path she had taken through the night, the path she had carved in desperation. If she squinted, she could almost imagine herself slipping back into the woods, vanishing once more.

But she wasn't foolish enough to believe that was possible

now.

Her eyes flicked downward, to the sheer gown draping her frame, and heat flared across her cheeks. She was practically bare. If she fled now, she wouldn't make it far before she was caught—whether by soldiers, bounty hunters, or worse. The mercenaries had been emboldened enough when she was cloaked and filthy. Dressed like this? She didn't want to imagine the outcome. And if she somehow evaded all of that, she would still have the Hollow Mist to contend with.

For years, the Mist had been an unlikely ally, shielding her cottage beneath its dense veil, her magical enchantments keeping her protected beneath its presence. But now that she was no longer bound to one place—now that she needed to run—the Mist would become an obstacle at best, and a terrifying end at worst.

It was a thick, suffocating fog that drifted wherever it pleased, creeping through woodlands and meadows, lingering for years in some places while vanishing in mere days in others.

No one understood the Mist, but everyone feared it. Those who stepped inside were swallowed whole, never seen again. Some claimed it was instant death, others whispered that it was a portal to another realm, but no one knew for certain. And no one was reckless enough to enter willingly to find out. The only thing that had kept *her* from being swallowed by the Mist was the enchantments she had woven around her dwelling before it passed through.

And to think—in her delirium last night, she had almost convinced herself it was a good idea to step inside. The memory lingered, hazy but persistent, the whispers nearly audible again: soft, insidious, beckoning—like something long forgotten. Like something waiting. She had known it was dangerous, and yet, standing at its edge, she'd felt unnaturally calm, as if sedated by its presence, as if it had cradled her in unseen hands.

If not for that rogue, Kierdan, she might have stepped forward. She might already be dead. Her body trembled, though she wasn't sure if it was from the fading adrenaline, the bone-deep exhaustion, or something far worse. The curse was spreading. Even now, she could feel it—the ache beneath her skin, the slow rot threading through her veins. She had been fighting it for years, holding back the inevitable with carefully measured doses of Valdoran sage. But her supply was gone.

She needed more, but she doubted Zakar had any on hand. The thought of asking him for it, of revealing just how weak she had become, made her stomach churn.

She could almost hear his laughter now, his voice smooth and derisive, savoring her slow, quiet suffering.

But without the sage, her body would betray her. The pain would worsen, creeping through her bones like fire, until even breathing became unbearable. And eventually, even the sage wouldn't be enough.

She needed the Syltharic Tome.

Her gaze shifted back to the chamber. It was empty, lavish, impossibly vast. The remnants of their earlier meal had been cleared, the table wiped clean, as if the feast had never happened. The entire room was a testament to Zakar's new life, his new throne.

The Arcane Citadel, his new castle to rule as its Master. The irony twisted in her gut. He was never meant to rule anything. He was meant to die. She was supposed to have killed him.

Draevok had killed Zakar's father—the king once known as the Butcher of Valthoria—on the night of a royal ball. With no living queen and no heirs beyond Zakar, there had been no one left to challenge Draevok for the throne after the murder. The remaining members of the royal bloodline were given a choice: denounce their claims or die.

Myrithia had been meant to end Zakar herself—plunge a blade into his back without hesitation. But when Draevok gave the order, she'd known in her bones she could never go through with it.

So when the ball began, and blood began to spill, Zakar never entered that ballroom. She had stolen him away before it all began—unaware, unarmed, unprepared. She had pushed him to flee, playing the role of traitor, forcing him to believe she had turned on him. Because it had been the only way to save his life.

But what did that mercy mean now?

What good had it done either of them?

At the time, he must have seen it as a cruel gesture, a twisted game. What kind of mercy was it to let a fallen prince live while his kingdom was ripped from his hands? What mercy was it to spare his life only to leave him in despair—exiled, broken, alone?

That was what she had given him. And then she had run away. And she had never truly stopped running.

She turned, her fingers trailing absentmindedly along the spines of the books lining the far wall, their gold-embossed titles gleaming in the soft light. She knew the tome wouldn't be here. Zakar wasn't foolish enough to keep something so powerful in his personal chambers. But the sheer nearness of it, the knowledge that it might be somewhere within these walls, made her pulse race.

It would be her salvation. If she could find it, she could sever the curse, free herself from Draevok's grasp once and for all. But escaping him didn't mean she would ever stop running. As long as he hunted her, she would never know peace. Hiding would be easier—possible—if she wasn't weak, if she wasn't wasting away, waiting to die. All the more reason to get the book. All the more reason to disappear. But Zakar would never allow that. Her lips parted, her breath slow, unsteady. Would he ever let her go?

Myrithia pulled away from the shelves, her gaze sweeping across the room that had become her gilded prison. No chains bound her, yet the walls felt as solid as iron.

She had spent her entire life as a slave, shackled to the will of a man who had carved his desires into her path, his commands shaping the very foundation of her existence. If she was to die, then she wanted—needed—to die free.

She wanted to live truly free from pain, free from fear, free to make her own choices. She wanted to feel the sun on her skin without the weight of her master's hand pressing into her back. She wanted to roam the land without fear of being hunted, of being dragged before a throne and sentenced like an animal.

She wanted to choose a lover. Not for duty, not for survival. But because she *chose* him. Sparks danced along her spine, settling somewhere deep. Because when she thought of choosing, when she let herself linger on the thought for even a moment...

She thought of *him*.

Of green eyes, sharp with mischief and a voice that had once carried devotion. She thought of the way his touch had once been gentle, before she taught him to be cruel.

Gods, she was a fool. A reckless, stupid, pathetic fool. How could she still want that with him? After everything, why did she still ache for the dream that had died the night she ruined them?

That life was impossible. She couldn't have a future with him. There was no hope of sharing a home with him. She would never have his hands mapping the shape of her body, would never fall asleep with his breath warm against her skin.

She was not meant for happiness.

And yet, some stupid, desperate part of her still wanted it. She still longed for a world where she was not his prisoner. Not his enemy. But his wife.

The thought was so absurd, so reckless that she wanted to scream at herself for even thinking it. She squeezed her eyes shut, exhaling shakily. If she didn't rest soon, she wouldn't make it to any sort of future with a real life. She turned, meaning to head for the bed, but as soon as she took a step, her vision swam. The room lurched, tilting beneath her feet.

Her breath snagged in her throat. The curse. It was sinking its claws deeper.

A sharp pulse of pain flared through her limbs, her body weakening under the invisible force that bound her. She reached for something—anything—to steady herself, but her fingers grasped only air. The world narrowed, sounds growing distant, her heartbeat thumping like war drums in her ears.

Her knees buckled. The floor rushed up to meet her.

A gasp left her lips as she hit the ground hard, her fingers trembling against the cold marble. She tried to push herself up, but the strength bled from her limbs. Her breathing came in shallow, uneven pulls, her body surrendering to the weight of exhaustion, the slow, creeping agony of the curse taking root once more.

No. Not now.

Her eyelids quivered. She could feel herself slipping, the world darkening at the edges.

And then—

THE ARCANE BARGAIN

The soft creak of a door opening.

She barely had the strength to turn her head, barely had the will to fight against the oblivion swallowing her whole. But before the darkness fully claimed her, she caught the faintest sound of footsteps approaching.

Then, nothing.

CHAPTER 12

Zakar

Zakar watched her sleep, his sharp green eyes tracing the steady rise and fall of her breath. She was still now, the restless twitch in her fingers quieted, her expression serene despite the strain he had seen on her face before she collapsed.

He hadn't planned to linger. He had only intended to check on her—to ensure she wasn't foolish enough to attempt breaking the windows, though even if she had, the enchanted barriers around the citadel's walls would have denied her any chance of escape. If she somehow shattered the glass, all she would accomplish was giving him an unnecessary mess to clean up.

But he had not expected this.

When he entered the room and saw her crumpled on the floor, his first instinct had been suspicion. Myrithia was cunning, after all. She had deceived him once, had made him believe in her, trust her, and then had stolen everything from him in a single breath. He had approached her slowly, watching for the telltale signs of a trick. But there was no deception here—only weakness.

Her breathing had been labored, her body trembling as if something unseen was wrenching at her insides. He had stood over her, watching, waiting, before his jaw tightened and he had bent down to lift her into his arms.

And still, he had not left her side.

At first, he told himself it was because she could not be trusted.

But trust had nothing to do with it. She could not leave, whether he watched her or not. The fortress was her prison, impenetrable and impossible for her to escape. And yet, instead of walking away, he had found himself seated in a chair beside her, his eyes on the delicate curve of her lips, the way her lashes trembled faintly with whatever unrest plagued her dreams. He had watched the breath fill her lungs, steady and rhythmic, ensuring that she would live.

Because he had not hunted her down just to watch her die.

He wanted her to suffer, yes—but he wanted her to endure it. He wanted her to wake up every morning knowing she belonged to him, to feel the consequences of her betrayal pressing down upon her with every breath. Death was far too merciful. She would serve him for as long as her life would last. That was the justice he demanded.

Zakar exhaled slowly, his hands fisting at his sides. Then, unbidden, a memory surfaced of her cottage. There had been a cup of tea she had made for herself, still warm where it had rested on the wooden table. And the scent of it—subtle, distinct, and familiar.

Valdoran sage.

A rare herb. Expensive. A healer's ingredient.

His mind turned back to the moment she had collapsed, to the way she had struggled to move, to breathe. He wasn't fool enough to believe she had simply fainted from exhaustion. This was something else. Something deeper.

A cold weight settled in his chest, his expression hardening. Why should he care? If she suffered, it should amuse him. He should relish her agony, revel in the knowledge that she was paying—*truly* paying—for what she had done to him. But a dead woman could not serve a sentence. If she was dying, if she wasted away in his bed before he had the chance to truly *own* her, then what justice would there be in that?

No, she needed to live. For a long, long time. And he would be the one to ensure it.

Myrithia stirred, shifting slightly beneath the covers before her lashes fluttered open. He watched the moment confusion gave way to awareness, the way her brows pulled together before her gaze landed on him.

Then, she jolted upright, eyes widening in alarm.

"Your Highness!" she squeaked, her long silver hair falling across her face, mussed from slumber.

Zakar chuckled, watching her scramble to gather herself, a brief ripple of nostalgia stirring within him. It had been a long time since anyone had addressed him by his formal title. His amusement deepened as he took in the subtle changes in her. The color had returned to her cheeks, her breath, though rapid, came steadily, and she looked far more lively than she had hours ago when he'd found her crumpled on the floor.

He said nothing of it, simply tilting his head as she continued to stare at him, her blue eyes narrowing in suspicion. His gaze slipped leisurely down her frame, the rose-tinted gossamer gown faint across her breasts, her smooth stomach, accentuating every lovely curve of her perfect body.

She looked down at herself then, as if suddenly remembering the sheer fabric of her nightgown. He caught the quick, startled motion of her hands yanking the blanket up to shield herself.

A soft *tsk* escaped him, his disapproval evident. "Your modesty is useless at this point, Myra," he mused, his voice smooth with amusement. "I've seen far more of you before. A pity we never took full advantage of those moments."

A flush of embarrassment crept up her neck, settling high on her cheeks, betraying her in the warm daylight. She forced herself to speak, her voice clipped, a little too quick. "Can we discuss our business now?" she asked, her tone carefully measured—a feeble attempt to reclaim control where there was none.

He leaned back slightly, stretching his legs out as he studied her. For a moment, he didn't respond. He simply let the silence rest between them, let her sit there stewing in her impatience. He wanted her unsettled, unsure of his next move.

Finally, he inclined his head in a slow nod. "Very well," he allowed, his voice carrying a casual laziness, as if indulging her request were an afterthought. "Let's discuss."

He propped his elbow against the armrest of his chair, resting his chin in his palm. "Tell me, Myrithia," he murmured, "why have you come to the Arcane Citadel seeking its master?"

Myrithia hesitated, clearly choosing her words with care. "I am in need of a book," she finally said.

Zakar tilted his head slightly, watching her—watching the way she held herself—controlled, wary, as if she expected him to deny her outright.

He had spent years hunting her. Yet, without any interference, her own path would have still led her straight to his doorstep, in need of the Arcane Master, in need of a mere book.

His lips curled. "What book?"

She swallowed, clearly fighting for composure. "The Syltharic Tome."

His amusement stilled.

A pulse of something sharp and electric ran through him. He had expected many things from her. This was not one of them.

He tilted his head, studying her now—truly studying her. "That is quite the artifact you seek," he murmured, his voice deceptively smooth. "A rather dark one."

Her grip tightened on the blanket wrapped around her chest, but her gaze remained defiant.

"What business do you have with such a dangerous thing?"

"That is my concern alone," she said coolly. "Do you have it?"

A foolish request. A naive one.

He let the silence stretch between them, watching the flicker of unease creep into her posture. He wanted her to feel the weight of what she had just asked. To understand.

Then, finally, he exhaled through his nose, shaking his head. "It's not the sort of book one simply borrows from a library, Myrithia." His voice turned mocking, dark amusement laced through every syllable. "You do understand what it is, don't you?" he asked, watching for the slightest tremor in her expression. "The tome is not knowledge, not power—it is death bound in parchment. A relic so volatile that even its guardians feared it."

He watched her, waiting, knowing the weight of her request would settle soon enough. Master Sorien had feared the tome falling into the wrong hands so deeply that he had ensured it was sealed away with him in death. If she wanted that book, she would have to descend into his crypt and take it from his grave.

Her jaw tightened, but this time, it wasn't defiance. It was uncertainty. "I know how dangerous it is," she said, voice quieter.

"Do you?" His brow arched, voice softening to something deceptively gentle—too smooth to be sincere. "Then tell me, Myrithia—what exactly do you want with it?"

A hesitation.

A second too long.

He saw it—the brief flicker of calculation, the way she tried to piece together a lie that wouldn't betray her true intentions.

Zakar sighed, shaking his head. "Don't bother lying." He had no interest in indulging her falsehoods. "Regardless, it's not here."

Her eyes snapped to his, frustration darkening her expression. "Where is it?"

"In a safe place."

She clenched her jaw, irritation flaring in her gaze. The frustration of knowing she was not in control. "And will you let me have it?"

A slow smirk crossed his lips.

"I'll let you *look* at it." He leaned forward, resting his elbows on his knees, relishing the way her breath caught, the way she sensed the noose tightening around her neck. Then, softly, he murmured, "For a price."

CHAPTER 13

Myrithia

Myrithia's fingers tugged at the sheets, her nails pressing into the fabric as frustration simmered beneath her skin. Of course, he wouldn't part with something so powerful without demanding something in return. He was not the same man she had once known. No. This man before her was different. He was calculating now, a master of manipulation.

And yet, she had still hoped, foolishly, that perhaps some part of him might offer her mercy.

Cautiously, she lifted her chin, forcing her voice to remain even. "And what," she asked, "is your price?"

Zakar leaned back in his chair, stretching out leisurely, as if he had all the time in the world. The slow, satisfied curve of his lips sent a warning shiver down her spine.

"What would you give me for it?" he mused.

She swallowed, her heart pounding. He was playing with her. Watching, waiting, to see how far she was willing to go. She had nothing—no gold, no treasures, nothing of worth except for herself. He knew that. And yet, he wanted to hear her say it.

After a long pause, she forced the words past her lips.

"Anything."

Zakar's smirk widened, his emerald eyes gleaming with amusement, with something darker beneath. He exhaled softly, his fingers tapping idly against the arm of his chair. "It has been a long time since I have seen such desperation in someone," he murmured, his tone a parody of reverence. "And I must say… I do love it."

Myrithia bristled, irritated by his enjoyment of her suffering. He was drinking in her misery like the finest of wines.

She clenched her jaw, forcing herself to remain calm. He was still her captor, and she was still at his mercy. "What do you want, Zakar?"

His gaze flicked to her lips, then back to her eyes, watching her closely. He let the silence stretch, letting her discomfort fester, before finally offering his terms.

"I want one thing," he said smoothly. "Your will."

Her inhale trembled, betraying her.

She stared at him, waiting for him to elaborate, to explain what exactly he meant, though she already knew. Dread curled in her stomach, a slow and suffocating thing.

"You will serve me," he continued, his voice soft yet firm, each word a brand against her skin. "In all things. My every whim, my every desire. You will be my personal slave from now until the end of your days." He tilted his head, watching the way her throat bobbed with her swallow, the way her fingers gripped the sheets like they might anchor her to something real. "And I expect you to do so willingly."

The weight of his words settled over her like chains.

Obedience. True submission. Total surrender.

A chill coiled down her spine, twisting into something hot and electric. Not because she wanted it. Not because she longed for it. But because it meant there was no escape.

Her mind raced, scrambling for a path forward, for a way out. There had to be a way out. She had spent her entire life in servitude, shackled to the will of another man, molded into a weapon never meant to belong to herself.

She could not—*would not*—spend the rest of her days as Zakar's possession, awaiting the day he grew bored of her and killed her. She needed to escape. Somehow. And she could figure out exactly what that would be once she was free of her curse.

Myrithia inhaled slowly, steadying herself against the weight of the unthinkable agreement, against the cold, creeping dread of what she was about to do.

She met his gaze—unwavering, firm—as she forced herself to say the words that would change everything.

"I accept your terms."

A slow, satisfied smirk tugged at Zakar's lips, his emerald eyes gleaming with something dark and victorious. He studied her for a moment, perhaps expecting hesitation, doubt—some sign that she wasn't truly committing to this.

But she held his gaze, refusing to show weakness, even as she reeled with uncertainty.

He lifted a single brow. "Do you truly understand what you're agreeing to?"

"Yes." The word left her lips too quickly, too forcefully, betraying the nerves she was desperately trying to bury.

His smirk deepened. He leaned in, his voice dropping to a smooth, silken murmur. "Good," he praised, adding, "Then you understand that I expect you to satisfy me, to give yourself to me whenever I want you."

Her brows furrowed slightly, a thread of desire mingled with fear flickering through her features.

"Your body now belongs to me," he clarified, watching her carefully.

A sharp pulse of something unnameable coursed through her—half dread, half something else entirely. Exhilaration. Shame. It tangled deep in her stomach, twisting in ways she couldn't fully grasp. *Gods.* Why did the sound of that send a shiver through her? Why did the way he said *your body* make her feel so—

She shoved the feeling down, locking it away behind every wall she still had left. This wasn't about *that*. This wasn't about whatever part of her still remembered the way he used to touch her, the way he used to look at her before she ruined everything.

She swallowed down her reservations, nodding slowly. "I understand."

Satisfaction flickered across his features. He stood to his feet, stretching with unhurried ease, as though reveling in the moment. He was basking in his victory, savoring her surrender.

Her stomach fluttered when he extended his hand toward her. She stared at it.

"We must seal the bargain," he said smoothly.

A thread of discomfort wove through her, but she hesitated only a second before slipping her hand into his. It was warm, firm, his grip gentle but steady. Her fingers trembled in his own, nerves skittering up her spine, uncertain of what would come next. A spell? A contract? A blood draw?

But what did come next shocked her.

Zakar pulled her forward with effortless strength, his other hand threading into the silver waves of her hair as his lips crashed against hers. The force of it stole her breath, her lips parting on a startled gasp—one he claimed instantly, deepening the kiss without hesitation. His grip tightened, possessive, his fingers fisting at her nape as if to ensure she didn't pull away.

But she didn't. She *couldn't*.

Heat burst through her, flooding her veins, scattering her thoughts like embers caught in the wind. He was demanding, relentless, his mouth moving over hers with an intoxicating mix of hunger and control. He kissed her as though she belonged to him—as though she had always belonged to him.

Her fingers pressed into his tunic, grasping for something solid to anchor herself, to stop the world from spinning. But instead of steadying her, it only pulled her deeper. Her lips parted further, a traitorous sigh escaping her as he took her willingness as an invitation, as permission. His teeth grazed her lower lip, coaxing, teasing—*taking*.

The room melted away. The past, the future, the looming consequences of what she was doing—all of it ceased to exist. There was only this. Only him. Only the impossible heat of his body, the dizzying way he overwhelmed her, consuming every breath, every thought, every lingering shred of resistance she should have had.

And then, just as suddenly as it began, he broke the kiss.

Myrithia barely had time to process the loss before he tugged at her hand, still locked within his own. He lifted it between them, his thumb brushing over the delicate skin of her wrist in a slow, maddening stroke. His lips remained slightly parted, as if savoring the taste of her, as if he had claimed something irrevocable.

Breathless, she whispered, "Is that how you seal all of your bargains?"

His eyes gleamed with amusement, his voice rich with satisfaction. "No."

"Then why—" she started, but the words died on her lips the moment she saw the way he was looking at her.

Because he *could*.

Because he *wanted* to.

Heat flared beneath her skin, a wildfire of fury and something far more reckless. Her mind screamed at her to recoil, to tear herself away before he unraveled her completely. But her body— traitorous, deceitful thing that it was—only swayed closer. Only craved more.

He smirked as if he knew the effect he had just had on her. As if he could *feel* the war waging inside of her. And somehow, she feared she had already lost.

Zakar reached into his pocket, and when he drew out a shining gold dagger into the space between them, Myrithia's breath faltered.

"I sign every deal in blood," he murmured, low and certain, like the slow pull of a noose.

A sharp snap of his fingers rang through the air, and her head jerked toward the sudden glow beside them. A parchment appeared, floating weightlessly, illuminated in a ghostly green shimmer. The edges were frayed, aged by time, yet the words written upon it gleamed in gold, their elegant script weaving the terms of their contract into something binding—permanent.

Her pulse hammered in her throat as he grasped her wrist, his hold firm but not cruel. The dagger's cool edge kissed her fingertip, and a quick, precise flick drew a bead of crimson. He pressed her hand to the parchment, smearing her blood against the ancient fibers.

It shimmered, absorbed into the page, the magic within it drinking from her as though it had been waiting for this moment.

Then, without hesitation, he turned the blade on himself. A single cut, a smear of his own blood beside hers. The gold ink pulsed, the contract flashing a luminous green before catching fire, twisting into nothing but embers that dissipated into the air.

THE ARCANE BARGAIN

Myrithia hadn't realized she had been holding her breath until the last wisp of parchment vanished. Her lips parted, her exhale shaky with the knowledge that she had just given something vital away.

When she dared to look at him again, she found his gaze already on her—slow, devouring, victorious. Then, with a slow exhale, he said, "We have a journey ahead of us, and you'll need to be prepared. My servants will bring your traveling clothes shortly."

Before she could respond, he snapped his fingers. In an instant, a lavish spread of food materialized on the table—fresh bread still steaming, ripe fruits glistening, meats and cheeses arranged in decadent portions. The air filled with the rich, tantalizing aromas of a feast conjured from nothing.

"Eat if you are hungry," he murmured, his voice edged with knowing. "We leave soon."

And with that, he turned and left, each step echoing the quiet confidence of a man untouched by urgency, as if he had all the time in the world.

Because he did.

Because she was *his*.

And with dark magic and her own blood, she had just sealed away her last hope of escape. A chilling thought crept through her— even if she managed to get her hands on the Syltharic Tome, she might never slip free of him again.

CHAPTER 14

Zakar

Zakar slipped on his black gloves with an air of satisfaction, the smooth leather molding to his fingers as he strode down the corridor. Beside him, Myrithia walked in measured steps, her discomfort evident in the way she tugged at the bodice of the gown he had selected for her. The deep red fabric clung to her form in all the ways he liked, embroidered with delicate golden filigree that made her look every bit the noble consort. A beautiful illusion, really, and one he intended to enjoy for as long as she remained at his side.

She huffed under her breath, shifting as though the weight of the dress alone was an unbearable burden. "This isn't very practical for traveling. I look like I'm dressed for a ball, not a day of riding."

Zakar hummed in amusement, his lips quirking as he glanced down at her. "I disagree. You look perfect."

She scoffed, shaking her head as they passed by the citadel's many mages and knights. The momentary silence in the corridor was broken only by the faint click of her boots against the polished stone floors—until he realized, abruptly, that she was being watched. Their gazes were subtle at first. Lingering. Curious. Appreciative.

Zakar's mood darkened instantly.

One sharp look from him was all it took. Every single head

turned away as if burned by the weight of his glare, their eyes snapping back to the floor or their duties, as if they hadn't dared look at her at all.

His jaw tightened, though he exhaled away the irritation. Perhaps he had overdone it with the dress. But even if he had, it pleased him. He enjoyed watching her like this, the color of the fabric rich against her pale skin, the way it moved with each graceful step she took.

She was meant to look beautiful—for him.

Not for them.

"The weather should be fair today," he said, forcing himself back into the ease of their prior conversation. "You won't need a cloak."

Myrithia only shot him an unimpressed glare but said nothing. A flicker of her usual fire had returned to her eyes, and he welcomed it. Good. He had no interest in seeing her cower every moment of the day.

By the time they reached the citadel's grand entrance, he could all but sense the anticipation thrumming through her. She stared at the looming doors like they were a promise, a gateway to something she'd been aching to reclaim. Beyond them, he knew, her magic would return—eager to flood back into her veins the moment the dampening wards fell away.

Zakar smirked, taking her hand in his own as he led her forward.

Together, they stepped past the threshold.

The moment they emerged into the open air, the towering trees of the forest stretched endlessly around them. A soft breeze wove through the clearing, rustling the leaves in lazy murmurs. Waiting at the foot of the steps was his black stallion, its reins held by a solemn knight who stood at rigid attention.

Zakar did not miss the relief that flickered across Myrithia's face. It was subtle, but there. Her shoulders loosened, her breath more measured.

And then—just for a moment—he saw it. The shimmer of her magic curling at her fingertips, faint but undeniable.

He clicked his tongue in mock disappointment. "If you try to flee, you may not like the outcome," he mused, his grip tightening ever so slightly around her fingers. "But by all means, do *try*."

Myrithia faltered, her fingers tightening, the faintest shimmer of magic sparking at her fingertips before it vanished once more. His challenge lingered between them, a dark invitation to test the bonds of her new servitude. Perhaps she was deciding against it, or perhaps she was simply coming to terms with the inescapable reality of what she had done. Either way, it didn't matter. If not now, she would learn soon enough what she had truly signed away in blood.

From the moment she set foot in the Arcane Citadel, her fate had been sealed. There was never a choice, never a path that led anywhere but here—her will surrendered, her servitude bound to him indefinitely. But he had savored every moment of her struggle, watching as she clung to the illusion of control, as if her defiance could ever change what he had already decided. He would have taken her either way, but this… this was far more satisfying. She had given herself to him, believing it was on her own terms, and that made his victory all the sweeter.

Zakar turned to his horse, the great black beast standing still and obedient as the knight at its reins stepped aside. Then, he turned to Myrithia, a knowing smirk playing at his lips as he caught the subtle retreat of her foot, the brief dart of her eyes toward the forest as if there might be another option.

There wasn't.

He stepped forward, slow and certain, watching as she stiffened when his hands came to rest at her waist. She sucked in a sharp breath, her body tightening beneath his touch, but she didn't step away. That was progress, at least. He could feel the heat of her through the luxurious fabric of her dress, could sense the rapid thrum of her pulse beneath his gloved fingertips.

Without a word, he lifted her effortlessly, feeling the way her fingers briefly clutched at his shoulders, betraying the instinctive desire for something solid to hold onto. He took his time, ensuring that his grip lingered just a little longer than necessary, his hands spanning her waist, appreciating the feel of her, savoring the moment. When he settled her onto the saddle, she immediately tried to create space, shifting forward as much as the horse would allow.

Zakar smirked. He mounted in one fluid motion, practiced and precise. He pressed forward, ignoring the way she tensed, the way she braced her hands against the pommel as if she could maintain even the smallest bit of distance. He let her pretend, let her hope—for just a breath. Then, he settled in fully, one arm wrapping around her waist as his other hand found her thigh, gripping her firmly as he pulled her back against him.

Myrithia drew in a sharp inhale, her spine going rigid against his chest. He felt it all—the stiff set of her shoulders, the shiver of discomfort that ran through her. It only made him grin.

"I should have my own horse," she said, her voice a breathy, frustrated whisper.

He leaned in just slightly, close enough that his lips nearly brushed the delicate shell of her ear. "A demanding slave you are," he whispered, "but you will ride in my lap obediently, won't you?"

She didn't answer. But she didn't pull away, either.

Zakar was many things, but a fool was not one of them. From the moment he'd told her that her body now belonged to him— that she would satisfy him with it—he'd seen it. The flicker. Fleeting, yes, but clear as day.

Desire.

She'd tried to hide it, bury it beneath defiance, but he'd caught it all the same. He had felt the way she melted against him in his chambers, had heard the soft, helpless sigh that escaped her lips when she gave in to the heat of his mouth on hers.

He hadn't kissed her to torment her. He had kissed her because he wanted to feel it—that—for himself. And he *had*. She could try to pretend she was unaffected. She could school her features, sit rigid in his arms, and act as though the press of his body did nothing to her. But it was far too late for that.

He had already seen the truth—in her breath, in her eyes, in the tremble just beneath her skin. And gods, how satisfying it was to know she couldn't hide it from him.

She hadn't forgotten how they once were together, and neither had he. But he would not mistake what was between them for love, because it had never truly been love in *her* eyes. However, he would not let her pretend there was *nothing*. Not forever. He would enjoy this, for all the pleasure it would bring him, for all the torment it would bring her. In the end, there would be no part of her that wasn't his to claim.

Zakar clicked his tongue, and the horse lurched into a steady trot, forcing Myrithia's body flush against his. A soft gasp escaped her lips, barely more than a breath, and in response, his thighs tightened around her, drawing her even closer. Her scent—delicate, floral, intoxicating—rose between them, filling his senses as the strands of her silver hair brushed against his chin.

She shifted, struggling to regain her posture, but every movement only pressed her further into him, her body unintentionally teasing the length between his legs. He exhaled slowly, willing himself to cool his lurid thoughts, smug in his victory, knowing that for the rest of this journey she would have no choice but to remain right where he wanted her.

CHAPTER 15

Myrithia

The sun dipped lower in the sky, streaking the horizon with hues of molten gold and dusky violet. Myrithia shifted slightly in the saddle, her body aching from the long ride. The silence had grown oppressive, filled with the unspoken truths of the bargain she had struck. She didn't know how to speak to him, not now—not when everything had changed.

She had sold her life away to him.

Even now, the enormity of it left her stomach twisted in knots. How different would things be from this moment forward? She didn't know. But she did know one thing—she needed to get her hands on the *Syltharic Tome*. If there was any spell in that book that could sever her ties to him, that could *break* the contract she had signed in blood, she would find it.

It was Zakar who finally spoke, his voice steeped in quiet mirth. "I recall you used to like making conversation, using your charm and your wit to amuse me. I didn't expect you to lose your voice when you became my slave."

Myrithia tensed, her fingers pressing into her lap as she kept her gaze fixed on the road ahead. "There's nothing to discuss," she said coolly.

He let out a low chuckle, the sound vibrating through his chest against her back. "Oh, but there's plenty," he countered easily. "For example—how exactly did you spend these last five years?"

THE ARCANE BARGAIN

The warmth in his tone vanished, leaving behind something cutting and raw. "How did you live after you abandoned me? After you played a role in wiping out my legacy?"

A sharp pang ran through her, his words unearthing ghosts she had tried to silence. He had every right to be angry with her. Wrathful, even.

Because he didn't know.

He didn't know that from the very beginning, Draevok had instructed her to seduce him—to make Zakar soft, compliant, blind. He didn't know she had never been told the full plan, that she had never imagined Draevok would order her to kill him.

She hadn't known he always intended for the Butcher's only son to die. But that didn't make her innocent. She wasn't blameless. She had played her part, spoken her lies, wove her deception until it blurred into something real. Into love.

Love she never dared voice aloud. Love that would've been mocked or twisted if she'd confessed it, especially on the night she left him to wander alone—bloody, hunted, betrayed.

No, he was right to hate her. Because on that night, she had been a traitor. And she had given him no reason to believe otherwise.

She forced the guilt down, burying it beneath a carefully measured breath. "I don't want to discuss it."

Zakar leaned in, his breath a phantom touch against the sensitive curve of her neck, sending an unwelcome shiver cascading through her body. His fingers found her thigh, resting there lazily—possessive, comfortable, as if he had every right to touch her.

Her pulse leapt in her throat.

"Every day for five years," he murmured, each word deliberate, drawn out, a slow unraveling of intent. "I have pictured the moment I would finally claim my vengeance."

A flush of heat pooled low in her belly, unwelcome, humiliating. She forced herself to steady her voice, to hold onto some semblance of control.

"I told you I would serve you," she said, though the words came out softer than she intended. "But I won't discuss the past."

His fingers tightened slightly, a quiet acknowledgment of her defiance. Then, just as easily, he withdrew, his smirk practically tangible.

"Oh, we'll discuss it," he assured her, as if it were inevitable. But for now, he let the matter rest.

He was toying with her—of that, she had no doubt. Likely relishing the fact that she now belonged to him, free to enact every desire and every cruelty he pleased.

She had never imagined it would come to this. Not after the courting. Not after the bloodshed that ended it all. If anything, she had expected a blade in her chest, his eyes locked on hers as the light faded from them. That would have made sense. That would have been justice.

But this? She hadn't expected this. And she certainly hadn't expected the way her body responded to it. *Pathetic*, really. Even after everything—even after the self-loathing and the years of running—her heart still leapt at the thought of him claiming her. Touching her.

She closed her eyes and forced herself to breathe, willing the old feelings back into their graves. They had no place here. No power. Not anymore.

He might think her story ended here, in his control. In his arms. But it couldn't. It *wouldn't*. She had come to the Arcane Citadel for one reason: to find the Syltharic Tome and rid herself of Draevok's hex. That purpose had not changed.

Her eyes opened slowly, fixing on the road unfurling before them. Master Sorien was gone now. Zakar ruled now, the title of Arcane Master resting on his shoulders.

After a moment of silence, she asked, "What happened to Master Sorien? Did he die?"

Zakar exhaled slowly, as if considering his words. "Yes, he died. Peacefully," he said at last. "Quietly. Just the way he wanted."

That surprised her.

She had only met the old sorcerer once, when she was barely a teenager, little more than a curiosity at Draevok's side. She had assumed a man of such power would meet a more violent end. A more fearful side of her worried Zakar had been the one to end it.

"Were you and he close?" she asked. It was a safer question than outright asking if he had taken the mage's life. Not that she believed he had—there had been too much gentleness in his voice.

He stifled a laugh. "As close as mentor and student can be, I suppose." There was something in his tone, a faint trace of amusement. She imagined he was smiling but didn't turn to confirm it. "He was an aggravating old man," he sighed, his voice dipping into memory. "A religious zealot. You probably know the kind."

She did. And despite herself, she smiled.

From what little she could recall of Master Sorien, she remembered his countless books on the old gods and goddesses. His devotion to them had been the reason she had risked this journey at all, the reason she had dared to ask him for a cursed book to undo a curse. She had once suspected that his interest in her stemmed from something beyond mere curiosity—that he had likened her to the deities he so revered. She had hoped that fascination would have been enough for him to help her.

But she had come too late.

"How long ago did he die?" she asked, surprised by the quiet grief threading her voice. She had never truly known the man, yet she mourned what could have been.

"It's been a couple of years now," Zakar said. "I was fortunate, really. When I sought out the Arcane Citadel five years ago, he happened to be in need of an apprentice. Maybe I wasn't his first choice, but he didn't have many options." He let out a soft chuckle. "He trained me hard, though. I learned a lot."

She didn't doubt it. Imagining Zakar as a willful student wasn't difficult. Sorien had likely found him an angry, broken prince and known he had his work cut out for him. Yet, despite whatever struggles there had been, the old mage had shaped him into something formidable. In a few short years, Zakar had become every bit as commanding as a true Arcane Master.

Her thoughts drifted, unbidden, to her first meeting with Sorien.

Draevok had brought her to him, demanding answers—wanting to know if she had any connection to the old gods or if it was mere coincidence that she looked the way she did.

Sorien had been intrigued. Fascinated, even. He had taken

her aside, away from Draevok for a rare, fleeting moment, and implored her to become his apprentice.

It had never been an option. Draevok would have never allowed it. But, how different could her life have been if she had made that choice? Would she have stood here now as an Arcane Master in her own right? Surely, Zakar would have already claimed his throne. Perhaps their paths would have crossed one day—not as enemies, but as equals. And maybe... just maybe, they could have become something else. Something real.

She forced the thought away. It was a fantasy, nothing more. Reality demanded her focus. The tome was all that mattered now.

"Where are we headed, anyway?" she asked after a long pause.

"Stonehollow," he said smoothly.

She blinked. "That's quite a distance. Where is the tome being kept there?"

Zakar's smirk deepened. "It is not being kept there. But don't you worry about that," he mused.

Myrithia let out a quiet sigh. There was no use pressing. He would tell her what he wanted, when he wanted.

Against her better judgment, she reclined slightly against him, the warmth of his body seeping through the fabric of his tunic. He was solid beneath her, all muscle and power, and as the cooling evening air settled around them, his warmth became inescapable.

She felt the steady rise and fall of his breath, the subtle flex of his arms each time he adjusted his hold. She swallowed against the tightness in her throat.

"How much further is Stonehollow?" she asked, forcing herself to focus on anything other than the way she felt in his arms.

"Not much further now."

She chewed the inside of her cheek before pressing, "And after we arrive there?"

He smirked. "A slave is not required to know every part of the journey."

She bristled. "You just don't trust me with the information."

"Correct."

She scoffed. "I'm bound to serve you. What's the harm in telling me?"

"I know you too well, Myra." He leaned in slightly, voice

dropping to something quieter, richer with amusement. "And I'd rather not tempt you with opportunity."

She went quiet at that, staring ahead at the path winding through the trees. He was right, of course. Given the chance, she *would* run.

But still, she muttered, "I have no intention of running from you."

Zakar laughed softly, the sound low in his throat. "Liar."

Her jaw clenched, heat flaring in her chest at his easy certainty. She hated this arrangement between them—this wretched bargain. She considered asking him why he wanted it, but the answer was obvious. And she had no desire to hear it spoken aloud.

He wanted her bound to him, a lifetime of servitude in payment for her betrayal. But death would have been the kinder mercy.

She should have died at Draevok's hand. She should have met the same fate as the family she helped dismantle, as the people she betrayed by standing idly at Draevok's side.

She deserved death.

After everything—after betraying Zakar, after taking his trust and grinding it into dust—surely that was reason enough. A small price to pay for the countless lives Draevok had stolen. Lives she had helped him take, because she had been complicit.

Because she had no choice.

But even as the thought crossed her mind, she knew it was a lie.

She had a choice.

She had made it the moment she chose to spare Zakar rather than strike him down. Why then? Why had she waited so long to find a conscience? Why warn him at the last second? Why not fight for him? Why not tell him she was *afraid*?

But she knew the answer. Because she hadn't wanted to lose him. She had clung to every moment, even knowing it was built on a fragile foundation of lies.

She had cared for him deeply, had fallen in love with him in spite of everything she had done. But she had been afraid of betraying Draevok, of what it would mean if she failed him. She was afraid of losing Zakar too soon.

Her time with him had been too *precious*. And she had been too *selfish*.

A long silence stretched between them, thick with everything unsaid. She bit her tongue, keeping her self-loathing buried deep inside of her, and looked ahead.

The last rays of sunlight had finally vanished beyond the horizon, leaving the sky draped in a rich tapestry of indigo and sapphire. The moon had begun its slow ascent, its silver glow illuminating the winding path ahead.

They rode on in silence, the weight of their conversation still pressing between them, unrelenting.

And then, as the distant glow of lanterns flickered through the darkness, breaking through the thick line of trees, Zakar finally spoke again.

"We are here."

CHAPTER 16

Zakar

The town of Stonehollow was exactly as he remembered it—seedy, restless, a place where shadows stretched long and danger lurked in every narrow alley. The streets were cobbled but uneven, reflecting the golden glow of lanterns swinging from wrought-iron posts. The buildings leaned together like old drunkards sharing secrets, some kept in fine repair, others sagging with age and neglect.

The people were just the same—a mix of traveling merchants, weary farmers, and those with less noble professions lurking in doorways and eyeing passersby with greedy intent.

And Myrithia stood out among them.

Zakar clenched his jaw as he felt the weight of lingering stares, saw the flickers of leering interest trailing her every movement. He should have given her a cloak—should have concealed her from view. But he hadn't.

He had wanted to see her in red, to admire her, to watch her squirm beneath the knowledge that she looked every bit the part of his possession. He had wanted word to reach Draevok—to make it known that his prized apprentice had been reduced to nothing more than a plaything in his hands. But now he was regretting that decision.

The men here were desperate. Greedy. He could feel the shift in their gazes, the slow calculation in their movements, the way a few took half-steps closer before meeting his eyes and wisely deciding against it. He didn't often travel to Stonehollow, so perhaps they were unaware of who he was.

His fingers itched to wrap around a throat or two.

He forced the thought away, focusing instead on why they were here.

It had been years since he'd last seen his old friend Calveren. He likely wouldn't mind the late hour—might even offer them a bed for the night. And in two more days they would arrive at Master Sorien's tomb, look at a dusty book, and their bargain would be complete.

Or, at least, his part of it would be.

Letting her actually have the book was out of the question.

The tome was dangerous. Even for him.

But she would *see* it. And that was all she had agreed to.

Watching her face twist with disbelief, with anger, when he kept it behind its seals and walked away—when he refused to let her touch the very thing she had gambled her freedom for—sent a ripple of satisfaction through him.

Let her suffer the consequences of her choices, for not questioning the terms, for not being more precise with her demands.

He pulled on the reins, guiding them through the winding streets, weaving past revelers and cutthroats, merchants closing their shops, and innkeepers ushering drunken patrons inside. His horse's hooves clattered against stone as they passed a gambling den, its doorway brimming with pipe smoke and laughter, the scent of roasted lamb and cheap ale curling into the night.

It wasn't long before they reached their destination—a manor nestled at the far end of town, set apart from the cramped buildings and bustling inns.

It was stately but modest, its stone walls draped in creeping ivy, the heavy wooden door carved with runic inscriptions that gleamed faintly under the lanterns lining the path. A black iron gate, slightly ajar, bore the emblem of an unfurling scroll—the mark of a scholar. Smoke rose gently from the chimney, and warm candlelight flickered through the arched windows, suggesting its owner had been expecting company.

Zakar smirked.

"Just a quick visit," he murmured, dismounting fluidly before turning to Myrithia. "I need something from an old friend."

Zakar dismounted first, his boots hitting the stone with practiced ease. A stablehand approached, taking the reins without a word, while another servant stepped forward, bowing his head slightly before addressing him.

"Master," the man greeted smoothly, his expression muted. "This way."

Zakar motioned for Myrithia to follow, placing a hand at the small of her back—if only to remind her that escape was a fool's notion. Together, they stepped inside the grand manor.

The interior was as he remembered—stately but not ostentatious, the walls lined with towering bookshelves, the scent of parchment and aged oak hanging in the air. A massive chandelier loomed above, its flames dancing as gilded light pooled across the dark stone floors. Plush chairs were arranged in intimate clusters, and woven tapestries draped the walls, depicting histories long forgotten by most. The atmosphere was heavy with quiet sophistication, a scholar's haven untouched by the chaos of the outside world.

Across the room, seated in a high-backed chair by the hearth, was Calveren Wren. His silver-streaked hair was tied neatly at the nape of his neck, and the lines etched into his face spoke more of wisdom than wear. A book rested open in one hand, a cup of tea in the other, steam drifting softly above the surface. He barely looked up as they entered, finishing his sip before closing the book with care and setting it aside.

Then, with a glance toward Zakar, he stood—tall for his age, his posture still proud despite the years. "Zakar." His voice was steady, carrying the weight of familiarity, respect, and a touch of exasperation.

A slow smile tugged at Zakar's lips as they met halfway, grasping forearms in a firm but friendly greeting, their mutual amusement unspoken but understood.

Before either could speak further, a small face peeked through a doorway across the room—barely visible, the top of her head just clearing the edge of the frame. She had a crown of soft brown curls and wide, curious eyes that darted between Zakar and Myrithia.

Calveren's expression softened instantly. "Back to your tea party, little one. I'll join you in a moment, once I've finished with our guests."

The girl gave a reluctant nod, vanishing back into the room like a shy shadow.

Zakar blinked, caught off guard. "You have a granddaughter?"

Calveren's smile deepened with surprising warmth. "Nessie finally settled down. Married a schoolteacher of all things. It's been nice," he said, his voice lower, almost wistful. "Slower pace of life. I find I don't mind it as much as I thought I would."

Then, like shutters snapping closed, the warmth disappeared from his eyes and he turned his gaze to Myrithia. His sharp eyes assessed her in a swift, practiced sweep before returning to Zakar. "I see you've brought a *traitor* to my home. Appreciate that."

His expression remained neutral, but Zakar didn't miss the slight twitch of his fingers—a silent debate over whether to reach for a warding spell.

Instead, his gaze slid toward the entrance. "Did anyone see you arrive?"

Zakar quirked a brow, but Calveren was already eyeing the striking crimson of Myrithia's gown. If the townspeople hadn't noticed that silver hair, they had surely noticed that dress.

A sigh left his lips before he muttered dryly, "Of course they did." His gaze turned toward the windows, already calculating. "I'll have to reinforce the wards. Otherwise, we'll have mercenaries clawing through the windows before the night's end."

Zakar chuckled. "No need to trouble yourself. We don't intend to stay long. I'm only here in need of a small favor."

Calveren shot him a knowing look, folding his arms. "There are no *small* favors that warrant a visit from the Master of the Arcane."

Zakar's grin widened. "Ah, but this one is relatively small. I just need to borrow the Nythera."

Calveren's expression darkened at the request, his lips pressing into a firm line. He sighed, exhaling slowly as if to smooth away his displeasure, brushing a hand over the sleeve of his fine tunic in an idle gesture of dismissal.

"And why, exactly, do you need that?"

Zakar gave a small, easy shrug. "A simple borrowing. I'll be gone few days at most, and I'll return it to you exactly as it was given."

Calveren's sharp gaze cut to him. "That does not tell me why you need it."

Before Zakar could decide whether he wanted to answer or keep the old fox guessing, Myrithia spoke up, her voice edged with impatience.

"Please, Sir, it's very important."

The urgency in her tone made Calveren's brows lift slightly in interest. He let the moment stretch before turning his attention fully to Zakar, ignoring her altogether. A slow smile curved at the edge of his mouth.

"And why is she in your company?"

Zakar blew out a long breath, already growing tired of the line of questioning. "She is not a threat. Calm yourself."

Calveren chuckled, shaking his head. "I never said she was. But I do recall the role she played in your downfall. A rather poetic reversal, don't you think? To see her standing at your side."

Zakar smiled, sharp and cutting. "She's not standing at my side, Calveren. She belongs to me now, as my *slave*."

Calveren's gaze slid back to Myrithia, taking his time as he appraised her once more. His eyes, keen as ever, caught the brief flicker of irritation she barely managed to smother.

His lips twitched, but he said nothing to her, instead looking back to Zakar with a considering tilt of his head.

"If you want the Nythera," he finally said, "then you'd best have something worth trading for it."

CHAPTER 17
Myrithia

Myrithia clenched her hands at her sides, unsettled by the prospect of Zakar having something valuable enough to trade. What was the Nythera, and why was it something he even needed to access a book? What could he possibly offer this man for it? A terrible thought crossed her mind.

She was his possession now. *She* was something he could trade.

Even as her anxiety flared, she reminded herself that Zakar wasn't likely to give her away so easily. She was too useful, after all. Too entertaining for him to discard after so many years of hunting her down. And yet, the thought still unsettled her, like a blade resting against her throat.

Zakar's green eyes flicked to her, then back to Calveren. "A servant might show her somewhere to wait while we conduct our business?"

Myrithia frowned. So that was his game. Whatever he was about to trade, he didn't want her knowing about it.

Calveren sighed, clearly reluctant to part with the item but also intrigued by what Zakar might offer in return. With a lazy gesture, he beckoned for a servant, a lean man in crisp evening attire, to step forward. "Show the lady to one of the sitting rooms. Make sure she is comfortable."

Myrithia's fingers twitched, silver light shimmering faintly at her fingertips before flickering out. She had ways of seeing what she wasn't meant to see.

She turned gracefully, allowing herself one final glance at Zakar. He hadn't so much as looked at her. Dismissed. Like a pet at his feet. She followed the servant through the hall, her mind racing with speculation.

The room they led her to wasn't the modest waiting room she expected, but a library—lavish in the way only old money could achieve. Dark-stained shelves climbed the walls, crammed with books whose spines gleamed with gold filigree. A low-burning hearth filled the air with the rich scent of cedarwood. Above it, murals stretched across the ceiling, weathered but still vivid— depictions of the old gods and goddesses, their faces beautiful and terrible in equal measure.

She had always wondered if they had ever truly existed, or if they were just myths carried forward by desperate men. If they had lived once… where were they now?

She caught glimpses of names as she passed: Altrien, the god of thresholds, often prayed to at births and funerals; Selvane, the goddess of storms and mourning, said to weep tempests when kings fell. Near the back of the room, half-obscured by shadow, was a smaller, darker figure whose mischievous smile was unmistakable. Nyxian, the trickster. A chill pricked at her skin despite the warmth of the fire.

There were holy books here too—stacked carefully on tables, their bindings heavy with age. Ancient prayers, lost rituals.

Draevok would have enjoyed this room. If she had more time, she might have lingered as well. Curiosity tugged at her even now, but she knew there were more pressing matters that demanded her attention now.

Myrithia tore her gaze away from the murals and exhaled softly, lifting her hands. Silver magic hummed at her fingertips. Carefully, she traced a small, circular glyph into the air, her magic weaving together to form a tiny portal window no larger than her palm.

The image wavered before coming into focus.

Zakar and Calveren stood below her, the spell giving her an aerial view of their exchange. Perfect.

You're a fool if you think I'll sit idly by while you keep secrets from me, she thought with a sneer. She might be his slave, but she wouldn't be ignorant. Information was an advantage, and she needed every advantage if she ever expected to escape this bargain.

Calveren folded his arms, expression dry. "I assume you aren't simply going to take it and leave?"

Zakar smirked. "Would I ever be so rude?"

Calveren gave him a look.

"Fine," Zakar relented, exhaling slowly as he reached inside his coat. Myrithia leaned forward, watching as he withdrew something small but gleaming. The spell's angle didn't allow her to see it very clearly, but when Calveren's brows lifted in surprise, she knew it had to be something of immense worth.

Calveren took the item from Zakar's hand and turned it over, weighing it with a discerning eye.

"You must be serious if you're giving this to me," Calveren mused. He tapped his fingers against what looked like a vial of red liquid. A potion? Blood?

Calveren's gaze flicked up to meet Zakar's, eyes unreadable. "Sentimental, isn't it?"

"Just enough," Zakar said smoothly. "And if I don't return the key on time, I'm sure you'll enjoy having the liberties that would provide you."

Calveren chuckled, then sighed, relenting. "Indeed, I would." He slipped the vial into his coat pocket and extended his hand. "Fine. You may borrow it, but return it in no more than five days. It's not something I need the Arcane Master to *accidentally* start thinking belongs to him."

Zakar chuckled, a dismissive nod signaling his acceptance of the terms. His amusement didn't waver, but something seemed to catch his eye—a faint glimmer of silver on his shoulder. With an idle flick of his gloved fingers, he brushed it away.

She barely had time to process the gesture before Zakar's head suddenly tilted upward, his smug grin widening.

"*That* will cost you, dear."

Her stomach plummeted.

He was looking directly at her.

Damn it.

She swiped her hand through the magic, instantly dissolving the spell, the image shattering like glass. Her pulse hammered against her ribs as she pressed a palm to her chest, trying to steady her breath.

Her intrusion had been noticed.

And Zakar, undoubtedly, was going to exploit it.

**

Zakar stepped into the waiting room, the door creaking open just enough for her to see the wry smile on his face. Myrithia stiffened, pulse quickening as she searched his expression for any sign of retribution. But he only cocked his head slightly, his smirk deepening.

"It's time to take our leave," he said smoothly.

She hesitated, unsure if he was simply toying with her or if there was truly some consequence lying in wait. But she swallowed her unease, forcing herself to nod. Without another word, she followed as he turned, her fingers briefly tightening into the fabric of her dress as she forced her features into careful neutrality.

"Where are we going?" she asked, hating the uncertainty in her own voice as they retreated to the main entrance of the manor.

Zakar barely spared her a glance. "Calveren was generous enough to offer *me* a bed for the night," he said airily, "but you, I'm afraid, are not welcome in his home."

Myrithia frowned, though she couldn't exactly blame the old mage for his refusal. Even if she didn't already suspect he disliked her, she understood why he might not want to endanger his granddaughter by harboring a fugitive. Her gaze drifted back toward the manor as they exited, the warm glow of its windows flickering like distant safety. Then, she looked ahead again.

"Did he at least give you the Nythera?"

Zakar gave a short nod, clearly uninterested in elaborating. "Of course."

She glanced at him. "What is the Nythera, exactly? Is it really that important? What does it do?"

"So inquisitive," he mused with a faint chuckle. "It's said the

Nythera was crafted by the first Arcane Gatekeeper—there's only one in existence. It's bound to the ley lines and allows a person to enter a place that would otherwise reject their presence."

Her brows furrowed. "You need it to access the book?"

"Precisely. Without it, getting inside would be significantly harder." He paused, then added with a faint smirk, "I'm sure Calveren had his own plans for it this year, but whatever they were can wait until next."

"Is it a one-time use?" she asked. "What does it actually do?"

"It grants instantaneous travel from one precise location to another—exactly one mile apart. But it's more than that. If I stand in the right place, I'll be transported directly into the location where the book is sealed away."

She blinked. "I could do something similar with my own magic. Not a full mile, maybe, but if it's just instant travel you need, I could do it."

"Ah, but what you can do pales in comparison to this," he said, his voice low with satisfaction. "This relic bypasses any charm, shield, or ward. With it, I could walk straight into Draevok's private chambers and kill him before he could lift a finger."

Her expression faltered, unsettled by the sheer power such a device held. No wonder Calveren had demanded a trade. "If that's possible... why haven't you done it already? It's been five years. He stole *everything* from you."

"Because that's not my style," he said simply. "There are countless ways we could kill each other. But I want him to know he lost. I want him to see it coming—and be powerless to stop it."

As they stepped into the night air, the stablehand was already approaching with Zakar's horse, not far from them.

"Where will we be staying tonight?" She asked.

"At an inn, I suppose," he said casually, as if the thought had only just crossed his mind.

She barely had time to respond before he unfastened his cloak, pulling it from his shoulders with an effortless grace. He didn't say a word as he settled it around her, the thick fabric pooling over her arms, the scent of him wrapping around her instantly. He clasped it at her throat with deft fingers, the smooth leather of his gloves brushing against her skin.

She looked up, only to find his gaze already locked onto hers. She swallowed. "What are you—?"

His fingers found her hood, guiding it over her hair with quiet intent. "Do you *want* to be recognized?"

Myrithia's lips parted, irritation flickering in her eyes. *Now* he cared about the bounty? *Now* he wanted to be cautious—after parading her through the center of town on his lap, dressed in vivid red? But as the frustration simmered, she couldn't focus on it—not when his hands lingered at the edges of her hood, his fingers brushing the sensitive skin beneath her ears with a touch that was firm and possessive.

He leaned in just slightly, enough that his breath ghosted against her cheek, and his smirk returned—this time, sharper, darker.

"I can't wait to punish you for spying on me," he murmured.

Myrithia's stomach dropped.

She drew back instinctively, her heart hammering as she stammered, "I—I was just curious."

Zakar chuckled, low and indulgent. "Curiosity is a dangerous thing, Myra." He reached up, smoothing an errant strand of her silver hair beneath the hood with a slow, measured touch. "And no apology will get you out of this."

A lump formed in her throat, his words settling over her like a silent vow.

"Let's go," he said smoothly, turning as the stable hand finally approached with his horse and presented the reins.

Myrithia remained still for a moment longer, her fingers tensing against the fabric of the cloak. Somehow, the night ahead felt far more dangerous than she had first anticipated.

CHAPTER 18

Zakar

Zakar shut the door to their new room behind them, his voice a low murmur as he wove an incantation under his breath. The air shimmered faintly, his protective seal snapping into place with an unseen force. Another flick of his wrist, and the window received the same treatment, a nearly invisible layer of magic locking the world out—and her in.

He had seen the way the inn's lower floors had stirred at their arrival, how eyes had lingered too long, whispers already carrying through the halls. No doubt her presence had made its way through Stonehollow by now. He had no delusions that they would be left undisturbed, but most would be deterred by his wards.

And if not?

Well, he wouldn't mind spilling some blood tonight.

But first, he had more pressing entertainment.

He turned, watching as Myrithia slipped his cloak from her shoulders and draped it over the back of a chair. She glanced around the room, her posture stiff with unease, her fingers tracing idly over the worn wooden table as if appraising the space. When she spoke, her voice was quiet but steady.

"Do you think we'll be safe enough here?"

Zakar smirked. "You are with the *Master of the Arcane*, Myra. You will be fine." Then, with a slow, measured step, he advanced.

THE ARCANE BARGAIN

Her body reacted before she did, backing toward the wall. His slow prowl across the room was effortless, savoring the way she shrank from him.

"It's time for your punishment," he murmured. Of course, there was no real punishment. He had no desire to bring her physical pain—he wasn't a sadist, at least not in that way. No, what he wanted was information. And perhaps a few other things.

She would be far more pliant if she believed she was avoiding a worse fate.

She backed away, her spine pressing against the wood. "Please, I—"

"I did warn you," he reminded her, his tone laced with the smallest thread of pity. "But if you'd rather avoid chastisement…" He paused, watching her pulse flutter against her throat. "Then perhaps you'd prefer to play a *game* instead."

She swallowed, wary.

His smirk deepened.

"The rules are simple," he continued. "We take turns. I ask you a question, and you must answer *truthfully*. Then, you may ask me one in return, and I will extend the same courtesy."

She narrowed her eyes slightly, as if searching for the trap.

Zakar's smile was slow, amused. "You may lie, if you dare," he said smoothly. "But I will know. And should you attempt to deceive me, well…" His gaze drifted lazily over her, as if already considering her punishment. "Then you'll be *mine* to do with as I please. No more games, no more choices."

She stiffened at that.

He reached up, brushing a gloved knuckle along the line of her jaw, reveling in the way her breath hitched.

"Do you accept?" he purred.

Zakar let his fingers trail away from her side, only to catch her wrist, his grip firm but unhurried. He could feel the tension humming beneath her skin, the barely contained nerves as he led her toward the hearth. He gestured for her to sit, watching as she hesitated only briefly before lowering herself onto the plush chair.

He settled into the chair across from her, the fire crackling between them as shifting shadows played across her uncertain expression. With a simple wave of his hand, a bottle of wine materialized on the small table between them, two glasses already filled with rich crimson liquid.

Myrithia glanced between him and the glass he now held out to her. He said nothing, merely offering it in silence, watching the war waging in her eyes. Cautious, she reached for it, lifting the goblet to her lips. She took a slow sip at first—testing, waiting—before tipping the rest back in a single swallow.

Zakar chuckled, swirling the wine in his own glass before taking a leisurely sip. He set it down with a soft clink and leaned back. "Let's begin," he murmured, his tone deceptively smooth.

She shifted, her grip tightening around the empty goblet, but she didn't protest.

He started simply, removing his gloves from his hands and draping them over the armrest of his chair. "How are you enjoying being my slave?"

Her lips parted on a sharp inhale, irritation flashing across her features. "I am not enjoying it at all."

His smirk deepened. "Are you sure?" He tilted his head, watching her closely. "You seemed to enjoy the kiss."

The reaction was instant. Heat flooded her cheeks, her lips pressing together as she turned her face away from him.

He saw an opportunity and took it. "Tell me, Myrithia—how did you enjoy it? What were you thinking in that moment?"

Her fingers clenched around the stem of the goblet. "I thought it was one question at a time," she shot back, her voice a little too controlled, too measured.

He laughed. "Very well. Your turn."

She exhaled, composing herself before speaking. "What item did you give to Calveren?"

He studied her for a moment, amused at the sharpness in her tone. "A vial," he answered easily.

Her brows knitted together. "And what was in the vial?"

He smirked and leaned forward slightly. "Ah, ah," he chided, "my turn again."

She exhaled harshly and leaned back in her chair, clearly displeased but unwilling to push the matter further.

Zakar's gaze never left her as he lifted his next strike. "The kiss," he repeated. "How were you feeling in that moment? Did you enjoy it?"

She was silent this time, staring into the fire, her expression carefully buried. But he *felt* it—the faint thrum of magic sparking under her skin, their bond stirring. She was preparing to lie to him.

He smirked, waiting.

"It was fine," she muttered, short, clipped, her voice betraying her irritation.

He arched a brow, letting the silence linger between them, pressing her with nothing but his patience. "Is that the answer you want to go with?" he asked smoothly. "Because if you're lying, Myrithia, I *will* carry out your punishment with no further delay."

She groaned, snatching up the bottle and pouring herself another glass. She downed half of it before speaking, her voice lower now, quieter.

"I have always enjoyed the way we kiss, Zakar."

Not a lie.

A swell of satisfaction filled his chest, his smirk tipping into something unmistakably victorious. It was good to know that had always been real between them. Then and now.

"What was in the vial?" she asked quickly, as if desperate to change the subject from her previous confession.

He tilted his head slightly, letting the anticipation linger before answering smoothly, "Blood."

Her body tensed. He could see it in the subtle shift of her posture, the way her fingers twitched slightly against the goblet. But she schooled her expression, forcing herself to feign disinterest.

"Blood from what?" she pressed, her voice steadier now. "From who?"

Zakar clicked his tongue, swirling the wine in his glass before taking another slow sip. "Ah," he mused, his voice smooth as silk. "You've already asked your question. Now it's my turn."

She huffed in irritation but leaned back, clearly displeased but unwilling to push the matter further.

He took his time, savoring the taste of the wine before his next question. "Why did you spare my life five years ago?"

The air in the room shifted. He saw it immediately—the way her body went still, the flicker of something unreadable crossing her face. It was a heavy question, and they both knew it.

She wet her lips, her fingers tightening slightly on the goblet. "I don't want to discuss the past," she muttered. "Is there a way to opt out of answering?"

His smirk deepened. "You can delay the question, but you *will* have to answer it eventually."

She exhaled sharply, looking away. "Fine. I'll delay it."

Zakar leaned back in his chair, watching her with lazy amusement. "Alright then," he mused, his voice dangerously soft. "Take off your dress."

Her reaction was immediate—her entire body stiffened, her head snapping toward him, her lips parting in utter disbelief. He relished it.

"What?" she choked out.

His smirk was wicked. "Or," he drawled, "you could just answer the question."

He could see the war in her mind—the frantic calculations, the attempt to decide which was the lesser evil. He took another slow sip of wine, watching her deliberate, thoroughly enjoying himself.

Finally, with a sharp exhale, she muttered, "Fine." She set her goblet down and reached for the laces at her back, fumbling.

Zakar chuckled, watching her struggle. "Come here," he instructed smoothly, setting his own glass aside. "I'll loosen them for you. *Unless*," he added with a smirk, "you'd rather just say your answer. It's an easy enough question."

Her glare was heated, but her stubbornness won out. She rose to her feet, stepping forward before sinking gracefully to her knees in front of him, turning her back to him, her long silver hair sliding over one shoulder to bare the delicate nape of her neck.

Zakar traced the laces with a slow drag of his fingers, untying them with a precision that dared her to move. His hands moved steadily, loosening the knots, his fingertips grazing the smooth fabric of her chemise beneath her gown. She was so close, her scent—soft, floral—filling his lungs.

Everything within him began to war against reason. He wanted her. He wanted her just like this, kneeling before him. He wanted to see her ivory skin bared in the firelight, sweat forming at the small of her back as she took him into herself, as her ragged moans might fill the air. He wanted to claim her in the way he had always wanted to, in the way he had dreamed of from the moment he first met her.

The first night he saw her had been the night of his engagement ball—a grand affair meant to celebrate both his imminent ascension to the throne and his intended bride, the Duchess of Evergrove. But Myrithia had stolen the night. She had stolen *him*.

A Chantress with no invitation, she had infiltrated the ball with purpose, seeking *him* out. And from the moment he heard her voice—sultry and hypnotic, weaving through the air like a spell—he had been ensnared.

She had bound him to her instantly, those siren-blue eyes and honeyed whispers leading him exactly where she wanted. He had been at her mercy from the very first glance, blissfully unaware of how deep her trap had already been set. One night. That was all it had taken for her to become his fixation, his hunger—his ruin.

And even now, he couldn't be certain if that had been the first of her spells or not.

His fingers lingered at her back for a second longer before he pulled back. "There," he murmured.

Myrithia stood, her movements stiff, her shoulders rising and falling with controlled breaths. She reached for the dress, beginning to slide it off her shoulders.

"Face me," Zakar commanded.

Her hands stilled. She turned slowly, her expression a mixture of embarrassment and anger, but she complied. Her chin lifted just slightly in defiance as she let the dress slip from her shoulders.

Zakar's gaze swept over her, leisurely, indulgent, taking his time drinking in the sight of her. He lifted his glass and took a long, slow sip, savoring every second.

"Slower," he murmured.

Her fingers tightened around the crimson gown before she obeyed, the fabric cascading down her frame in a slow, reluctant descent until it pooled at her feet.

Only a thin, cream-colored undergarment remained.

He took his time observing her, letting his eyes roam over the curves of her body highlighted crisply by the flames behind her, the delicate shift of her breath, the way her lips pressed together as if resisting the urge to speak.

Gods, he wanted to drag her into his lap, to grip her hips and sink into her until he forgot every reason he was supposed to hold back. Until there was nothing left but the sound of her moans and the feel of her wrapped around him. He swallowed, closing his eyes to regain his composure. Pitiful, really, that his game with her was torturous even for himself.

Finally, he gestured lazily to her chair while he readjusted his posture in his own. "Sit," he murmured, lifting his goblet once more. "And ask your question."

CHAPTER 19
Myrithia

Myrithia tried to steady her breath, her fingers grazing the rim of her wine goblet as she attempted to ignore just how sheer her underdress truly was. She had reminded herself—over and over—that he had already seen her in even less, the crimson nightgown he had so wickedly chosen for her back at the citadel. This was no different. She shouldn't feel exposed.

And yet, under the weight of his gaze, she did.

She needed a distraction.

Pouring herself another generous helping of wine, she finally asked, "Whose blood is in that vial?"

Zakar, who had been watching the flames dance in the hearth, turned his head slightly, his expression nonchalant. "Mine."

She stiffened.

Blood magic. That was the only logical reason for it. Blood magic forged the strongest bindings—contracts that could not be undone without powerful countermeasures. And yet, he had given it away, placed it in the hands of another. He must truly trust that Calveren wouldn't betray him.

Or, her mind whispered, if she could get her hands on that vial, she might very well be able to forge her own freedom.

She barely had time to school her expression before his sharp green eyes flicked to hers. As if he had plucked the thought straight from her head, he smirked.

Myrithia's stomach twisted uneasily.

Before she could say a word, he spoke—his voice measured, composed, and unmistakably in control. "My turn again. Why did you spare my life five years ago?"

Her breath caught.

She had known he would return to this. Knew, deep in her bones, that he would never let it go.

A slow, cruel smile curled his lips.

"You must pick a new question," she insisted, her voice clipped, her fingers tightening around the goblet. "I chose not to answer that question and you allowed me to delay it."

He made a sound of amusement. "Ah, but I never said how long your delay would last. I only said it could be delayed."

She clenched her jaw. "That isn't fair."

His gaze darkened. "Answer the question."

Myrithia sucked in a sharp breath, feeling herself slipping beneath the weight of it. Five years. Five years of evading this very moment, of suppressing the memories, the truth, the unbearable guilt. But she couldn't say it. She couldn't give him that piece of herself—not when she knew what he could do with it.

To admit she had loved him would be to hand him a weapon. And if he twisted her confession into something cruel, something to laugh at, it would shatter what little pride she had left.

He already owned her body. She would not let him own her heart. Not when it could be used to break her.

She forced the word past her lips. "Delay."

Zakar's smirk deepened, wicked and knowing.

Gods, she had made a mistake.

"To delay the question again, dear," he murmured, his voice rich with amusement, "you will have to give me a kiss."

Her heart lurched.

Of course. *Of course*, he would make her do this.

Her mouth parted, forming silent protests that refused to pass her lips. She felt trapped beneath his expectant gaze, pinned in place by the smoldering intensity in his expression.

It would be easier to just answer the question. To peel away the layers of deception and truth she had so carefully built over the years. But answering it would undo her. She would no longer have a shield to wield against him. He would know.

Surely, a kiss was the lesser of two evils.

"Fine," she muttered, swallowing back her apprehension.

She stood, each step slow, cautious as she closed the distance between them.

Zakar watched her approach with the patience of a hunter, his gaze sharp, his lips slightly parted as if already anticipating her taste.

Her pulse pounded as she leaned down, bracing herself with one hand against his chair. Her breath mingled with his, the space between them vanishing, and then—softly, hesitantly—she pressed her lips to his.

The touch was fleeting, barely more than a whisper of contact. But as she pulled back, relief flooding through her at having completed the task, Zakar did something that sent a wave of ice down her spine.

He patted his thigh. And with a wicked gleam in his eye, he murmured, "No, I want you here as you do it." He tilted his chin, his smirk deepening. "I want you on my lap, and I want you to kiss me like you used to… when it was all just a game to you."

Myrithia's breath caught in her throat.

He was savoring this—her hesitation, her inner turmoil, the storm raging within her. She inhaled deeply, summoning whatever remained of her shattered composure, and stepped forward.

Slowly, hesitantly, she placed her hands on his shoulders and climbed onto his lap, her knees pressing against the firm muscles of his thighs. Heat radiated from his body, wrapping around her, suffocating her, drowning her in the scent of spice and magic. The sheer intimacy of their position was unbearable, yet she forced herself to settle against him, her breath hitching when she felt how solid he was beneath her.

His hands, large and possessive, skimmed up her sides before resting on her waist, fingers flexing in lazy possession. He was enjoying this far too much.

"Go on, then," he murmured, his voice a silken thread of command. "Kiss me, Myra. Like you used to."

A shiver danced down her spine.

Like she used to. When she had whispered honeyed lies in his ear, when she had kissed him in hidden corridors, weaving her spell of deception so masterfully that even she had fallen prey to it. When she had been the one leading him to ruin, never anticipating that she would be the one to fall.

She inhaled deeply and leaned in, pressing her lips to his.

At first, it was tentative—a slow, cautious meeting of mouths, her lips soft against his, testing, lingering. He didn't push, didn't seize control as she expected. He let her lead, let her taste him, let her remember.

It was that memory—the way he had once been hers—that made her reckless.

The kiss deepened.

A soft sigh slipped from her lips as she tilted her head, her fingers threading into the dark strands of his hair. His hands tightened at her waist, and then, with agonizing slowness, they trailed lower, smoothing over the curve of her hips, his grip firm, possessive. He pulled her flush against him, against the rigid column beneath his trousers, the movement drawing a gasp from her—one he swallowed greedily as his lips moved against hers, coaxing her into a slow, sinful rhythm.

Warmth rushed through her, sending a throbbing, dull ache of need between her legs as she rolled her hips against him, feeling his groan of approval shiver through her. His fingers slipped beneath the gossamer fabric of her chemise, coarse fingertips gliding up her thighs in possession, squeezing the soft curve of her round backside as he met the undulation of her hips.

She shouldn't be doing this. She shouldn't be enjoying this.

But gods, she was.

His tongue swept against hers, tasting, claiming. He kissed her like he had five years ago—like he had never stopped wanting her, never stopped craving her.

And for a moment, just a moment, she allowed herself to melt into him.

Her body continued to betray her, pressing closer, her thighs tightening around him as her fingers grazed the nape of his neck. He groaned again into her mouth, a sound that sent heat pooling deep in her stomach. He wanted her. And worse—she wanted him, too.

Panic seized her.

She broke away, breathless, her fingers trembling where they still clutched his hair. His lips were flushed, his breathing ragged, his pupils blown wide as he stared up at her with something dark and knowing.

"You're a fool if you think I'll let you stop there," he murmured, his voice roughened with something almost dangerous.

She stiffened, willing her thundering heart to settle.

"I upheld my end," she whispered, her voice not nearly as steady as she wanted it to be. "I kissed you."

His lips curved into a slow, victorious smirk.

"Yes," he agreed, dragging his hands back down her thigh, his touch igniting sparks along her skin. "You did. And unless you pull away now, our little game will be over and I'll make use of our bargain and claim your body tonight."

Myrithia shot up from his lap as if she'd been burned, nearly knocking over her goblet in the process. Her breath was unsteady, her pulse a frenzied rhythm she couldn't seem to calm. She turned away from him, smoothing her hands down her sheer underdress as if that would erase the memory of his touch, of his mouth on hers, of the fire that still burned low in her stomach.

Damn him.

Damn herself for enjoying it.

She dropped back into her chair, her hand firm around the stem of her glass, though she made no move to drink from it. Zakar was watching her, his gaze still heavy with hunger, his lips still parted slightly as if he was tasting the ghost of their kiss.

She needed to say something. Anything.

"It's my turn," she said, her voice quieter than she would've liked.

Zakar exhaled slowly, lifting his goblet, and took a long sip of his wine as if to steady himself. "Ask it."

The question left her lips before she could stop it.

"Do you hate me?"

She stiffened.

Why had she asked that?

Of all the things she could've asked, why had she chosen the one question she didn't want the answer to? The one answer she feared? Of course he hated her. He had every reason to. How could he not?

Her fingers flexed around her goblet, considering draining the rest of the wine in one long gulp, hoping to drown out whatever venomous truth was about to fall from his lips.

But then, he did something unexpected.

Zakar smiled. Not a cruel smirk, not something laced with amusement at her expense. Just... soft. Quiet.

And then, in a voice equally as gentle, he murmured, "I do not."

Her breath stilled.

She blinked at him, unsure if she had heard him correctly.

Her heart betrayed her, stuttering in a pathetic, unsteady rhythm. She couldn't speak, couldn't demand an explanation, couldn't even ask what he meant by that.

Because it wasn't her turn.

And when he exhaled, his gaze darkening, she knew exactly what he would say next.

"Why did you spare my life five years ago?"

Damn him.

Damn this question.

She tightened her grip on the goblet, nails pressing into the delicate glass. She hated the way he looked at her—so patient, so knowing. He knew she had been trying to avoid this. He knew it unraveled her.

She clenched her teeth and muttered, "Delay."

Zakar leaned forward slightly, his voice lowering into something rich edged with warning. "Answer it."

"Delay," she snapped, more insistent this time.

He chuckled darkly, shaking his head. "I will drag you to that bed and show you what you will do for me next," he murmured, tilting his head as his eyes traced over her, drinking in her flushed skin, the rapid rise and fall of her chest. "And then, when I am sated, you will answer that question."

A shallow gasp escaped her.

Gods.

The worst part was that she couldn't even begin to unravel why that threat made her dizzy with want. Why it sent heat curling through her veins, making her thighs press together beneath the sheer fabric of her dress.

She swallowed hard, steadying herself. "I spared your life because I couldn't bear to kill you," she blurted out. "I didn't want you to die. I couldn't let that happen."

Zakar's expression didn't change.

He simply stared at her, as if reading every part of her. And then, softly, "Why?"

Myrithia stiffened.

"That is a new question—" she began, but he cut her off.

"It is the same question," he said, his voice low and unflinching. "Why did you spare me?"

Her throat ached.

The words were there, pressing against her tongue, threatening to break free. And gods, she couldn't say them.

Her eyes burned. She felt the weight of it all pressing against her chest, suffocating her, unraveling her, leaving her exposed in ways she couldn't afford to be.

She took a breath.

Then another.

And then, voice barely above a whisper, she forced out the only word she could.

"Delay."

CHAPTER 20

Zakar

Zakar stared at her, his fingers clenching into a fist as the word echoed in his mind. *Delay.*

Again. She had dared to say it *again. This maddening woman.*

His grip tightened around the stem of his wine glass, the urge to shatter it between his fingers almost too tempting to ignore. But instead, he set it down with sharp finality, the sound slicing through the charged silence between them. And then, before she could even react, he was on his feet.

Myrithia barely had time to inhale before his hand wrapped around her wrist, yanking her up to stand before him. A sharp gasp parted her lips, but he didn't let her speak, didn't give her the chance to utter another damn *delay.*

Instead, he crushed his mouth to hers in a kiss that was anything but gentle.

It was punishing, bruising, his tongue moving against hers with a fury that was only matched by the possessive grip of his hands. He backed her up, forcing her against the wall, feeling the way her breath seized, the way her body stiffened beneath his touch before it softened—before she *yielded* to him.

The past, the betrayal, the shattered pieces of what they once had—none of it mattered in that moment. Only this. Only her.

Her fingers dug into his tunic, dragging him closer, and that single act sent a violent thrill through him. She *wanted* this. She *wanted him.* And damn her, damn her completely, because he wanted her even more.

With a growl of frustration, he tore his mouth from hers just long enough to grab her arm and drag her toward the bed. She stumbled, but he caught her, pushing her down onto the mattress with effortless strength, his body following as he kissed her again, harder, deeper, consuming her. He could feel her trembling beneath him, her fingers gripping his sleeves, her breath coming in soft, desperate pants.

His hands found the hem of her dress again, pushing it up around her waist as he pressed against her. His trousers were tight, strained against his arousal as he let out a low rasp into her neck. He let his fingers trace her sex, already finding her slick, and he dipped inside of her with a satisfying exhale from his lips. She moaned into his ear, a sultry sound that coiled around him like a silk ribbon tightening with every breath.

She was just as lost in this as he was.

And that was *exactly* why he had to stop.

He pulled away abruptly, forcing his body to still, to *breathe*. His hand still rested low against her, his fingers ghosting along her damp skin, his own breath uneven with restraint. Myrithia stared up at him, dazed, her lips parted, her cheeks flushed.

And he nearly lost himself all over again.

He forced himself to step back, his fingers slowly closing into fists as he turned from her. He needed distance. He needed control.

"The game is over," he muttered, his voice lower, rougher than he intended. His pulse was still thundering, his body still demanding more, *demanding her,* but he would not be weak. Not again. When he would take her, and he *would* take her, he would be in control. He would be the one to toy with her and bring her to ecstasy, all the while savoring how she felt as she surrendered to him, to the shame of her desire for him.

This was his game, and damn it all if she thought she was the master of it.

He reached the door and gripped the handle, looking back at her just once—just enough to see the way she still lay there, stunned, her chest rising and falling in quick, uneven breaths, her sheer gown still bunched around her waist.

"You *will* give me an answer," he told her, his voice edged with finality.

And then he left, slamming the door behind him before he

could make the mistake of turning back.

Zakar descended the stairs with measured steps, his expression carved from stone. Around him, the low hum of drunken voices and clinking tankards filled the inn's dimly lit common room, firelight flickering against worn wooden beams. He ignored the glances cast his way—the wary, the curious, the ones who knew exactly who he was but pretended not to. It didn't matter. None of it mattered.

He barely had a single glass of wine, while Myrithia had indulged in at least two—perhaps three—but yet, he was the one who felt intoxicated. Drunk on the taste of her. On the fire in her gaze. On the maddening, infuriating way she still had power over him, despite being entirely at his mercy.

He stepped outside, inhaling deeply as the crisp night air cooled his burning thoughts. He needed to clear his mind. To forget the way her body had fit against his, the way she had melted under his touch, the way he had wanted—needed—her to keep kissing him.

Weak.

He grit his teeth, lifting his gaze to the moon, a fragment of cold silver against the deep indigo sky. Last night, he had been in control. When he set out through Farenvayle Forest, his purpose had been clear. He had stalked her through the shadows, followed her every misstep, and when he finally caught her, he had relished every delicious flicker of terror in her eyes.

She had been his from the moment he wrapped his fingers around her wrist.

And now? Now he was right back where he had been five years ago. Wanting her. Needing her. Being unraveled by her.

No.

He would not be desperate for her.

He would not be weak for her.

She was his slave. He was her master. She would bend to *his* will.

He exhaled slowly, willing himself to cool, to center himself in the truth that had carried him these long five years. He would make her answer him. He would make her say it—to admit that she spared him only because she wanted to prolong his suffering.

That's not true.

The thought seared through him like a blade, cutting into the carefully constructed walls of his mind.

Of course, it was true. She had toyed with him. She had fed him lies, and then she had led him straight to ruin. She wanted him to live, not out of mercy, but so he would suffer—so he would wake every day knowing that he had been the fool who loved a woman who never truly existed.

It's not true.

His jaw clenched, his breath sharpening. He had told himself this for years. He had forced himself to believe it because anything else was too dangerous.

Suddenly, something tugged in his blood. Zakar's eyes snapped open, a keen awareness sobering him instantly.

She was running.

His blood simmered in anticipation as he felt it—the bond tightening, pulling like an invisible chain woven from the very magic she had surrendered to him. He turned his palm over, letting his fingers shift and tighten, attuned to the pulse of her defiance. It was like a plucked string in a symphony only he could hear, a sharp vibration against the inside of his ribs.

He had wondered when she might try to flee. He exhaled slowly, letting the cold night air settle into his lungs, relishing the familiar, intoxicating thrill of the hunt. Did she truly believe she could slip away from him? He had warned her, dared her, even invited her to try—and now she had.

Did she truly think she could outrun him?

How adorably naive.

He exhaled, casting a glance at the moonlit sky before setting off after her, unhurried, assured—because this was not a chase.

This was a retrieval.

And soon enough, his disobedient little servant would learn that there was only one direction she was allowed to run.

Straight back to *him*.

CHAPTER 21

Zakar

Zakar moved through the shadows of Stonehollow's winding alleys, the pulse of their bond guiding him with unerring precision. The thread of magic linking them tugged insistently at his core, and as he closed the distance, he heard it—low, jeering voices slicing through the night like rusted daggers.

"What's the matter, sorceress? Run out of magic?"

His amusement evaporated instantly.

His steps quickened, silent as death, his breath measured even as something searing and *violent* roared to life inside of him. He turned the corner and saw them—four men boxing Myrithia in, like wolves circling a wounded doe.

One of them had ripped his cloak from her body, letting it dangle from his fingers like a discarded rag as he let out a low whistle. "Pretty little thing," he murmured. "Didn't know we'd be getting a reward *and* a show."

Another had his fist knotted in her silver hair, yanking her head back as he leaned in and ran a lecherous tongue along the exposed column of her throat. Her fingers glittered weakly with magic, but the sparks fizzled before they could take form. She swayed, her limbs sluggish, her chest heaving with exertion.

Zakar's stomach twisted in something dark and deadly. She was *not* a woman easily overpowered. He had seen her sharpness, her cunning—had spent years hunting the memory of a creature that had always managed to slip through his grasp.

But she wasn't slipping now.

She was wilting.

Weak. Deteriorating. And he still didn't know why.

His fury thickened, hot and consuming.

His hand shifted slightly at his side, magic simmering at his fingertips as he advanced a step, voice cutting through the alley like a blade.

"Evening, gentlemen," he murmured. "What seems to be your business with the lady?"

The mercenaries turned, their expressions flickering from irritation to dismissal. They had made the mistake of not recognizing him.

"Get lost," one of them spat. "Can't you see we're busy?"

Another smirked and tightened his grip on Myrithia's hair, tugging her closer. "Her bounty's going to buy me a new house."

Zakar wasn't looking at them anymore. He was watching her—watching the way she barely managed to keep herself upright, how her head lolled as if the weight of it was too much to bear. The stubborn, taunting creature he'd spent years chasing looked *fragile*.

And he loathed it.

Because Myrithia was *not* fragile. She was a siren, a menace, a viper in silk. She had outwitted him once, had commanded his every thought and dream. And now she was this—wilting in the grip of men so far beneath her they should have never even gotten close.

She should have torn them apart.

She *would* have torn them apart, if she could.

That revelation sent something sharp and electric sparking down his spine.

They had caught him in a foul mood. And now, they would suffer for it.

A slow smirk curled at the corner of his lips. "What luck," he said, exhaling a long, measured breath. "I was in need of a proper distraction." His fingers twitched, magic humming in anticipation. "And you've all so kindly volunteered."

He moved before any of them could even blink.

A flick of his wrist, a slashing arc of power—one man gurgled, clutching at his throat as blood spilled between his fingers. A second followed, his chest pierced by an unseen force, his body slumping gracelessly to the ground.

The third barely had time to process his impending death before Zakar reached him, fingers closing around his jaw in a vice grip. With a mere thought, the man's spine shattered from the inside out, and he collapsed, a broken, lifeless heap.

Only one remained.

The one still holding *her*.

Zakar turned slowly, his emerald eyes cutting through the night like shards of ice.

The mercenary swallowed thickly, his confidence crumbling as he looked at his fallen comrades. His grip on Myrithia tightened in some desperate, feeble attempt at leverage.

Zakar's expression darkened.

That was a *mistake*.

He raised a single hand, and with an invisible force, the man was ripped away from her, sent flying backward and slamming into the opposite alley wall with a sickening crack.

He didn't even let him hit the ground before he struck again.

Another flick of his fingers, and the man's limbs snapped in multiple places. He howled, writhing, a pathetic, broken thing.

Zakar closed the distance slowly, savoring the sheer terror in his eyes.

"Hurts, doesn't it?" he mused softly, his tone almost gentle. "Not nearly as much as what you *would* have done to her, but…" He knelt, gripping the man's chin and forcing his gaze up. "I think you get the idea."

And then, with an absent hum, he ended it.

Efficient. Bloody. A fitting lesson.

The moment the man crumpled, all fight gone, Zakar turned.

Myrithia was swaying, her breath uneven, her body visibly trembling.

He was beside her in an instant, catching her just as her knees buckled. She sagged into his arms, her weight sinking into him, trusting him, needing him.

His hold on her tightened instinctively. He exhaled sharply

and swept her up effortlessly into his arms.

Their night had just taken a very different turn.

***

The fire burned low in the hearth, its glow pooling along the wooden beams on the ceiling of the secluded cabin. Zakar sat beside a bed, one arm draped over a chair's back, his fingers tapping a slow, measured rhythm against the worn wood. His gaze lingered on Myrithia's sleeping form, her breath rising and falling in shallow, uneven intervals.

He had left nothing to chance. Wards sealed the cabin, weaving a near-invisible veil over the structure, hiding them from prying eyes and ensuring that anyone who wandered too close would see nothing but an empty clearing.

They were safe here. For now.

The ward wouldn't be strong enough to withstand the Hollow Mist if it crept too near—but if it did, he would take her and flee before it could swallow them both.

His eyes flickered to her face, tracing the delicate curve of her cheek, the faint crease between her brows. *She looks fragile like this*, he thought bitterly. She had never been fragile before.

His jaw tightened as his thoughts drifted back to their escape.

After slaughtering those mercenaries in the alley, he had wasted no time retrieving his horse. The stable boy had paled at his demand, his hands fumbling with the reins, too afraid to question the red staining Zakar's sleeves. He had mounted in one fluid motion, Myrithia limp in his arms, her body unnervingly warm. She had stirred only once, a faint, fevered whimper against his chest before slipping back into unconsciousness.

He had ridden hard through the dark, putting as much distance between them and Stonehollow as possible before dawn could break and rumors could spread. He knew they would be looking for her. He had no intention of making their search easy.

That brought him to *now*.

This small, long-abandoned lodge in the forest would serve its purpose. His Sentinels would be scouring the area as guardsmen, alerting him to any danger through the night. This cottage wasn't the luxury he was accustomed to, but it was private. Quiet. The wards were set, and the fire was warm. They would rest here for the night, and at first light, they would be gone.

With any luck, they would reach the tome in two days' time. But returning to the Arcane Citadel would be the safer option. The East Citadel wasn't far—he could at least stop there for supplies before pressing on. This brief journey was already stretching longer than he had intended.

He exhaled slowly, raking his fingers through his hair before leaning forward, studying her.

His eyes roamed over her, searching for any visible signs—an injury, a clue, *anything*—but there was nothing. No wounds, no marks. Just the same stubborn woman who had evaded him for five years, only now, she was barely clinging to consciousness.

He reached into the inner pocket of his coat, fingers curling around a small sachet of Valdoran sage. He pulled it free, inspecting the dried leaves inside.

A precaution. He had snatched it from the apothecary before they left the citadel, anticipating she might need it.

How long has this been happening?

His first instinct had been to blame the contract. But no—she had been weak *before* she signed her name in blood. Before she gave herself to him. Before he had *claimed* her.

His grip tightened around the sachet.

What's killing you, Myra?

His mind churned, piecing together fragments of what little he knew. She had been Draevok's apprentice. That much was certain. He had always assumed she had followed orders *willingly*—had played her role as the seductress with no regret. But there had always been *more* to it, hadn't there?

She didn't want to speak about those missing five years. She didn't want to speak about what he made her do. She had never told him *why* she betrayed the man.

His body reminded him of another pressing reality—he hadn't slept in nearly two days. His muscles ached from the ride, and though adrenaline had carried him through the fight, the weight of exhaustion was beginning to settle into his bones.

He let out a slow breath and stood, tugging off his boots before pulling his shirt over his head. The mattress creaked slightly as he settled onto it, and without hesitation, he reached for her.

Even in sleep, she melted against him.

His arm looped around her waist, drawing her close, pressing her back against his bare chest. She let out a breathy sigh, a soft, helpless sound that sent heat curling through his gut. It almost sounded... content.

His fingers twitched against her hip.

This is not what she deserves.

She should be shackled, kneeling, begging for his mercy. She should be suffering for what she did.

And yet, here he was. Holding her close. Keeping her warm.

Fool, he chastised himself.

Still, as the fire crackled and the night stretched on, he allowed himself this one indulgence—letting his eyes close, letting her scent lull him into a fragile kind of peace.

Tomorrow, she would give him answers.

Tonight... he would allow himself to rest.

CHAPTER 22

Myrithia

Myrithia stirred at the gentle intrusion of morning light filtering through the cabin's windows, washing the wooden walls in a warm glow. Her mind felt sluggish, body weighed down by an unfamiliar warmth. She blinked slowly, taking in the room—a modest yet cozy space, with a roaring fire crackling in the hearth, its embers shifting with each flicker of enchanted flames. The scent of cedar lingered, layered with something darker, more alluring. It slipped over her like a whisper, coaxing her into a security that felt too easy.

Then she noticed it.

The heavy weight draped over her waist. The slow, steady breath at the back of her neck. The press of firm, solid muscle against her back.

Her heart lurched as realization struck, her breath catching in her throat. She tried to shift away, her limbs sluggish, but before she could so much as turn, a low, velvety growl vibrated at her ear.

"Good morning, Myra."

Zakar's voice was thick with sleep, deeper, lazier—more intimate than it had any right to be.

Heat flooded her face. Her breath came uneven, her pulse a frantic thing. How had this happened? What had happened?

She stammered through a hesitant, "Good morning," barely

above a whisper, attempting once more to pull away. But his arm, firm and possessive, only tightened around her, anchoring her against him.

He exhaled slowly, the breath fanning against the nape of her neck, sending an unwelcome shiver down her spine. "How do you feel?" His tone was softer now, less teasing, more direct. He wanted an honest answer.

Myrithia swallowed. She was still trying to piece together the fragments of last night. "I... I'm fine."

A long pause. Then, as if to test the truth of her words, he breathed her in. The sound was slow, almost indulgent. The kind of thing a man did when he knew exactly how to unsettle a woman.

Then, finally, his hold eased.

She took the opportunity, pushing herself up from the bed with too much urgency, as if burned by the contact. She turned to face him—and nearly tripped over herself at the sight of him reclining against the pillows, shirtless, the sheets resting low on his hips.

Gods.

She had known he was strong, had *felt* it in the way he carried her, the way he handled her. But seeing it laid bare was another thing entirely. The broad expanse of his chest, the sculpted muscles that had not been there so many years ago, the sharp lines of his abdomen—he was a vision of power. Hardened, honed. Every inch of him forged from years of discipline, every part of him lethal.

He stretched, slow and languid, rolling his shoulders, dark hair tousled from sleep. His sharp green eyes found hers immediately, taking in her wide-eyed stare with a knowing smirk.

"Enjoying the view?"

Myrithia snapped her gaze away, embarrassment searing through her as she busied herself with smoothing down the wrinkled fabric of her underdress. "Where are we?" she asked, attempting to redirect the conversation, her voice a touch too sharp. "What happened?"

He stood slowly, the kind of slow that made it impossible to look away, amusement playing at the edges of his mouth and curling through the air like smoke. He was reveling in this—her discomfort, her helpless fluster. He stepped closer, his bare feet silent against the wooden floor, until he was near enough that she could feel the warmth radiating from him.

"We are in an abandoned cabin in the woods," he answered easily. "I did improve it for us, of course. It was hardly hospitable before I arrived." His gaze flicked toward the glowing hearth, the candles burning gently on the table. Magic pulsed faintly in the air, evidence of the charms he had placed.

Then, his gaze slid back to hers, sharp, knowing. "Though, I assume you have experience with such things—considering the little cottage you lived in for the past five years."

Her stomach turned.

So he had known. He had known exactly where she had hidden herself. He had found her. The menacing presence that had rattled the air, the unseen force that had sent her fleeing into the night—it had been him all along. She had assumed Draevok's spies had finally closed in on her. But no. It had been Zakar. Hunting her.

She barely had time to react before he took another step, closing the distance, and she instinctively backed up—only to hit the edge of an old wooden chair, her legs giving way beneath her as she stumbled into the seat.

Zakar smiled, slow and predatory, then leaned in, placing a hand on the back of the chair, trapping her between the armrests.

"What happened to you last night, *my dear slave?*" His voice was a whisper of velvet over steel.

Myrithia's heart slammed against her ribs.

She was still trying to piece everything together, to *separate* the chaos of the night before from the undeniable heat of the moment now. But the memories surged anyway.

The room at the inn. The wine. *Him.* The firelight flickering against his sharp features. His touch—her own hands threading through his hair, her lips parting for him—

No. Not that. *After* that.

Zakar leaving. The heavy silence. The restless frustration. The wine humming in her veins, making her reckless.

She had *thought* she was thinking clearly when she moved to the door, when she realized the seal had been broken upon his departure. She had *thought* she was making the smart decision.

"I was going after you," she tried weakly.

Zakar's hand closed over the wood, his grip tightening. He let out a slow, deliberate sigh before murmuring, "Liar. You were trying to escape me."

Myrithia averted her gaze. "*At first.*"

His silence demanded more.

She clenched her jaw, inhaling shakily. "I—I was going to leave," she admitted, voice quieter now. "But I realized how foolish that was the moment I reached the stairs."

It was true. The moment she had descended into the inn's lower levels, she had *felt* it—the danger, the predatory eyes tracking her movement. She had turned back, but it was too late.

She had tried to use her magic.

She had *failed*.

"I tried to vanish," she admitted, voice hollow. "I made it outside. A few buildings away."

"And?" Zakar's voice was calm, but there was something lethal lurking beneath the surface.

She swallowed hard. "I landed in an alley." The words tasted bitter. "An unlucky coincidence that there were more men there, bounty hunters. They had been drinking, but they knew me instantly."

A dark shadow flickered across Zakar's face, his expression chilling, but he remained quiet.

She forced herself to keep speaking, though her voice was tight, strangled. "They were playing around with me. And when I tried to use my magic again…"

Nothing.

She had been utterly defenseless.

Zakar was still staring at her, but his gaze sharpened, as if he was analyzing every detail, dissecting every truth and every lie she might be feeding him.

"How did those pathetic men corner you?"

Myrithia flinched.

He knew.

He *had* to know. He had seen the state of her body when he

found her—had *felt* the weakness in her limbs when she collapsed against him. He was too perceptive not to suspect something.

"I don't know," she lied, hating the way the words felt on her tongue. "It all happened so quickly."

Silence.

Then, he lifted her chin with two fingers, forcing her to meet his eyes once more.

"Try again."

She swallowed, but said nothing.

Because she couldn't tell him.

Because to tell him would be to admit the truth—that she was weak. That she was *dying*.

For a long, drawn-out second, Myrithia felt like she had forgotten how to breathe.

The room was still, save for the crackling fire and the weight of his expectant silence pressing down on her. She could feel his stare burning into her, waiting, demanding.

After a few more moments of waiting, she swallowed and forced herself to speak.

"I don't know."

Zakar's expression barely flickered, but the air around him thickened. He didn't believe her.

He didn't like that answer.

Without a word, he stood upright, pulling away from her, his movements slow and measured. Myrithia watched as he walked across the room, stepping toward his discarded, bloodstained tunic. He reached into a pocket and retrieved something small, something she recognized the moment he turned back toward her.

A sachet of Valdoran sage.

A sick heaviness settled behind her ribs.

Zakar reached the table, his sharp gaze locked on her, and dropped the small pouch in front of her with an unforgiving thud.

Myrithia inhaled sharply, her pulse drumming against her throat.

She knew what this meant. Knew what it confirmed.

She'd spent the last few years drinking that very same tea, using it as a feeble crutch to stave off the inevitable. And now, he *knew*.

Zakar tilted his head slightly, studying her reaction. His voice was quiet, but absolute.

"You're going to tell me what's wrong with you."

Her breath trembled as he took a slow step forward.

"You can do so willingly," he continued, his tone cool, *measured*, lethal. "Like the obedient servant you are." His gaze flicked over her, daring her to deny it. "Or I can wrench the answer from you in any way that delights me."

A shiver coiled down her spine.

She clenched her jaw, her fingers twitching toward the sachet, but before she could take it, his hand shot out, closing around her wrist. His grip was firm, yet absent of cruelty or force.

"What is happening to you, Myra?"

The question lanced through her, a blade cutting too close to the truth.

She dropped her chin, drawing her fingers inward, exhaling a slow, trembling breath. The words *would not form*.

Zakar's patience cracked. With a growl of irritation, he yanked her to her feet. She staggered, colliding against his bare chest, heat radiating from his skin like a furnace.

She gasped, hands catching against the hard muscle of his torso, her fingers brushing over the taut ridges there. Her face flamed at the contact, but he was relentless, keeping her trapped against him.

"This is your last chance to answer me honestly." His voice was lower now, quieter—dark with *promise*. "Fail to do so, and I *will* force the words from you."

Something inside her shuddered—something bound in blood and magic.

A ripple of power slithered through her veins, responding to the *command* in his voice. He *owned* her now. If he willed it, she would *answer*.

Myrithia swallowed hard, her hands tightening around the hardness of his shoulders, her heart thundering against her ribs. She wanted to fight him. To keep her walls up, to keep the truth buried where it belonged. But it was already clawing its way up her throat.

THE ARCANE BARGAIN

A sudden crack split through the air—sharp, unnatural.

Zakar's head snapped up, his entire body going rigid.

The air in the cabin shifted, the magic around them rippling like a disturbed pond. A low, reverberating hum pulsed against the walls, vibrating through the floorboards, signaling something—or someone—tampering with his enchantments.

Myrithia felt it too, her breath hitching. Whatever battle had just been playing out between them vanished in an instant, replaced by something colder, more urgent.

Zakar released her so quickly she nearly stumbled, already turning toward his discarded tunic. He snatched it up, shaking out the fabric before pulling it over his head in one fluid motion. Even as he did, his magic crackled at his fingertips, barely leashed.

Then, from the shadows near his feet, something moved.

Myrithia's breath seized in her throat as a skeletal figure rose soundlessly from the floor, its form shifting between solid and spectral, draped in tattered black robes that swayed with an unseen wind. Hollow eye sockets gleamed with an eerie blue light, and though its bony features were twisted and charred, its presence exuded something ancient—something wrong.

She took an instinctive step back, her pulse hammering.

The creature leaned toward Zakar, whispering in a voice that barely seemed to belong to this world—soft, distant, layered in echoes, as if multiple voices spoke at once.

Zakar's expression sharpened, his eyes narrowing in understanding.

"Wait with the others nearby," he commanded, his tone quiet but firm. "I'll call upon you shortly."

The Sentinel's glowing eyes flared briefly, its skeletal form bowing slightly in acknowledgment before it shifted back into the floor, vanishing as seamlessly as it had appeared.

Myrithia exhaled sharply, her entire body stiff with unease.

Zakar turned to her, expression subdued as he spread his fingers, dispelling the remaining energy coiling at his fingertips. "Get ready," he said, voice smooth, steady. "We're not alone."

CHAPTER 23

Zakar

Zakar stepped onto the porch of the cabin, his fingers flexing at his sides, his body coiled with readiness. The morning light cut through the trees in fractured beams, stretching long shadows across the clearing, but none were as dark as the figure waiting just beyond the shimmering boundary of his wards.

General Garron Blackvale.

The traitorous knight stood at ease, arms folded, the picture of relaxed confidence. But Zakar knew better. Knew the careful control of a man who could kill without hesitation. The easy grace of someone who had long since stopped questioning his own cruelty. His dark leather coat, reinforced with enchanted plating, bore the scuffs and scratches of battle, the hilt of his curved blade worn from countless draws. His chestnut hair, tied loosely at the nape of his neck, was tousled by the wind, a few strands falling into his sharply cut face. Amusement glinted in his eyes—dark, shrewd, assessing—as if he had just stumbled upon a particularly entertaining turn of fate.

Garron smirked. "Thought I recognized those wards of yours, old friend." His tone was almost genial, but there was a knowing edge to it, a hunter who had just found his quarry. "How have you been?"

Zakar exhaled a quiet chuckle, slow and mirthless, as he leaned a shoulder against the doorframe. "Quite well. And how about you?" His smirk sharpened. "How is life under another mage-murdering tyrant?"

Garron's grin widened, his white teeth flashing like the snarl of a wolf. "Ah, let's not pretend you stand on any moral high ground, Zakar." He sighed, tilting his head with exaggerated remorse before arching a brow. "You, the son of the Butcher of Valthoria, are condemning *my* allegiances? That's rich."

Zakar's jaw tensed, but his smirk didn't falter. "My father deserved his death." His voice was deceptively calm, though magic simmered beneath his skin, crackling at his fingertips. "But your new king? He deserves a much worse end."

Garron's expression darkened slightly, though his posture remained at ease. "Draevok is correcting what should've been done long ago. Mages have never had their rightful place in this world. He's ensuring that changes."

Zakar scoffed, stepping down from the porch. The very air around him pulsed with his presence, thick and oppressive, pressing outward like a force of nature. "Is that what he told you? That he's *liberating* mages?" A humorless laugh left his lips. "I expected better of you, Garron. My father at least knew what he was—he never lied about the slaughter he unleashed. Your king, though?" Zakar's lip curled, his voice dripping mockery. "He's far more insidious. Quietly culling you all. Killing those who could one day challenge him while keeping the rest too weak to fight back. And you? You serve him eagerly." He tilted his head, as if considering. "Tell me, Garron, do you bow before him willingly, or did he just carve out the spine you used to have?"

A muscle in Garron's jaw twitched, his fingers tightening over the hilt of his blade before he let out a slow breath, smoothing his features into something unreadable. "You always were one to twist the narrative in your favor," he mused. "Even while you stood atop the bones of the people your father crushed."

Zakar didn't respond, but for a brief moment, something fierce flashed through his eyes.

"But I'm not here to trade philosophy with you," Garron continued, his voice cooling, shedding any traces of amusement. "I know she's inside." He lifted his chin, his gaze steady. "You can hand her over *now*, or wait until my men arrive to drag her out by her hair—while you choke on your own blood."

The magic in the air thickened. The runes of the warded barrier pulsed, glowing faintly in response to the power rising in Zakar's blood.

His smirk was gone.

"You won't so much as touch her."

Magic crackled through the air like a storm ready to break.

Zakar wasted no time. The moment his refusal left his lips, his power surged outward, a pulse of raw energy rippling through the space between them. Garron was ready. A barrier of seething dark magic erupted around him, absorbing the impact as he surged forward. In the same breath, an enchanted longsword coalesced in Zakar's grip, the hilt cool and familiar in his fingers.

Their blades met in an explosion of steel and sorcery, the impact ringing through the air as sparks scattered like embers in the morning light. Zakar pivoted smoothly, dodging Garron's counterstrike as he twisted his wrist, aiming a slash at Zakar's ribs. A narrow miss. Zakar smirked.

"Sloppy," he taunted, sidestepping another strike, "or did all that groveling make you slow?"

Garron snarled, pressing his advantage with a quick succession of brutal strikes, his blade carving through the space between them with lethal precision. Zakar met every blow, their magic igniting the air with each impact.

Garron flicked his fingers, summoning a blast of dark energy. Zakar barely had time to shift, the force of it sending him skidding backward, boots digging into the dirt.

Garron smirked. "Still think I'm slow?"

Zakar rolled his shoulder, feeling the sting where the magic had burned through his tunic. "Only compared to me."

He lunged this time, closing the distance with a burst of speed, summoning a glowing dagger of arcane energy in his left hand while his sword locked against Garron's. He drove the dagger toward his opponent's ribs, but Garron twisted, evading just in time, retaliating with another sweeping arc of his sword.

Zakar ducked, feeling the blade slice through air just above his head.

A flicker of movement behind Garron caught his eye—

Myrithia.

Her fingers pulsed with magic, silver light swirling around them. An illusion took form, a perfect copy of Zakar appearing to Garron's left, lunging forward with a blade poised for a killing blow.

Garron reacted instantly, pivoting to strike.

It was a mistake.

Zakar took the opening, sweeping his leg beneath Garron's feet and swiping his sword across his chest, sending him crashing to the ground. Without hesitation, he lifted his hand and called upon the shadows beneath them.

His sentinels rose like spectral wraiths from the earth, skeletal hands curling around Garron's arms and legs, holding him down. Their hollowed eyes glowed, their whispering voices an ominous chorus of torment.

Zakar stepped forward, looming over him. "Keep him company for a while," he commanded, his voice a rich, velvety threat. "But let him go once we've departed. I want him alive—so I can savor his death personally."

His Sentinels could have ended Garron in an instant, but that would be far too merciful. No—his suffering would be exquisite, drawn out when Zakar had the time to savor every second of it. And right now, with more enemies closing in and Myrithia still weakened, time was a luxury he couldn't afford.

Garron thrashed against his spectral captors, but his curses were swallowed by their hollow, bone-chilling wails.

Zakar turned, his eyes locking onto Myrithia. He lifted a hand, power pulsing through his veins as he summoned their bond, compelling her body to move.

She gasped, magic pulling her toward him like an unseen current.

She stumbled into his arms, breathless, and he wasted no time. He grasped her hand, leading her quickly to his waiting horse.

Before she could protest, he caught her by the waist, lifting her easily and settling her onto the saddle. He swung up behind her, his arms caging her in as he seized the reins.

"Hold on," he murmured at her ear, then spurred the horse into a gallop, vanishing into the depths of the forest.

CHAPTER 24

Myrithia

Myrithia gripped the saddle, her fingers trembling as she reached for her magic again.

Another burst—thirty feet ahead.

Another—fifty.

Her vision blurred at the edges, her breath coming too fast, too shallow. She pressed closer to Zakar, drawing from every last reserve she had left. They had to get away. Garron was too strong, and his threat still echoed in her mind. *You can hand her over now, or wait until my men arrive to drag her out by her hair—while you choke on your own blood.*

She couldn't let that happen. They needed more distance.

Another burst, another fifty feet.

Again—

Suddenly, Zakar's firm hand clamped over her wrist, halting her mid-cast.

"Enough," His voice was steady, firm with quiet authority. His fingers pressed against her skin, magic curling subtly around hers, stilling it. "Stop wasting your energy. I'll get us somewhere safe."

She tried to push against him, tried to summon another spell, but her limbs were too heavy. Her magic flickered weakly at her fingertips before fading entirely. A wave of dizziness crashed over her, and her body slumped against his, forced back by the rushing wind atop his horse.

The last thing she felt was the warmth of his hold, anchoring her as everything went dark.

***

The scent of Valdoran sage tea drifted through the air, warm and familiar, followed by the rich aroma of food—something spiced, roasted, indulgent. Myrithia stirred, her mind sluggish as she blinked against the soft glow of enchanted sconces lining the walls.

The bed beneath her was too soft. The sheets were fine, luxurious. Not the forest. Not a haphazard hiding place. Slowly, her vision adjusted to her surroundings—ornate furniture, dark stone walls, and a large fireplace where flames flickered, painting the room with shifting light. And standing by the far end of the room, smoothing out the sleeves of his pristine black coat, was Zakar.

His presence hit her like a spell breaking. Her pulse leapt, memories slamming into her all at once—Garron, the fight, her magic failing, his arms catching her before the world went dark.

She sat upright too quickly, the room tilting slightly, and he immediately turned, his sharp green eyes locking onto her.

Without a word, he strode forward, lifting a steaming cup of tea from the table and placing it beside her. He also gestured to a tray of golden-crusted bread, roasted meats, fresh berries, and soft cheese.

"Eat." His tone was curt, commanding, and edged with something that seemed a bit like concern.

Her fingers braced the cup, but she could feel it—anger simmering beneath his composed facade. She waited, but he said nothing more. Instead, he turned, his coat billowing slightly as he moved across the room.

Myrithia watched as he picked up a sword resting atop a velvet-draped sofa, lifting it with practiced ease, inspecting the edge in the late afternoon sunlight.

"We're in the East Citadel," he said finally, his voice calm but laced with tension. "A smaller one that Master Sorien used to retreat to when the politics of the Arcane Citadel became too bothersome for him."

She took a sip of the sage tea, the familiar taste soothing some of the tremors in her limbs, but not enough to settle the unease clawing at her.

"Will we be safe here?" she asked.

Zakar cast her an incredulous look, as if she had asked whether the sky was blue. "Of course." He gestured slightly, the air thrumming around them. "This place—like the Arcane Citadel—is veiled under some of the strongest wards in existence. No one will find us unless I want them to." He turned the blade in his hands. "We can stay for the rest of the week. Let the heat of your bounty cool. Then, we return to the Arcane Citadel."

The Arcane Citadel.

Her fingers clenched around the delicate stem of the teacup.

He was delaying. He was changing their course.

Her heart thudded painfully in her chest as she sat up straighter, eyes darting toward him.

"But the tome—"

Zakar's head snapped toward her, his emerald gaze sharp and final.

"It will have to wait for another day."

Her breath stilled in her chest. She had known—known deep down that he wouldn't make this easy. But hearing him say it so dismissively, like it was some inconsequential thing, something she could afford to wait for.

Her heart crashed against her ribs.

She set the teacup down and shoved the blankets back, standing too quickly, her body moving before her mind caught up. Her voice trembled, strained and unsteady, as if speaking might tear something loose. "That wasn't our bargain."

Zakar didn't flinch. He simply watched her, unmoved, his expression cool. Then, with a kind of slow, measured calm, he set the sword down and stepped toward her.

"My dear slave," he murmured, his tone laced with faint amusement, as if tasting the words. "You don't dictate the whims of your master."

Her core felt like it had caved in on itself.

"Maybe not," she said, her fists tensed at her sides. "But you bound me in a contract. And I expect you to uphold your end of it."

He tilted his head slightly, studying her like something beneath glass.

"Did you give me a time limit, Myra?"

She opened her mouth, but no answer came.

His smile grew—slow, quiet, certain. A man who knew exactly how the pieces moved on the board.

"No," he said softly, "you didn't. Which means I could wait years before retrieving that book. Decades, even. And you'd have no power to stop me."

He leaned in slightly, his voice dropping to a near-whisper, the softness of it only making the cruelty more precise.

"Perhaps I will."

The words struck deeper than they should have. She stayed still. Silent. Her body held rigid, but something inside her shifted—fracturing, splintering beneath the weight of it.

Tears burned hot behind her eyes, her breath caught high in her throat. A tightness wrapped around her chest, crawling up her spine, coiling in her ribs. The air felt thin. The room, too small. It was panic. Rising. Slow and suffocating.

He was toying with her. Smiling. Controlling the tempo of her unraveling like it was nothing more than another game. And worse—he had no idea what he was withholding from her. What it was costing her.

Her fingers clenched around the teacup, knuckles white. She tried to breathe. To think.

Not yet. Don't say it. Don't let him see—

"I don't have years," she said.

Too loud. Too raw.

Zakar stilled. The edges of his grin softened, his focus narrowing like a hunter catching the faint rustle of prey.

He stepped toward her—slow, deliberate, eyes sharp.

She flinched, her back bumping the edge of the bed. The room felt smaller.

"Why?"

The word landed with quiet weight, sharp and controlled.

She turned her face away, but he closed the space between them, slow and patient, until she could feel the heat of him, the press of his presence.

"Myrithia." Her name in his voice made her chest tighten. It wasn't tender. It wasn't cruel. It was sharp—like a knife laid flat against the skin. "Tell me. Why?"

She hesitated a fraction too long.

His eyes narrowed, a flicker of suspicion cutting through the cold green. He was piecing it together—slowly, methodically.

She shook her head, but the panic was already climbing higher.

"I need that book," she whispered, barely able to steady her voice. "I need it now."

His jaw tightened. His expression didn't shift. "That's not feasible."

The dismissal was calm. Clean. Like she'd asked for something trivial. Her chest was tightening. Her vision narrowing. She couldn't breathe. "Then I'll get it myself." The words tore out of her like a spark thrown to dry grass.

A low laugh answered her—quiet and unhurried. "You?" He tilted his head slightly, as if she'd just offered to scale the moon. "You'll do it yourself?" Another soft chuckle followed, curling in his throat like smoke.

He was right to laugh. She had no idea where it was. He'd never told her, never trusted her with so much as a hint. Tears stung her eyes. Humiliation bloomed like fire under her skin. She pressed a shaking hand to her forehead. Her lungs ached.

"I have to have that book," she whispered. "And if you were any kind of decent human being, you'd honor your bargain. You'd keep your word."

The shift in him was subtle—barely more than a flicker in his eyes. But it was enough.

"I am not a decent human being," he said, voice flat and final.

A tight breath caught in her throat.

She hated him.

He turned away without another word, walking back to the table, fingers brushing over the weapons laid out there like none of it mattered. He selected a dagger, sheathing it at his hip with practiced ease.

"Eat," he said. "Rest. We leave for the Arcane Citadel in a week."

She didn't move.

Didn't touch the food.

Her hands stayed clenched at her sides, shaking slightly, her chest rising and falling with shallow, uneven breaths. The silence between them stretched—heavy, suffocating. Her throat burned. Her vision blurred.

And before she could stop herself, the words slipped out quietly, bitter and broken. "It would've been better," she whispered, "if I had just done what Draevok said."

Zakar paused, unmoving.

A slow, lethal turn.

She looked up just in time to see it—the full force of his fury unfurling like a storm.

Oh, she had said the wrong thing.

CHAPTER 25

Zakar

He couldn't believe the words had left her mouth. Zakar moved toward her, footsteps heavy with the weight of her admission, as if the words had anchored him to the earth. She had always been merciless. Always been pitiless. But now she had given voice to the truth he had always known—the truth that had lived in his head like a haunting whisper for five years.

She wished she had killed him.

She wished she had *ended* it.

Not because she was wracked with guilt, not because she thought he had suffered too much—no.

Because he hadn't suffered at all.

She could see it now, couldn't she? That he had thrived in her absence. That while she had withered into weakness, he had risen from the ashes she left behind and built himself into something far greater, and she *resented* it.

He stepped in close, forcing her backward until her back hit the wall, his hand slamming against the stone beside her head.

Air stalled in her lungs, her lips parting, but no words came.

Her fear was intoxicating.

"You regret not ending it?" His voice was low, cruel, simmering with barely restrained wrath. "Not killing me, Myra?" He leaned in just enough to watch her tremble. "You should."

For a moment, he felt justified. He had been right. She had

wanted him to suffer. And now, she was the one suffering.

But then she spoke.

"Not that," she whispered, voice tight with frustration, with pain. "I still wouldn't have killed you." Her throat bobbed in a tense swallow. "But I regret leaving Draevok. I regret running."

Zakar's fury flickered, a sliver of intrigue cutting through it. She was shaking. Not from him, but from the memories. She wasn't talking about him anymore.

She exhaled, her voice raw. Honest. "I should have faced my punishment. Should have faced what I'd done. That would have been the merciful end. Not this." Her breath faltered, every nerve alight beneath his presence. "Not this slow torture."

Zakar tilted his head, considering her. "Say more."

She clenched her jaw. "I told him that I didn't kill you," she went on. "And he was furious."

Zakar's grip on the wall tightened.

"He wanted to deal with me. I was supposed to accept my fate, accept the consequences of betrayal." Her voice was quiet, broken. "But I ran."

Zakar stared at her, studying her closely. It was the truth. Every piece of it, and it surprised him.

For years, he had assumed that Draevok had ordered his life to be spared as a calculated maneuver. But if Draevok himself had been enraged by her choice, if she had been meant to wait for death, and if she had run…

His gaze flickered with something dark.

He had only begun to question her role in it all when he first started seeing the wanted notices, watching as her bounty climbed higher and higher. He had begun to wonder if she had defected, if Draevok had wanted her back—not as a loyal subject, but as a prize to be punished.

The implications unsettled him.

He straightened slightly, his expression unreadable. "Why is Draevok hunting you?"

She hesitated, her fear palpable.

Zakar lifted her chin gently with his fingers. "Speak."

Her lips trembled, her pupils blown wide with distress. "I think…" She swallowed. "I think he wants to kill me himself."

Zakar locked in place.

"He wants to deal with the traitorous servant who dared to defy him." Her voice shook. "And if he's sending Garron, then he means to finish it."

Zakar exhaled slowly, his magic coiling within him. His grip on her loosened.

Draevok would destroy her. That much he already knew. Myrithia wasn't just a traitor—she had been his apprentice. And Draevok's apprentices did not live after failing him. And yet she had. But only because Zakar had gotten to her first. She belonged to him now.

"I won't give him the satisfaction," Zakar said, his voice a low promise. He leaned in, his thumb brushing the tear on her cheek. "You are mine."

She exhaled sharply, as if a weight had lifted from her chest. When he looked into her tormented eyes, he saw something he hadn't expected.

Relief.

She was relieved—that he had claimed her. His head tilted. She truly saw him as the better alternative. But, he supposed that should not have surprised him. Draevok would have made a spectacle of her execution, a brutal display of what befell those who betrayed him. And yet, despite knowing she had sealed her own fate, despite the satisfaction he should have felt in watching her suffer, a sliver of something unwanted twisted inside him. He shouldn't pity her. But, against all reason, he did—if only a little.

The question burned at the edge of his tongue, demanding to be spoken. Why had she spared him? Why had she defied Draevok's will? He could force the answer from her—he knew it as surely as he could feel the quiet, inescapable pulse of their bond thrumming beneath his skin. One command, and the truth would be his.

But instead, he asked something else. His voice was silken, dangerous. "Tell me, Myra..." He dragged his knuckles along her cheek, watching her quiver beneath his touch. "Why are you weakened?"

He saw it immediately—a flash of raw terror in her eyes. She tried to look away, but he caught her chin, forcing her to face him.

"Answer me," he murmured, his voice velvet and venom. "Why?"

She inhaled sharply, parting her lips, "I need the Syltharic Tome."

"So you've said." His grip tightened, his voice low, unimpressed. "But that's not what I asked."

She winced, and he felt the thrum of her magic warring within her—an instinct to flee, to lie, to evade him.

"Why are you weakening?" His voice darkened. "Why did those men get the better of you?"

She sucked in a tight breath, her expression cracking just enough for him to see her defeat. A single tear slipped from her eye, resting against his thumb.

"Because I have been cursed, Zakar."

Silence.

Not a lie.

Zakar's eyes narrowed. "Who cursed you?" But he already knew the answer. He knew it before she even spoke his name.

"Draevok."

His grip faltered. He didn't have to ask why. She had disobeyed him. She had defied her master, and Draevok did not tolerate defiance.

Myrithia clenched her fists. "Please." Her voice shook. "I need the book. It has the counterspell within it."

Zakar studied her, calculating.

"Without it, I don't know what will happen to me," she whispered. "I'm so weak now, Zakar. I can hardly—" She swallowed. "I can hardly live at all."

Zakar held her gaze. His mind whirled with too many questions, but answers would not come freely. And if he wanted her broken enough to answer him, if he wanted her humiliated with her own truths bared before him, then she had to *live*.

But the Syltharic Tome would not be so easily obtained—not with Draevok's hounds closing in. Another two days of riding, and they would reach it. Sealed behind layers of ancient magic within a hidden tomb, it would have remained untouchable—if not for the Nythera in his possession, rendering those defenses meaningless.

He had been prepared to simply view it and walk away, but if she truly needed a spell from within it to survive, then he didn't have much choice. He would have to pry it from the dead man's hands himself.

He leaned in, his lips barely a breath from hers. "Very well, Myra. We will retrieve your tome."

CHAPTER 26

Myrithia

The morning outside was calm, peaceful even. The sky stretched in soft hues of dawn, the lingering fog rolling gently over the trees, dissolving as the sun crept higher. Myrithia stood by the window, fingers resting lightly on the ledge, tracing idle patterns against the cool stone as her thoughts wandered.

She had been left alone the night before—a small mercy, though she wasn't sure if it was because Zakar was angry with her or because, against all odds, he pitied her. Either way, she had taken full advantage of the solitude. She had eaten well, taken a much-needed bath, and—for the first time in what felt like forever—slept without fear of what the next moment would bring.

But now morning had arrived, and with it, the inevitable journey ahead. She wasn't looking forward to it, knowing full well the dangers that awaited them beyond these walls. Mercenaries, bounty hunters, and Garron himself were still out there, and she was in no condition to outrun them, not with the curse eating away at her. But she had only one goal—to survive long enough to get the tome. If she could do that, she would live. And maybe then, she would finally figure out what came next.

She let out a sigh, smoothing her hands down another of Zakar's carefully chosen gowns—one he had no doubt instructed to be laid out for her to wear today, despite it being hardly something to wear for a day of travel. It was a deep burgundy, the fabric rich and clinging, its sweetheart neckline accentuating the curves of her bust. The sleeves were fitted, elegant, and everything about the dress was designed to remind her of who she once was—the seductress, the whisperer of lies, the woman who had ensnared him five years ago.

Her gaze drifted over the vast treetops stretching beyond the citadel grounds, her mind circling the same inescapable thought: *How much longer until we retrieve the tome?*

Zakar knew now. He understood what she needed. And for all his torment, for all his sadistic pleasure in controlling her, he seemed willing to allow her that much. He would let her access the counter-curse to spare her life.

She exhaled slowly, her breath fogging faintly against the glass.

Would it be so terrible to remain his slave?

The thought struck her with quiet horror, but she did not immediately dismiss it. If she was freed from this curse, she would have to run. Always look over her shoulder, always fear the day Draevok's hunters finally caught up to her.

But with Zakar, she wouldn't have to. She would be owned, yes, but she would also be protected. His cruelty, his possessiveness—it was no secret. But neither was the fact that he would sooner burn the world to ash than let another man take what belonged to him.

Her fingers recoiled against the stone ledge, nails scraping against its rough surface. *No. Stop this.*

It was madness. A weakness born of exhaustion. Zakar was not her savior. He was her captor, and his brand of protection would be nothing more than a pretty cage. He wanted her subservient, kneeling, stripped of all dignity until there was nothing left of her but obedience. He would not shield her from Draevok out of kindness—he would do it for his own satisfaction, his own control.

That was no life.

Even if she had to live in the shadows, constantly on the run, it was better than spending the rest of her days groveling at his feet. Because that's what this arrangement was. A master and his slave. She was his enemy, and he would never forgive her. Never.

The soft creak of the door broke the silence.

Myrithia turned, her pulse steady but her breath catching just slightly at the sight of him.

Dressed in black with deep green embellishments, his attire bore the subtle yet unmistakable touches of nobility—regal embroidery at his cuffs, the gleam of silver fastenings along his vest, the perfectly fitted layers of his coat. He looked… composed. Commanding. Handsome.

Her heart skipped a beat despite herself.

He approached her with a measured, steady gait, as if he had all the time in the world. "The horses are ready," he told her, his voice smooth as silk. "Are you?"

Her brows pulled together slightly at that. Horses? Plural? She tilted her head. "More than one?" she questioned, glancing toward him. "You're letting me ride my own?"

His lips quirked into a knowing smile. "We'll move faster that way," he said, amusement flickering in his green eyes. "And I remember you being an exceptional rider."

She exhaled softly, a memory stirring in her mind of when they were once courting, when he had invited her for a ride through the countryside…

She had arrived at the stables with her own horse—a striking silver-gray mare, quick as the wind. He had expected a leisurely ride, a quiet escape from the pressures of court, but she had other ideas. She had flashed him a wicked smile and nudged her horse into a full gallop, leading him on a spirited chase across rolling green hills and sun-dappled fields. He had pursued her relentlessly, laughing, cursing, pushing his horse faster, but by the time he caught up to her, they had found themselves far from the castle—at the very edge of the Cliffs of Morrowynd.

The view had been breathtaking. The ocean stretched endlessly below, the sky painted in hues of amber and gold. It was there that everything had changed for her.

She had expected Zakar to be a man like his father. The heir to the Butcher of Valthoria, a prince raised in a kingdom built on fear and bloodshed. A man groomed to rule with an iron fist.

But then, they had found a wounded mage that day.

A young man, barely past boyhood, slumped against the rock, blood seeping through his tattered robes. A rogue mage—unaffiliated, unclaimed, unprotected. By law, Zakar should have turned him over to the king's men. That was the order for all unaligned magic-wielders. To serve, or to be destroyed.

She had watched him closely then, her heart pounding as he crouched beside the young sorcerer.

But instead of hauling him back to the castle, he had bandaged him. He had given him water and told him how to slip past the patrols and get out of Valthoria undetected.

That was the moment Myrithia had known—truly known—that her mission was now complicated.

She had been sent to seduce a prince, to bring about his downfall as well as the king's. But how could she bring ruin to someone who had already defied the very cruelty he was supposed to uphold?

That had been the first time she had doubted everything.

And now, standing here in this suite with him, staring at the man who had once made her question the path she had been set upon, she felt it all over again.

She straightened, pushing the memory aside, lifting her chin as she met his gaze. "Good," she said, steadying her voice. "Let's go, then."

"Before we go," Zakar said, amusement flickering in his eyes.

Myrithia hesitated. That look never meant anything good for her.

He stepped closer, his presence as commanding as ever. "The road ahead will be dangerous. We'll be hunted relentlessly. You'll need every advantage you can get." His gaze raked over her, his expression turning more serious. "And I cannot afford to have you fainting every day from your curse."

She stiffened. The words should have stung, but they were true. She hated that he saw her weakness so plainly.

"So," he continued, tilting his head slightly, enjoying the way she stiffened under his gaze, "I'll be lending you a portion of my power."

Her brow furrowed. "You'll what?"

His amusement was subtle, carefully restrained beneath the

surface. "Don't get excited." He leaned in slightly, voice smooth, weighty with finality. "I'll only share enough to keep you useful. This is a privilege afforded to you through our contract."

His smirk lingered, his voice turning almost bored, as if the warning was hardly worth mentioning.

"And if, for even a moment, I suspect you might use it against me…" He let the words hang, watching her carefully. Then, with a measured shrug, he finished, smooth and unbothered, "then I suppose I'll have no choice but to take back what's mine. And perhaps… a little *more*."

He let that sink in, savoring the flicker of fear in her expression before adding, softly, dangerously, "You'll need me if you want to survive the week, so be a good girl and do as you're told."

Before she could muster a response, he pulled her hand into his own and pressed his palm against hers, threading his fingers through her own, holding her in place.

Their hands fit together perfectly.

Their eyes locked.

Then, in a voice barely above a whisper, he spoke the incantation.

Heat slammed into her chest.

It spread through her veins like wildfire, a rush of warmth that nearly stole the breath from her lungs. Strength flooded her limbs, burning away the ever-present fatigue of her curse. She gasped softly, her fingers tightening around his instinctively. The frailty that had plagued her for years—the aching, the weariness, the slow, suffocating decay—felt like nothing more than a distant memory.

For the first time in years, she felt strong.

And then she felt something else.

A second heartbeat.

It pulsed within her, an echo against her own. She knew instantly it wasn't hers. The steady, thrumming beat belonged to Zakar.

Her breath faltered. She could feel him.

Not just his heartbeat. Not just his breath, which now matched hers in rhythm. But something deeper. Something raw and unspoken.

THE ARCANE BARGAIN

Pain.

Resentment.

The weight of it pressed against her mind, heavy and suffocating. It wasn't her emotion—it was his.

Her gaze snapped up to his, searching. For a moment, she swore she could feel it, something fragile beneath the storm of his usual arrogance.

And then, just as quickly as it came, it was gone.

Zakar pulled his hand away, severing the connection.

Myrithia stared at him, breathless. The sensation still lingered in her chest, that strange awareness of him, as if he was still standing inside her skin.

Had he felt her too? Had he known what she was thinking?

She wanted to ask. She wanted to know if this was normal, if she would feel such awareness of him every time he shared his power with her.

But she bit back the words.

Zakar exhaled slowly, opening and closing his hands with quiet precision, as if testing something beneath the surface. "Alright. Let's go."

CHAPTER 27

Zakar

The forest stretched before them in endless shades of green and gold, flecked light slipping through the canopy as their horses moved along the winding path. Myrithia rode just ahead of him, her silver hair catching in the breeze, glinting in the setting sun like spun moonlight.

Zakar hadn't spoken much to her all day. Not because he didn't want to—he had intended to—but beneath his usual smug amusement lay something else. Something far more inconvenient. A quiet, gnawing concern he refused to acknowledge.

Myrithia was dying.

She could call it whatever she pleased, but the truth was unchanging. The curse was meant to kill her, and it was winning.

He wanted to pretend it didn't matter. That her fate was nothing more than the consequence of her own choices.

He wished it didn't matter. But it did. And he hated that it did.

For reasons he refused to name, she needed to live. There was no future quite so satisfying, quite so deliciously complete, as a future where she belonged to him. And so, he would give her what she needed.

Not out of kindness. Not out of mercy.

But because he would not allow her to slip from his grasp again.

He would weaken, to an extent, the longer he shared his

power with her. But it was negligible. A week, perhaps two, and it would have no lasting effect on him. The cost was worth it if it meant ensuring that Myrithia didn't crumble under the weight of her curse before they could retrieve the tome, or find some other way to cure her curse.

That was the rational side of it. The part of him that dealt in logic, in power, in control.

What he hadn't anticipated, however, were the other effects.

He had known they would be connected a little more deeply now—that his magic would flow into her, that he would determine when and how much she could wield. But what he hadn't expected was everything else.

Her pulse, a steady rhythm echoing against his own. Her breath, measured and even, matching the cadence of his own inhales and exhales. The warmth of her body, distant yet close, a phantom sensation just beneath his skin.

Her emotions.

When he had felt them, it had startled him. A sudden pang, heavy and aching, settling deep in his chest. A sorrow so consuming, it nearly took his breath away. It was not his own. It was hers.

He clenched his jaw, his hands tightening around the reins.

Was it because she was dying? Was it simply self-pity, knowing she now had to rely on him—knowing she had no choice but to take his magic to keep herself standing?

He didn't know. And he didn't care to keep feeling it.

But whether she wanted to admit it or not, she was further connected to him now. She was bound.

And now that she could feel her own strength again—his strength—flowing through her, she would realize what she already should have known.

She *needed* him.

She wasn't foolish enough to try to run again, not when her very survival depended on him. And she would hate it.

Myrithia turned to glance over her shoulder, her blue eyes fastening on him with mild exasperation. "How much longer do you intend to ride?" she asked. "And are we making camp tonight, or are you planning to push through until we collapse off our horses?"

Zakar smirked. "We can stop for the evening." He flicked the reins, urging his horse forward. "I need to scout the area anyway."

She nodded but said nothing, slowing her horse until she was riding beside him, matching his pace. "And how far are we from the book?"

"About three more days."

She let out a small sigh, adjusting her grip on the reins. "I could get us there faster, you know. I can transport us both—cover large distances in seconds."

"I'm aware," he said coolly. "But I'm not in the habit of wasting my magic for convenience. Especially not when you're borrowing it." His gaze cut to her, sharp and knowing. "Besides, I don't entirely trust you not to drain my power on purpose and make a run for it."

Her lips twisted, but she said nothing.

The silence that followed was telling—and damning. The steady clop of hooves against the road filled the growing space between them, every beat a reminder that trust had no place here.

Then, after a few moments, she spoke again. "Thank you."

Zakar glanced at her, brow arching.

"For the power you're letting me borrow," she clarified. She hesitated, then admitted, "I feel good. Like how I used to feel before the curse."

His smirk faded. He looked ahead, brushing off the statement as if it were of no consequence. "I am merely doing what must be done to ensure that my slave lives long enough to properly serve me."

Her expression darkened, displeasure flashing across her face. But she didn't argue.

Probably for the best. He was hardly in the mood for a squabble.

"We can stop over there," Zakar said, gesturing with his chin toward a small lake nestled between the trees just ahead of them. The water reflected the dying sunlight in rippling bands of silver and gold, the surrounding reeds swaying in the soft evening breeze. It would do.

He pulled on the reins, slowing his horse to a stop near the water's edge before dismounting with effortless ease. The earth was soft beneath his boots, damp from the lingering chill in the air. Behind him, he heard Myrithia follow suit, sliding down from her saddle with far less grace, though she made no sound of complaint.

Zakar unfastened the reins from his stallion's bridle, then held them out to her.

"Give them water," he said simply, not waiting for an answer.

She blinked at him, momentarily startled, before taking the leather straps in her hands. The color was better in her cheeks now, but he could feel the way her magic clung to his, borrowed, insufficient.

She was holding on. But only because of him. She knew it, too. He considered, briefly, cautioning her against trying anything foolish.

Stealing his horse. Running into the woods. Disappearing into the night like a wisp of smoke.

But she wouldn't. She wouldn't dare.

Not because she didn't want to—he had seen the way she still bristled against his control, the way her mind still searched for an out.

But because she had none. Not anymore. She was a dead woman without him, and she knew it.

Smirking faintly, he turned on his heel and strode toward the treeline. "I'll take a quick look around. Stay put."

She would. She had no other choice.

***

The wards were set. The seals in place. No eyes would find them here, no unwanted company would stumble upon their camp.

Zakar exhaled, rolling his shoulders back as he surveyed the darkened tree line one final time. Satisfied, he turned back toward the clearing—and then he heard her.

Soft. Low. A voice made of silk and secrets.

The sound stopped him in his tracks.

Myrithia was singing.

It wasn't loud, nor meant for an audience. It was the kind

of song meant only for the night itself—private, instinctual, something she had likely hummed to herself a thousand times before.

Zakar's breath came slower, deeper.

It took him back to nights when she had sung him to sleep, her voice drifting through the dim glow of candlelight, her fingers threading through his hair as he lay with his head in her lap, her touch lulling him into a peace he had never known before her.

She used to sing for him often.

She never had to. She never had to do anything. But when he returned to his chamber late at night, exhausted and frayed from the burden of politics and war councils and the weight of expectations, she had welcomed him into the quiet.

Into her arms.

Into the lull of her voice.

The night they had first met, he had actually heard her first. The mysterious Chantress who had enthralled the guests with her song. The sound of her voice had wrapped around him like a vice and never truly released him.

And much like that night, he found himself again turning his head, seeking the source, and there she was through the trees—his siren. And he, always the foolish sailor, already being drawn to the rocks.

Zakar moved soundlessly through the brush, drawn forward before he could stop himself. She stood by the water's edge, framed by silver moonlight, the soft glow reflecting off her hair.

She was brushing her fingers along the flank of one of the horses, lost in her song, unaware that she was being watched.

He could have announced himself. He could have interrupted the moment with a cutting remark, with something smug or playful, something to remind her that she was not the girl she had been, and he was no longer the fool who loved her.

But instead, he stayed.

Silent.

Listening.

Just for a little while longer.

CHAPTER 28

Myrithia

Singing had always soothed her. Even as a child, before she understood what peace should feel like, it had been her solace.

Draevok had never forbade it. It was one of the few things he had tolerated—perhaps even enjoyed—though he never explicitly said so. He had offered no praise, only silence. And silence, from him, had been the highest approval she could hope for.

She stroked the horse's mane absentmindedly, her voice carrying softly over the water in a melody that had no name. Something simple. Something soothing so that the beasts would be a little calmer than they'd been moments before. The horses lowered their heads to drink, the soft pull of water and steady swallows the only other sound in the quiet of the night.

Her fingers trailed through the coarse strands, her mind drifting elsewhere—to the magic stirring in her blood.

Zakar's magic.

It was a strange thing, how it had worked through her, subtle yet undeniable. As promised, he had given her little. Just enough to keep her upright, to keep her well.

But even that small portion had made a difference.

More than she had grown used to.

And gods help her, she was grateful for it.

Being his slave was never the life she would have chosen. Not after spending her entire existence shackled to the will of another. And yet, it should have felt unnatural. She should have felt restless, eager to leave, eager to escape. She should have longed for a life that was her own.

But she didn't know if she would ever leave him. Not truly. Because something about being with him felt disarmingly natural. Far more natural than the life she had lived before.

Zakar had always been easy to be with. Even when he was arrogant. Even when he was impossible. He had adored her once. Teased her, doted on her, given her the kind of attention that had melted through her like the first touch of summer after a long winter.

And now...

Now, his playfulness was edged with bitterness. His attentiveness was laced with control. His touch, when he allowed himself the indulgence, was no longer one of devotion, but of possession.

Yet, somehow, it still felt like home.

And it didn't help matters at all that she hadn't stopped thinking about Stonehollow, about how close they had been in the inn. She should have let it go, let it sink into the abyss of regrets she refused to examine too closely. But the memory of it lingered, waiting in the corners of her mind, rising to the surface even now.

She had kissed him because he had told her to.

Like you used to, he had said.

And she had.

The moment her lips had touched his, something had unraveled inside her. A string pulled too taut, snapping beneath the weight of all that time apart.

Her body still remembered.

She had responded to him the way she always had. As though no time had passed at all. It had been like returning to a dream that she had never wanted to awaken from.

The taste of him had been so divine, so utterly, maddeningly familiar that she hadn't wanted to stop. He hadn't wanted her to stop. So why had she?

Perhaps it had been fear.

Not fear of him—fear of herself. Fear that if she let herself fall too deeply, she wouldn't care to climb back out. Because what was freedom if it meant a life without him?

Her heart clenched, even as her voice carried on, weaving the melody across the water. If she had any self respect at all, she should want to leave. If for no other reason than to be truly free.

She hated him.

Hated him for demanding so much of her.

But she hated herself more for wanting to give it all away to him.

Then—a snap.

A twig breaking underfoot.

Her song faltered as she looked up sharply, her breath catching.

Zakar was approaching. His eyes were on her, and judging by the look in them, she hadn't been alone in her thoughts.

"The charms are in place, and we are protected for the evening," Zakar informed her, his voice steady as he beckoned her forward.

Myrithia moved toward him, handing back his reins without a word. They worked in silence as they tied their horses to the nearby trees, securing them for the night.

She could feel him watching her.

She didn't dare look up.

Did he hear me?

The thought sent a flicker of unease through her, tightening in her chest. She had never been shy—not truly. Not about herself, not about her voice.

But where it concerned *him*? She felt raw, exposed in a way that had nothing to do with power or pride, but something deeper. Something painfully fragile.

The thought of him speaking on it—of him teasing it, twisting it into something careless—made her stomach knot.

So she kept quiet, hoping he would, too.

And yet, some foolish, reckless part of her still wanted to know. What had he thought of it? Did he remember how many nights she had sung him to sleep—or was that something he had long since cast aside?

She let out a slow breath, forcing the thought away. His opinion shouldn't matter. She hated that it did. But of course it did. Because his was the only opinion left that truly held any bearing.

He was the man she had betrayed more than anyone. The man whose life had unraveled because of her.

She expected him to despise her, to never forgive her, to let her suffer the wages of her sins. That was what she deserved, after all. And if he never forgave her, then maybe she would never have to forgive herself.

Because she wasn't sure she ever could.

Myrithia exhaled softly, loosening her grip on the leather reins before stepping away from her horse. The night was silent, but the weight of their actions lingered in the air, unseen but undeniable.

Ahead of her, Zakar lifted his palm, his fingers relaxed yet brimming with control as tendrils of black and green magic swirled above his hand. The energy pulsed, shimmering with a serpentine grace before unfurling outward, expanding into a dome around them. It flickered once—a brief, iridescent shimmer—before vanishing entirely, leaving nothing but the quiet hush of the forest around them.

Myrithia recognized the spell instantly. An invisibility shield.

She had woven the very same magic for years, concealing her cottage in plain sight, making it untouchable, undisturbed. It was a subtle magic, requiring precision and focus. That Zakar could summon it so effortlessly—without so much as a murmur of incantation—only reinforced what she already knew. He was beyond powerful.

But he wasn't finished.

With another fluid motion of his wrist, Zakar retrieved a small, rune-etched token from his belt—obsidian black, with faint threads of green magic pulsing beneath its surface. He rolled it between his fingers, murmuring something under his breath before flicking it forward. The token dissolved into the air, vanishing in a whisper of energy.

Immediately, the space before him wavered, as if reality itself were bending to his will. From that shifting void, a door took shape—ornate, dark, and utterly out of place against the wilderness surrounding them. Its polished black surface gleamed, adorned with swirling gold and deep red embellishments that coiled like veins of molten fire. The handle, delicate and gilded, caught the moonlight like a sliver of captured starlight.

Myrithia's breath caught, awe tightening in her chest as she took in the sight before her.

Zakar turned, his green eyes glinting as he gestured toward the door with a slow, knowing smile. "I only gathered a few of these before we left the East Citadel. Best not to waste them, but tonight, I suppose we can indulge." He flicked a hand toward the door with an air of theatrical indulgence. "Behold—our sleeping arrangements for the evening."

Myrithia blinked, her gaze flicking between him and the conjured doorway, her mind turning over what she had just witnessed.

He had not pulled this sanctuary out of thin air—not entirely. The magic had been stored, waiting, bound to that small obsidian token until he decided to unleash it. A prepared spell, not a spontaneous feat of raw power. And yet, that did little to diminish the majesty of it.

Even with constraints, this was an extravagant display— where others would be left with bedrolls and firelight, he could summon opulence with a flick of his wrist. It wasn't arrogance, nor was it meant to impress. It was simply *efficiency*. A calculated use of his resources as the Master of the Arcane.

And tonight, she would be stepping through a door of his choosing.

CHAPTER 29

Zakar

The room unfolded around him with seamless perfection, a near-exact replica of his suite in the Arcane Citadel. Jewel-toned drapes of deep sapphire and emerald fell from the high canopy, their folds shimmering in the flickering firelight, which poured a soft amber glow across the polished marble floor. The grand onyx bed stood at the heart of it all, carved with intricate gold filigree, its sheets smooth as untouched silk.

Even the window—though he knew it was nothing more than an enchanted illusion—offered the familiar sight of treetops stretching toward the night sky, the moon pouring silver light across them as if they stood high above the world.

Zakar exhaled, pleased with the efficiency of the magic. The room was exactly as it should be. At least for tonight, they would sleep well.

A rustle behind him drew his gaze over his shoulder. Myrithia stepped into the chamber, her movements slow, measured, as if uncertain whether to trust what she was seeing. Her attention drifted over the grand space before settling on the table at the room's center, where an abundance of food awaited them.

He studied her reaction, noting the flicker of awe beneath her composed exterior.

She likely understood the magic at play—this was no mystery to her. She had cloaked her carefully forged cottage in an invisibility ward for years, after all. But as he watched her take in the sheer *luxury* of it, he wondered if Draevok had ever spared such enchantments for her in the past.

No, he decided almost immediately.

Draevok was a cruel and miserly man, unpleasant in all the ways that mattered. He had no interest in comfort, only power. Whatever indulgences he allowed himself, they were not extended to others, least of all to an apprentice he saw as disposable.

Myrithia turned to him then, her expression muting into something more neutral. "How many of these do you have?" she asked, gesturing toward the conjured room—more specifically, the magic that had created it.

"Enough," he answered smoothly.

It was a convenient answer, but not entirely a lie. *Enough*—if they met no further delays. If the path ahead remained clear.

But if Garron caught up to them, delays were inevitable. And *considerable*.

A muscle tightened in his jaw at the thought. He should have stayed long enough to finish the job. He'd had his sheathed dagger at his hip—he could have buried it in Garron's throat, ended him once and for all.

But some selfish part of him had wanted something *worse* for his old friend.

A simple stab wound would have been too swift. Too easy. Garron deserved to *suffer*. And Zakar had been willing to wait for the right moment.

His men would have arrived to that lodge at any second. *Perhaps*, he thought, the opportunity for revenge had not passed just yet.

Zakar leaned casually against the table, watching as Myrithia drifted toward the far end of the room. She moved with quiet intent toward the door that—if this truly was his suite in the Arcane Citadel—would lead to the bathing chamber.

She hesitated briefly before testing the handle, and when the door swung open to reveal the adjoining room, he caught the flicker of relief that crossed her face. Without a word, she stepped inside and closed the door firmly behind her.

He smirked.

Was she truly going to just take a bath? *Just like that?* Without asking for permission? What a presumptuous slave.

Shaking his head in amusement, Zakar waited just long enough to estimate how much progress Myrithia had made in undressing before following after her, pushing the door open without hesitation.

Inside, she stood with her ivory-skinned back to him, her dress draped over a chair, her chemise bunched loosely around her waist. The flickering candlelight cast golden highlights along her bare shoulders, tracing the gentle slope of her spine, the soft curve of her hips. She had just begun to tug the delicate fabric lower when she heard him enter.

She turned abruptly, the motion sending a subtle, mesmerizing shift through her body, her full breasts rising before settling once more.

Zakar stilled.

A sharp, hungry need twisted through him, seizing him with the kind of tension that was both unbearable and thrilling. Every muscle in his body went taut, a deep, instinctive heat unfurling in his core.

A wolfish grin curled across his lips.

"Would you like any help with—" he began, his voice thick with amusement, but she cut him off with a frantic gasp, yanking the chemise back over her chest—only to inadvertently expose herself to him from behind.

His grin deepened.

"Get out!" she screeched, spinning once more to face him, her expression burning with outrage.

Zakar chuckled, entirely undeterred, and began loosening the buttons of his coat. The first few came undone easily, the fabric parting to reveal the dark tunic beneath. He tugged at the laces near his collar, his fingers moving deftly as he admired her tousled appearance. The thin, gauzy chemise did little to conceal the shape of her, the soft swell of her curves still visible through the fabric.

Her eyes widened.

"What are you doing?" she demanded, her voice edged with alarm as he shrugged off his coat and let it drop to the floor.

He met her gaze evenly, his smirk deepening. "You had a

good idea in taking a bath," he said smoothly. "I'd like to bathe as well."

Her expression darkened with immediate disapproval. "You'll have to wait," she huffed, arms crossing over her chest in a feeble attempt to shield herself. "I'm bathing alone."

Zakar merely smiled, the kind of smile that made her wary. "We've bathed together before," he reminded her casually.

Color exploded across her face, her composure shattering in an instant.

"That—" she sputtered. "That was different! We did *not* bathe together!"

He arched a brow. "No?"

"No!" she snapped, flustered beyond measure. "You *pulled* me into the bath! *Soaking my dress through!* And then you *laughed* at me!"

At that, he did laugh, the deep, knowing sound filling the chamber.

"You barged into *my* bath," he reminded her, his voice rich with amusement. "Where I was *entirely naked*, I might add. You fully intended to put *me* on edge."

Her lips parted, undoubtedly to argue, but he pressed on.

"Only it didn't quite work, did it?"

He took his time unlacing his tunic, sliding it over his head in one smooth motion before tossing it aside. Now clad only in his pants, he grinned as she gaped at him, utterly unapologetic.

"You wanted to watch me become embarrassed," he mused, his voice laced with dark amusement, "but instead... you watched *me* bare myself before *you*—and you lost your voice."

Myrithia's face turned a deeper shade of red as her gaze flicked—unintentionally, but noticeably—to the front of his trousers, as if the memory of his body was resurfacing in her mind.

"You were *naked!*" she squeaked, her voice just as high and mortified as it had been that day.

Zakar smirked. *Utterly priceless.*

"Indeed, I was," he agreed smoothly.

With practiced ease, he tugged at the laces of his trousers, undoing them with slow, deliberate precision. As the seam parted, he let them slip down, stepping free of the fabric with effortless grace. He didn't look at her at first—he didn't *need* to.

He *felt* her gaze.

Her sharp inhale. The way her body locked up entirely, paralyzed between instinct and propriety.

And then, as realization struck her like a lightning bolt, she spun around so fast she nearly tripped over herself.

Zakar smirked. *Adorable.*

His eyes roved leisurely over the delicate curve of her lower back, the gentle swell of her hips. But just as he had predicted, she seemed to remember herself—and her current state of undress. With a strangled noise, she spun again, facing him once more with her eyes *tightly* shut, her entire body wound with frantic tension.

Zakar chuckled and turned toward the bath, unfazed by her dilemma. The large basin was already filled, steam rising from the surface, scented lightly with enchanted oils—just as it would have been in his suite at the Arcane Citadel. The water lapped gently at the marble edges, inviting and warm.

He sank into it with a low, satisfied sigh, stretching out, the heat working into his muscles. Then, without so much as a glance at Myrithia, he spoke.

"Join me if you want," he offered lazily, trailing a hand through the water, watching the ripples shift around his fingers. "But once I leave this bath, I'll be making sure there's no water left for you."

Behind him, he heard her bristle.

She was predictable in her defiance—her immediate need to push back against his every whim. He could almost hear the stubborn lift of her chin before she even spoke.

"I can do without a bath," she snapped, already striding toward the door. "Enjoy your privacy—"

"Actually," he interrupted, his voice low, smooth as silk.

She stopped mid-step.

For a beat, she didn't turn. But then, as if unable to resist, she glanced back at him, her blue eyes wary.

Zakar smiled. Slow. Knowing.

"I think I would like your company," he said, watching as color crept back into her cheeks. "Get in the bath with me."

Her embarrassment was consuming her, her expression a battle between horror and indignation. Her lips parted, already shaping a protest—

But he was faster.

"As my slave," he reminded her, voice dark and edged with amusement, "you are obliged to fulfill my *every* desire."

He leaned back against the marble, watching her with sharp, wicked interest.

"Now," he murmured, tilting his head, *just* suggestively enough, "come join me."

CHAPTER 30

Myrithia

She could hardly believe what she was hearing. Of all the things he could have commanded her to do—scrubbing floors, emptying chamber pots, polishing his boots—he chose *this*?

She had agreed to this arrangement. She had *given* him her obedience, sworn to serve his every whim. But *this*?

Heat crawled up her neck, her thoughts outright rebelling against the words that had left his lips.

Get in the bath with me.

Myrithia knew he was enjoying this. *Reveling* in her hesitation, in her torment. His smirk burned through her, sharp and taunting, as if he could hear every frantic thought screaming inside her head.

Her teeth clenched as she exhaled, marching forward with reluctant, measured steps. The closer she got, the heavier the weight in her chest became. She stopped just before the edge of the sunken marble bath, her toes grazing the cool stone.

The water rippled slightly as Zakar shifted, all lazy ease, his dark hair dampened by the mist in the air. Steam softened the edges of his form, but not enough to dull the way his broad chest gleamed beneath the firelight, or the way his arms stretched against the rim of the tub.

A tremor of something electric rolled through her middle.

"Could you at least *look away*?" she asked stiffly, arms folding tightly across herself, her entire body wound with tension.

Zakar held her gaze, unwavering and unapologetic, his eyes fixed on hers with an intensity that refused to relent.

"Why?" he asked, his voice as smooth as the surface of the water. "It's clear. You're going to be naked in front of me, dear. Turning away now won't make you invisible beneath it."

Her irritation spiked like a blade to her ribs. He was right. She had no argument, no logic to wield against him. A hushed whimper of aggravation slipped from her lips before she could stop it.

She exhaled sharply, then—before she could talk herself out of it—released her hold on her chemise. The fabric slipped from her shoulders, cascading down her body in a whisper of silk.

She *did not* look at him.

But she *felt* his gaze.

It swept over her like a lingering caress, unapologetic in its touch, drinking in every inch of exposed skin before she slipped beneath the water's surface. Her chest rose, trembling with restraint, heat searing through her that had nothing to do with the bath's warmth.

Sinking into the basin, she kept her gaze trained downward, her fingers instantly seeking out the long strands of her silver hair, tugging them forward in a futile attempt at modesty. The water lapped at her bare skin, its heat soothing, yet doing nothing to ease the tension in her spine.

Slowly—*reluctantly*—she forced herself to meet his gaze.

Zakar looked as if he had never been more at ease in his life.

Leaning back against the marble, he stretched his arms across the edge, utterly relaxed, his confidence suffocating the space between them. He watched her, his expression entirely too pleased with himself, his smirk both infuriating and insufferable.

His body was equally at ease, his broad chest shifting slightly with each slow inhale, the firelight playing against every defined plane of his torso.

With the exception of one very *not* relaxed part of him.

Her breath caught, her eyes betraying her for a fraction of a second.

A slow, knowing grin curled across his lips.

"Now," he said smugly, voice thick with amusement, "isn't this nice?"

Myrithia's lips pressed into a thin line, her irritation warring with the heat forming low in her stomach. How was he so confident?

He sat there, *fully aroused* and yet utterly at ease, watching her with that insufferable smirk, as though this were the most natural thing in the world.

Had he no shame at all?

She refused to answer his question. The bath was *not* nice. It was *not* comfortable. She didn't want to be in the water with him—especially not now, when her thoughts were tangled in memories she had no right to be thinking about.

The inn at Stonehollow. The memory refused to die.

She could still feel the press of his hands on her hips as he'd pulled her onto his lap, the bruising hunger in his kiss as he'd ground against her, his arousal thick and insistent beneath her.

And then—further still—the way his desire had turned punishing. How he had pinned her beneath him on that bed, his fingers slipping between her thighs, pressing against her, *feeling* her.

She had expected him to take her right then. Expected him to undo her completely, to push inside her and shatter the last of her resistance.

But he'd *stopped*.

And now she couldn't resist thinking about how to make him reckless again.

Heat coiled in her core, an unwelcome pulse of longing. She swallowed hard, squeezing her thighs together beneath the water, as if she could will away the sensation, will away the memory.

She needed to survive this bath. *Survive this night.*

If he ordered her to have sex with him, she would have to obey. That was their agreement. But *why*, then, did the thought of that make her impatient with eager anticipation?

Shame warred against reason, clawing at her, desperate to reel her back from the edge of something far more consuming than this bath.

"Something on your mind, Myra?"

THE ARCANE BARGAIN

His voice broke through her thoughts, low and playful, his amusement curling around the edges of her name.

She startled, her gaze snapping to his, only to find him watching her closely. The knowing glint in his green eyes sent a shiver down her spine, as if he could see straight into her thoughts, unraveling them thread by thread.

Could he?

He certainly *looked* like he could. She wanted nothing more than to wipe that arrogant expression right off his face.

"Now that you have me in this bath with you," Myrithia began coolly, willing her voice to remain composed, "what do you expect now? And when can I leave?"

Zakar clicked his tongue in mock deliberation, as if considering her words carefully. But the mischief in his eyes said otherwise.

"I think," he mused, stretching out in the water like a man wholly unbothered by her distress, "*a good slave* would see that her master is properly cleaned."

Her stomach dipped.

A spike of heat licked through her, followed swiftly by a flood of mortification.

He wants me to —

She swallowed hard, her throat suddenly dry.

"You want me to clean you?" she asked, incredulous.

He didn't seem the least bit fazed by her horror. Instead, with an infuriating amount of ease, he lifted a hand, conjuring a cloth out of thin air. The soft material shimmered, imbued with enchanted soap, its scent rich and intoxicating as it rested in his open palm.

Zakar offered her the cloth, a knowing smirk tugging at his lips, his eyes dancing with teasing intent. "Be sure not to miss any spots."

Heat flared in her cheeks, spreading down her throat like wildfire.

She *seethed*. Not because she would refuse — she *couldn't* refuse — but because he *knew* how much this would unnerve her.

Gritting her teeth, she snatched the rag from his palm, determined to maintain her composure.

It was just cleaning.

Just. Cleaning.

Slowly, she reached out, pressing the cloth against his forearm, dragging it over the defined muscles of his arm. She kept her movements measured, methodical, trying to focus on the task rather than the way he was *watching* her.

The heat of his gaze burned against her skin, unraveling her carefully constructed defenses, sinking into every space she tried to keep untouched.

Then came the soft click of his tongue against the roof of his mouth—a quiet, deliberate sound that made her pulse stutter. Mock disappointment dripped from the gesture, settling in her stomach like a lead weight.

"You should be closer," he murmured.

Before she could react, his hands found her waist.

A startled gasp escaped her, but it was already too late—his grip was firm, effortless, and suddenly the water shifted around her as he pulled her forward, closing the small space that had separated them.

Her body collided with his, and she was on his lap before she could even think to resist.

Myrithia sucked in a sharp breath, every muscle in her body locking up—because between them, his length lay thick and heavy against her stomach, *undeniable*, branding her with the knowledge of exactly what she was doing to him.

Oh gods.

Her mind was a battlefield, a violent clash of warring thoughts, logic desperately trying to hold the line against the primal, all-consuming sensation of being *this* close to him.

His skin, slick from the bath, was hot beneath her palms, the ridges of muscle shifting with every slight movement. The hard plane of his chest was *firm* against hers, his breath fanning over her damp skin, sending a traitorous shiver down her spine.

Her thighs clenched instinctively around him, the warm water swirling between them, teasing every sensitive place they touched.

How was she supposed to focus? How was she supposed to think *at all* when her body was betraying her so completely?

Her lips parted on a shaky inhale.

She had momentarily forgotten how to breathe.

CHAPTER 31

Zakar

Zakar was pleased. So very pleased to have her exactly where he wanted her—perched in his lap, her soft stomach pressing against his rigid need, her bare breasts flush against his chest.

Pleased to feel the warmth of her, the slick glide of her skin against his, the delicate tremor in her frame as she struggled to compose herself.

Pleased, most of all, to know that she would have to touch every part of him—because he willed it.

His smirk deepened as Myrithia moved stiffly, the cloth gliding over his skin in motions too careful to be anything but forced. She started with his arms, then over his chest, the soapy lather gliding over the ridges of his muscles. Her touch was careful, cautious. Almost too careful.

Zakar let her continue, watching the tension in her brow, the way her lips pressed into a firm, irritated line. He knew her well enough to recognize her defiance, even in something as simple as this.

But then, she hesitated. The cloth paused near his waist.

Zakar arched a brow, his amusement flaring. "Why are you stopping?" he asked, voice smooth, but edged with something darker.

She swallowed. "You can clean that part yourself."

His smirk widened. "No," he said, utterly unbothered. "I want you to."

A quiet groan of frustration left her lips.

For a moment, he thought she might refuse. But then—slowly, hesitantly—she obeyed.

The cloth brushed over his length, tentative and featherlight.

And Zakar immediately regretted everything.

A sharp, unforgiving wave of heat tore through him. Damn it.

Even with the rag separating them, he felt it—every bit of it. The firm pressure, the slow drag of the fabric against his aching hardness.

His thoughts fractured.

Everything inside him suddenly coiled, tense and starved, every muscle locking as a primal, devastating need took hold.

All he could think about—all he wanted—was to grip her hips, lift her, and force her down onto him, burying himself deep inside her until neither of them could breathe.

A low, unbidden growl rumbled from his chest.

His fingers found her hips, gripping her instinctively, holding her there as his body betrayed him, his restraint dangling by a thread.

Myrithia gasped.

Her hand shot away from him, abandoning the rag entirely as she steadied herself against his chest.

He looked at her, startled by his own reaction—but he masked it quickly, smoothing his expression into a careful, lazy smugness.

"Perhaps I'm clean enough," he murmured, his voice still slightly strained.

She didn't reply.

She studied him, her blue eyes sharp, calculating.

Then, slowly, she shifted.

Her hips tilted forward, her stomach brushing against him, teasing the rigid length of his arousal against her skin.

Zakar tensed, need snapping through him like a live wire. A fierce, hot pulse hit before he could brace for it, and he barely caught the groan at the back of his throat. What the hell was she doing?

Had she done that intentionally?

His gaze snapped to hers—just in time to catch the soft, ghost of a smile curving at the corner of her lips.

She did it again.

A barely-muted growl vibrated in his throat, his pulse slamming, blood rushing thick and heavy below. Her skin was flushed, her chest rising and falling slightly faster now.

And then she pulled back. Not entirely. Just enough. Teasing him. She *was* doing this on purpose.

The realization sent something dark and feral tearing through him.

A slow, dangerous grin spread across his face.

Without hesitation, he gripped her hips—this time with force—and yanked her forward, pressing her flush against him, trapping his length between them, his thick girth grinding against her stomach.

A soft, breathy moan slipped from her lips at the friction, at the way he rolled his hips greedily against her, his base pressing firmly against the delicate nerves between her legs.

His control was slipping. Fast.

A low, guttural growl escaped him as he bit down gently at her neck, his lips tracing the flushed heat of her skin.

"Tease me, Myra," he murmured against her throat, his voice a deep, wicked promise, "and I will ruin you right here in this bath."

She gasped at his threat as she instinctively pushed back from him, as if that alone could sever the tension choking the air between them. But she didn't push too far, and perhaps that was because her face looked almost desirous.

He was certain that's what he saw there, no matter how desperately she tried to mask it behind shame, behind propriety, behind whatever fragile resistance she still clung to.

Zakar drank in the sight of her, savoring the way her long silver hair clung to her damp skin, rivulets of water tracing over the smooth expanse of her collarbone, slipping lower, pooling between the soft swell of her bare, perfect breasts.

The pale curves were untouched by the water's concealment, unapologetically visible, her pink nipples taut from the heat of the bath, or perhaps—he hoped—from something else entirely.

He clenched his jaw.

He wanted to ruin her.

Not just out of vengeance. Not just because he wanted to watch her break beneath him, to make her surrender completely.

No—this wasn't just a want.

It was turning into a craving.

A need.

He needed her. Every inch of her, every sound, every breathless whimper. He needed to possess her, to claim her, to leave no space between them until she was his in every sense of the word.

This was a mistake.

A disastrous, aching mistake.

His face remained impassive, cool, betraying nothing of the war raging inside him. He let out a slow, measured breath, then met her gaze evenly.

"You should leave," he said smoothly, voice perfectly controlled despite the chaos within. "Your master is now clean."

She hesitated. Just for a second.

Then she backed away from him, nervously reaching for the rag, her voice muttering something about needing to wash herself quickly.

Zakar watched as she turned, her movements rushed, her hands skimming over her skin as if she could obscure his view, as if she could hide from him.

As if he couldn't see everything.

Every shift of her body, every subtle motion—it was maddening.

His eyes traced the smooth, dripping curve of her back, the gentle swell of her hips, the soft weight of her breasts as she reached across herself, lathering soap over her skin.

And when she dragged the cloth down between her thighs, a curse fell low under his breath.

Heat curled in his core, molten and rising, his entire body tensing with immediate, excruciating need.

If he didn't stop this, he was going to spill himself right here in the water like some desperate, untouched fool.

His fingers pressed against the marble edge of the bath, barely holding himself together, barely stopping himself from yanking her back into his lap and grinding his aching length against her until she begged for him.

Enough.

His voice was calm—too calm—when he spoke, but his restraint was hanging by threads.

"Unless you want to be bent over the edge of this bath, Myra," he murmured, low and steady, the heat in his voice impossible to ignore, "you should get out. Now."

Panic flashed in her blue eyes.

Without hesitation, she rose from the water, the movement abrupt and stunning, the droplets cascading down her glistening skin as she rushed to grab a towel.

Zakar swallowed hard, willing himself to not look—and failing.

She wrapped the fabric around herself, too late, and fled from the bathing room, the door clicking shut behind her with unceremonious finality.

For a long, agonizing moment, Zakar remained in the bath, unmoving.

His pulse pounded in his ears, his breath uneven.

Then, slowly, he looked down at the hardened traitor between his legs with pure, unfiltered resentment.

This.

This was the source of all his problems.

CHAPTER 32
Myrithia

The cool night air drifted through the chamber, brushing against Myrithia's skin as she stood by the enchanted window, her arms wrapped loosely around herself. The illusion of the treetops stretched endlessly before her, bathed in moonlight, the sky a deep, velvet black.

What had she been thinking?

Her cheeks burned as the memory flickered through her mind—the way she had moved against him, the way his body had reacted, the sounds that had escaped his throat.

She had *made* him do that.

A simple movement, a subtle shift, and Zakar—the unshakable, all-powerful Master of the Arcane—had groaned beneath her touch, his restraint unraveling.

A strange sense of satisfaction swelled in her chest.

It was dangerous. Reckless. Stupid.

Her arms tightened around herself.

When they had courted years ago, she had wondered, *then*, what sex would be like. She had never intended to give herself to the man she was destined to betray, but at the same time, she had never felt these things with another.

But then again, serving Draevok had left no space for romance.

Zakar was the only man who had ever truly seen her. The only one who had ever touched her in a way that wasn't meant to hurt or manipulate.

Before him, there had been nothing—just a short-lived courtship in her girlhood, a brief, innocent glimpse of what love was supposed to look like. A kiss. A hand to hold. That was all.

Until Zakar.

With him, she had tasted something more.

They had shared *many* kisses. *Many* touches. But he had been a gentleman then—had told her he wanted to marry her first, as was the proper custom.

And when he had proposed, she hadn't given him an answer.

Draevok had been pleased. Zakar *adored* her, and that had been enough to ensnare him. The hardest part of her task had been completed.

But *she* had hesitated. Because, despite everything, she had wanted to say yes. The idea of marriage—to him—had been *so* tempting.

But it had never been real.

It had been a dream—a dream built on a *lie*, and when he had woken from it, when he had seen what she had done, there had been no salvaging what they had.

How could he ever separate the truth from the lie?

How could he ever forgive her for the role she had played in the destruction of his legacy?

A quiet, shaky breath escaped her as she rubbed her arms absently, as if the motion might soothe the ache in her chest.

She was being foolish.

Hearing him groan under his breath as his arousal thickened between them, wanting to feel *all* of him, teasing him just to watch him come undone—it was all so foolish.

Because this wasn't love.

Zakar didn't want her the way he once had. He wanted to exact his claim, to humiliate her. He probably knew by now that she wanted it, and he was *cruel* enough to withhold it—just to make her suffer.

Or worse.

Perhaps he would decide he had no interest in her pleasure at all. Perhaps he would simply rut against her, seeking only his own satisfaction, reducing her to nothing but a vessel to take what he needed.

And *still* she wanted it.

Myrithia clenched her teeth, a curse slipping from her lips as she squeezed her eyes shut.

What had she become?

A soft creak broke the silence.

She stiffened.

The door to the bathing room swung open behind her, releasing a faint gust of warm, perfumed air into the chamber.

She turned her head slightly, her pulse quickening as Zakar stepped inside, his gaze immediately finding her.

He was barefoot, his dark hair still damp from the bath, a single droplet of water trailing along the cut of his collarbone before disappearing against his bare, sculpted chest.

He was only wearing his trousers. Myrithia groaned internally.

As if the night hadn't already tested her limits, now he had gifted her with the sight of his perfect, bare upper body, on full display for her suffering.

And, as if that weren't enough, he had left her only this flimsy, nearly sheer nightgown to wear—one that clung to the dampness of her skin, doing absolutely *nothing* to conceal her body from his view.

If she managed to keep her virginity intact by the end of this evening, she would honestly be surprised.

His sharp green eyes were dragging over every inch of her slowly, savoring her, owning her with nothing but a glance.

Then, just as easily, he looked away.

He strode toward the table where the feast still steamed with lingering heat, unbothered, unaffected, as though the tension between them didn't exist at all.

"You should eat if you're hungry," he advised, selecting a few things from the table before turning back toward her. "I'll be sleeping in the bathing room, if you need me."

Myrithia blinked, momentarily thrown off by the statement.

Sleeping in the bathing room?

She frowned. "Why? You can have the bed." She gestured toward it, watching him carefully. "It *is* your bed, after all. Besides, I assumed you'd want me next to you all night."

At that, he paused mid-step.

A flicker of amusement crossed his face as he turned to look at her, studying her.

"Is that what you assumed?"

She shifted, suddenly uncertain.

"You've slept beside me every night since I became your slave," she pointed out, forcing herself to hold his gaze. "Should I be anticipating I'll be getting my own quarters when we return to the Arcane Citadel?"

The corner of his mouth lifted just slightly, but the look in his eyes was anything but kind—predatory, dark, and claiming.

He set the food down on the bedside table, then—without a word—began walking toward her.

Myrithia swallowed as he closed the distance, step by slow step, until her back met the cold, smooth post of the onyx bed.

Towering over her, trapping her.

"No," he murmured, the word sinking into her bones like a promise. "No, you will not have anything to call your own. No quarters. No bed. Nothing."

His fingers lifted, his palm brushing against her jaw, forcing her chin upward so she had no choice but to meet his gaze.

"You have a bed tonight because I say you do."

Myrithia's breathing stuttered, her pulse thundering.

"Why?" she blurted out, unable to stop herself, even as her mind screamed at her to shut up. "Because of what happened in the bath?"

His lips twitched, a spark of wicked intent glinting in his eyes.

"The bath?" he echoed, his tone mocking.

Before she could react, his mouth was on hers, claiming her with a kiss that was searing, relentless, and utterly consuming. His hands gripped her body with possessive intent, fingers kneading, exploring, taking, as if he had every right to her.

She gasped against his lips, but he swallowed the sound, pressing her harder into the bedpost, his strength undeniable, his desire a force that surrounded her. His tongue swept past her lips, stroking deep, leaving no space between them untouched.

His hands mapped her curves with unhurried precision, dragging over the sheer fabric of her nightgown, teasing the barrier as if deciding whether to remove it entirely. His grip was firm and demanding, his touch sending shivers down her spine as heat coiled low in her stomach, leaving no question as to what he wanted—or how much she was beginning to want it too.

Then—suddenly—he pushed her, pressing her down firmly into the mattress below.

The world tilted, her pulse hammering wildly, but there was no time to think.

Zakar was on top of her, his body heavy, commanding, his mouth devouring hers once more as his hand slid between her thighs.

She gasped, her breath shattering against his lips as his fingers pressed between her legs, gliding through her wetness with maddening precision. A low, feral growl vibrated in his throat as he pulled back just slightly, his mouth moving down, tracing hungry, open-mouthed kisses along her jaw, her throat, and lower.

His fingers slid past the thin fabric of her nightgown, pushing inside her—a slow, torturous stroke that made her arch, her moan slipping free before she could stop it.

His other hand gripped her hip, pinning her beneath him, keeping her exactly where he wanted her.

He kissed lower, dragging her nightgown down beneath her chest, exposing the delicate curve of her breast.

His tongue traced over her nipple with a soft, teasing touch before his lips closed around it, sucking gently.

A shuddering moan ripped from her throat, her hands flying up to clutch his shoulders, fingers digging into his damp skin.

Zakar groaned deeply, grinding against her as his fingers slid in and out, slow and agonizing, building the pressure inside her until she was trembling, desperate.

Then—just as suddenly as it had started—he stopped.

Myrithia let out a sharp, frustrated whimper, her hips twitching beneath him, seeking him.

Zakar chuckled darkly, kissing her once more—deep, punishing—before biting her lip gently, just enough to make her breath catch.

When he pulled away, his eyes were heavy-lidded, his

expression wholly unapologetic.

"How does it feel, Myra?" he murmured.

She panted, her pulse frantic, her body aching. "Good," she barely managed to whisper. "Why did you stop?"

He smirked. "Why?"

His voice was husky, strained, his breath uneven as he pulled back, his pants visibly tight.

"Because now you'll know how it feels," he murmured, eyes glinting with dark amusement, "to be teased and left *wanting*."

Myrithia stared at him, wrecked, still aching for him—but he simply stood, adjusting his pants with an air of infuriating control.

"Goodnight," he said smoothly.

Then, without another word, he walked away, leaving her in his bed, wanting nothing more than for him to return and finish what she'd started.

CHAPTER 33

Zakar

The rhythmic thud of hooves against the damp earth filled the quiet morning, the dense canopy of trees stretching endlessly above. Sunlight filtered through in golden slivers, drawing soft shadows along the narrow path as Zakar rode through the woods, his posture relaxed, his mind anything but.

A few paces ahead of him, Myrithia rode in silence.

He hadn't spoken much to her since the night before, nor had he exchanged many words over breakfast.

He hadn't planned for *this*.

At the outset, he had known exactly what he wanted—to claim her, to take her body as his, to finally have her the way he had always imagined. It was about vengeance, about power, about owning what had once been denied to him.

But something had changed.

That night, just before she had signed her life to him in blood, he had felt it—desire. Real and unbidden, slipping past her carefully controlled exterior, sinking into her kiss, betraying her even as she surrendered her fate.

She *wanted* him.

She perhaps hadn't realized it then. But she was surely aware of it *now*, which only complicated his desire to claim her.

He no longer wanted simply to bury himself inside her for his own gratification. That was too easy. Too simple.

Now, he wanted her to beg for it.

But she had bolted from the bath like a frightened doe at the mere *threat* of it, clutching the towel to her body as though it could shield her from what had nearly happened.

Zakar exhaled slowly, his fingers tightening briefly around the reins.

She wasn't desperate enough yet.

She desired him—he had felt it in the way her body had moved, the way she had moaned beneath his touch. The way she had hesitated before pushing him away, her body betraying her even as her mind screamed for her to flee.

She had wanted him, but not enough to beg. Not enough to surrender.

He wouldn't take her until that last shred of defiance cracked—until she was as desperate for him as he had once been for her.

Back then, he had *yearned* for her, *ached* for her, imagined her in his arms as his, only to be left in the wreckage of her betrayal.

He had suffered for years, drowning in the torment of knowing that she had played him. That she had lured him in, kissed him sweetly, touched him gently, only to shatter his world the moment it had served her.

Now, he would make her understand that torment.

He would make her suffer for it.

He would own her need, the same way she had once owned his.

In bed with her, he had nearly given in, nearly lost control when her body had responded so beautifully to him. The way she had gasped, the way she had tightened around his fingers, the way her silken moan sounded when he had taken her nipple into his mouth.

But even as he denied her, as he left her wanting in that bed, she hadn't followed him.

She hadn't sought him out, desperate for him. She had laid there, clinging to the memory of his touch, her body burning for him—yet still unwilling to plead for him to finish it.

As if he would give her the satisfaction of pleasure without first humbling herself before him.

Zakar's jaw tightened. He wouldn't simply take her. That

would be *too easy*, too merciful. No, he would make her suffer first. He would make her beg.

She would come to him, pleading for relief, gasping his name, aching for him to claim her completely—and *only then* would he give her what she craved.

"Zakar," Myrithia called ahead, her voice tight with concern.

He barely glanced up at first, still tangled in his thoughts—until he caught the way her posture had stiffened, the way her horse had slowed to a near halt.

His gaze followed hers.

A breath curled in his lungs, heavy with irritation.

To the east, the Hollow Mist was creeping across the land, swallowing their path in a slow, soundless tide. The pale, colorless fog devoured the forest in its wake, reducing it to nothing but a ghostly blur of shadows. Even from here, he could feel the unnatural stillness—the way the air itself seemed to recoil from the mist's touch, as if even nature refused to fight against it.

Their path was gone.

Zakar exhaled sharply, suppressing the groan of frustration that threatened to escape.

The Hollow Mist was an uncompromising force, an entity that yielded to no one, not even him. Even his magic—vast as it was—could do nothing but shudder and dissipate if tested against its hunger.

To enter would be suicide.

But to turn west—toward Hawthorne Reach—would be an invitation for bounty hunters to descend upon them like starving wolves.

Myrithia had come to a full stop now, her hands tight on the reins, her expression carefully unreadable.

She was waiting.

Waiting for him to speak.

But she already knew. She had to.

There was only one way left to go.

And it would lead them straight into the hands of the very people who wanted them dead.

He sighed, breaking the silence at last. "Have you ever been to Hawthorne Reach, Myra?"

Apprehension flickered across her features. "No."

"Well," he mused, betraying none of his displeasure, "it's lovely weather this time of year. And it's certainly more level terrain."

She didn't rise to the bait. Her gaze remained wary. "It will be crawling with mercenaries."

He nodded, appearing unbothered, his tone almost bored. "Yes, it will. And perhaps it will make our journey a little more… invigorating."

She didn't look reassured.

Not that he expected her to be.

She had been hunted for years, and the weight of it was beginning to show. The last few days had taken a toll on her body, draining her strength in ways she had been reluctant to admit.

But she didn't need to worry.

He would protect her, whether she liked it or not.

***

The town was larger than most, sprawling across the valley with a steady hum of life and movement. It carried an air of indifference—efficient, practical, a place built for commerce and routine rather than warmth or charm.

The streets were lined with cobblestone and timber buildings, many adorned with fresh-painted signs for taverns, apothecaries, blacksmiths, and market stalls. Townspeople moved briskly, engaged in their daily trade, though today, there was an undeniable sense of excitement in the air.

Strings of lanterns and colorful pennants were being fastened between buildings, swaying lightly in the afternoon breeze. The scent of freshly baked bread and sugared pastries mingled with the richer aroma of spiced meats roasting over open flame. Vendors were arranging artisanal wares—intricately carved jewelry, handwoven textiles, fine glasswork—on display as if anticipating heavy foot traffic.

Zakar rode in silence, his cloak drawn tight over his shoulders, the hood shadowing his face. Beside him, Myrithia kept her head low, her own cloak obscuring the features that would make her too recognizable.

For the most part, they blended in.

The townspeople were too preoccupied with their preparations to spare them more than a glance. But Zakar scanned every movement, every face, his sharp gaze sweeping over the bustling streets like a predator watching for a break in the herd.

He would have to use a glamour to alter his appearance, but maintaining one for Myrithia would be beyond his reach. She would need a different solution. Muttering the incantation under his breath, he felt the shift take hold—his raven hair draining to stark white before settling into a soft blonde beneath the shadow of his hood.

They rode deeper into town, eventually stopping at an inn that appeared reputable enough. The exterior was well-maintained, the carved wooden sign swinging lightly in the wind, the scent of braised meat and mulled wine wafting from within.

Zakar dismounted first, handing his horse over to the waiting stablehand, flicking him a coin without a word. Myrithia followed suit, though her movements were slightly sluggish, her exhaustion barely concealed. He ignored the flicker of concern that rose unbidden in his chest.

Inside, the inn's interior was luxurious, warmer than the outside world. The floors were polished dark wood, the walls lined with deep emerald drapes and gold candle sconces. The scent of burning cedar and aged brandy filled the space, mingling with the low hum of conversation from well-dressed patrons.

Near the fireplace, a group of young women sat in a cluster, their voices bright with excitement.

"I still haven't chosen a dress," one of them lamented, sighing into her wine cup. "I'll have to borrow something from my sister."

"You've had months to prepare!" another laughed, shaking her head. "The festival is tonight! What if you don't find anything in time?"

"Then I'll dance in rags," she declared, flipping her golden braid over her shoulder. "As long as I get to dance, that's all that matters."

The others giggled, clinking their glasses together in agreement.

Zakar turned his attention away, letting their chatter fade into the background.

"But we need a place to stay," the man in front of Zakar was insisting, his voice edged with frustration as he gestured toward the woman beside him.

She was draped in finery, her gown rich with embroidery, but she reeked of strong perfume, the scent overbearing, over-sweet, desperate.

The innkeeper's expression remained unchanged.

"This is a fine establishment, young sir," he said flatly.

Then, with a pointed glance at the woman, he lowered his voice, his tone carrying the quiet weight of finality.

"If you wish to stay somewhere with your... *whore*, then you'll have to stay somewhere else."

The man flushed, clearly humiliated.

"There is nowhere else!" he pleaded, hands gesturing wildly. "Every inn is full!"

The innkeeper did not budge. His arms folded across his chest, rigid and unmoving, a silent testament to his resolve. "You should've booked your room earlier, then." His silence stretched just long enough for the man's hope to wither. "Perhaps you'll find the stables more welcoming than the streets."

And with that, the conversation was over. He turned his attention to Zakar and beckoned him forward. "Next."

Zakar stepped up with effortless confidence, circling an arm around Myrithia's waist as he did so.

She remained tense beside him, her fingers clutching the edge of her hood, keeping her face concealed.

Unbothered, he tightened his hold, drawing her against him.

"My wife and I would like a room, please."

CHAPTER 34

Myrithia

Myrithia nearly jumped at the word *wife* tumbling so easily from Zakar's mouth. It sounded so natural, as if it weren't a lie at all. She bit her lip to keep from correcting him.

She had seen what had happened to the man before them, sent away for bringing a whore to the inn. It stood to reason that a man and his *slave* would have fared no better.

The innkeeper studied her warily, eyes narrowing with concern before shifting to Zakar.

"Is she alright?" He looked back to her, tone softening. "Miss, are you feeling well—"

"My wife is newly pregnant, good sir," Zakar interrupted, effortlessly drawing the man's attention back to him.

Myrithia's breath caught. *Pregnant?* She barely had time to recover from the absurdity before he continued.

"She has spent much of the day atop a horse and really needs to rest awhile. Do you have a room?"

The innkeeper's eyes brightened immediately. His entire demeanor shifted, and for the first time since they arrived, he smiled.

"Pregnant, you say?" Beaming, he grabbed a key from the wall behind him and gestured for them to follow. "My daughter just gave birth a few days ago to a beautiful little boy!" he said proudly as he led them down the hall.

Myrithia's heart was still racing, but not from fear, but from the thrill of the deception. She caught Zakar's smirk out of the corner of her eye as he followed behind the innkeeper, slipping effortlessly into the ruse.

"Oh, congratulations!" he said smoothly. "You must be so proud."

The innkeeper nodded, his chest swelling with pride. "Yes, he is my first grandson! Hopefully the first of many grandchildren." He reached the end of the hall, inserting the key into the door before turning back to them.

Zakar didn't hesitate. He slid an arm around her waist again, drawing her flush against him. "I hope so," he said warmly. "Just as I hope my wife and I will have a great many children of our own."

Myrithia felt a wild surge of something unnamable lodge in her chest. It was nonsensical, but for a fleeting moment, she was his wife, pregnant with his child, and he had expressed a desire for a family. It was a lie—one he told with such conviction that even she was tempted to believe it.

For just a moment.

"Will you be attending the festival this evening?" The innkeeper turned his attention to her, his excitement infectious. "My daughter will be there with my grandson. I think you'd get along well."

Myrithia opened her mouth, uncertain of what to say.

Zakar, of course, answered before she could.

"We would love to attend," he said smoothly. "That's the very reason we came to town."

She clenched her teeth behind a practiced smile.

"In fact," he continued, "my wife makes the very best Umberkern pie. Perhaps we could make some to contribute?"

Myrithia's stomach dropped. She fought to mask her shock, smoothing it into feigned enthusiasm. "Oh, yes," she forced herself to say, "it's delicious."

The innkeeper lit up further, patting his round belly. "I would never turn down a pie!" he declared with a hearty laugh. "You can use our kitchens downstairs to bake as many as you wish." Turning to Zakar, he handed over the key. "Let that wife of yours rest up a little before you start." And with that, he turned and strode back down the hall.

The room they stepped into was quaint but refined, a perfect blend of comfort and quiet luxury. A four-poster bed, draped in soft linen and deep emerald quilts, took up most of the space, its carved wooden frame polished to a subtle sheen. A small writing desk sat beneath a leaded-glass window, the panes reflecting the soft glow of the lantern hanging beside the bed.

The hearth had already been lit, its flames spilling golden light across the warm oak floors, filling the room with the rich scent of pine and spiced wax. A silver tray rested on a low table near two well-cushioned chairs, holding a carafe of mulled wine and two delicate goblets. It was the kind of place meant to lull a weary traveler into ease, though Myrithia doubted she'd find any rest tonight.

The moment the door clicked shut behind them, she pulled her hood down and turned toward Zakar, arms crossed. "I am now your *pregnant* wife who makes *Umberkern pie*?"

Zakar smiled broadly, shrugging as he slid a hand over the back of an ornate chair. "You're not even showing yet, and already you have that *pregnancy glow*," he mused sarcastically.

She rolled her eyes. "I don't know how to make Umberkern pie," she scolded. "You could've picked *any* other pie, but you chose one of the hardest ones to make."

Zakar stepped toward her, his fingers trailing lightly over a strand of her hair, tilting his head as he studied her.

His nearness carried the warm, heady scent of cedarwood, making her stomach tighten.

"The Umberkern," he said smoothly, "is to dye your hair."

She stared at him, realization dawning. Umberkern seeds were a deep, dark mahogany, and when boiled, they produced a thick, rich dye capable of staining fabric, as well as hair.

She had always relied on glamour spells to disguise her appearance—like what he was relying on now—but maintaining an illusion had always been exhausting to sustain for more than an hour.

And that was back when she was at full strength.

Now? She wouldn't last ten minutes.

"That's brilliant," she blurted before she could stop herself.

The triumphant smirk that stretched across Zakar's lips made her regret it instantly.

"I thought so," he murmured, releasing her hair and stepping back. "I spied a shop in town that sells Umberkern," he added. "I'll stop in and buy some."

Myrithia narrowed her eyes. "I still can't make the pie." She exhaled sharply. "The innkeeper will be expecting one, don't you think?"

Zakar waved a dismissive hand. "Don't worry about the pie. I'll make it. If for no other reason than to spare my poor pregnant wife the unnecessary *burden*."

She blinked, momentarily caught off guard. "You bake?" she asked, suspicious.

Zakar adjusted his cloak, turning toward the door. "I am a man of many skills, Myra."

Then, after a pause, he cast a glance over his shoulder, his tone laced with teasing warmth. "Now go on, be a good little wife, and get yourself ready for the festival."

The words shouldn't have meant anything. It was a game, a performance, nothing more. And yet, warmth bloomed in her chest at the endearment, comforting her.

She could get used to this.

Even knowing it was a fantasy, she would let herself indulge — just for tonight. Pretend she was his. Pretend she was something to be cherished.

***

A few hours later, Myrithia wrung the last of the dye from her hair, twisting the damp strands through an old rag, watching as dark threads bled into the bucket below.

She had already rinsed it twice to rid herself of the excess stain, but still, the scent of Umberkern lingered, warm and earthy. She reached for a comb, dragging it slowly through the strands, marveling at how foreign she looked in the flickering candlelight. The dye had clung to her silver roots, softening the color into something rich and warm, a tawny brown with deep undertones of gold.

She had never known what it was like to appear ordinary—to be unremarkable, unassuming. From her first breath, the world had looked at her and known she was different—that silver hair, that gaze like stormlight caught in still water. There was no blending in. She had always been set apart, as if shaped by a story too old to remember.

Draevok had told her once that when he first found her, it wasn't pity or chance that had drawn him in—nor even fate. It was a colder thing: a hunger dressed as curiosity. She reminded him of the old myths—the silver-veiled goddesses lost to time. A being with immense, enviable power who had been sought after by many—both gods and men—though they were always a step behind, always searching.

Draevok was like those men—always searching and collecting souls who showed promise and power. He'd taken one look at her and decided. She would be formidable. He had expected it, had demanded it even.

Unfortunately for him, she had never fully risen to the place he had envisioned for her. She had never been good enough—not in the way he had wanted, in the prodigy that he had expected her to become.

A near-wasted investment, until he found another use for her. Until he saw the opportunity in dangling her before Zakar, in using her to snare the prince's interest. That, at least, had satisfied him. Until she betrayed him and became his greatest disappointment.

She rose to her feet and walked over to a tall mirror, hardly recognizing herself. It was a strange feeling—to look into her own reflection and see someone who could be anyone. She no longer looked like the phantom of Zakar's past, nor the traitor the world hunted. She was common, yet still striking. Still... *beautiful.*

And perhaps, if she ever truly escaped, if she could someday live a life unchained, this was a look she could grow accustomed to. She reached back, gathering the damp strands into a long braid down her spine, fingers working deftly as she secured it in place.

Her gown was just as unfamiliar. Cerulean blue, fitted at the waist, its embroidered sleeves trailing delicately past her wrists. It was ornate enough to belong to a noble lady, but not so fine as to draw unwanted attention. Zakar had brought it for her before disappearing downstairs to bake the pies, along with the Umberkern seeds that had transformed her hair.

She understood why they were going to the festival. It was the simplest explanation for their presence in Hawthorne Reach. Any other excuse—passing through, seeking shelter, merely travelers—would have required a more elaborate story, one riddled with unnecessary complications.

Why not blend in? Why not let coincidence be their ally? She had considered asking Zakar if it was entirely necessary to go through the trouble. Wouldn't it have been easier to camp on the outskirts of town and use another one of his magic tokens to conjure them shelter?

But she knew the answer already. He didn't have many of those tokens left. And if mages were already searching for spells and charms in the area, then a conjured dwelling might draw unwanted attention. It was safer to disappear in plain sight. Her thoughts were interrupted by the sound of the door opening behind her.

She turned hastily, her braid swaying, as Zakar entered the room. The faint aroma of Umberkern pie clung to him, warm and spiced, hanging in the air like an old memory. Myrithia inhaled involuntarily, her body responding before her mind could stop it.

She hadn't grown up in a normal home. She hadn't known the warmth of a mother baking in the kitchen or the comfort of returning to a place that felt like hers. She had been an orphan until Draevok took her in—not as a daughter, but as something to be shaped, honed, and wielded. He had crafted her into a weapon, a tool of his design, meant for utility, never love.

As a girl, she would walk through the crowded vendor stalls of the capital, catching hints of baked goods cooling in the sun. Occasionally, if Draevok was in a generous mood, he would allow her to have one. But only if she pleased him that day.

And then, later, there had been Zakar. When she played the

role of his mistress, he had fed her like a queen, clothed her like one too. Perhaps that was the only time in her life she had ever been treated like something adored. Her abdomen tensed, the feeling so alien it made her uneasy.

Then, Zakar flashed her a smile. "The pies have been made, and you look beautiful, little wife."

Her heart leapt into her throat. She tried to tamp it down, to pretend the words didn't affect her.

But really, what was the harm in indulging—just for one night? Could she not allow herself this small sliver of happiness, even if it was only an illusion?

Completely unaware of the excitement unfurling in her chest, Zakar casually began stripping off his clothes.

Myrithia let out a sharp breath and spun around, blushing fiercely. She refused to look at him. She listened as he moved effortlessly about the room, the rustle of fabric, the quiet click of clasps unfastening.

When she finally dared to turn back, he was already fully dressed, fastening the last few buttons of his coat.

They matched.

His black coat was edged in the same cerulean blue as her gown, their outfits coordinated like true husband and wife. The sight of it unraveled something small and secret inside her. She couldn't fight the smile that crept onto her lips.

For just one evening, she could allow herself to believe it—believe that she had married him, that she was cherished, that in this quaint little town, on this simple festival night, she belonged to him in a way that had nothing to do with chains.

CHAPTER 35

Zakar

The glamour had settled easily over him, the magic hardly fatiguing, but still, he disliked it. His hair had been black as ink his entire life—a defining trait, an unshakable part of his identity. Now, the strands were a pale golden blonde, light enough to seem unremarkable, blending him into any number of nameless men wandering through the festival.

It felt wrong. Unnatural. His green eyes flicked sideways, catching the way Myrithia kept eyeing him. Did she prefer him this way? He couldn't quite place her expression—curiosity, maybe. Amusement? Disdain?

Did it matter? Of course not. And yet, the idea of her finding his new look entertaining left a peculiar itch of annoyance in the back of his mind. He turned his focus to the world around them, shifting through the sea of bodies, lantern light, and celebration.

The festival was in full swing, and Hawthorne Reach had come alive with it.

Laughter and animated chatter wove through the streets, voices raised in friendly haggling, in drunken songs, in sweet murmurings between lovers.

The scent of spiced cider and roasted almonds drifted through the air, blending with sizzling meats, herb-dusted breads, and honeyed pastries. Red and gold banners fluttered overhead between lantern-lit posts, their glow dancing gently across the bustling square.

Vendors called out from carts and stalls, offering trinkets, dyed fabrics, carved figures, and glinting jewelry. Children dashed past, laughing, their faces painted with foxes, birds, and flowers, ribbons and sweets clutched in their hands.

The steady pulse of a drum mingled with flutes and lutes, weaving lively, inviting melodies through the crowd. At the heart of it all, couples danced in graceful twirls, their laughter rising beneath the starlit sky.

Zakar let his gaze roam over it all, taking in the movement, the shifting faces, the easy joy painted across them.

It was so unlike the world he had known. A world where power was survival. Where a misplaced step could cost you everything. Here, there was only festivity, only warmth, only people celebrating something fleeting and fragile.

"Derek!"

He turned, spotting Julian, the innkeeper, weaving through the crowd, a small newborn cradled in his arms, calling out the false name Zakar had given him.

It wasn't until that moment that he realized—he had never given Myrithia a false name for the evening.

Quickly, he slipped on a broad smile, circling an arm around her shoulders, pulling her against him as if it were the most natural thing in the world. A husband and his wife, completely at ease.

"Hello again," Zakar greeted smoothly, his voice light, casual.

Just behind Julian, a young woman hovered close, her eyes locked on the infant in his arms. Julian beamed, shifting the baby slightly as he stepped forward. "I wanted to show you my grandson!" he said delightedly, holding the tiny bundle out slightly so they could see him better.

Zakar glanced at the child, schooling his features into an expression of feigned interest, then leaned into Myrithia, sliding a wide palm across her stomach. "Soon, we will have a little one of our own, my dear." He pressed a soft, lingering kiss to her cheek, his lips brushing warm against her skin.

And though he knew it was part of the act, though he was merely securing their story, the sight of her flushed cheeks and stunned expression nearly knocked the breath from his lungs.

Because for a fleeting moment, he couldn't tell if she was playing along... or truly lost in it.

Her eyes softened as she gazed at the baby, her fingers sliding over his hand, where it still rested against her stomach.

Slowly, she looked up at him.

And smiled.

A gentle, radiant smile—so convincing, so damn believable, that for half a second, he felt his entire world tilt.

"I can hardly wait," she murmured, her blue eyes shining with something that could only be described as adoration.

His chest tightened.

Julian chuckled, nodding approvingly.

His daughter, the young woman beside him, stepped forward, resting a hand on Myrithia's arm. "Would you like to hold him?"

Myrithia nodded hesitantly, a quiet eagerness peeking through her careful restraint. Zakar watched, pleased. She needed to play along, and so far, she was doing admirably.

Julian's daughter carefully placed the tiny, sleeping child in Myrithia's arms, and she held him as if he were made of glass.

"He's so light!" she whispered, wonder flickering in her tone, though she kept her voice soft enough not to wake him.

Julian's daughter laughed, nodding. "Yes, he is!" she agreed, then eyed Myrithia's slim waist with a knowing smirk. "A lot lighter to hold than he was to *carry*. You'll be feeling that in a few months, to be sure."

Myrithia nodded, brushing her knuckles lightly along the baby's cheek.

Zakar observed the way she cradled the child, the way her fingers moved with careful reverence, as if afraid of disturbing something fragile and precious.

Something she had never known before.

Julian's daughter shifted, glancing toward the buffet tables in the distance.

"Would you mind holding him another minute or so?" she asked, smiling. "I'd love to grab a slice of your delicious pie." She pointed to the tables about thirty feet away, watching as Myrithia nodded in agreement. "I'll be just over there," she assured before gently pulling Julian with her, leaving them alone.

Zakar let the silence settle between them, watching as Myrithia held the child with an ease that made something strange coil in his chest.

He studied her carefully, then spoke. "This cannot be your first time holding a baby."

She smiled sheepishly, her gaze still locked on the sleeping infant. "It is."

He frowned. He hadn't had much experience with babies himself, but he had at least held them before.

For her to have never even done that…

It occurred to him that while all he knew of her had been a lie, there were things he had simply never known at all.

"I had assumed you were an only child," he said after a pause. "I suppose that's true, then? No siblings, no nieces or nephews?"

She shook her head. "I was an orphan," she explained, her voice softer than before. "I lived at the Home for Innocents until Draevok took me. I hardly remember it."

Zakar raised a brow. "You were raised by him?"

"Not as a daughter or anything like that," she corrected gently, a flicker of something dark and distant in her tone. "He was adamant that I knew he was not my father. He said I had a gift for magic, and so he trained me. Molded me."

His stomach hardened. "Were there others?" he asked. "Other children he took in?"

She shook her head again. "He said he regretted taking in a small child," she murmured. "That it was too much work to put up with a child's needs. I was his biggest regret."

A strange, ugly feeling twisted inside him.

Pity. Anger. A seething disgust.

He knew she wasn't lying.

She couldn't lie.

Draevok had taken a child—a small, innocent child—and crafted her into this. Into a weapon. The implications of it threatened to upend his core. Threatened to unravel the rage he had carried for five years. He swallowed it down, pressing it into something harder, sharper, quieter.

"Do you want to hold him?" Her voice was softer now, her

blue eyes lifting to his, hesitant yet oddly warm.

Zakar looked past her, toward Julian's daughter in the distance, sitting with her father, watching them with a careful smile. He forced a smile of his own, knowing they had an audience. And because appearances mattered, he extended his arms and took the baby from her. The infant was small, barely a weight in his hands.

A quiet moment passed between them as Myrithia leaned in close, standing on her tiptoes, her breath fanning softly over his neck. "I'll go get us some pie," she murmured, voice just above a whisper.

Then, without waiting for his reply, she turned and walked away. Zakar watched her go, something aching in his chest. Something he had no name for. Something that felt too much like regret.

CHAPTER 36

Myrithia

Gods, what a delicious pie. Myrithia finished her slice of Umberkern pie with such ferocity that she startled herself. Zakar chuckled, now seated beside her at the long wooden table, his posture lazy, smug, fully at ease. Across from them, Julian's family sat comfortably, the infant now nestled in his mother's arms, quietly nursing beneath a soft blanket.

Zakar glanced at Myrithia's empty plate, the corner of his mouth twitching with amusement. "You want another slice, darling?" he asked, reaching for her plate.

She gave an enthusiastic nod, catching herself too late, her hand darting to cover her mouth in a feigned attempt at modesty.

Zakar's laugh was warm, rich, undeniably pleased. He stood, plucking the plate from the table with a smirk. "I'll be right back."

Myrithia watched him retreat, still flushed with the humiliation of her obvious hunger.

Why was he so good at this? Playing the adoring husband, teasing yet doting, indulging her without hesitation. She should have been used to it—his convincing ease, his effortless charm—but it still unnerved her.

Kala, Julian's daughter, leaned in with a conspiratorial grin. "He is so handsome."

Myrithia's stomach flipped.

"Wherever did you find him?"

She froze. They had never picked a backstory. And now, Zakar wasn't here to hear it. For a fleeting second, panic gripped her—but she smoothed her expression into something soft and demure, forcing a sheepish smile.

Best to keep things simple. Best to let him lie.

"Oh, I should really let my husband tell the story." She let out a light, practiced laugh. "He tells it so well."

Kala giggled, nodding, utterly charmed by the notion.

By the time Zakar returned with a fresh slice of pie, Kala was already bursting with anticipation.

"Your wife tells me you do a lovely job of telling the story of how you met." She clasped her hands together, practically vibrating with excitement. "Please, indulge us!"

Myrithia went rigid.

Zakar cut a side-eyed glance toward her, suspicion flickering briefly before he masked it expertly.

She quickly took a bite of pie, using it as an excuse to keep her mouth full and remain silent.

He didn't miss it. But, to his credit, he only smirked, then lowered himself back into his seat.

"It's really quite ordinary." His voice was smooth, relaxed—as if he had all the time in the world. "But sure. I'd be happy to tell it." He set the plate before her, then leaned casually back, his green eyes gleaming with something mischievous. "It started, as most great love stories do, with complete disaster."

Kala let out a delighted gasp, settling in, and Myrithia felt her pulse stutter.

Zakar continued, effortless, weaving the words with a natural rhythm. "We met in the rain," he said, his voice lowering just slightly, drawing them in. "The kind of storm that sends most people running for cover. But not my Myra."

Myra.

It had been years since she had heard him say it like *that*.

So easily.

So fondly.

"No, she stood in the middle of the street, ankle-deep in water, waving a broken shoe at a man who had just splashed her with his carriage."

The table erupted with laughter, even Julian chuckling into his drink.

Myrithia blinked, mouth parted in disbelief. He was lying. And he was so damn good at it.

"I was minding my business—" Zakar went on.

"Doubtful," Julian muttered, making his daughter giggle.

Zakar grinned.

"—when I saw her. A vision, soaking wet, absolutely furious, cursing like a sailor. And I thought…"

He paused, his gaze falling on Myrithia, his voice barely above a whisper, threaded with something achingly gentle. "I need to know this woman."

Her heart lurched. She had no idea how he was doing this, how he could craft something so beautiful, so convincingly romantic in mere moments. Her hands trembled slightly, forcing her to press them against her lap beneath the table.

"I offered her my cloak," he continued, tilting his head toward her. "She refused. Of course."

That earned another round of laughter.

Kala shook her head. "Oh, you poor man."

"I know." Zakar sighed dramatically, feigning long-suffering patience. "But I was persistent. I followed her home—"

"Oh, that's not charming," Julian's wife teased, shaking her head.

Zakar smirked. "Not like that. I walked with her. And eventually, she let me." He exhaled softly, gaze flicking to Myrithia as if he were seeing the moment all over again. "She told me she didn't believe in love."

The words hit something deep inside her. Something raw, something painful. Because there was truth in that. A truth that had once belonged to her. A truth she had shaped into a weapon to pierce his heart.

Zakar, seemingly oblivious to the tension twisting inside her, simply smiled. "So, naturally, I made it my life's mission to prove her wrong."

A breath of silence passed, soft and warm, before Kala sighed wistfully. "You did, though, didn't you?"

Myrithia's throat tightened.

The fantasy was so rich, so carefully spun, so devastatingly perfect that for a moment, she forgot.

Forgot that none of it was real.

Forgot that this was a story crafted for an audience, a beautiful lie wrapped in gilded words.

Her eyes burned.

Before she could stop herself, tears welled up, glistening just enough to be noticeable.

Zakar caught it first.

His gaze narrowed, his smirk fading slightly, replaced with something quieter.

Julian's wife gasped softly. "Oh, she's crying!"

Kala placed a hand over her chest, sighing. "That is the most romantic thing I've ever heard."

Myrithia snapped back to reality, horrified.

Gods, what is wrong with me?

She tore her gaze away, blinking rapidly, forcing out a breathy laugh.

"Forgive me," she said quickly, dabbing at her eyes, her voice trembling in humiliation. "I don't know what's come over me."

Kala squeezed her hand. "Don't be embarrassed. If my husband had told me something so sweet, I'd cry too."

Myrithia forced a laugh, her fingers tightening beneath the table.

She had let herself get lost in an illusion. And worse—she had wanted to believe it.

Zakar, still watching her, said nothing. Because he knew. He knew she had fallen for it, even if just for a moment.

She braced herself before glancing his way again, expecting to find his face smug with satisfaction, but instead, she caught something unexpected.

A flicker of tenderness. Almost... concern? Perhaps that, too, was a lie. But for tonight—for this one, fleeting evening—she could allow herself to pretend it was all true.

Zakar's gaze drifted past her, scanning the main dancing area, listening as the music shifted into something softer, slower. Then, without hesitation, he looked back at her and stood, extending a hand toward her. "Would you like to dance, my love?"

Myrithia's heart thudded, traitorous and eager.

She should have been used to his sweet endearments by now, should have known they were nothing but an act, but they still struck her like arrows.

She nodded, graciously rising to take his hand.

"Please excuse us," Zakar said smoothly to the table.

Julian and his family smiled, nodding, waving them off with cheerful encouragement.

Soon, he was guiding her toward the main square, moving through the crowd with practiced ease, his grip on her gentle yet unrelenting. And then, as if it were the most natural thing in the world, she was drawn into his arms.

The moment their bodies met, he took the lead—fluid, instinctive, like he had been waiting for this all evening.

One of his hands pressed firmly to the small of her back, the other tangling with hers, guiding her through the movements as if she belonged there.

"You're really quite convincing," he mused, voice smooth, calculated. His fingers flexed against her spine, his palm hot through the fabric of her dress. "But I suppose you've always been convincing."

Myrithia's chest ached, the words cutting through the delicate illusion she had so foolishly let herself indulge in. Of course. This was still a game to him. The smiles, the whispers, the gentle touches—All of it was fabricated. A mirror of the lies she had once spun for him. She should have expected it, maybe even been immune to it by now.

And yet, the sting of it spread through her ribs like slow poison. Because she knew the truth. She had played her role convincingly not because she was a master manipulator. Not because she had been skilled in deceit, but because she had loved him. Long before he had loved her. Long before he had even known what she truly was.

It had all started as a lie—that much was undeniable. But the moment he had touched her, kissed her, whispered soft confessions into her skin, it had ceased being an act. She had adored him. She had wanted him. She had been his long before he had ever been hers.

"Are you quite comfortable?" His voice rumbled through his chest, warm, steady, threading through her bones like an enchantment.

It wasn't until he spoke that she realized she had rested her head against him, her cheek pressed to the broad plane of his chest. As if it were natural. As if it were safe.

Heat flooded her face, burning down her neck as she snapped her gaze upward, only to find his eyes already watching her.

"Just playing along," she said, feigning innocence. "They can still see us."

His smile softened. "Yes, indeed they can."

She wondered if he knew she had forgotten, and felt the moment she sank into him just as much as she had. She tried to rein in her breath, tried to silence the pounding in her chest, but the moment had already unraveled her.

She needed distance. She needed to break the illusion before it broke her. "How long will we be playing along, anyway?" she asked, forcing lightness into her tone, praying he wouldn't hear the desperation beneath it.

Say forever.

Gods, say forever.

"Another hour should suffice," he mused, unconcerned, unbothered. "You are pregnant, after all, and you'll need your rest."

Myrithia exhaled a soft laugh, shaking her head. She couldn't help it. It was ridiculous. The idea of being pregnant with his child. A fantasy so impossible, so utterly unrealistic, that it almost felt cruel to even joke about it.

And yet, hearing him say it so offhandedly, as if it were some inevitable truth, was oddly amusing. And for some stupid, reckless part of her, maybe even a little cruelly tempting.

The music began to slow, signaling the end of the song. She pulled back, breathing easier now, ready to retreat, to create some distance, to ground herself back in reality.

But Zakar didn't let go.

His grip stayed firm, and when she looked up, something in his face cracked—just faintly, just for a heartbeat. A softness in his eyes. A hesitation at the edge of his smirk. It was there and gone, but she caught it. Not teasing. Not hunger. Could it be longing? Or was this an act, too?

Her chest ached with it, a need so sharp she could barely breathe. The warmth of his hands on her waist, the press of his body against hers, the easy rhythm they'd found as they danced like any ordinary couple—like husband and wife—was unbearable. Because she didn't want it to be a lie. She wanted to stay here, in this small illusion spun between lantern light and laughter, where his voice was warm and his eyes didn't spite her and the story he told of how they met was sweet and untainted and theirs.

This wasn't real. It never had been. But her body had memorized the weight of him, the scent of his skin, the impossible thought of belonging to him. And the truth—sharp and bitter and undeniable—was that she did belong to him, just not in the way she wanted.

Her fingers curled slightly into the fabric of his coat before she realized what she was doing. She forced herself to look away, to blink hard and breathe deep, willing her heart to be quiet. But it was no use. Her traitorous mind had already remembered what it was like to lean her head against his chest late in the evenings. To fall asleep beside him. To wake to the sound of his voice.

She wanted it back. She wanted something *real*.

And then he spoke—his voice low and far too gentle. His lips tilted upward as he murmured, "One more dance."

CHAPTER 37

Zakar

It had been years since his last dance. But this—this moment, this music, this woman in his arms—only reminded him of the dance that had been denied to him.

That night. The night everything slipped away. That evening, he had been prepared to announce their engagement.

The Duchess of Evergrove, his betrothed by arrangement, would have hardly cared—she was too self-absorbed, too wrapped up in her own affairs to concern herself with the idea that her intended loved another.

But perhaps she would have been embarrassed.

Ashamed that he had planned to shock the nobles, to upend the expectations of the court by declaring his intentions to marry his mistress.

His father would have been furious. He had never approved of Myrithia. He had allowed his son to indulge in her, tolerated her presence without enthusiasm, but *never* would he have blessed that union.

And Zakar hadn't cared. He had been in love with her. Truly, completely, devastatingly in love. He had believed every beautiful lie she had spoken. Had trusted every tender caress. He had been ready to make the entire world know just how much she meant to him. Just how much he wanted her as his queen. They were supposed to share their first dance that night.

A real one. Not one hidden behind closed doors, not stolen in secret corridors, but one that was theirs.

Instead, before he could even step into that ballroom, she had caught him in the corridor and pleaded with him to follow her.

And he had obeyed. Because he always had. Because if she had asked, he would have given her the world. And if he hadn't... If he had ignored her, brushed past her, walked through those doors—

He would have died there.

The music of the festival shook him from his thoughts, pulling him back to the present. To the tawny brown hair on Myrithia's head, the color still unfamiliar even as it blended into the crowd.

They were in hiding. They were being discreet. Or, at least, as discreet as they could be at a public event. He pulled her closer, holding her as he might have that night—the night they never had. She was so soft against him, her body small, warm, her breath gentle as she rested against his chest once more.

And he let her. He didn't mind it. He didn't care if it was real or not. But he could feel the sincerity in her body and in her blood. Could he have been wrong? Could she have loved him all this time?

The thought threatened to undo him. He rejected it instantly. His jaw tightened. His eyes shut. He forced himself to remember.

She was still his enemy.

Even as he bent her to his will, even as she moved so naturally in his arms, even as the past blurred with the present in a way that made his chest ache, he knew. She was not to be trusted. She would betray him at her first opportunity. She would run at the first glimmer of escape. She would hurt him again. The thought infuriated him.

His grip tightened. His hold hardened, pressing her firmly against him, a silent reminder, a warning, a promise.

Her breath faltered. He felt it. Felt the shallow hitch of her inhale, the way her fingertips pressed just a little more firmly against his chest.

She tilted her head up, her eyes bright, perplexed, searching his face as if she could read his thoughts. As if she had any idea what she was to him now. As if she had any idea that she would never slip away again.

"Are you alright?" Her voice was gentle, uncertain, barely above the sound of the music, yet it reached him too easily, sinking its way under his skin, into his bones.

Zakar let a cold smile form, each inch of it sharpened with intent.

Alright?

He was exactly where he wanted to be.

Because she was *his*.

And it didn't matter in what capacity—his queen, his wife, his slave.

She belonged to him. She was bound to him. And he would never let her know another reality.

The thought sent a pulse of hunger through him, coiling deep in his gut, heating his blood, making every slow sway of their dance something unbearable.

He wanted to whisk her away.

To mutter some feeble excuse to Julian, to escort her back to the inn with the polite civility of a devoted husband, only to lock the door the moment they were alone. To pin her between himself and the soft silken sheets of their bed.

To hoist her skirts above her hips, to hear the soft, breathy sighs that would slip from her lips as he rolled his body into hers, taking what had always been his. Because he knew she had never belonged to anyone else. He knew that no other man had ever touched her, had ever laid claim to her body. She was inexperienced, untouched, completely unknowing of what she had denied him.

It was infuriating.

Infuriating that such a naive woman—one who had never known a man's touch—had seduced him and brought him to ruin. She had played the part of his lover, stolen his trust, manipulated his desires, and yet had never once been with him.

Not truly.

He had once cherished her innocence. Had once considered it carefully, tenderly, thinking of the moment he would claim her, how he might coax her into lovemaking after she became his betrothed.

But now?

Now, he didn't want to be careful. Didn't want to be slow, sweet, patient. His desire burned hotter, rawer, crueler. He wanted her. He wanted to consume her, ruin her, make her tremble beneath him.

He could feel her desire too. He could feel it in the way she melted against him, in the way her breath caught when he touched her, in the way her lips parted whenever their gazes held too long. She wanted him.

And when he took her—as he always intended to—he wouldn't be gentle. He wouldn't coax, or ask, or ease her into it. No, he would take. He would drive into her, deep and relentless, until she understood. Until she felt it in every fiber of her body.

Until she knew she was his. Until she never even thought to run again. Until the idea of life apart from him became unfathomable. Until she knew—with every gasp, every moan, every arch of her body—that no one else could ever touch her the way he would. That no one else could ever bring her to such madness. That no one else would *ever* have her.

She was so close, so soft, so easy to claim.

And yet—

A sudden explosion in the sky shattered his thoughts, a crackling boom that sent gold and crimson light cascading through the darkness. For a split second, his instincts sharpened, his body tensing, prepared for an attack. But then another burst of color followed, and another, painting the festival in brilliant, shimmering light.

Myrithia gasped softly, her head tilting back, her eyes wide with wonder. "Oh," She turned toward him, smiling, a rare, unrestrained joy lighting up her face. "Kala mentioned there would be fireworks soon."

Zakar should have returned his gaze to the sky. He should have admired the brilliance of the display, the artistry of the colors. But he didn't. Because his attention was caught elsewhere. The golden light danced across her skin, catching in the strands of her hair, reflecting in the depths of her blue eyes.

She was genuinely entranced, a rare moment of unguarded wonder.

THE ARCANE BARGAIN

It was...

Nice.

The thought struck him unexpectedly, irritatingly. And yet, for a moment—just a moment—he allowed himself to simply look at her.

She must have felt his gaze.

Because when she turned back to him, her smile faltered, just slightly. Her lips parted like she wanted to speak, but hesitated.

Zakar said nothing. Didn't smirk. Didn't mock. He only watched her.

For a fraction of a second, something unspoken passed between them, something too quiet, too fleeting to name.

And then the shifting crowd broke them apart. Festival-goers brushed past them, voices murmuring, laughter bubbling up between the bursts of fireworks.

"We should get a better view," someone called. "Come on, there are seats near the fountain!"

A gentle bump to Myrithia's shoulder made her blink, breaking whatever had just settled between them. She glanced at the moving crowd, then back at him, her expression still softened beneath the flickering glow of the fireworks. "Would you like to get a better view, too?"

Zakar inhaled slowly, tearing his eyes from her, willing away the faint, nagging warmth in his chest.

He smirked, tilting his head slightly. "Lead the way, little wife."

CHAPTER 38

Myrithia

Myrithia's fingers tightened around Zakar's hand, her heart racing as she led him through the festival, weaving past flickering lanterns and lively bursts of color.

She needed a distraction. The warmth of his touch, the way he had held her so close, looked at her so intently—it lingered too much, made her feel too much. Had the fireworks not interrupted them, had the crowd not broken the moment—She might have kissed him.

Gods. She needed to calm down. Yes, she could indulge in the fantasy of the night, in the illusion of what they were pretending to be. But there were limits.

She slowed as the path bottlenecked, coming to an abrupt stop against the wall of people crowding forward, vying for a better view. Bodies pressed in from all sides, blocking them completely.

Sighing, she turned back toward Zakar and murmured, "I guess this will have to do."

Zakar clicked his tongue, disapproving. "No, I think not."

Before she could ask what he meant, he tugged her along, his pace swift, his hand firm against hers as he led her down an empty alleyway.

Then, without warning, she felt the pull of his magic. A sharp pulse of emerald light, a rush of movement that wasn't movement at all, and suddenly they were twenty feet higher. Myrithia gasped, blinking as she regained her footing. They were atop the roof of the very building they had just been standing beneath.

She laughed, startled and delighted. The entire sky stretched before them, unobstructed, a sweeping canvas of fire and starlight. She smiled brightly, breathless at the view, before she quickly ducked behind the chimney, ensuring that no wandering eyes from below would catch sight of them.

Zakar smirked at her reaction, then sat down casually beside her, his long legs stretching out against the sloped tiles. "Now, this will do."

For a while, they sat in silence, watching the sky together. It was strangely comfortable, she couldn't help but think. The festival buzzed with life below, but up here, it was just them, wrapped in the glow of the fireworks, the distant echoes of laughter and music a soft hum in the background.

Then, after a long moment, her voice broke the stillness.

"I liked your story," she said softly. "The one you told Kala and the others."

Zakar turned his head, brow lifting as he studied her. "Is that so? It didn't seem like you cared for it."

She knew what he meant. He was referring to her reaction, to the way her eyes had welled with tears she had tried—and failed—to suppress.

Still, she nodded. "It was so romantic. I wish it had been true."

A quiet chuckle left him, but there was no real humor in it. The irony was thick between them. She had woven a love story for him once, spun a beautiful lie between them, only to tear it apart with the truth.

"I wish it had been true, too." His voice was smooth, easy, but she was grateful—grateful he had spared her his usual biting remarks, grateful he didn't use this moment to twist the knife. "Perhaps it would have been better if we had met under different circumstances."

She swallowed, watching the way the golden glow of the fireworks illuminated his sharp, beautiful face. "Oh?" she asked, tilting her head. "You would have liked that? You, a common man? Me, a common woman? Meeting as strangers on a rainy day?"

He gave a slow nod. "We would have had a small ceremony," he mused. "Perhaps you would've carried white lilies in your wedding bouquet, tied off with a red ribbon." A sly smile tugged at his lips as he glanced at her. "I know you would've worn white, but I so prefer you in red."

Something in the way he was looking at her shattered her.

It wasn't his usual cruel amusement. It wasn't taunting. It wasn't sharp or laced with mockery.

It was something else.

Something that made her heart lurch painfully in her chest.

For a moment, beneath the crackling fireworks, he looked at her the way a husband looked at his wife. There was almost something worshipful in the way his eyes traced over her, a silent adoration in his expression that sent her stomach twisting into knots.

The air felt different.

Lighter.

Brighter.

Like the illusion of the festival had fully wrapped around them, ensnaring them in something fragile and golden, something so unbearably beautiful that she couldn't bear to breathe too deeply lest it shatter.

She forced a quiet laugh, though it came out unsteady. "Tell me more of what our wedding would have been like. Our marriage."

Zakar exhaled, tilting his gaze back to the sky as if considering it. "I think we would've had a little party afterward, if we could've afforded such a thing. Let everyone dance." His lips curved slightly. "And our marriage... I imagine it would have been nice. Not perfect, of course. You would have driven me mad, no doubt."

She let out a soft huff, shaking her head. "Oh, certainly."

He hummed. "But I can see us with a few small children running around."

Her breath caught.

The words should have meant nothing.

But they did.

She could see it. The image formed so easily in her mind that it physically ached—a small girl with green eyes staring up at her, clutching a flower in her tiny hands, beaming with laughter.

A life that would never be.

The fireworks above them exploded in dazzling bursts of color, but she didn't see them. She was already lost in the cruel dream her mind had conjured for her. She could hear the children's laughter, feel the warmth of Zakar's arms wrapped around her in the quiet of a winter night, see the glow of candlelight on the walls of a home that had never existed.

Her chest twisted, tightening, burning.

"Myra?"

Zakar's voice pulled her back, and only then did she realize she was crying.

She hastily wiped her cheek, her breath trembling as she blinked rapidly, trying to force herself back into reality. But Zakar was watching her now, his brow furrowed, his expression indiscernible.

She wanted to tell him.

She wanted to tell him that she had loved him all these years. That she had never stopped. That every smile, every laugh, every stolen touch—none of it had been an act. That being with him had been as natural as breathing. That it still was.

But what would it matter now?

She sighed, her breath vanishing into the cool night air. There was no point in convincing him. She had lost the right to prove herself a long time ago.

And even if she could, it was already too late.

A quiet breeze curled through the night, chilling her. Without thinking, she raised her hands to rub her arms—a futile, self-comforting gesture rather than a response to the cold.

She wasn't ready for the illusion to end. Not yet.

She wasn't ready to slip back into reality, to feel the steel of her captivity pressing against her ribs again, to remember that none of this was real.

She closed her eyes for a moment, trying to will it all away.

And then something warm and heavy settled over her shoulders. Myrithia's eyes fluttered open, her breath catching. Zakar had draped his coat around her, saying nothing.

She turned to him, slowly, hesitantly. He wasn't looking at her at first, staring out at the firework-lit sky, his expression carefully composed, his jaw set, his shoulders tense.

Then, as if feeling her gaze, he lowered his eyes to her.

And for a moment—just a single, fragile moment—there was nothing between them but the quiet, and the beautiful way the golden light flickered across his face. The space between them felt smaller than it should. Her fingers tightened on the edges of his coat, its scent wrapping around her, warm, familiar, achingly intimate.

Neither of them spoke. Neither of them moved. And then—

Shouting.

Distant at first, then closer. She jerked her head downward, toward the festival square below. People were shoving past one another, murmuring, gasping, being corralled by dozens of knights bearing the sigil of Valthoria.

Draevok's knights.

Torches flared, illuminating a sudden shift in the energy of the festival. A hollow ache opened in her gut.

A man's voice boomed across the square. "By order of the King, no one leaves this festival until all have been accounted for."

Zakar swore under his breath.

Myrithia felt the tension coil between them, sharp and immediate.

The illusion was over.

Reality had found them once again.

CHAPTER 39

Zakar

Draevok's knights had planned this well. They had likely tracked the Hollow Mist, deduced where it would force them, and anticipated their arrival in Hawthorne Reach. A clean, calculated ambush. Zakar's gaze flicked to the city gates, jaw tightening at the sight of armored sentries stationed at every exit.

No way out. The city was locked down, cordoned off like a cage.

A smart move. A necessary move. If he had been in Draevok's position, he would've done the same.

His gaze returned to the square, sweeping over the soldiers barking orders, the way the crowd tensed and parted beneath their advance. Draevok's army was no ordinary force—every captain was a skilled mage, trained to hunt and subdue. By his estimation, there were at least four or five among them. His Sentinels could dispatch the foot soldiers and a mage or two, but he would still have something of a challenge on his hands with the remaining captains.

An illusion spell, cast wide enough, could serve just as well. But he wasn't operating at full capacity. His magic was still tethered to Myrithia, sustaining her, and he couldn't risk sending out his wraiths and weaving illusions without severely weakening himself. And if he faltered, she would too.

That was a risk he wasn't willing to take.

A direct confrontation wasn't the answer. But they were running out of time. His fingers instinctively found his pocket, seeking something small—something he'd nearly forgotten about. Cool glass met his touch. Relief flickered through him as he pulled it free. Between his fingers, a small, enchanted marble glowed faintly in the dim light. Inside, magic swirled like captured stardust—threads of blue and gold twisting in a slow, hypnotic dance.

Myrithia's eyes snapped to it immediately. She was still clutching his coat around her shoulders, her breath hushed and uncertain. "What are we going to do?" she asked, her voice edged with quiet urgency.

Zakar didn't answer. He had only one of these. He had planned to use it later, when the need was greater—when they were truly out of options. But this was as good a time as any. If he was going to waste it, he might as well waste it now. Otherwise they could very well end up dead or in chains by the end of the night. His thumb brushed over the marble's surface, murmuring a low incantation.

Myrithia barely had a second to react before he caught her wrist, pulling her against him.

Then—

A blinding rush of color.

Magic unfurled like a shockwave, swallowing them whole, ripping them from the rooftop. Wind howled in their ears, the world around them folding in on itself, space bending and stretching—then, silence.

Cool grass met their feet. The city's distant glow flickered behind them. They were outside the walls now, a mile into the forest, wrapped in the hush of midnight.

The only sound was Myrithia's sharp inhale. Zakar released her, watching as she swayed slightly, disoriented, her fingers clutching at the remnants of vanishing magic in the air.

She exhaled, slowly. Then, she looked at him, speechless.

"You're welcome," he said, giving a slight flourish as he swept into a mocking bow.

Myrithia didn't react. She only blinked, her gaze shifting past him, turning toward the distant glow of Hawthorne Reach—now a mere flicker against the horizon.

She spun back toward him, eyes wide, breath unsteady. "How—?!" she gasped, her voice catching. "How far away did you take us?!"

He shrugged, adjusting the cuffs of his gloves as if it were hardly worth noting. "A few miles at best. Certainly gives us a bit of a head start." His gaze flicked to the treeline, sharp and assessing. "Speaking of—" he turned smoothly, beckoning her to follow. "We need to start moving. We have a long night ahead of us. Eventually, they'll realize we're no longer in Hawthorne Reach, and then they'll start to expand their search."

She hesitated a second longer, still thrown by their sudden relocation, but fell into step beside him.

It grated him, having abandoned everything—the horses, the supplies, the comforts of an inn. A frustrating loss, but not a devastating one.

He still had the Nythera. Small mercies.

Still, the journey ahead would be unpleasant. What should have been a manageable trek would now be agonizingly slow on foot.

Damn it.

He'd be back for those horses eventually. Just not for days.

Myrithia's hand suddenly clasped around his forearm, pulling him to a stop. "If we need to move quickly," she said, her voice steady, "then lend me a little more of your power and I'll make up the distance."

He stared at her, remembering. She had a rare gift. One he had dismissed due to her weakness, but one that could be beneficial if fueled properly. The offer was logical, but he hesitated.

His fingers twitched.

He hadn't forgotten how much she craved freedom. How every breath she took was edged with rebellion.

Could he trust her with his power?

He was silent for too long.

Her gaze sharpened, as if reading his hesitation. "Zakar," she pressed, more insistent now. "Please."

A faint smile began to shape his lips, too controlled to be anything but calculated. "Very well, Myra." He plucked her hand from his sleeve, interlacing their fingers, locking their palms together. He let his gaze hold hers, unwavering.

Then, with a deep inhale, he unleashed the flood of magic into her veins. Her breath caught, her fingers trembling against his own as the magic rushed into her like a storm.

Then—a flicker of something.

Panic. A tremor of fear. Regret. Determination. And something else—something sharper.

Opportunity.

His expression darkened. His grip tightened. In a single, forceful motion, he yanked her forward, crushing her against him.

One hand curled around the back of her neck, fingers digging into the fine hairs at her nape. He felt the tremor of her pulse, the way her body stiffened, caught off guard.

His lips brushed the curve of her ear. "Planning to steal it and run?"

She froze. A single, sharp intake of breath. Her shock rippled through him as if it were his own breath caught in his throat.

His touch firmed against her skin, his voice sinking into a lethal whisper. "Would you really run and hide?" His tone was bitter, laced with scornful disappointment. "Knowing full well you're only running into your own grave?"

She was pressed against him, trembling. He could feel everything. Her pulse fluttering, a rapid staccato against his chest. Her breath catching in panic, her body yielding just enough to show that she knew she had no escape.

"No," she whispered, shaken. "I wouldn't. It was a fleeting, stupid thought."

He said nothing.

She swallowed thickly. "Please, let me help us," she pleaded, her voice a soft, desperate whimper. "I can get us far from here. Just tell me which direction to run."

He laughed. Cold. Amused. Bitter. "It's good to know that death is somehow preferable to me."

Her breath shuddered. "You don't understand," she argued, her body growing fainter in his arms.

He did. He did understand. She was terrified of him. And that should have pleased him. It didn't. It only deepened the ache in his chest, the ugly twist of frustration and something far too close to resentment.

His jaw clenched. They didn't have time for a battle of wills. Her knees buckled. She was too weak to withstand this standoff much longer. And, damn it, he needed her abilities.

He exhaled sharply. "Fine," he muttered. Then, with a final surge of magic, he pushed more power into her.

Her eyes illuminated, deep blue flashing in the dim light.

Then, without hesitation, she tightened her grip on him and they vanished into a blur of silver and shadow. Each burst of magic carried them fifty feet in an instant, the world vanishing and reforming with every flickering step.

North. Again. And again. And again.

Until—

She collapsed.

He caught her before she hit the ground, her limp form slumping against his chest. Her breath was shallow. She had overdone it.

His arms tightened, lifting her into his hold, her head falling against his shoulder. The world around them was silent. No distant glow of Hawthorne Reach, no echo of knights in pursuit. Only shadows and trees. They were safe. For now.

But she was too fragile. Too drained. He had one obsidian token left. A final emergency reserve. He didn't want to use it so soon. But he had no choice.

Zakar glanced down at Myrithia's pale face, her breath shallow, her body weak. Then, with a sigh, he reached for the token. They needed shelter.

And he'd make damn sure she survived the night.

CHAPTER 40
Myrithia

Myrithia inhaled slowly, the steady rise and fall of her breath grounding her as awareness stirred. The air smelled of incense and charred cedar. Familiar. She opened her eyes, her vision blurring before sharpening into focus.

The towering bookshelves, the gleam of obsidian furniture, the soft flickering glow of enchanted lanterns.

The Arcane Citadel. Or rather, another replica of his suite. Zakar must have used one of his tokens. She sat up, slowly, feeling no pain, no fatigue—only the lingering disorientation of travel.

A flicker of movement caught her eye.

Zakar.

He strode toward her from across the chamber, his expression inscrutable, his gaze sharp as ever. "How are you feeling?" he asked, voice low, smooth, carrying none of the resentment she knew had to be there.

She turned toward him, instinctively searching his face for any trace of the bitterness she had felt through their connection before she collapsed.

Nothing. His face was unreadable. Composed. Like a wall she couldn't scale.

"I feel excellent, actually," she admitted, her voice barely above a whisper. The words felt strange on her tongue, knowing how close she had been to collapse, knowing how much of his power had surged into her veins.

Then, it all came back in fragments. The festival, the dancing, the fireworks, the frantic escape, until finally she recalled it. The ugly, fleeting treachery of her own thoughts. Her breath caught. She could still feel the echo of it. That desperate, wretched desire.

Run.

It had slammed into her like a tidal wave of guilt, so brief yet so damning. She hadn't meant it. She wouldn't have acted on it.

But he had felt it. Through the thread of magic linking them, Zakar had felt her longing to use him, to break free, to take his gift, his power—and vanish. Even if it meant dying alone.

Her hands fisted into the sheets. He had felt it all. The self-loathing, the grief, the unbearable truth she couldn't even admit to herself. Zakar didn't love her. He never would, and she was a fool for ever having hoped otherwise. She swallowed hard, forcing herself to lift her gaze to his. But he wasn't looking at her. His expression remained impassive. Cold. But she knew the truth.

She had felt his pain, his resentment, and his bitter, aching grief. It had pierced through him like knives, just as it had five years ago. And now? Now, he would never trust her. Not even an inch.

"You need to eat," Zakar's voice broke the silence, smooth, detached. He gestured toward the end of the room, where a feast of rich meats, fruits, and breads awaited. "Gather your strength."

Myrithia exhaled slowly, forcing her legs over the edge of the bed, her fingers gripping the sheets just a little too tightly.

She didn't deserve the food, much less his help. She didn't want to feel this crushing weight in her chest, knowing she had wounded him yet again. But she would do as he said. She would eat. She would gather her strength. And she would live with the knowledge that she had damned herself in his eyes all over again.

Myrithia approached the table, settling into the chair with a quiet breath, willing herself to think of anything else—anything but the wretched ache of guilt festering inside her. She forced her hands to move, selecting food, tearing off pieces of warm bread, scooping soft slices of fruit onto her plate. Eat. Swallow. Pretend.

It was a bitter thing, pretending to be normal in a world where she had ruined every good thing she had ever been given.

"You can take a bath, too, if you'd like," Zakar said, his voice smooth but distant.

She glanced toward him, watching as he adjusted the folds of his black tunic near the armoire. His movements were measured, practiced, as though this moment—this entire night—had not shaken him in the slightest.

"I have clean clothes for you to wear," he added.

Myrithia's fingers stilled against her fork. She would need to change, of course. By now, the knights would know their disguises—the brown-haired wife and her blonde-haired husband.

Zakar had dropped his glamour at the soonest opportunity, his raven-black hair restored the moment they were free from the city. But her disguise had not been so easily shed. She would need to bathe the dye from her hair, return to her silver-haired self, back into the face of a traitor.

Her chest tightened. She had been a pregnant wife, at a simple festival in a simple town. It had all been such a beautiful lie. She had felt safe in the lie. And then Draevok ruined it.

No—*she* ruined it.

Fate had an ugly way of reminding her that she was the reason she would never be happy.

"I had a resupply of various needs in here, but this is our last token," Zakar continued, drawing her back. "When we stop again, we will have to camp out under the stars. We are close to the tome, though. Another day or two, on foot."

She nodded, relieved that last night's magic had at least served its purpose. They were close. The book was close. But traveling on foot wasn't ideal. They did need horses, especially because they were being hunted.

"It would waste time for us to trek and find horses," Zakar mused as if reading her thoughts. "So, we will simply have to walk."

Myrithia considered him for a moment. Was his magic restored? She felt fine. More than fine. He was still sustaining her—enough to keep her steady, enough to keep her whole. But how was he faring?

"How are you feeling?" The words left her before she could stop them.

Zakar turned to her fully, sliding his black coat over his shoulders with a slow, practiced ease. Something about the way he stood there, back straight, hands clasped behind him, exuding confidence so absolute it nearly silenced the question itself.

His smile was cold. "How am I feeling?" he echoed.

Myrithia regretted asking.

He moved toward her, each step steady, like a man who knew she had nowhere left to run. "I am well, Myra," he said smoothly, stopping just before her. Too close. Close enough that she could see the cruel glint of satisfaction behind his green eyes.

"I am focused," he continued, voice low, "strong."

Another step.

"Ready to fulfill my end of the bargain."

The bargain.

The unbreakable contract binding her to him, sealing her fate in endless servitude. There would be no way out. No mercy. No forgiveness. Air caught, sharp and sudden, as his fingers found her chin, his touch deceptively gentle, a mockery of tenderness.

"So, please," he murmured, his voice a soft, dangerous thing, "I'm impatient—so eager to have you restored, dear slave, so that you will have all the strength you need to fulfill my every want."

Myrithia swallowed, throat dry.

The mask was flawless. There was no pain in his gaze. No lingering ghosts of what they had once been. Only control. Only the mocking weight of his ownership pressing down on her like iron chains.

She held his gaze, though she didn't want to. Not like this. Not when the words threatened to tear from her lips before she could stop them.

"I'm sorry for last night."

Zakar faltered, the moment catching him off guard. A flicker of something—something raw, something dark, something unspoken—flashed in his eyes. And then, just as quickly, it was gone. He released her, turning away, his expression carefully neutral.

"Please do make haste," he said briskly, his voice lighter now, as though her words had never even reached him. "We need to stay ahead of Draevok's men. Perhaps," he mused, already walking away, "if they catch up to us, we can acquire a couple of their horses."

***

The forest terrain was unforgiving beneath her boots, a constant tangle of roots and loose stones that seemed determined to trip her at every step. The uneven ground sloped in places, forcing her to brace herself against the incline, while other stretches dipped into soft, moss-laden patches that gave slightly beneath her weight. It should have been beautiful—the sunlight filtering through the thick canopy overhead, the rich scent of earth and pine mingling in the cool air—but all she could focus on was the ache in her legs, the dull throb in her feet, and the way each step sent fresh pinpricks of pain up through her heels.

She should have walked more.

She should have spent less time confined to her cottage, pacing the same rooms over and over, and more time wandering the land that surrounded it. She had explored, yes—gone into town for necessities, stretched her legs when the solitude of the Hollow Mist grew too heavy—but it had never been enough to prepare her for this.

And what made the journey all the more agonizing was knowing it could have been different. She could have crossed vast distances with him in mere moments, moving leagues ahead with the power he had once willingly given her. They could have reached the tome a full day sooner, spared themselves the slow, grueling march through the wilderness.

But no.

Because she had entertained the thought—just for a moment—of taking his magic and escaping, and now he wouldn't trust her with it. So they walked. Step by step, mile by mile, bound to this slow, pitiful pace... all because she had proven herself unworthy of his faith.

Judging by the position of the sun—now hanging high overhead, beating down in golden slants through the trees—it was well past midday. Four hours, at least, of uninterrupted walking. The hunger nagging in her belly confirmed it. She wasn't sure how much longer she could keep going without collapsing into the dirt. She was grateful he had given her something practical to wear. A pair of black pants and a reasonably fitting cream colored tunic. It was simple, and easy enough to walk in, but yet she struggled.

She forced herself to look up, to focus on the man a few paces ahead of her. Zakar moved with effortless ease, his stride unbothered by the uneven path, his cloak barely shifting with his steps. His posture was relaxed, but she knew better—every motion was calculated, aware. Always aware. Even now, he was scanning the terrain, listening to the sounds of the forest, ensuring they weren't being followed.

If she slowed, he slowed. But he never turned back to look at her.

He had barely spoken to her since they left the Arcane suite that morning. Their only exchanges had been brief, to the point. Nothing more, nothing less. And that, more than anything, made the trek stretch on endlessly. It was bad enough that her feet felt like they were on fire, that every step sent a dull pulse of pain through her arches—but the silence, the absence of *anything* to distract her from the discomfort, was unbearable.

Finally, after what felt like another eternity, his voice cut through the quiet.

"Do you need to rest?"

Her pride bristled, but she knew the answer was yes.

She needed food. She needed to rub the pressure from her feet before her blisters worsened. She needed a moment of stillness before her body forced one upon her.

But she *hated* this. She hated feeling *weak*. She hated that she was slowing them down.

She had once been strong—once wielded enough power to make even the most ruthless men wary of her. Now, she was barely a shadow of what she had been. A worn, fragile thing with nothing left but her own stubbornness.

She swallowed hard, forcing steel into her spine. "I can make it another mile, I think," she said, lifting her chin. "Do you have any water?"

Zakar didn't hesitate. With a simple flick of his fingers, a canteen materialized in his hands—a sleek black vessel, emblazoned with the sigil of the Arcane Citadel.

She took it without a word, bringing it to her lips and drinking deeply. Cool, crisp water filled her mouth, soothing the dry ache in her throat. She exhaled softly as she wiped her lips, letting the canteen lower against her chest.

And then, without another glance at him, she stepped forward. Past him.

She wasn't going to be the reason they were delayed. She would keep moving. She would ignore the sting in her feet, the gnawing ache in her stomach, the fatigue pressing into her bones.

Because they were so close.

And she *could not* be the one to slow them down.

CHAPTER 41

Zakar

Zakar watched the steady sway of her long silver braid, the subtle hitch in her stride betraying the pain she was undoubtedly feeling. Even though she tried to hide it, he could see the faint stiffness in her steps, the way she adjusted her weight ever so slightly to compensate for the blisters that must have formed on her feet.

She was being stubborn. He sighed, tilting his head to the sky as he walked. Perhaps he was being stubborn too.

Every time he had considered breaking the silence, only cruelty had threatened to leave his mouth. Bitter, humiliating cruelty that would serve no purpose other than to twist the knife he had already buried deep.

She had been desperate last night. Desperate to prove she could be trusted, even as the thought of escape had flickered through her mind like a dying flame.

But he *knew* it had been fleeting.

Just an impulse. A brief, fragile thing crushed beneath the weight of her own remorse.

Because even as he had begun to withdraw his magic from her, even as he had held her against him and accused her of wanting to run—she had pleaded with him. *Begged* him to believe her.

And the worst part? She had meant it. Because what choice did she really have? What had he *given* her, except another cage to rot in? He clenched his jaw, his gaze flicking briefly to her before cutting back to the path ahead. She had betrayed one master only to find herself under the weight of another.

Him.

And hadn't he made that *abundantly* clear? Hadn't he reminded her at *every opportunity* that she belonged to him? That her will was his to command?

All of it fueled by his own spite. He was cruel.

His father had once told him that cruelty was the easiest way to keep power. That fear and suffering bound far more effectively than love ever could. But, all he had observed was that her fear had only urged her to keep pulling away.

If their positions were reversed, if he were in *her* place—he would have left his so-called master behind without a second thought. He wouldn't have hesitated. Wouldn't have pleaded for trust. He would have run. Because he was merciless. More so than her. More so than anyone.

But the only way he could ever hope to keep her near him was this. This leash of magic. This contract. This slow, insidious breaking of her will. If he were kind to her—if he softened—he would have to let her go.

He would have to let go of his bitterness. Of his need to own her. But he knew himself too well. That would never happen. Because he wanted her.

Needed her.

And that truth unsettled him more than anything else. Maybe he was more like his father than he realized. His eyes darkened. Any resemblance to the Butcher of Valthoria was a blight—one he refused to acknowledge.

Perhaps it wasn't the fact that she wanted to run that truly unsettled him—but that it had come on the heels of such a perfect night.

Despite himself, despite his grudges and thirst for vengeance, he had let the fantasy consume him. For a fleeting moment, she had been his wife. They had spent an ordinary evening at a simple festival, and she had danced in his arms as if she belonged there.

The story of how they met in the rain, the wedding, the children—it had all been a lie. And yet, it had felt so real. So effortless. So deeply satisfying.

And he had fallen for her all over again.

Like a fool.

Had he learned nothing in these past five years? Did he even truly want her as a slave? The answer was painfully obvious now. He had never wanted that. He had been chasing a dream he could never have. And she had proven that, hadn't she? Even after a night like last night, she had still thought to run, still considered leaving him again. And he couldn't even blame her.

Zakar was shaken from his thoughts abruptly, noticing her the moment before it happened. Myrithia's foot caught against an exposed root, her balance faltering—just enough for him to react. He seized her waist, steadying her before she could fully stumble, his grip firm and unwavering.

"We should stop," he said.

She wrenched herself from his grasp, pulling away with unnecessary force. "We keep going."

His jaw ticked. Stubborn woman. "We can afford five minutes."

"We can't." Her tone was clipped, curt. "I'm fine. It was just a loose root. Let's keep going."

Zakar's gaze sharpened, studying the way her shoulders tightened, the way she pressed forward despite the clear limp in her step. She was lying to herself, and to him, and that grated at him.

He watched her for another moment, debating whether or not to just hoist her over his shoulder like a sack of flour.

"We should stop for food," he tried again, reaching for her arm.

She ripped it away from him, spinning on him with fire in her eyes. "I said I'm fine! Another mile."

She turned sharply, walking ahead, and something in him snapped.

"Then I will carry you for a mile," he said, voice flat, just before he caught her again—this time with no room for argument.

She yelped as he effortlessly lifted her from the ground and threw her over his shoulder, her weight nothing to him. Immediately, she squirmed, hands bracing against his back as she kicked her feet. "Put me down!"

"After we have walked another mile, dear," he said, his grip iron over her thighs. "Then I will set you down, and you *will* eat." A pause. Then, with an infuriating amount of ease, he added, "Continue to struggle against me, and I will spank you."

A strangled sound left her throat.

Zakar smirked.

She stilled instantly. Not out of fear—no, he could feel the heat of her mortified indignation. It simmered beneath her skin, filled the air around them. Delicious.

Her voice, when it came, was sharp with warning. "You wouldn't dare."

He hummed in amusement, drawing one large palm up her thigh before giving the curve of her backside the softest, most condescending tap. "I would love nothing more than to show you how serious I am."

"Put me down," she hissed, though she was much more careful now, not daring to fight against him further.

"I will put you down if you agree to eat," he countered smoothly.

She groaned, frustration evident. "Fine! I will eat!"

"Excellent," he said, voice maddeningly gentle as he lowered her down with ease. Her feet met the forest floor, but she refused to meet his eyes, her hands clenched at her sides. *Adorable.*

He took his time studying her. The color in her cheeks was deeply satisfying, the way she burned with embarrassment and ire. It was a welcome change from the look of *remorse* she had worn all morning.

This was better.

"Take off your boots," he ordered, reaching into the pouch at his belt. A small grain rested in his palm, and with a flicker of magic, it swelled into a fresh loaf of bread. He extended it to her.

Myrithia eyed the bread before flicking her gaze back to his. Suspicious. "Why do you want my boots off?"

"I want to see your feet," he said simply, reaching into another pocket and pulling out a small glass vial, no bigger than his palm. A thick, silvery liquid sloshed inside. "If you have blisters forming—and I *know* that you do—this will help."

She hesitated for a moment, her pride warring against

practicality. But, inevitably, she loosened the laces on her boots and slid them off.

Zakar knelt before her, his movements fluid and unhurried as he removed his gloves and lifted her foot into his hands. He marveled, briefly, at the delicate structure of it—small, soft, and utterly unfit for this kind of travel. His jaw tightened. In their five years apart, they had lived entirely different lives. His had been grueling, his days spent sharpening his magic and strength for the moment he would seize back what was his. Hers, on the other hand...

She had been hidden away in her cottage, weak and withering, underneath the Hollow Mist.

He exhaled, not looking up at her, perhaps to spare her the humiliation of how pitifully unprepared she was for this journey. Instead, he focused on the angry blisters marring her skin. Three on one foot alone.

The sound of bread tearing filled the quiet between them. He could hear her chewing slowly, trying not to make a sound. As if that would keep him from noticing her discomfort.

Without a word, he uncorked the small vial in his palm, smoothing a bit of the ointment onto his fingertips. Gently, he massaged the oil into her foot, feeling the blisters shrink and disappear beneath his touch. The blend was a masterful concoction of alchemy and magic, capable of sealing wounds and accelerating healing. He had only brought a few vials, meant for dire situations. But she needed to keep up with him. And no matter how amusing it would be to carry her through the woods like a petulant child, he had no intention of slowing their pace.

A soft, breathy moan escaped her lips.

Zakar paused.

His eyes snapped to hers just as her cheeks flushed crimson, her gaze darting away in mortified silence. She jerked her foot back, tucking it beneath her as if she could somehow erase what had just happened. "Thank you," she muttered stiffly, likely praying to Vyria, goddess of mercy, that he would let the moment pass without comment.

He smirked, amused, but said nothing.

Instead, he reached for her other foot.

She immediately yanked it away, extending her hand out to him instead. "Just give me the ointment. I'll do it myself."

Zakar ignored her, catching her ankle with ease and pulling her foot into his grasp. His touch was firmer this time, deliberate. When he met her eyes, he held them. "Eat."

Her chest rose with a deep inhale before she released an irritated breath, relenting with obvious frustration. Tearing off another piece of bread, she shoved it into her mouth, chewing with more force than necessary.

Good girl.

He hadn't meant for it to feel so soothing. But knowing that it did—that *he* did—sent a dark satisfaction curling in his chest. He wanted to pull more sounds from her. He wanted to find all the ways he could reduce her to breathy, helpless whimpers under his hands.

She kept her gaze averted, but he could see the subtle way her body eased. She was barely aware of it herself, her shoulders losing their tension, her fingers relaxing against the loaf of bread in her lap. By the time he released her, the blisters were gone, and comfort had melted into her limbs like a slow, creeping warmth.

Carefully, she pulled her foot back and slid it into her boot.

"Can we walk now?" she asked, standing quickly, eager to escape the moment of vulnerability she had unintentionally let slip. She held out the remaining half of the bread to him, her voice steadier than before. "I've eaten half. Surely you're hungry too."

Zakar smiled, slow and knowing. "We can carry on."

Accepting the bread from her, he turned and started ahead, leading the way once more.

CHAPTER 42

Myrithia

More hours passed, the rhythmic crunch of their footsteps filling the spaces between their conversation. It wasn't much—just idle chatter, fleeting remarks about the terrain, the occasional exchange of sarcasm—but it was better than the suffocating silence that had stretched between them earlier.

Myrithia welcomed the shift. It felt... normal. Almost.

But she wasn't foolish enough to think Zakar had let go of last night just yet—let alone the past five years. His voice was easy, his tone deceptively light, but beneath it all, the weight of their history still lingered.

The sky ahead had begun to darken, heavy clouds creeping across the expanse of gray. The air thickened with humidity, dense and charged, the scent of impending rain seeping into the forest.

Zakar glanced upward, his pace steady but thoughtful. "We should find shelter soon," he remarked, voice even. "It'll start coming down any minute."

She sighed. *He's right.*

She had walked in wet boots before, and the thought of trudging the rest of the day soaked through was miserable. Not to mention the weight of damp clothes, the chill that would settle into her bones as the temperature dropped.

They walked a little farther before Zakar slowed his stride, veering slightly off the path.

Myrithia followed, frowning as she took in their surroundings. The forest around them was shifting in elevation—just beyond their trail, the ground sloped upward, forming a natural rise about ten, maybe twenty feet above them. Thick tree roots curled over the edge, gripping the rock and earth like skeletal fingers, and beneath the overhang, the land dipped into a sheltered alcove of sorts. It wasn't quite a cave, but the way the ridge jutted out above them, dense with tree growth, it would provide enough cover to keep them mostly dry.

As if to confirm his foresight, the first few drops of rain began to fall.

Zakar glanced back at her, then toward the overhang. "This will do."

She exhaled, stepping under the shelter of the rock and tree cover just as the rain began to intensify, the steady patter growing louder against the leaves above.

It wasn't perfect, but it would keep them out of the worst of the storm. And for now, that was enough.

The rain had only just begun to fall when the ground before them darkened—not from the storm, but from something else entirely.

Myrithia took an instinctive step back as the earth rippled, an unnatural distortion spreading like ink in water. The shadows deepened, stretching impossibly, and then *they* rose.

Four figures emerged from the darkness, skeletal forms draped in tattered black cloaks that barely seemed to exist, shifting between solidity and mist. Their bones were blackened, charred with something ancient, and through the gaps in their decayed ribcages, faint blue light pulsed like dying embers. Their hollow eyes gleamed with the same eerie glow, flickering as if caught between realms.

She recognized them. The same spectral creatures from before.

A cold dread slithered down her spine.

Zakar, however, remained completely unfazed. He exhaled as if mildly inconvenienced, his stance relaxed even as the nearest wraith glided forward, its movements silent, unnatural.

When it spoke, its voice was a layered distortion—deep and

echoing, as if a chorus of the dead spoke in unison. The sound sent ice through her veins.

Zakar nodded once, seemingly understanding them, then cast a glance her way before looking back to the wraith. "Understood," he murmured, tone even. "Thank you. You are dismissed for now."

At his words, the four figures dipped their heads in a slow, almost reverent bow before receding. Their bodies dissolved into the mist, vanishing as if they had never been there at all.

For a long moment, Myrithia remained quiet, the rhythmic patter of rain filling the silence. Then, unable to hold back any longer, she finally asked, "What... are those things?"

Zakar turned his gaze to her, the faintest smirk tugging at the corner of his lips. "My Sentinels," he answered smoothly. "Four wraiths—once arcane masters themselves, hundreds of years ago. Now, they live to serve the Master of the Arcane."

Her skin prickled. "They look terrifying."

"They're quite friendly once you get to know them."

She narrowed her eyes, trying to determine if he was jesting or serious.

"What did they say to you?" she asked warily, watching him as he stared out into the rain, the steady downpour drenching the earth around them.

Zakar exhaled slowly, his gaze fixed on the water pooling in the dips of the forest floor. Myrithia watched him, noting the way his expression darkened, the way his shoulders tensed beneath his cloak. Whatever his sentinels had whispered to him, it wasn't good.

"The Hollow Mist is drawing nearer." His voice was low, contemplative—but beneath it, there was an undercurrent of unease. He straightened from where he sat, his jaw tightening. "It's begun to spread."

Her gut churned, restless and uneasy. "What? But I thought it was outside of Hawthorne Reach—"

"It is," he interrupted, his eyes darkening, "but it also moves when it wants to. And right now, it's moving toward us."

She sat up straighter. "How close?"

Zakar dragged a hand through his damp hair, scanning the

shadows between the trees. "Close enough that if we don't keep moving, we risk being swallowed by it. If it reaches the tome before us..." He trailed off, expression grim.

Myrithia's pulse quickened. "We'd lose access to the book."

He gave a slow nod. "Possibly for a long time. Longer than you have."

The weight of that settled between them. This wasn't just a threat. This was a looming catastrophe. If they lost the tome, her fate was sealed—there would be no breaking the curse, no escaping the slow, agonizing death waiting for her.

She swallowed, glancing up at him. He was already moving, already making the call before she could even ask.

"We need to keep going." His tone was firm, final. "We don't have the luxury of stopping anymore."

Myrithia hesitated for only a moment before nodding. She wasn't thrilled about pushing forward through the rain, but the alternative was far worse.

As if that wasn't enough, his next words sent a chill down her spine.

"One more thing," Zakar murmured. "Our pursuers are still far enough that they're not an immediate concern—yet. But there's a small army of them." His lips pressed into a thin line. "Led by Garron."

Her chest constricted as panic crept in. She had known Draevok would send forces after them. But hearing that name made her stomach churn.

She clenched her fists, forcing herself to focus. "How far?"

Zakar glanced toward the darkness of the forest, then back at her. "A day behind. Maybe less, depending on how hard they ride."

Myrithia forced down her rising dread. Between the Hollow Mist closing in and Garron on their heels, there was no time left to hesitate.

"Then let's move."

But even as she said it, something gnawed at her, something that had lingered since the lodge, since Zakar had let Garron live.

Her expression darkened. "You kept him alive." The words slipped out, edged with something bitter. "Why?"

THE ARCANE BARGAIN

Zakar didn't even look at her as he adjusted his coat, pulling the hood over his head. "You don't care for your old comrade?" His voice was cool, laced with a mockery that made her blood simmer.

She scoffed. "He was never my comrade."

That at least made him glance at her, the corner of his mouth tilting slightly, but the amusement in his gaze didn't quite reach his eyes.

She turned away, her fists clenching as she started walking again.

Garron had served Draevok, flawlessly playing the role of Zakar's closest friend while secretly aiding in his downfall. And yet, despite being a liar, Garron had never struggled with his deception the way she had. His loyalty to Draevok had been unwavering, his ability to hate Zakar effortless. That had always unnerved her—how seamlessly he could pretend, how easily he could discard someone he had once feigned brotherhood with.

She had never been able to do that.

Worse still, Garron had wanted *her*—something Draevok had been all too willing to exploit. He had promised her to Garron as a *prize* once the royal family was destroyed. As if she were something to be owned, to be given away at a whim.

"I never cared for him," she said over her shoulder, her tone dismissive. "But I am surprised *you* didn't finish him off. You're so brutal, after all."

Zakar chuckled, low and dark. "Brutal, am I?" He caught her subtle eye roll as he stepped into stride beside her and he smirked. "I *will* kill him, Myra. But I prefer to take my time with such things."

"You don't need to elaborate," she muttered, hoping he wouldn't. She hated Garron, but she didn't need the gory details of his inevitable demise.

But Zakar wasn't done. He tilted his head slightly, studying her. "What did he do to earn your hatred?"

Her fingers tensed into fists at her sides. "He wanted a courtship. I did not."

Zakar straightened at once, his posture shifting from amused to something much sharper. He looked down at her, his voice cool and precise. "Courtship?"

Myrithia swallowed, knowing he had already deduced the truth. Garron wasn't the type to want an actual courtship. She gave him a knowing look, then glanced away, unwilling to say the words aloud.

The silence that followed was heavy. Tense. Then she felt it—his rage, slow and building like a storm on the horizon.

"Say the word," he murmured, his voice quiet but dangerous. "Say the word, and I will find him, small army or not, and I will carve the life from his body."

She let out a breath, unsettled by the cold finality in his tone. "He never forced me, Zakar," she clarified. The words felt foul even as she said them, but she needed him to understand.

It didn't help. His expression only darkened further, his muscles coiled tight.

He slowed, his jaw like iron, and she instinctively looked back at him. "Draevok wouldn't have allowed it," she added quickly. "Not because he cared, mind you. But because I was to be *earned*."

Zakar went unnervingly still. "Earned?"

Myrithia shifted where she stood, feeling the weight of his gaze. Her chest ached with something between indignation and humiliation. "Draevok promised to give me to Garron as his reward—after the royal family was slaughtered. That hadn't stopped Garron from touching me, cornering me when he pleased, taunting me at what he would do to me when it was all over."

His breath came slow and measured, but the air around them changed.

"I thought you were Draevok's prized apprentice," he said, his voice deceptively smooth. "And he would give you away like that to a man like him?"

She lifted her chin, her spine rigid. "I was never his apprentice. I was his indentured servant. And yes," she met his eyes without wavering, "he *would* give me away like that."

The rain fell steadily between them, the world narrowing to the space where they stood.

"I'm certain that if Draevok captures me now, he will make good on his promise to Garron," she continued, her voice quieter now. "And then, after that, I will be executed for treason."

The ground trembled with a low, almost imperceptible vibration. She felt the tension in the air before she even looked up.

Zakar's hands twitched at his sides, emerald wisps of energy licking up his arms, crackling in warning. The fine hairs on her skin stood on end, and her pulse quickened.

He was *angry*.

She had seen him furious before, but this was different. This was cold, merciless, deadly.

His hands clenched into fists, power thrumming just beneath his skin, the forest itself seeming to pulse in response to his fury.

Myrithia swallowed hard. For the first time since this journey began, she feared what he might do.

CHAPTER 43

Zakar

Zakar remembered his courtship with Myrithia in flawless detail, every moment turned over and over in his mind like a blade being sharpened against stone. Years of reliving every glance, every touch, every whispered promise—only to have it all shattered by her betrayal. And yet, as vivid as those memories were, another recollection clawed its way to the forefront.

Garron.

He had boasted often of the women he pursued, spinning his conquests into crude, elaborate tales over drinks and laughter. Zakar had never thought much of it—Garron was a lecher, after all, and women were drawn to his easy charm. Nobles and concubines alike had lined up for him, and he had indulged them all, never once pretending to be the type of man to settle down.

But there had been one time, one particular story, where his tone had been different. He had spoken of a woman who enraptured him, a woman promised to him—a future wife, he had claimed, one whose father had arranged the match. He had boasted of her beauty, of her body, of the things he intended to do to her once she was his.

Zakar had only half-listened at the time, dismissing it as Garron's usual indulgence. He had pitied the woman, assuming she was some naive noble's daughter being sold off to a man who would never love her, who would use her until he grew bored and found another. But any woman agreeing to marry Garron must have understood what she was in for.

Only now did he realize—that woman had been Myrithia.

He hadn't known it then, of course, but there was no doubt in his mind now. Garron had spoken of her, of his Myra, before Zakar had even begun to court her. And all this time, Garron must have known. Known who she was, known she would belong to Zakar, and yet had smiled in his face, had watched him fall deeper under her spell while knowing that Zakar's death would deliver her into his waiting hands.

The memory curdled in his stomach like poison.

He had laughed about it—laughed while describing all the ways he would enjoy her once she was his.

Zakar inhaled slowly, forcing the air through his lungs even as his hands pulled into fists at his sides. A mistake. He had made a horrible mistake.

He should have killed Garron back at the lodge.

A slow death, a quick death—it didn't matter. He had to die.

He *would* die.

A soft hand grasped his sleeve, and his body tensed at the touch.

"Zakar."

Myrithia's voice was low, steady, soothing. "I'm sure there will be time for dealing with Garron later, but we must keep moving forward."

Zakar looked at her with a smile that he hardly felt. "You can't expect me to hear such a story and just do nothing about it."

Myrithia hesitated, her posture stiff, as if she were carefully weighing her next words. "You'll have to push those feelings aside for now. They aren't important."

His expression darkened. "Not important?"

"That's not what I meant." She fumbled, the urgency in her voice betraying her caution. "Your emotions *are* important, it's just that we don't have time to dwell on them. Sometimes you just have to bury your feelings and keep pressing on."

His fingers tightened as he placed a firm hand on her shoulder, forcing her to meet his gaze. "I know how to bury feelings, Myrithia."

She stiffened beneath his touch before pulling away, turning sharply from him. "If you're just going to foolishly head the wrong direction to go slaughter a pathetic traitor, then you can do it alone." She started walking again, her voice curt. "I'll be outrunning the Hollow Mist and finding the tome, or die trying, I suppose."

He stared after her for a long moment, rain soaking through his clothes, before her voice cut through the downpour—cool, distant.

"Garron shouldn't concern you anymore, anyway." She didn't look back, as if needing the distance before saying it. "If what we had was a lie, then you should hardly fault him. After all, I'm the one who hurt you. Far worse than he ever could." A breath, then quieter, "If anything, you shouldn't care at all. I am nothing to you. Nothing but a slave."

Before he could think better of it, he moved—closing the distance between them in an instant, fingers clenching tightly around her arm. She turned sharply at the contact, blue eyes blazing beneath the veil of rain, her face a mask of calm fire.

"You know you are more than that." His voice was low, taut with something he couldn't name.

She let out a quiet scoff. "Am I?"

With a quick, defiant jerk, she wrenched her arm free, her chin lifting as resolve steeled her features. "I am not your wife, or your mistress, or even your lover. I am nothing more than your slave. And a disobedient one at that."

His lips twitched in annoyance. "You are mine, regardless of what I may call you." His gaze darkened, voice thick with warning. "And I don't care for Garron wanting what is mine."

"You're really this upset that I was promised to him?" She demanded, tilting her head up at him. "You, who has already taken the last of my will—"

"You gave it to me," he corrected icily.

"I had no choice!" she shot back.

He smirked. "Well, you're not wrong there."

His hand slid up, fingers threading through her wet hair, gripping at the base of her skull as he tugged—tilting her chin up, forcing her to hold his gaze, to feel the weight of his claim on her.

"From the moment you stepped into the Arcane Citadel," he murmured, his voice a dark whisper between them, "there was never a choice."

Her breath caught, teeth clenched behind her lips.

He leaned in, gaze flicking between her eyes and mouth, as if daring her to deny it. "You were my prisoner long before you ever accepted it."

Gods, he couldn't help himself. The cruelty, the need to keep her bound to him—it was instinct, a sickness he could never seem to cure. He was pathetic. He masked the bitter taste of self-loathing behind cool, impassive eyes.

"So the bargain," she said slowly, her voice laced with something fragile, something teetering on the edge of realization. "The agreement we made..." She exhaled, a trembling breath lost to the storm. "That was just for your amusement, wasn't it?"

He didn't answer. He didn't have to.

She already knew.

Her expression twisted, fury flashing across her face like lightning splitting the sky.

And before he could even take a breath, she was gone—her body dissolving into a breathtaking mist of silver light, glittering against the downpour before vanishing entirely.

CHAPTER 44
Myrithia

She hadn't truly believed she could escape him. She wasn't that naive. She needed both of them to continue in the correct direction or risk being lost to the Mist, and she would lead him on a chase if she had to. And gods, she needed to get away—from his eyes that saw through her so easily, from the shame curling like hot iron in her chest. She didn't want him to witness the humiliating unraveling of what little defiance she had left. She needed distance, even if only for a fleeting moment.

There had never been a deal. Not a real one.

She had walked into the Arcane Citadel with empty hands, and he had taken *everything*. The tome was not a fair trade—it was merely his amusement, his indulgence. He was only letting her have it because he didn't want his little slave to die before she had properly served her sentence.

Again, she flashed in hurried bursts of glittering silver light—twenty feet, ten, six…

A sharp pull yanked through her chest, wrenching the breath from her lungs. She gasped, stumbling as she felt the power drain from her body, slipping from her like water cupped in trembling hands. *He was taking it back.*

He was letting her run, and now, like a patient master reclaiming his wayward pet, he was simply calling her home.

"Myra," his voice rolled through the rain like a slow, indulgent purr. "What are you doing?"

"We have to keep going," she snapped, pressing forward even as the ground turned to thick, treacherous mud beneath her boots. "So, either lead or leave me alone."

But she wasn't angry at him. Not really.

She was angry at herself.

Why couldn't she just accept it? Why did she have to fight him at every turn? Why couldn't she simply obey and be content with what little he offered? She would never escape him. She would never find freedom. Her life with him—his possession, his plaything—was infinitely better than the execution awaiting her if she ever did manage to slip through his grasp.

But she was greedy.

She didn't want to be his slave.

She wanted to be *his*.

His *wife*, his *lover*—his *something* beyond a servant bound by magic and vengeance. But that was impossible. *She* had made it impossible. To remain his slave would be to fall deeper into him than ever before, helpless against the pull, helpless against herself—and the agony of loving without hope, of giving without return, would one day break her beyond repair.

And so, like a child throwing a tantrum, she forged on.

"Enough," his voice came from behind her, firm and unwavering. Before she could react, his arms braced around her, lifting her effortlessly off the ground. She yelped, her hands instinctively grasping at the soaked fabric of his cloak as he carried her through the rain.

The transition was seamless, his hold unshakable, making it clear that struggling would be in vain. His hold on her was not the rough, punishing grasp she had expected—it was sure, possessive, as if she weighed nothing at all in his arms. Rain clung to their skin, rolling in rivulets down his sharp jaw as he walked with her held against his chest.

"We will forge on," he said, his tone clipped, agitated. "I was never going to chase after him," he muttered. "But I was considering having my Sentinels wait for him. While I would prefer to savor his slaughter myself, at this rate, I'd settle for the comfort of knowing he is dead."

She exhaled sharply, grateful that the rain blurred everything—the trees, the path ahead, the way her face must've burned with mortification at being carried like a wretched bride through the storm. "It's good to know you weren't going to let it slow us down," she mumbled, still fuming.

She was still angry. But at least they were moving again. At least they were heading in the right direction.

"If we are to make it to the tome, we need to move quickly," he said. Then, after a pause, he added, "That is why I will be lending you my power."

She stiffened, surprise flickering in her chest.

He finally stopped, his breath steady despite the exertion. "Can I trust you?" His voice was low, but there was no accusation in it this time. Only urgency. Need.

There was no time for hesitation. No time for stubbornness.

She met his gaze and nodded.

He sighed, lowering her to the ground. Her boots sank slightly into the muddy earth, the rain making every step slick and unsteady. Then, without further preamble, he reached for her, linking their fingers together.

Magic pulsed between them.

The world slowed, the sounds of the storm dulled, and all that existed was the deep, coiling warmth spreading from his touch. It was more than just power—it was connection. His breath became her breath. His heartbeat, a steady drum inside her own chest. His anguish, his unspoken thoughts, the raw, relentless force of his will—it flooded through her, thick as ink, settling into her very core.

Then, they moved.

With each burst of power, the forest blurred, rain becoming streaks of silver as they crossed vast distances in a blink. The ground vanished beneath them, their bodies flickering forward in long, fluid leaps through space, reappearing and vanishing again in rapid succession. The weight of it built in her limbs, pressing into her muscles, but she pressed on, covering mile after mile with each pulse of magic.

Then, just as her breath started to tremble, she slowed.

THE ARCANE BARGAIN

Zakar's grip tightened slightly, steadying her. "Are you alright?" There was genuine concern in his voice, one she could feel as surely as if it were her own.

"I'm fine," she said hastily, already preparing to push them forward again.

But his gaze had shifted, fixed on something past her.

"Stop."

The way he said it made something cold coil in her chest. She furrowed her brows and turned, following his line of sight.

And then she saw it.

The Mist.

Her pulse stuttered. Further north... was it already too late?

Not fifty feet away, a churning wall of unnatural darkness crept toward them, rolling over the earth in thick, swirling tendrils. It moved like a living thing, reaching, consuming. There was no sound—no whisper of wind, no rustling of leaves. Just silence. A vast, stretching nothingness devouring the world ahead.

Again, she could almost hear it—that whispering voice. Soft, elusive, beckoning. If she didn't know any better, she would almost think it was hunting her, wanting to entrap her within it.

Her heart should have been heavy as lead in her chest, but instead, she stood transfixed, held captive by the mist shifting before her. It loomed, vast and impenetrable, yet something within her stirred at its presence.

Every fiber of her being urged her forward. It wasn't conscious. It wasn't a choice. It was instinct—deep, inexorable, inevitable.

The earth trembled.

A low, eerie hum vibrated beneath Myrithia's boots as shadows unfurled from the ground, seeping through the cracks of the damp forest floor like spilled ink. The mist coiled and thickened into shapes—long, spindly fingers, hollowed ribs, cloaked figures that flickered in and out of existence like dying embers.

Then, with a whisper of shifting air, Zakar's Sentinels rose. The very air around them twisted, the temperature dropping as their presence bled into the space around them.

She went still, lungs holding too much and not enough. Gods, she hated those things.

They stood motionless for a long moment before the one in

front—slightly taller than the rest—turned its gleaming eyes onto Zakar. When it spoke, its voice was layered, distorted, as if it echoed from a hundred different mouths at once. The sound was indiscernible hissing, but she knew Zakar could understand them.

Zakar's shoulders tensed. His gaze flicked toward the mist in the distance, his face a calm veneer, before slowly shifting back to his Sentinels. He remained still, watching them, his fingers twitching at his sides as if suppressing the urge to summon more power.

He looked over his shoulder at her. And for the first time, there was something close to unease in his expression.

She had never seen him look uncertain. Even in his anger, his arrogance, his amusement, there was always confidence—always control. But now? Now, there was doubt.

He turned back to the Sentinels and gave a single nod.

The creatures bowed in perfect unison, lowering their skeletal heads as their cloaks swirled with unnatural movement. Then, without another sound, they sank back into the ground, vanishing into a mist of black and blue, the last flickers of their glowing eyes disappearing into the abyss.

The forest was silent once more.

Myrithia exhaled shakily. The rain drummed against the leaves, but the cold feeling lingering in her bones had nothing to do with the storm.

"What did they say?" She asked warily.

He was quiet another moment, the weight of his silence pressing down on her before he finally spoke.

"We will have to enter the Mist."

The words sent a chill through her, colder than the rain soaking through her clothes.

CHAPTER 47
Zakar

His Sentinels were strange creatures—he had always known that. Old, dead souls, warped by time and tethered to a duty that outlived their mortal bodies. Once, they had been Masters of the Arcane, just as he was now. And in death, they continued their service, bound by magic, their existence dedicated to the Master who claimed them.

Master Sorien had never made the pact. He had refused them, insisting that his soul was meant to pass onto the next realm, the afterlife, alongside the gods and goddesses who ruled it. Zakar had thought him foolish for it. Who would turn away such power? Who would deny the chance to command forces so absolute? He hadn't hesitated—hadn't even considered hesitation—when he took his place as Master. The exchange had been simple. Unlimited power in life, in return for servitude in death.

A fair trade, for someone whose only purpose had been vengeance.

But now, standing at the edge of the Hollow Mist, he wondered.

Which of his Sentinels was waiting for true rest? Which one had spent centuries longing for release? Which one was watching him now, knowing his time would come, knowing the cycle would continue?

Enter the Mist.

The Sentinels had said it so plainly, so certainly.

"The tomb is within. The book is within. There is no danger to you."

Zakar's breath stilled in his chest.

For the first time in years, true fear sank its claws into him.

The Sentinels served him, yes, but they were not mindless. They had their own thoughts, their own desires. They had been human once, and they had not lost that part of themselves. They had lived for centuries, perhaps longer. And one of them, surely, was waiting for release.

This was something Sorien had feared. And perhaps, for the first time, Zakar understood why.

Was he walking into his own death?

Should he turn away? Should he take Myrithia and go, let the Mist pass, find another way to keep her alive? He could. He could hold onto her long enough, find some other solution—no matter how forbidden, how dark. He would do anything to ensure she lived.

His mind was unraveling too fast, a storm of thoughts colliding and twisting within him, until—

"Zakar?"

Myrithia's voice was soft, hesitant. A quiet anchor pulling him back from the brink.

"They told you to enter the mist?" she asked, her voice tight with worry. "Did they at least tell you what was in there?"

He didn't fault her for her fear. He feared it as well, though he was loath to admit it, even to himself. Nobody knew what lay beyond that dense, creeping shroud. Those who entered never returned. It was not just certain death—it was an unknown, an abyss beyond reason or understanding. The Hollow Mist had existed for as long as history could recall, swallowing the unfortunate and leaving behind only whispers of what might become of them. Even the most powerful sorcerers avoided it.

Yet here he was, expected to walk willingly into its depths.

The rain pounded against him, soaking through his clothes, sliding down his face. He had yet to answer her. He knew it. He knew she was waiting.

"Zakar?" Her voice cut through the storm, pressing him for words, for certainty, for something to ground her against the dread creeping into her bones.

THE ARCANE BARGAIN

If he turned back now, if he abandoned this course, he could take her south. Find shelter. Buy time. His Sentinels could deal with Garron and his men while he sought another way. He could return to the Arcane Citadel, scour its archives, search for another means to sustain her life—another talisman, another spell. And when the Hollow Mist receded, when the path was clear once more, he could retrieve the tome on his own.

It was a logical plan. A safer plan. But as he looked at her—soaked, trembling, waiting—he knew the truth. She didn't have that time.

Every time he lent her his power, she needed more of it. The curse was a ravenous thing, devouring whatever strength she was given, gnawing at the edges of her life. If he turned back now, if he hesitated, she would never live long enough to see the tome. He could sustain her for a while, maybe weeks, maybe longer if he was careful—but he wasn't a fool. He wasn't naive enough to believe any talisman or enchantment would hold indefinitely.

This was the only chance.

He drew in a slow breath, forcing the tension from his shoulders. "There's nothing to fear, Myra," he said, his voice smooth, easy—practiced. A gentle, almost charming expression settled over his features, betraying nothing of the unease that clawed at his gut.

A lie. But she needed it.

He couldn't afford to let her panic.

If they fled, she would die. He would live. If they entered the mist, there was a chance—however small—that they might both survive.

It was a gamble.

And he had never been one to fold.

So he extended his hand to her, fingers steady despite the storm raging around them. "Come," he murmured. "It's time."

She hesitated only a moment before slipping her hand into his, her fingers cool and delicate against his own. Together, they turned toward the mist.

It loomed before them, a churning veil of dense, silver-gray fog, stretching endlessly in both directions. The trees at its edges curled inward as if recoiling from it, their branches gnarled and lifeless. It was unnatural, foreboding—yet it called to them, beckoning like an abyss that had been waiting for them all along.

Zakar stepped forward.

Closer.

Closer.

The mist swirled around him, thick and impenetrable. He drew in a breath, steadying himself as the icy dampness coiled around his skin, smothering every sound—every sense—until—

Warmth.

Sunlight.

He blinked, startled by the sudden brilliance of golden light streaming through the trees, his clothes no longer damp but pressed and pristine, his boots polished to a fine gleam. Beneath him, the earth was soft, vibrant green, and the scent of fresh blooms and summer air filled his lungs.

This place—it was familiar. Too familiar.

A lush forest clearing stretched around him, the dappled light flickering through the canopy above. Songbirds trilled sweetly in the distance, their melodies soft and uninterrupted. A gentle breeze stirred the leaves, carrying the scent of honeysuckle and rain-washed earth. The peaceful serenity was a stark contrast to the storm that had battered them mere moments ago.

His pulse pounded in his ears.

He knew this place.

It was Myrithia's haven. The one she had crafted in her years apart from him. He half expected to see her cottage just beyond the trees, its ivy-covered walls bathed in golden light.

His fingers curled reflexively around hers, grounding himself in the only thing that still felt real.

Myrithia.

He turned his gaze down to her, stunned.

She wasn't drenched in rain, nor coated in mud. Her silver hair cascaded in long, shimmering waves down her back, free of her braid. She wore crimson—deep, rich red, trimmed in gold filigree—an elegant gown that clung to her frame, regal yet inviting. She was resplendent. Ethereal. Breathtaking.

And she was smiling.

All traces of fear, of exhaustion, of the weight she had carried for so long—gone.

"You were right," she breathed, stepping closer, her arms sliding around his waist as she nestled her face against his chest.

Zakar's heart betrayed him, stumbling at the soft, effortless way she fit against him, as though she had always belonged there.

His arms hovered at his sides, stiff, uncertain.

This wasn't real. It couldn't be.

His gaze flicked around them, catching the faint glimmers of iridescent light floating lazily through the air, the leaves swaying in an unfelt breeze. No, this wasn't what he had expected. He had anticipated darkness, suffering, horrors beyond comprehension.

Not *this*.

Not this beautiful lie.

Myrithia lifted her head, looking up at him with a tenderness that stole the air from his lungs.

"Let's go," she whispered, her fingers lacing through his as she gently tugged him forward, deeper into the impossible dream waiting beyond the trees.

CHAPTER 46

Myrithia

Myrithia could hardly comprehend what lay before her. It was nothing like she had imagined—nothing like it should have been. She had spent years living beneath the Hollow Mist, existing on its edges, surrounded by its presence but never stepping inside.

And yet, she could have never anticipated this. The world around her was ethereal, bathed in soft, shimmering white, iridescent waves rippling through the air like the surface of a disturbed lake.

The whispers—the ones she had heard the first time she had stood at its threshold—returned. Soft. Faint. Beckoning.

Everything felt warm, weightless, pleasant, like that fleeting, drowsy moment when you first wake from a long dream, hovering between reality and something else entirely.

A voice, disembodied, cutting cleanly through the whispers.

"You resemble her."

She stilled.

She spun toward the sound, her breath uneven. Not far from her, she saw a man standing amidst the gleaming white of their surroundings.

Only… He was not human.

Something about him felt untethered, ethereal in a way that defied explanation. His skin was pale, a shade too light to be natural, gleaming in the white expanse around them. Tousled strands of reddish-gold hair framed his sharp, elegant features, falling haphazardly over his forehead as though the wind had just touched him. But it was his eyes that unsettled her most— solid, gleaming gold, ringed with intricate runes that pulsed faintly like the heartbeat of some ancient magic.

He wore a red and gold tunic embroidered with strange symbols, cinched at the waist with a thick golden sash, and fitted trousers that spoke of ease and authority. The way he stood—poised, unhurried, utterly certain—made it clear he was something powerful. Something that didn't belong to her world.

And yet... there was something familiar about him. Myrithia's mind raced back to the tapestries she had glimpsed in Calveren's study—the depictions of the old gods. One in particular: the trickster.

Nyxian.

The resemblance was there, undeniable. Though no mural, no book had captured the sheer beauty of him. They had painted him as sly, cunning, beautiful in a cruel way. But they hadn't done him justice. The real thing was infinitely more breathtaking—and infinitely more dangerous.

Her throat tightened. "Who are you?" she asked, though she already knew.

"Nyxian," he confirmed, pleasant but distant, his expression only mildly genial, as if the introduction was a formality rather than a necessity.

Her heart skipped painfully in her chest. She hadn't been wrong.

Myrithia licked her lips, her nerves tightening in her chest. She had no idea how to interact with him, no sense of what he wanted. Only that he was real.

"Do you live here? In the Mist?" she hesitated. "Do you control it?"

Nyxian's lips curled into a small, amused smile. "I was hoping *you* would."

Her brows drew together. "That I would..." she echoed, her voice trailing off. Then came the realization, sharp and sudden, threading disbelief through her thoughts like a splinter. "That *I* would control it?"

The moment the words left her lips, he moved. Within a blink, he was suddenly before her.

She staggered back, her breath catching.

His gaze swept over her, a glint of cold calculation stirring behind those golden eyes.

"You do not have her eyes," he murmured, almost sullen, as if disappointed. Then, with a sharp click of his tongue, he leaned back, folding his hands casually behind him. "Still, though. Very, very similar indeed."

Myrithia's fingers curled and uncurled at her sides. She didn't like this—the way he studied her, the way he moved, as if she were a curiosity, not a person.

"Who is this woman I'm being compared to?" she asked warily, her gaze following him, wary of every smooth, calculated step.

Nyxian barely glanced at her. "A goddess." He said it simply, dismissively, as if the word meant nothing.

A goddess.

Her mind reeled at the comparison. So fitting, yet so foreign.

The white abyss around them dissolved, revealing towering black stone as flickering torchlight played over the arched windows in restless shadow. The Valthorian castle. But not as she remembered it. The corridors were longer, endless, moonlight spilling through the vast stained glass, illuminating dust motes suspended in the air.

Her clothes were now dry, pristine—more than that, they were magnificent. A regal gown of deep purple and crimson cascaded down her frame, the luxurious fabric pooling behind her in elegant ripples. Gold embroidery shimmered in delicate patterns along the bodice, and the weight of a jeweled pendant rested against her collarbone, as though she had always worn it.

She lifted her hands, tracing over the impossibly smooth silk. How...?

It was an illusion.

She turned back to him, her posture rigid, shoulders tight with restraint.

"What do you want?" she asked, her voice steady—a stark contrast to the uncertainty twisting in her chest.

Nyxian smirked, golden eyes gleaming with lazy amusement,

as if her question wwas a source of mild entertainment rather than concern. "I'd like to play a little game with you, Myrithia."

"A game?" She asked, narrowing her eyes at the god before her. "I don't have time for games. I'm here for one purpose only, and that—"

"—is to acquire the Syltharic Tome, yes," Nyxian interrupted smoothly, his golden eyes gleaming. "I know."

She stiffened. He knew too much, as if he had access to every thought and memory in her head.

"Why?" she asked finally. The word escaped her lips in a quiet breath, heavy with layers of meaning. Why was she here? Why did he want to entangle her in this absurdity? Why her?

Nyxian studied her, the corner of his mouth twitching as if he enjoyed her uncertainty. "If you win my little game, Myrithia, I will answer any question you have." He spread his arms, as if offering her the world. "And, of course, I will give you your tome."

There would have to be a catch. There was always a catch.

"And what about Zakar?" she asked, her voice quiet.

The silence pulled tight around her, heavy as stone, until Nyxian's lips curved into a slow, cruel smile.

"If you win my game," he murmured, "you will be free of him. I will void your blood contract."

Freedom.

The word sent a sharp, dizzy thrill through her. True freedom. True independence. But...

Her lips parted. "And Zakar?" she pressed, cautious now. "He would be... alright, wouldn't he?"

Nyxian chuckled under his breath, the sound curling like smoke through the corridor. "Let us begin our game."

Then, with a snap of his fingers, he was gone.

The air was still, save for the faint hum of something unnatural pressing at the edges of her senses.

At the end of the corridor, tall, hooded double doors glowed with a soft orange light, leading into the ballroom beyond.

"I'm giving you a rare opportunity," Nyxian's voice echoed around her as she neared the doors. "This is a chance to choose differently. A chance to rewrite your past."

CHAPTER 47

Zakar

The cottage was alive with warmth and movement, the scent of baked apples and spiced cinnamon curling through the air like a welcome embrace. Laughter echoed from the halls, light and unburdened—three small children darting past him, their tiny footsteps thudding against the wooden floorboards as they played.

Myrithia's voice carried from the hearth. "Would you like some?" she asked, glancing over her shoulder with a bright smile as she bustled toward the oven, reaching for a fresh pie.

Zakar watched, momentarily caught in the simplicity of it all. The kitchen was quaint, filled with the quiet hum of domestic life—the faint crackle of the fire, the soft clinking of dishes, the golden glow of candlelight flickering against the walls. Myrithia looked so at home here, effortlessly moving between the table and the hearth, the soft red fabric of her dress swaying around her ankles.

Something tugged at his coat.

He glanced down, startled to find a small boy standing before him, grinning up at him with wide, green eyes. His green eyes.

Zakar inhaled sharply, frozen.

The boy giggled, stretching his arms upward in silent demand, and without thinking, Zakar obeyed. He lifted the child with ease, feeling the warmth of his small body press against his chest.

The boy squealed in delight, throwing his arms around Zakar's neck in an exuberant hug.

His heart slammed against his ribs.

"Myra," he murmured, watching her as she cut a slice of pie, placing it neatly on a plate.

She turned, still smiling, but before she could speak, the child in his arms wriggled free, sliding down to the floor and scampering toward the table. He grasped the slice of pie with chubby fingers and bolted, his laughter trailing behind him.

"You'll ruin your supper!" Myrithia scolded playfully, though her tone was thick with affection.

Then she turned back to Zakar, stepping closer, her touch warm as her fingers ghosted along his jaw. "But you," she purred, her voice low, teasing, "you can have as much dessert as you want."

His lips curled into a smile—a real one. Unburdened. At peace. His wife. His *Myra*. She leaned in to kiss him.

His hand caught her wrist.

Confusion flickered in her eyes as he held her still. His smile was gone, his gaze sharp, calculating.

"What have you done with my Myra?" His voice was cold, measured.

She blinked. "What?"

"Where is she?"

The illusion shattered.

Like glass, the world around him collapsed into void, the warmth of the cottage dissolving into darkness. The scent of pies and firewood vanished, replaced by silence, thick and suffocating. The only thing left was him—and Myrithia.

Or whatever she was.

The illusion of Myrithia smiled—soft, knowing—before vanishing entirely, dissolving into mist like a breath against glass.

Then, a voice, smooth and rich, drifted through the void.

"Well, well," it mused, the sound coming from everywhere and nowhere at once. "I have never had the pleasure of meeting a Master of the Arcane."

Zakar remained still, his sharp gaze scanning the darkness around him. Unamused, but ever the performer, he let a grin stretch across his face and swept into a mock bow, all flourish and disdain.

A chuckle echoed in response, warm and indulgent.

"What possessed you to enter here?" the voice continued, its amusement palpable. Then, as if answering its own question, it hummed thoughtfully. "Let me guess."

A shimmer in the air, a flicker of silver light—and suddenly, she was there.

Myrithia.

Or rather, another illusion of her.

She stood before him, bathed in ethereal moonlight, her silver hair cascading over the delicate white fabric of her gown. A vision of purity, of haunting beauty. Her blue eyes were soft, filled with something near reverence, a look she had never truly given him.

"You fell in love with a dying creature," the voice sighed, a soft tsk following. "And you think an old book will save her."

Zakar exhaled slowly, tilting his head before lifting his hand in a lazy flick. The illusion scattered like smoke in an emerald burst, tendrils of his magic slashing through it with ease.

"Since you already know why I'm here," he said coolly, his patience thin, "perhaps you might tell me how to acquire Myrithia and the tome."

The world shifted.

The void melted away, replaced by the warm glow of firelight. A small, cramped cottage materialized around him—humble, weathered by time, the scent of old parchment and burnt wood lingering in the air. A crude fire flickered in the hearth, the flames dancing lazily against the stone walls. Two wooden chairs sat near it, worn from use.

A man occupied one of them, his back turned to Zakar.

The firelight caught the strands of his hair, a deep gold threaded with rich auburn, like a sunset frozen in time. He exuded an otherworldly presence, something old and ageless, something that didn't quite belong in the realm of mortals.

Slowly, the man turned.

Zakar studied him, his gaze sharp, dissecting. The golden runes around his eyes glowed faintly, symbols of power, of divinity. Understanding settled over Zakar like a weight.

This was a god.

THE ARCANE BARGAIN

Which one, he wasn't certain. But he had learned enough about them under Sorien's tutelage. Sorien had revered them. Worshipped them.

Zakar had never been so easily impressed.

The man's lips pulled into an infuriating smirk, his golden eyes glinting with something far too knowing. He gestured to the empty chair across from him.

"Take a seat."

Zakar approached, his movements slow, measured. He lowered himself onto the chair, keeping his posture relaxed but his mind razor-sharp. His gaze never wavered from the god's.

The smirk deepened, as if pleased.

"My name is Nyxian," the god drawled, leaning back with effortless ease, amusement threading his voice. "It's so nice to make your acquaintance, Arcane Master."

Zakar leaned back in the old wooden chair, feigning ease, though his muscles were coiled tight beneath the surface. His tone was casual, but pointed. "For a god, I should think you'd conjure up better chairs."

Nyxian chuckled, tilting his head slightly. "Oh, this isn't for my benefit. It's for yours."

Zakar studied him for a long moment, taking in the languid posture, the smug amusement that flickered behind those golden eyes. Then, he looked away, into the fire.

"What is your game?" he asked, voice even.

Nyxian smirked. "You assume I'm here to play games?"

Zakar's gaze flicked back to him, sharp as a blade. "Nyxian, a god of mischief, are you not?"

The god's smirk widened, the golden runes at his temples glinting in the firelight. He didn't confirm nor deny it.

Zakar continued, his tone deceptively light. "Do you live in the Mist? Do you control it?" His eyes narrowed. "Or does it control you?"

Nyxian let out a soft sigh, shaking his head as if Zakar were asking all the wrong questions. "I am here to play a game with your slave, Arcane Master." He rested his chin in his palm, studying Zakar with something between curiosity and amusement. "If she wins, I'll give you the tome."

Zakar's expression didn't shift. "And she will be free to go."

Nyxian's mouth tilted into an easy, confident smile. "If she wins my game, then *yes*, she is free to go."

Zakar forced himself to remain still, to keep his expression impassive despite the unease tightening his chest.

"Can I take her place? Will you play your game with me instead?"

"Oh, no," Nyxian said lazily, his fingers tracing the rim of an empty goblet that hadn't been there a moment ago. "Playing a game with the Arcane Master is no fun. You know too many spells. But, playing a game with *her*?" His grin turned wicked, predatory. "I do hope she fails. It has been a while since I've seen a woman so beautiful. I'd love to trap her here with me forever."

Zakar's jaw tightened. Rage burned through him, low and seething, but he refused to give the god the satisfaction of a reaction.

Instead, he smiled, dark and cold. "Start your game, god."

Nyxian tilted his head, studying Zakar with quiet amusement. "Oh, but the game has already begun."

Zakar's expression didn't shift, though his hands curled into loose fists on the wooden armrests of his chair.

"She's going to be given a choice between *you* or *freedom*," Nyxian murmured, watching Zakar's reaction carefully. "A rather generous one, don't you think? I wonder what she'll choose."

Zakar's jaw clenched, his unease mounting.

Nyxian smirked knowingly, enjoying the tension coiling between them. He lifted his goblet of deep red wine, offering a toast rich with dry amusement.

"Good luck, Arcane Master," he purred. "But between you and me? I wouldn't get my hopes up."

CHAPTER 48

Myrithia

Myrithia hesitated, her fingers brushing the gilded handle within the illusion of the Valthorian corridor. Nyxian had just told her that she had a chance to rewrite her own history. Memories surged through her mind in rapid succession, so vivid they nearly stole her breath. She could hear Draevok's voice, commanding, inescapable. *You will seduce the crown prince of Valthoria. Make him love you. And when the time comes—dethrone him.*

Her heart pounded. This was the night she met him. The night that changed everything.

She glanced down at herself, the deep crimson of her gown glimmering under the candlelit chandeliers. It was the same dress, identical in every way to the one she had worn that evening. She smoothed a trembling hand over the fine silk, her mind warring with itself.

Was this real?

Could this god truly manipulate time? Or was this simply a cruel illusion, an elaborate snare to test her?

She swallowed and pushed open the doors.

Music swelled around her. A grand waltz, rich and full-bodied, wrapping around the air like a spell of its own. The ballroom was alive with movement—gilded nobles twirling across the polished marble, laughter weaving between the notes of the minstrels' instruments. It was breathtaking.

THE ARCANE BARGAIN

Her gaze drifted instinctively to the raised platform at the far end of the ballroom—the dais where she had once stood, the place from which she had first bewitched him. It was waiting for her now, just as it had been then.

Like a marionette moved by an unseen hand, she walked toward it, her steps light, her breath steadying. The minstrels glanced at her expectantly, and she lifted her hands, murmuring a soft incantation. Power rushed through her like fire, flooding her limbs, effortless and intoxicating. Her magic obeyed her without strain, without hesitation. The music rose at her command.

She opened her mouth and sang.

It poured from her like spun silver, filling every corner of the vast chamber. The melody was rich, clear, captivating. She had forgotten how *good* it felt to sing like this—to wield her voice like a weapon and a caress all at once. The notes weaved through the air, drawing in her audience, holding them rapt.

And then she saw him.

Zakar stood near a grand pillar at the edge of the ballroom, half-hidden in shadow, a glass of wine dangling loosely from his fingers. His posture was relaxed, almost bored—ignoring his guests, uninterested in the swirling mass of nobility before him. But his attention was fixed *entirely* on her.

Her pulse skipped.

His green eyes burned through her like an ember smoldering beneath the weight of his gaze.

Even now, even here, he looked at her as if she had *already* ruined him.

The song ended. The ballroom erupted into applause, and yet all she could hear was the wild thrumming of her own heart.

She descended from the dais, moving toward him as if drawn by a force stronger than herself.

"You have a lovely voice, Chantress," Zakar murmured, that same gleam of interest sparking in his eyes. "Will you be singing more this evening?"

She smiled. She knew what Draevok had ordered her to do. She knew what she was supposed to say, how she was supposed to ensnare him, how she was to play this role flawlessly and weave a perfect lie.

The words hovered on her lips. But something inside her *balked*.

Zakar watched her expectantly, sensing the hesitation.

Her gaze flickered past him—past the gilded finery, past the lavish ballroom—to the great doors at the far end of the hall.

She was in the past.

She could leave.

She could turn away from it all. She could disappear into the night, vanish into nothing, escape. She didn't *have* to meet Zakar. She didn't *have* to destroy him.

She could walk away.

Her throat tightened, her decision forming like a storm in her chest.

"Excuse me," she murmured, dipping her head in feigned politeness before stepping past him.

She could *feel* his eyes following her as she strode toward the doors, her heart hammering wildly in her ribs. She eased the door open and slipped into the cool, silent corridor, the music behind her fading into a distant murmur as the heavy door clicked shut.

Her footsteps quickened. She knew exactly where the stables were. She had passed them earlier that evening, and even now, she could see the sliver of flickering torchlight illuminating the courtyard outside.

Freedom was right there. *Right there.*

She reached the window, her hands pressing against the cold glass as she gazed out at the darkened yard below. Her horse would be waiting, saddled and ready. It would take *nothing* to slip out unnoticed. Draevok was preoccupied, Garron was undoubtedly somewhere lurking in his shadow. They wouldn't suspect a thing until morning.

A rare chance. A clean escape.

She would still be cursed—she had always known that. Draevok carried a vial of her blood at all times, his own personal fail-safe, a means of control through blood magic. She had never been naïve about what that meant. If she ever defied him completely, if she ever truly broke free, he would hex her beyond repair. Because he had.

Retrieving that vial was impossible.

But she could still run, and she knew she would at least have five years of life left in her.

In this version of events, no one else had to die. Zakar could claim the throne at last. Maybe this time, in this reality, she'd find Master Sorien sooner—break the curse before it consumed her. She could become a Master of the Arcane herself. Maybe even meet Zakar again, not as enemies, but as equals.

The thought lifted her chest, her heart soaring at the glimpse of a different life. A better one. If she was fast—if she was careful—she could still have it.

She lifted her hands, summoning her magic to her fingertips, already feeling the familiar pulse of energy gathering, preparing to whisk her away in a breath of silver light.

"Chantress?"

The voice sent an immediate jolt down her spine. Her entire body went rigid. She turned, slowly, finding Zakar standing in the dim light. His head tilted slightly, those sharp green eyes narrowing in question.

She was *supposed* to be inside. She was *supposed* to be seducing him.

"Where are you going?" he asked, his voice deceptively calm.

"G-Going to get some fresh air, I think," she said innocently, forcing a polite smile. "Please excuse me." She turned swiftly, eager to put distance between them.

"I shall join you, then," he said smoothly, effortlessly matching her pace, his tone light, casual—yet laced with intrigue.

She fought the inward groan that threatened to surface, grudgingly accepting his company. "If it should please His Highness," she murmured, keeping her tone neutral. The longer she indulged this conversation, the harder it would be to walk away. She needed to end this. Now.

She slowed to a stop, turning to him with a practiced smile. "This is probably far enough, Your Highness," she said softly. "I didn't want to be rude, but I'm quite tired. I should really retire for the evening. I hope I haven't offended you."

"You didn't seem tired just now—singing." His words were edged with amusement, but his eyes studied her more intently now.

She quickly opened a nearby door, stepping halfway inside as she spoke. "Yes, well, I'm also not feeling well. So, please excuse me."

Then, before she could let herself hesitate, she gently closed the door between them, and magic flew from her fingertips.

A moment later, she materialized in the stables, the scent of hay and damp earth filling her lungs. Her heart pounded, an erratic rhythm against her ribs, her breath shaky as she forced herself to focus. She was doing the right thing. It would be better if he had never known her.

She urged herself to move, her legs carrying her toward her horse, hands trembling as she reached for the reins. The familiar weight of the leather steadied her, grounding her, but it did nothing to ease the ache in her chest.

She mounted with practiced ease, gripping the reins tightly as she urged her horse into a slow trot, the soft thud of hooves against packed dirt the only sound in the quiet night.

Then, abruptly, her path was blocked.

Nyxian stood before her, his reddish-gold hair glinting under the moonlight, a knowing smirk playing at his lips. His golden eyes gleamed, mischief and something unreadable swirling within them.

"This is a good decision," he commended smoothly, tilting his head. "You will truly be happy after this."

She swallowed hard, her hands tightening around the reins as she wiped the moisture from her lashes. "It's all I've wanted for so long," she murmured, her voice unsteady. "To prevent all the slaughter and suffering."

"Yes," he purred, his voice like silk and smoke. "And in this path you choose, Draevok will never rise to power. Zakar will rule as the new king in due time, as it was meant to be. And you *know* he will be a good monarch."

She nodded firmly, forcing herself to believe he would be fine without her. This was right. This was the only way.

"Only," Nyxian offered, feigned disappointment laced in his tone, "that's not entirely true, is it?" His slow smile sharpened. "You were Draevok's pawn in seducing the prince, but he's a crafty sort, isn't he?" His golden eyes gleamed with something cruel. "He will find a way to kill the royal family. We already know he has Garron and countless others in his employ."

A breath wavered between her lips.

No.

That wasn't true. It couldn't be.

But—could she truly say that?

Draevok was relentless, patient, methodical. He had been planning this coup for years, long before she was ever part of it. If not her, then another woman. If not through seduction, then through another means. He would succeed, with or without her.

And then—who would be there to protect Zakar? If she wasn't there to stop Draevok, to stop Garron—Zakar would die. Strong as he was, he was not yet the Master of the Arcane. He would never become the Master of the Arcane.

Nyxian sighed, stepping aside with an exaggerated flick of his wrist. "Ah well," he mused, as if the outcome were little more than a passing curiosity. "At least this way, you get to save yourself from your own guilt."

His voice shifted, growing almost wistful. "Though I imagine things will unfold just as they did before. You'll return to your little cottage beneath the Mist, and you'll die—slowly, quietly."

He paused, tilting his head. "Unless, of course, you manage to find the old Arcane Master, beg for his cursed book, and convince him to make you his apprentice. I'm sure that will be nice and simple."

A sinking weight dragged through her gut as she looked past him, toward the darkened horizon, the dense forests beyond where she could disappear into nothingness.

"Don't you worry about him," Nyxian continued, his smirk widening. "It's not like you can tell him his fate. If you did, he'd likely have you executed." His voice lowered, smooth as honey, yet venomous. "Your only real choice here is the one you're making."

Myrithia took a deep breath, closing her eyes with finality. Then, muttering a curse under her breath, her magic flickered at her fingertips, silver light coiling in her palms. In an instant, she vanished.

She reappeared in the corridor she had fled from, the echo of her own heartbeat pounding in her ears.

Footsteps.

She barely had a moment to brace herself before a familiar voice hissed through the dimly lit hall.

"Chantress."

Then he was there—at her back, his fingers clamping around her arm in a firm grip, wrenching her around to face him.

"You are a sorceress," Zakar said, his voice a low, venomous growl, his green eyes ablaze with something raw. "And whatever game you think you are playing with me—"

"You can imprison me tonight," she interrupted, voice flat, every word chosen with care. She forced them out despite every instinct in her body screaming at her to run, to escape, to disappear before it was too late. His father, the reigning King of Valthoria, did not allow magic-users to be free in this world. They either served him or they were brought to death. "You can have me executed by morning if it pleases you," she added, her voice barely audible in the darkened corridor.

The fury in Zakar's expression flickered. A moment of hesitation. The briefest glimpse of uncertainty. "I—" he faltered, his grip on her arm tightening.

She met his gaze with cold, implacable determination. "I was sent to seduce you," she said plainly, her voice hollow, barely recognizing it as her own. "And in due time, lead you to your death."

His hold on her tensed, his whole body going rigid.

She forced herself to continue.

"Garron," she bit out, the name like poison on her tongue, "your friend—he is aligned with my master. And he, along with many others, are conspiring for the death of the royal family."

Shock flickered across his face. Disbelief. But she pressed on, knowing that if she faltered now, if she let fear steal the words from her lips, she would lose everything.

"If you keep me alive," she said, her voice steady despite the ache in her chest, "I will point out every dissenter. You will live. But if you have me killed too soon, if you ignore my warnings," she swallowed, her breath trembling, "Draevok *will* kill you after he kills me. You have my word on that."

A silence fell between them, heavy and suffocating.

Her heart clenched, agony lancing through her.

"And when my usefulness has run out," she finished quietly, her voice barely more than a whisper, "you may dispose of me as you wish."

Her blue eyes burned with regret, with something deeper, something unspoken.

And still, she held his gaze.

Zakar's grip remained firm around her wrist, his gaze sharp with disbelief. His breath came slow and measured, as if he were attempting to piece together a puzzle that shouldn't exist.

"You expect me to believe this?" he murmured, his tone tightly controlled.

She didn't answer.

He exhaled, his free hand dragging through his hair before his expression hardened once more. "Then I'll take you to the dungeons," he decided, his voice low. "You will answer my questions in full. And if I find even a sliver of deception—" His grip tightened slightly, "—I will have your head for it."

She didn't resist as he tugged her along, his stride purposeful, his mind clearly working through the implications of her words. The weight of everything pressed down on her chest, the reality of what she had done, of what she had just admitted.

But before they had taken more than a few steps, she caught a flicker of movement beside her.

Nyxian.

He walked leisurely at her side, unseen by Zakar, his golden eyes glittering with amusement. He smirked, giving her a knowing glance before lifting his hand.

A sharp snap of his fingers.

The world collapsed.

The grand marble halls, the chandeliers overhead, the music in the distant ballroom—all of it vanished in an instant.

Darkness.

Then, sensation.

Cold. Wet. Heavy.

The weight of rain-soaked fabric clung to her body, her breath sharp as she gasped, blinking against the sudden onslaught of reality. The storm still raged overhead, the scent of damp earth filling her lungs.

She wasn't in the palace anymore.

She stood alone in a small clearing of a forest, mud clinging to her boots, her chemise and pants damp and clinging to her skin.

Was she still within the Hollow Mist? Still trapped?

Nyxian was gone.

And the only sound was the relentless downpour, hammering against the canopy above.

CHAPTER 49

Myrithia

The rain had softened to a steady patter, but the chill still clung to Myrithia's skin as she stood at the base of the mountain, her arms wrapped tightly around herself. The sky was a muted gray, casting the landscape in an eerie stillness, save for the occasional rustle of wind through the trees. She shifted uneasily, exhaling a shaky breath, her pulse thrumming with uncertainty.

Had she won?

Before she could dwell on the thought, Nyxian materialized beside her with a lazy stretch, his sudden presence jolting her.

"Well, my fascinating little mortal," he said, his voice carrying its usual note of amusement. "Congratulations."

A snap of his fingers, and a horse appeared beside him, standing obediently as though it had been waiting all along.

"You've won my game," he continued smoothly, dusting off the crimson sleeve of his tunic as if this were all terribly mundane. "And now you're free to go."

Myrithia's body tensed. She studied him warily, waiting for the trick, the catch—the inevitable twist. Her heart skittered against her ribs, and her voice was slow when she finally spoke.

"The tome."

Nyxian clicked his tongue in mock disappointment. "Oh, that's right."

With a flick of his wrist, the air between them shimmered, and in an instant, the Syltharic Tome took shape in his outstretched hands.

The book was ancient, bound in weathered black leather that seemed impossibly dark, as if it drank in the light. Silver filigree sprawled across the cover in elaborate symbols that pulsed with an eerie glow, as if the magic within was alive, restless. A heavy clasp, adorned with an obsidian gem, kept the book sealed, and the very air around it seemed to hum with latent power.

Myrithia hesitated, then cautiously reached for it. The moment her fingers brushed the leather, a dark energy rippled up her arm, sending a cold shudder through her spine. It felt… wrong. Like something that shouldn't be touched, shouldn't be wielded. But still, she held it tight.

Slowly, her gaze lifted back to Nyxian. "And Zakar?"

The god tilted his head, feigning mild surprise. "Oh? Did you want him too?" A smirk played at the edges of his lips, his golden eyes gleaming with mischief. "I would've thought—since you're now free and all—you'd want to get a head start on your life anew."

Her brow furrowed. "I'm free? How do you mean?"

Nyxian sighed as if bored with the question, waving his hand in a flourish. "I voided your contract for you, as promised." He gave an exaggerated nod of acknowledgment. "You're welcome."

Myrithia inhaled sharply, something uncoiling in her chest, a tightness she hadn't realized she'd been carrying. A strange, unbidden smile touched her lips, disarming even herself.

"And he…" she hesitated, voice barely above a whisper. "He will be alright?"

Nyxian chuckled, rolling his eyes. "Oh, stop your needless worrying." Another careless wave of his hand. "He's fine. Alive and well. Soon, he'll be on his way." His smirk returned, sharper now. "And I suggest you take advantage of this time and put some distance between you both. Maybe go look for your countercurse, hm?"

Nyxian's smirk deepened as he watched her gaze drop to the book in her hands, her fingers tightening around the worn leather.

"The power he was sharing with me," she started hesitantly,

her voice barely above a whisper. "Is it—"

"Gone?" He finished smoothly, his golden eyes gleaming. "Yes, you no longer have access to it." A performative sigh slipped from him as he tilted his head. "So, best be hurrying along with your book, and use your magic sparingly in the meantime. Once you find your cure, you should be able to live freely, without a care in the world."

Freely.

The word should have felt like salvation, but all it did was stir something uneasy in her chest. A hollow, sinking dread that twisted against her ribs.

She was alone now. Truly alone.

Doubt crept in, gnawing at the edges of her mind, insistent and unrelenting. Could she really do this? Could she truly imagine a life without him—a life stripped of the fire in his touch, the pull of those sharp green eyes that left her breathless and bare? Would that even be freedom? Or just another kind of prison—one where she spent forever running from what she couldn't forget?

As if sensing the turmoil unraveling inside her, Nyxian clicked his tongue and mused aloud, "You will never be his wife, Myrithia."

Her breath stalled, emotion tightening her throat, but she didn't look at him.

He grinned, slow and knowing, stepping closer, his voice dropping into a velvet purr. "You know this in your soul, do you not? He wants a slave. A plaything. A life of vengeance acted out upon the one who betrayed him."

The words sliced through her, carving deeper than she had expected. But they weren't lies, were they? No different than the man who had loathed her for five years, who had promised her servitude and nothing more.

The same Zakar who had told her, just moments ago, that he would drag her to the dungeon without a second thought.

Nyxian gave a soft, almost sympathetic sigh. "You know now, don't you?" He murmured, watching her with feigned concern, his eyes alight with amusement. "He will never forgive you. And why would he?"

She inhaled sharply, but it did nothing to quell the ice spreading through her veins.

"You led a murderer to his father," Nyxian continued, his words gentle, but merciless. "You allowed his best friend to deceive him time and again. You knowingly played a pivotal role in the destruction of his throne, his birthright." He leaned in slightly, the final blow slipping past his lips like silk. "Do you truly believe he would ever marry someone like that?"

Tears burned hot behind her eyes, glossing her vision, blurring the edges of the world.

No.

He was right.

She forced herself to swallow the lump in her throat, her voice hoarse when she finally answered, "No, I don't think he ever would."

Nyxian smiled, clasping his hands behind his back, utterly indifferent to the storm of emotions tightening in her chest. "Well, then, that's settled. Be on your way." He gestured lazily to the horse beside him. "I'll even grant you a head start and release you close to Farenvayle Forest. Be mindful of the road ahead."

She nodded, the weight of everything pressing down on her, making her feel strangely... gray. Hollow.

"The goddess," she said, startled by the sound of her own voice breaking the stillness. She glanced at him, hesitating only for a moment before continuing. "Could you tell me more about her?"

Nyxian's ever-present smile remained, though dimmed, as he stared back at her.

"You said you'd answer any questions I had after I won," she reminded him, her voice low, respectful. "You said I resemble her. I'd like to know more. What was her name?"

"She's dead," he said curtly, his eyes cold despite the ghost of a smirk. "No sense in learning about a dead goddess."

"But for a moment, you thought she was alive, didn't you?" she pressed. "When you first saw me?"

His expression didn't waver. "This was not the first time I have seen you, Myrithia."

She frowned. "What?"

He folded his arms across his chest. "You've been living

beneath the mist for the better part of five years. Do you really think I wouldn't have peered past your little charms and enchantments?"

A chill ran through her. She hardly knew what to make of that. "So you've known me all this time?"

His gaze held something unreadable, something that resonated deep within her—like the whispers in the mist. "I have known you for a very, very long time."

The words settled into her bones, an eerie echo threading through her soul.

"When you were born, you were feared." His voice was quieter now, almost distant. "So much so that you were abandoned to die. I couldn't let that happen, of course."

The mist thickened around her, its whispers curling closer, wrapping around her like unseen hands. She swallowed hard, barely able to process what she was hearing. "You saved me?"

Nyxian let out a soft laugh, shaking his head. "I'm not your savior, Myrithia." He tilted his head slightly, watching her reaction. "And I didn't look out for you because I'm a kind man." His lips twitched into the barest smirk. "In fact, if I had believed— even for a moment—that you truly were her… let's just say your life would have turned out very differently."

Unease prickled down her spine, and she took a small, instinctive step back. "Could you at least tell me her name?"

For a moment, she thought he might leave her in silence, letting the question hang between them, unanswered. He didn't like this goddess—that much was clear.

Just as she began to accept the quiet as his only response, he finally spoke.

"Sylara."

The name fell from his tongue like a melody, smooth and effortless.

She loved the sound of it. It lingered in the air, soft yet powerful, stirring something deep within her. But she didn't dare press him further. His patience was thinning by the second, a tension coiling beneath his otherwise lazy demeanor. She should go— before she tested him any further. Reaching for the reins, she hesitated, stealing one last look at the god.

"Did you play a game with Zakar too?"

He let out a soft chuckle, seemingly pleased with the topic change. "Yes, yes, I did."

A flicker of concern crossed her features. "And did he win?"

Nyxian sighed, his expression masked, whatever he was thinking hidden behind a placid stare. "That remains to be seen." Then, after a pause, he looked back at her with a sly grin. "But either way, he'll be just fine. He is an Arcane Master, after all. And such fun, too."

Her fingers tightened around the leather straps. "You promise he's well? That he's free?"

He let out a long-suffering sigh, waving her off like a bothersome child. "Would you stop worrying? I'm merely stalling him at the moment. Giving you time to make your grand escape. Please don't waste this generous opportunity I've given you."

Her brows knitted together, irritation creeping through the haze of her emotions. "You promise?"

At that, his golden eyes darkened, the runes surrounding them flickering with something ancient, something that sent a cold pulse of unease down her spine.

"I must ask you," he murmured, his voice like silk laced with steel, "to stop questioning me."

She swallowed, but he wasn't finished.

"He is your former master, is he not? If you are so concerned for him, then by all means... stay." His smirk curled, cruel and knowing. "Await your chains. Waste your freedom. Waste your future as his plaything."

A sharp breath pushed past her lips, and she forced herself to steel her spine, squaring her shoulders, though she still wisely took a step back.

Without another word, she turned and mounted the horse, the leather creaking softly beneath her as she swung her leg over the saddle. Her grip tightened around the reins, knuckles paling, as if grounding herself in the weight of her decision.

One last glance.

She cast her gaze past Nyxian, to the mist looming in the distance, to the trees and everything she was leaving behind. A whisper of doubt formed in her chest, but she shoved it down.

THE ARCANE BARGAIN

There was no future for her with him. No children. No little house. No warm, quiet life filled with stolen laughter and soft touches.

This was the only way.

With a kick, she urged the horse forward, riding hard into the night, desperately hoping she had made the right choice.

CHAPTER 50

Zakar

Nyxian swirled the wine in his goblet, tipping it lazily, watching the deep red liquid catch the firelight as if it were the most fascinating thing in the world. The room was still, eerily so, and Zakar had no way of knowing how much time had passed in their silence.

Then, finally Nyxian spoke.

"Would you like to hear a story?" he mused, his gaze flicking toward Zakar, amber eyes glinting with firelight.

Zakar wasn't in the mood for riddles. He had no time to waste. But this was a god, and for now, he was trapped in this illusion of a cabin, forced to endure whatever game Nyxian had decided to play.

He exhaled slowly, betraying none of his irritation. "I suppose that's a fine way to pass the time."

Nyxian chuckled, tilting his goblet as if already amused by what was to come.

Then, as if summoned, the door creaked open.

A figure stepped through. Dressed in opulent black robes, lined with intricate silver runes, his presence was unmistakable.

Zakar's blood turned molten. His magic surged to his fingertips as he shot to his feet, his voice sharp as a blade.

"Draevok." The name left his lips like a curse.

And yet—there was no reaction.

Draevok walked toward him, completely unbothered. No sign of recognition. No acknowledgment. Then, just as easily, he walked right through him.

Zakar stilled, a sharp pulse of confusion twisting through him.

"It's a memory," Nyxian spoke with idle amusement, still seated, still utterly at ease, watching from his chair as if this were a casual evening of entertainment. He swirled his goblet, unmoved by the sudden weight pressing down on the room. "Her memory, specifically."

Zakar turned back just in time to see Draevok moving through the dimly lit cottage, his steps purposeful as he reached a small, closed door. He pushed it open. Inside, Myrithia stood waiting. She was wearing a gown fit for royalty, the same one she had worn the night she left him. The deep crimson fabric caught the dim candlelight, draping over her form with regal elegance—and yet, she looked small. Fragile.

Her tear-streaked face lifted, her eyes locking onto Draevok, wide with pleading trepidation. "I'm sorry, I couldn't do it." Her voice shook. "I sent him away."

Zakar felt something in his chest lurch, though he didn't know what.

Draevok went still for a moment, and then suddenly his rage ignited. The air crackled violently, black energy seething from his form, coiling around the room like a living thing. Myrithia staggered back, a small whimper escaping her lips.

He had never seen her cower before. *Never*. And yet, here she was—terrified. She wasn't just wary of Draevok. She wasn't just fearing punishment. She was petrified of him.

"I knew you were useless," Draevok sneered, his tone like venom, "but I didn't know you were also that stupid."

Myrithia flinched but held her ground, her voice trembling as she desperately tried to reason with him. "He isn't like his father," she whispered. "He wouldn't be a threat to you. He's a good man—"

Draevok's hand lashed out. The slap cracked through the air like a whip, the force of it snapping her head to the side.

Zakar's rage lanced through him.

Myrithia crumpled, the impact sending her sprawling to the

floor. A small, pained cry escaped her lips as the shockwave of the blow rattled through her bones. She didn't have time to recover.

Draevok loomed over her, his expression dark with unforgiving fury. "Fool!" he spat. "He is the heir to the throne! My throne! If he lives, he will never stop pursuing it!"

Zakar's fists clenched uselessly at his sides. He couldn't touch Draevok. Couldn't break him for what he had just done. He could only watch.

Watch as Myrithia crumpled, her body curling inward, her hands gripping the skirts of her gown as she shrank beneath Draevok's shadow.

Zakar's pulse roared in his ears. His magic flared, every muscle in his body aching to do something, to intervene, to strike Draevok down where he stood. But he couldn't. Because, this was already written. This had already happened.

"What reason could you possibly have had to let him go?" Draevok demanded, his voice sharp as a blade, his towering form casting her in shadow.

Myrithia looked up at him weakly, her breath coming in broken gasps, blood slipping from her split lip where his ring had torn through her skin. Her silence only stoked his fury.

"Answer me!" Draevok growled.

A tremor passed through her, but she did not flinch. Instead, her lips parted, and with soft, raw finality, she whispered, "Because I love him."

Zakar froze.

The words slammed into him, ripping the breath from his lungs. If he were not here to witness it, he would have mocked her confession. He would have thought it a cruel joke, another manipulation. But not now. Not *this*. Not when she lay battered at her master's feet, professing a truth that should have gotten her killed the moment it left her lips.

Draevok's laugh was a brutal, grating thing, dark with disbelief and sadistic amusement.

"You love him?" he repeated mockingly, his mouth curling in disgust before he barked a sharp, angry obscenity.

Myrithia made a soft sound—not quite a sob, but something fragile, something that made Zakar's skin crawl. She wasn't begging or pleading for mercy. She was waiting for the next blow. Waiting for punishment, like an *obedient slave*.

Grief punched through Zakar's center like a blow. He hated it. He hated the taste of it, the reality of it, the sheer injustice of it.

She had been a slave her entire life—used, bartered, owned—and even now, after everything, she had only traded one cage for another. She had tried to escape, tried to fight, had risked everything to save the man she loved, only to be met with hatred, chains, and betrayal.

His hatred. His chains. His betrayal. His chest heaved, thick with revulsion, fury—disgust.

But he wasn't sure who he hated more: Draevok... Or *himself*.

"You know what?" Draevok sneered. "Perhaps you won't be so useless after all." He lunged, yanking her upright by the arm, ignoring the sharp, pained gasp that slipped from her lips.

"I will turn you into an example." His grip tightened, his voice changing into something vicious, gleeful. "When I parade you before the crowd—when your head rolls lifeless from the dais—they will know." He leaned in, his breath hot with malice. "They will know that I am not to be disobeyed."

A frightened sound escaped her as she wrenched free, silver sparks snapping from her fingertips.

In the blink of an eye, she vanished, reappearing near the door—her breathing ragged, her gaze fixed on the wall. But Zakar stood there—directly in her line of sight. She was looking through him, her expression a war between terror and defiance.

"Your impudence!" Draevok snarled, rounding on her. "You would dare to evade punishment?"

She flinched, eyes squeezing shut, her body coiled tight with indecision. Zakar saw it—the fracture between old habits of obedience and the burning instinct to run.

Draevok felt it too. His sneer deepened as he stalked toward her, his movements calm and exact. "If you dare to flee, Myrithia," he taunted, his voice thick with cruel amusement, "you know what will happen to you."

She stood frozen, her breaths coming fast, panicked.

"I will find you," he continued. "And your suffering will be slow. Painful. Absolute." He stopped just feet from her, his dark eyes glittering with the promise of violence. "But if you accept your fate, I will be merciful." He spread his arms in a grand, exaggerated gesture of false generosity. "Your death will be brutal, but quick."

Zakar's rage boiled over. Draevok had to suffer. Needed to suffer.

But before he could even process his fury, Myrithia moved. Her eyes snapped open, fever-bright, a shuddering breath slipping past her lips. Her voice came steady and unshaken. "Goodbye, Draevok."

Silver glittered in the air as she vanished, leaving behind nothing but the static hum of expelled magic.

And then the scene collapsed. The walls of the memory disintegrated, bleeding into nothingness, leaving Zakar standing alone in the suffocating dark.

"A bit of a sad story," Nyxian mused, his voice now behind him, too smooth, too amused. "But I do hope it was enlightening."

Zakar turned sharply, muscles taut, but the god only smirked, sipping from his goblet as if they had simply finished watching a theatrical performance.

"She never really stood a chance," Nyxian continued, tilting his head as though the thought delighted him. "He unleashed a curse on her after that, you know. Easy enough, considering he had a vial of her blood with which to weave his little hex."

He sighed, shaking his head with mock sympathy. "So sad."

Zakar's hands flexed at his sides, his magic coiling hot beneath his skin. He didn't care for Nyxian's amusement or for his flippant tone. He didn't care for anything except one thing.

He turned to face the god fully, his voice low, unyielding, absolute.

"I want to see her. Give her to me."

CHAPTER 51

Zakar

"So demanding, Arcane Master," Nyxian mused, laughter threading through his words, smooth and unbothered. His golden eyes glittered, sharp with delight. "Tell me—are you more displeased with me, or with yourself at this moment?"

Zakar's glare hardened, turning glacial. "I want to see her. Has she won your game?"

Nyxian's smile barely lifted, quiet and condescending, like a parent humoring a petulant child. "Yes, she has. But, before we get to that, you will likely want what you came here for."

With a snap of his fingers, the world around them reformed into a cold, cavernous space. A single source of light illuminated the chamber—an enchanted, eerie glow that pulsed over a stone slab at the center of the room.

Zakar's boots echoed against the stone floor as he stepped forward, his gaze narrowing at the sight before him.

Master Sorien lay motionless atop the slab, his body preserved by ancient magic, as though he had only just closed his eyes. Clutched in his lifeless arms, bound tightly against his chest, was the Syltharic Tome, held not like a mere relic, but as if it were something precious, sacred. The very source of chaos, revered even in death.

He was finally here. Deep within the mountain, within the tomb that had sealed away the former Master of the Arcane. This was the end of their journey. This was the book that Myrithia had risked everything for. The Nythera he had borrowed from Calveren was supposed to have navigated through every charm and seal upon this place, and yet this god had led him here with a literal snap of his fingers.

Zakar reached for the book, but Nyxian's voice sliced through the silence.

"It won't heal her." His tone was mild, indifferent, as though he had simply mentioned the weather.

Zakar's hand stilled. He turned, his gaze sharp. "She told me there was a counter-curse within it."

"She *hoped* there would be a counter-curse within it," Nyxian corrected, his voice silk over glass, his expression laced with indulgent condescension. "Hope is such a fragile thing, isn't it?"

A slow, simmering fury began to coil within Zakar's chest. The god of mischief had known from the start that the book was useless. And still, he had entertained himself, toyed with them, dangled false hope in front of Myrithia like a scrap of food to a starving beast.

Zakar's fingers twitched, emerald magic crackling at his fingertips. "Then tell me, oh *powerful one*," he bit out, his voice edged with venom, "what will heal her curse?"

Nyxian grinned, flashing white teeth. "Oh, there is no spell. No talisman. No ancient blood magic that will undo what has been done." He leaned against the slab as though they were merely discussing a trivial matter.

Zakar's patience was razor-thin, his jaw tight as he took another measured step forward. "I sat through your little game, and she won. You know what we came here for. I am not leaving until I have what will free her from her curse."

Nyxian sighed as if burdened by the conversation, idly inspecting his nails. "You will leave when I say you can. And I could keep you here a very *long* time," he said darkly. His golden eyes flicked toward Sorien's lifeless body. "But at least you'll have good company." He gestured toward the corpse with a lazy wave. "Perhaps he'll keep you entertained." He smirked, adding, "Or, if that fails, you can always read a *book*."

A pulse of emerald energy crackled at Zakar's fingertips,

barely restrained. His voice was low, edged with threat. "Do not toy with me, Nyxian. I will have what I came here for."

Nyxian met his gaze, entirely unfazed, his smirk growing. "Oh, would I ever toy with *you*?"

Zakar took another step, his magic thrumming at his skin, pushing against the very air around them. "You are an ethereal being, with access to magic beyond mortal comprehension. You're telling me there is nothing that can undo a curse cast by a mere man?"

Nyxian's smirk held steady, but a flicker of patronizing delight danced behind his eyes.

And then, he chuckled. Low. Amused. Predatory.

"Oh, Arcane Master," he purred, tilting his head as if considering something. "You're finally asking the right questions." He let out a long exhale and ran his hand through his hair. "Draevok *is* a mere man. And since that is all he is, that's good news for you. You can kill him."

Zakar clenched his jaw. "I had already planned to do so. Are you telling me that the only way to break the curse is to kill the one who cursed her?"

Nyxian chuckled, amused. "Yes, that is precisely what I'm saying. And how convenient that is for you, since it already aligns so well with your aims. All you'll need is a certain fatal weapon, and all your goals will be attained."

The god began to pace slowly, trailing his fingers over the cold stone walls of the tomb. "Draevok is quite a vindictive sort. Any curse he inflicts upon another is quite powerful, and will only result in a painful, slow demise." His golden gaze flicked toward Zakar, a cruel smile touching his lips. "It's a wonder Myrithia has lasted this long. Isn't it?"

A cold thread of unease coiled through Zakar's spine. Myrithia had lived in Farenvayle Forest, which had been mostly swallowed by the Hollow Mist, receding and returning as it willed for nearly five years. He had always known that. The Mist was something he had tracked closely, watching as it shifted over the land, swallowing villages, dissolving from the map like ink bleeding into water. Yet the cottage she had hidden in had remained untouched, an island in an otherwise devoured landscape. He had suspected it was due to her own enchantments, but...

His gaze sharpened.

"You protected her?" Zakar asked, his voice low.

Nyxian exhaled an amused breath, shaking his head. "Please, I am not one for sentiment." He turned, glancing toward the tome in Sorien's lifeless grasp. "I do not control the Mist in the way you might think. I go where it leads, and I play with whatever mortals are foolish enough to be caught within."

"But not Myrithia," Zakar pressed, his voice like steel.

Nyxian's smirk deepened. "What can I say? She gained my interest."

Zakar's expression darkened.

Nyxian continued idly, pacing the length of the tomb as if this conversation was of little consequence to him—already shifting the topic.

"If you want Draevok's death and Myrithia's subsequent cure, then..."

With a flick of his wrist, an object materialized in his grasp—sleek, black, humming with dark energy.

A dagger.

Zakar's gaze flicked to it, his brows furrowing. The air around the blade *hissed*, the magic within it twisting, writhing, *hungry*.

Nyxian turned it over in his palm, his golden eyes glinting with something eerily close to satisfaction.

"This will do quite nicely." His voice was smooth, each word carefully measured. "A weapon crafted of *Emberstone* will strip him of power the moment it pierces him, nullifying his curses, severing his magic as he dies. And, in turn..." He smiled faintly. "It will set your little Chantress free from an untimely death."

Zakar stepped forward, his gaze never leaving the dagger.

"And you're just going to *give* this to me?" he asked coolly. "And then what?"

Nyxian's grin widened. "Then I'll let you go. You can't kill him if you're stuck here, can you?" He tilted his head, as if amused by the very idea. "And we *certainly* can't let your songbird die now, can we?"

Zakar's jaw tightened. The question gnawed at him, sharp and unrelenting.

"What's your interest in Myrithia?" His tone was measured, but there was an edge to it, a quiet demand. He didn't expect honesty from a god, but something in him *needed* to ask.

Nyxian chuckled, shaking his head as if the answer were obvious.

"I'm not interested in *her*, per se," he corrected smoothly. "But rather, in her *past*." He lifted his gaze, meeting Zakar's with something unreadable. "And also... in her *future*."

A muscle in Zakar's jaw twitched.

He didn't like the sound of that.

A god taking interest in a mortal was *never* a good thing. And he sure as hell didn't want Myrithia's future tangled in whatever whims Nyxian was entertaining.

The god twirled the dagger lazily between his fingers.

"I have lived a *very* long time, Arcane Master," he mused. "And if there is one game I have enjoyed above all others, it is this one. *You* and *Myrithia*." He exhaled as if recalling something fond. "You two have been my greatest source of amusement."

Zakar's fingers curled at his sides.

Gods playing with mortals—*toying* with them, using them for their own entertainment—was nothing new.

But this?

They had been nothing more than a diversion to him.

Nyxian's smile was slow, sharp—*cruel*.

"Now," he murmured, lifting a hand. Magic shimmered, shifting the dagger from his palm to Zakar's. "Take your weapon." His golden eyes gleamed with something knowing, something wicked. "And do try to make this interesting."

Zakar exhaled sharply, a dismissive sound under his breath, before sheathing the weapon at his hip.

The god snapped his fingers, and the world shifted around them in an instant. Gone was the tomb, the eerie stillness of Sorien's resting place. Now, Zakar stood in the small clearing of a forest, the dark night sky stretching endlessly above him, the scent of freshly fallen rain lingering thick in the warm air.

His head turned sharply toward Nyxian, his patience waning. "You're forgetting something."

"Am I?" Nyxian's expression was an exaggerated mask of

contrition, his golden eyes gleaming with mischief.

Zakar faced him fully, his gaze piercing and unwavering. "Where is she?"

"Oh," Nyxian exhaled, his tone shifting into a mockery of sympathy. "Yes, about that..."

"You said—" Zakar began, but the god lifted a hand, silencing him with a single look.

"What we agreed upon," Nyxian corrected smoothly, "was that you would have the tome, and that she would be free to go if she won my game." He tilted his head, his smile sharpening. "You, of course, rejected the tome. But as promised, she *is* free."

Zakar's jaw locked, fury tightening in his chest.

"And she has gone, rest assured," Nyxian added, his voice laced with casual amusement.

A slow, seething rage built within him. "Where," Zakar asked through gritted teeth, his voice dangerously low, "has she gone?"

Nyxian clicked his tongue, feigning thoughtfulness before offering a lazy shrug. "Is it really your concern anymore?"

"She is mine." Zakar's voice cut through the air like steel. "Of course, she is my concern."

"No," Nyxian corrected, his expression shifting, his gaze filled with something that almost resembled pity. "No, she is not your slave anymore." He let the words settle between them before delivering the final blow with a devilish grin. "As part of our agreement—she and I made—I granted her freedom. From you."

Zakar went still, as though something had struck him.

Nyxian's grin widened. "So sorry about that."

Zakar's patience snapped like a frayed string pulled to its end. Magic crackled up his arms as fury rolled through him in waves, dark and seething. "You have overstepped, god."

Seemingly thrilled by the reaction, Nyxian grinned wider. "No, I'm merely doing what you don't have the strength to do."

"And what is that, exactly?" Zakar bit out, his voice a blade's edge.

"Setting your dearest love free." Nyxian's tone was light, almost playful, but the meaning behind it was a vicious twist of the knife. "Letting her choose for herself what she truly wants. And apparently, that is a life without you."

At his sides, his fingers stirred, the quiet thrum of power alive beneath his skin. "You had no right to do that. My bond with her was keeping her alive. You have given her a death sentence!"

"You will not dictate the rules of my game, Arcane Master," Nyxian said smoothly, the runes around his eyes pulsing with energy, his expression dark but utterly delighted. "She made her choice."

"You have doomed her." Zakar's words came low, growled between his teeth, each syllable brimming with barely contained wrath.

"Oh, don't be so dramatic. I did give her the tome, or at least a *replica* of it. Though, more importantly, I've given her enough protection to keep her alive for another week. Surely it won't take you *that* long to kill Draevok." Nyxian remarked, tilting his head as if inspecting Zakar like a particularly amusing specimen. "Tell me, are you more enraged that I set your slave free, or that the love of your life simply doesn't want you?"

Zakar stepped forward, close enough to feel the hum of Nyxian's energy licking at his skin like static. He knew better than to engage, knew he was outmatched, but his fury was near blinding.

"Where is she?" he demanded, his voice a lethal promise

Nyxian laughed, low and rich with amusement, utterly unfazed by the storm raging in front of him. "By now?" He tapped his chin, considering. Then he smirked. "Who knows?"

Zakar turned sharply, his fury manifesting in the surge of magic that lashed from his palms like snapping tethers, striking the earth with crackling force. The ground trembled beneath the weight of his will as his Sentinels coiled up from the darkness, their forms solidifying from shifting tendrils of black mist. Hollowed sockets gleamed with eerie blue fire, their skeletal figures draped in the frayed remnants of spectral cloaks, awaiting his command.

"Find her," he ordered, his voice a razor's edge, his green-lit eyes burning with rage and possession.

In perfect, soundless unison, the wraiths bowed their heads, then dissolved into the night like shadows torn from reality, vanishing into the trees with unnatural speed.

Behind him, a rich, velvety laugh filled the air. He didn't turn.

THE ARCANE BARGAIN

He refused.

"Oh, this is exquisite," Nyxian mused, his voice dripping with satisfaction. "A little delicious drama before the grand finale." He sighed, mock wistful. "You two really have been my favorite mortals in ages."

Zakar clenched his jaw, forcing his eyes to remain fixed ahead, scanning the dense woods. He might no longer feel Myrithia through their connection, might no longer track the pulse of his power through her veins, but he would find her. He had found her once before. He would do it again.

Without another word, he stormed forward, vanishing into the thick shadows of the forest, his cloak snapping behind him. The god's laughter lingered in the air, a chilling melody fading into the night as Zakar disappeared into the hunt.

CHAPTER 52
Myrithia

The wind bit at her skin, the night air thick with the remnants of the storm as she rode deeper into the unknown. It had been hours since the god had granted her freedom, hours since she had left everything behind.

She had cried at first. Silent, bitter tears that streaked her face as she let the wind dry them away. But now there was nothing left to feel except exhaustion.

Her thighs ached from riding, her body sluggish with weariness. Every muscle burned, her magic drained from the day's relentless torment. She needed to stop. Just for a while. Just long enough to rest.

That was when she saw it.

The manor loomed in the distance, a monstrous silhouette against the darkened sky. Abandoned, decayed, half-swallowed by the forest, its windows stared like hollow, vacant eyes. Ivy strangled the stone, wrapping the towers in a slow, suffocating death.

She slowed her horse, unease prickling along her spine. It had been left to ruin. No firelight. No signs of life. But it would be a shelter until the morning. A risk, but a calculated one.

She nudged her horse forward, intending to at least shelter under the broken archway leading toward the entrance. She was too exposed here. The Mist may have been behind her, but Zakar would not be far.

Then, the ground trembled.

A sickening shift, like the earth exhaling beneath her.

Her horse snorted violently, muscles locking as the air grew deathly cold.

A whisper.

No, not one. Many.

Breathy, fractured voices curling through the night, slithering past her ears—words she couldn't understand, but could feel in the marrow of her bones.

She turned, pulse hammering.

Black smoke coiled up from the ground, swirling like mist before hardening—solidifying. Shadows took form. Long, skeletal limbs. Tattered black robes hanging like decayed funeral shrouds.

Her breath strangled in her throat.

They rose around her, their glowing blue eyes burning from the depths of their skulls, fixed unwaveringly on her.

Sentinels.

Zakar's protectors. His undying shadows.

Her horse screamed, rearing back in terror.

"Easy!" Myrithia clutched the reins, heart hammering—

The beast bucked hard.

Her body slammed into the earth, the wind knocked from her lungs as she tumbled, pain exploding across her side.

Dirt and rain matted her skin, but she barely had time to register the impact before her horse fled, hooves pounding against the earth as it vanished into the night.

No. No, no, no—

A low voice rippled through the dark.

"Myra."

Her blood turned to ice.

She whirled onto her knees, panting, scrambling back as her wide eyes locked onto the figure now standing just beyond the Sentinels.

Zakar.

Towering. Unyielding. The storm winds lashing through his black hair, his emerald eyes burning.

He was silent and still. His gaze pierced through her, cutting through the space between them like a sharpened blade. The sentinels did not touch her, did not move—but they waited. Waited for his command.

His voice was cold, absolute.

"Why did you run away, Myra?"

Her stomach plummeted.

She was trapped.

"Zakar, please understand, I—"

"Oh, I understand." His voice was a blade, cutting through her plea before it could fully form.

His stride was slow, measured, the storm-lit night wrapping him in shadow and emerald fire as he advanced on her. The hunter closing in.

"You thought you could gain your freedom from that impish god, but your freedom was never *his* to give."

Myrithia's breath shuddered as she forced herself upright. The weight of his presence threatened to swallow her whole.

"I cannot live as a slave to you forever, Zakar!" she snapped, her voice raw, every ounce of pain, of exhaustion, breaking free.

He was in front of her now, towering, merciless in his claim.

"You must," he said simply, his voice forged in iron and finality. "It was our bargain that was keeping you alive. So you must bear it a little longer."

Rage flared through her like wildfire, twisting through the pain that had been festering inside her for too long.

"I am *free*, Zakar!"

His lips twitched, his jaw tightening.

Then—he moved.

His fingers closed around her wrist, yanking her toward him so fast her breath left her in a soft gasp. His body was heat and dominance, a force as immovable as the storm itself.

Her chest rose hard against his, their anger sizzling between them like lightning in a bottle.

"A god may have severed our bond, but you still made a vow to me," he murmured, his voice like dark velvet, laced with something primal. His grip tightened. "You will honor it."

"You may want my obedience," she sneered, voice shaking,

hands trembling as they curled into fists, "but you can wait for an eternity."

His expression darkened.

"No," he murmured, his grip loosening just enough to send a shiver down her spine. "I will simply take it." Before she could react, his lips found hers—an explosion of fire and fury, heat and hunger. His hands were possessive, framing her jaw and throat, fingers threading through her damp silver hair as he pulled her closer, crushing her against him.

She fought at first.

Not to escape—but because she wanted to consume him just as he was consuming her.

Her hands clawed at him, fingers digging into his shoulders, his chest, desperate for purchase, for control—as if she could tame the storm that had been building between them for five years.

His tongue brushed against hers, a hot, merciless demand, and her resolve shattered like glass.

She moaned into his mouth, and he drank the sound like a man starved.

No hesitation. No restraint.

His grip shifted, his hands raking down her body, cupping her waist, pressing her against him until she felt every hard, unrelenting inch of him.

She arched into him, every nerve igniting at the sheer desperation of it.

He broke the kiss, his lips trailing to her jaw, her throat, grazing her skin with the scrape of his teeth.

"Myra," he murmured, voice thick with possession, with need.

Her knees buckled, but his hands held her firm, refusing to let her fall.

She was lost, unraveling, burning alive in his hands.

And gods help her, she never wanted it to end.

The sentinels vanished into the night, leaving only the heavy sound of their breathing and the crackling tension between them. Without a word, Zakar scooped Myrithia into his arms, holding her tightly against his chest as he strode up the worn stone steps of the manor.

"Where do you think you're taking me?" she demanded

breathlessly, fingers gripping his tunic.

He didn't answer. The doors groaned open at his command, and with a mutter of an incantation under his breath, magic flared through the air. Candles sparked to life as they passed, bathing the corridors in flickering gold. The manor was old, untouched, its beauty dulled by time, but the master suite was still grand — black marble, silk drapes, a fire roaring to life in the hearth.

Zakar kicked the doors shut behind them and carried her straight to the bed, laying her down against the plush sheets. His hands lingered on her waist, his gaze steady and heated, like he was memorizing her in this exact moment.

"Just because I kissed you back doesn't mean I'll be your slave," she said, voice tight.

He smirked, brushing his fingers along her jaw. "Well, lucky for you, tonight I don't require a slave." His lips ghosted over hers, a slow promise of what was to come. "I want a *lover*."

Her breath caught at the word *lover*, at the way he said it so effortlessly, as if it were the most natural thing in the world. As if she were capable of loving him. As if he were capable of loving her.

She stared up at him in the golden glow of the firelight, her pulse thrumming wildly. He was devastatingly handsome, his damp black hair falling in loose waves around his face, his tunic clinging to the hard lines of his body. Shadows danced over his sharp features, making him look every bit the dark, untouchable force she had once feared.

But there was nothing untouchable about him now.

"You can bed me, Zakar, but I will never stop running," she whispered, hoping the words carried conviction. Hoping she could still convince herself. Wishing she wasn't so weak, so pitiful as to accept the inevitable — the morning would come, and with it, her usefulness would run out.

He smirked, wicked and knowing, one hand fisting in her hair, tilting her head back just enough to claim her mouth in a kiss that shattered all reason — raw, searing, and possessive.

Between breaths, he murmured into her lips, each word a brand against her skin. *"I will bed you,"* he promised, the weight of it sinking into her bones. His hands found her hips, dragging her against him, his thickened length pressing firmly between her legs, teasing her through the thin barrier that remained.

"And if you dare to run again," he continued, his voice low, sinful, "I will *remind you exactly* of where you belong. *Beneath me.*"

The words sent a violent shudder through her, pleasure spiking before he had even truly touched her. Gods, what had he done to her? What had he always done to her? Even now, when she should resist, when she should claw for the freedom she had so desperately sought—she *ached* for him instead.

CHAPTER 53

Zakar

Gods, she was stunning. Her bare breasts rose and fell with frantic breaths, the firelight dancing over her skin like an artist's final, perfect stroke. Her pink nipples were peaked, her soft stomach quivering beneath his touch. The damp chemise hung from her frame, askew and unnecessary, a whisper of fabric he wanted gone. He needed her bared to him completely—skin glistening, body pliant, her form nothing short of a masterpiece.

But it was her eyes that undid him.

The way she looked at him, raw and wanting, as if there was nowhere else she would rather be—no one else she would rather be with.

A deep growl rumbled in his chest as he crushed his mouth over hers, the kiss wild, consuming, filled with the kind of hunger he had spent five years denying. He unfastened his pants in one swift motion, yanking at her waistband to free her from the last barrier between them.

Then her fingers wrapped around him.

A hiss tore from his throat, pleasure lancing through him like a brand. His grip tightened on her hips as he stripped her free of her trousers, his hand sliding between her thighs, finding her slick and ready.

His breath came sharp. *Mine.*

She moaned at his touch, her thighs parting in quiet invitation, her body yielding to him with an eagerness that unraveled him completely.

He pulsed his fingers inside her, feeling her, stretching her, his tongue sweeping through her mouth with the same slow, devastating precision. She was intoxicating, a drug he had craved for too long, and he was finally taking his first forbidden taste.

His slick fingers withdrew, gripping the soft curve of her waist, pressing, bracing, positioning. And then, with a slow, deliberate thrust, he pushed into her, the tight, wet heat of her enveloping him in a rush of pure euphoria.

A delighted moan tore from her lips as he filled her, as if she had been waiting for this just as long as he had.

He drew back, the slide of him against her making his head tilt back in pleasure, then thrust in again—slow, controlled, savoring.

His hands flexed against her waist as he moved, each stroke agonizingly deep, as if he could imprint himself into her very being.

A ragged breath escaped him, a low, shuddering groan.

She was everything. Every wicked fantasy, every fevered dream, every moment of agony he had spent craving her.

And now she was his.

He would never let her go. She could try—*gods, he would dare her to try*—just so he could chase her down, catch her in a blink, press her up against the nearest wall, and take her all over again. He would spread her wide, force her to moan his name, and remind her—*with every punishing thrust*—that she belonged to him. Not as a slave. Not as a plaything. *His.* In the truest, most undeniable sense.

His fingers dug into her hips, controlling, claiming, guiding her to meet each forceful snap of his body against hers. His eyes devoured her—the way her flushed breasts bounced with every relentless thrust, the way her parted lips trembled with every desperate moan.

She was pure sin, exquisite and wild, her slick heat wrapped around him like a vice, drawing him deeper, pulling him under.

This siren—this beautiful, maddening, impossible woman—was *his*.

His pleasure. His mistress. *His wife.*

He would make it so.

"Zakar!" she moaned, her voice raw, desperate, a plea and a demand all in one as she rolled her hips to meet his deep, indulgent thrusts.

He groaned low in his throat, the sound of it vibrating against her skin as he tangled his fingers into her silver hair, pulling her head back, baring her throat to him. He pressed fevered kisses along the delicate column of her neck, his tongue tracing each heated pulse of her racing heartbeat.

"Yes," he murmured against her skin, his lips brushing soft before he bit down, savoring the way she gasped beneath him. His thrusts slowed, deeper now, indulgent. He pulled nearly all the way out before driving back into her, dragging out every sensation, every maddening ounce of pleasure.

"You will know just how much you belong to me, Myra," he whispered against her throat, his voice dark silk and heated steel. His hips moved with perfect precision, measured, devastating. "And you will never be able to live without me."

She gasped, her body arching, trembling against his. He claimed her mouth then, capturing her soft, open lips in a searing, possessive kiss. His tongue swept inside, tangling with hers, tasting her, drinking in every sound she made.

She met him with equal fervor, her fingers twisting into his hair, pulling him closer, needing him just as much as he needed her. Their bodies moved in perfect rhythm, her hips lifting to take him deeper, his grip tightening on her waist to hold her where he wanted her.

His pace quickened, his control slipping as her nails raked down his back, as her thighs tightened around him, as she whispered his name against his lips like a prayer.

He was losing himself in her. And he never wanted to be found.

Her breaths were unsteady, gasping, frantic, her pleasure mounting steadily as he drove into her with relentless precision.

He smirked against her jaw, pressing slow, indulgent kisses

along the delicate skin before murmuring into her ear, his voice a deep, velvety taunt. "You are rather obedient when you want to be."

She scoffed, or at least tried to, but the sound dissolved into a helpless moan as he thrust into her deep, stealing the breath straight from her lips.

He chuckled, slipping in and out of her slick, welcoming heat with an ease that was utterly maddening.

"This is not obedience," she choked out between his thrusts, the pleasure in her voice betraying the defiance in her words. "This changes nothing."

Oh, she was trying to goad him. His grin was all sharp teeth, dangerous delight curling through him. Stubborn little woman. He thrived on it.

Without warning, he pulled out of her, flipping her effortlessly onto her stomach. A gasp escaped her as he pressed her down into the soft mattress, his weight caging her in, his large hands smoothing down her spine before tangling in the damp waves of her silver hair.

He tugged, just enough to make her gasp again, just enough to hear the sweetest moan slip past her lips.

Then, with one smooth, powerful thrust, he slid back inside her, burying himself to the hilt.

Her groan was loud, helpless, a sound of sheer, reckless pleasure that echoed through the candlelit chamber.

Again and again, he drove into her, each thrust steady and controlled, savoring the way her body tightened around him, the way she trembled beneath his hold. One hand gripped her hip possessively, steadying her, while the other remained tangled in her silken hair, keeping her exactly where he wanted her.

The firelight bathed her in a golden glow, illuminating the arch of her spine, the perfect curve of her hips, the roundness of her ass as she yielded to him completely. Gods, she was breathtaking—every inch of her, his to claim.

He slowed, breath shuddering, his grip tightening as he watched where they connected, mesmerized by the way he filled her, the way her slick, welcoming heat took him in with every deep thrust.

She cooed softly, her fingers fisting into the plush pillows, her thighs quivering as she braced herself against him.

A deep, possessive growl rumbled through his chest as pleasure rippled through him like a slow-building storm. The sight of her, the sound of her, the way she was unraveling beneath him—it was maddening.

With a sharp snap of his hips, he picked up speed again, the raw need to overtake her searing through him. Harder. Faster. Deeper. He needed her to feel him, to know that no matter how far she ran, no matter how much she fought, she would always belong to him.

"Still think this changes nothing?" he taunted, slamming into her with ruthless, agonizing precision.

A broken moan tore from her throat, her body writhing beneath him, caught between pleasure and stubborn defiance. "You are insufferable," she panted, but then gasped as he thrust deeper, her nails digging into his arms. "But gods... you feel good."

A dark, satisfied laugh rumbled through his chest. "That's more like it."

Without warning, he withdrew from her only to flip her onto her back, his strength effortless as he grasped her thighs and spread her wide beneath him. He eased into her again, savoring the flutter of her lashes, the soft gasp at her lips, the greedy pull of her body around him.

"Look at you," he murmured, his pace unrelenting, savoring the way her body surrendered, the way she gasped with every deep thrust. "Come now, *tell me*, Myra," he demanded, voice like silk laced with iron. "Tell me how good it feels."

Her lips parted, a soundless cry caught in her throat.

"Tell me you won't beg for this again," he challenged, driving into her harder, deeper, pulling every ounce of pleasure from her body as she arched beneath him. "That you won't crave the way I will break you apart, night after night, day after day."

He leaned in, his lips grazing the delicate curve of her jaw, his voice a velvet snarl. "Lie to me, Myra..." His breath was molten against her skin, each word drawn out like a promise wrapped in sin. "So that I can drive into you so deep, you'll submit like you were *made* for it."

THE ARCANE BARGAIN

Her eyelids fluttered open, heavy with exhaustion and pleasure, her lips curling into the faintest, wicked smile. Breathless, she met his gaze, eyes dark with invitation.

"If you want my submission, your highness… then *claim* it."

CHAPTER 54

Myrithia

She knew the moment the words left her lips that she had invited a ravenous beast to consume her whole. She felt it in the way he thickened inside her, in the way his eyes darkened with raw hunger, blazing with a fire that would leave her utterly undone. A sharp gasp tore from her throat as he seized her wrists, pinning them above her head into the satin pillows, trapping her beneath him, a prisoner to the merciless pleasure he promised with every devastating thrust.

He buried himself deeper, stretching, filling, claiming—his thrusts purposeful, relentless, stripping her down to nothing but sensation. Her thighs spread further of their own accord, her body welcoming the pressure, craving the sheer force of him as he thrust into her, again and again, with a possession that stole the breath from her lungs.

This wasn't just pleasure. This was ruin. This was worship.

The usual weight of guilt—the shadow of betrayal, the ache of regret—vanished beneath the onslaught of his touch, the undeniable rightness of his body pressed into hers. For the first time, she wasn't Zakar's temptress, his traitorous little Chantress. No, she was something more. Something cherished, something claimed, something divine beneath the crushing force of his desire. Perhaps she *was* made for submission—crafted to be worshiped like this, to be unraveled beneath his hands, his lips,

THE ARCANE BARGAIN

his unrelenting need.

The sounds pouring from her throat were ones she didn't recognize, high and desperate, shameless. He rocked into her, deep, hard, thorough—her body arching, tightening around him, greedily milking every inch of him as dampness pooled beneath them, proof of her surrender, of her utter devastation.

"Submission looks good on you, Myra," he murmured, his voice thick with satisfaction, laced with dark amusement. A bead of sweat trickled between the hard planes of his chest, disappearing beneath the fabric of his black tunic, and she realized—she wanted to see him. *All* of him.

Her fingers found his tunic, grasping at the buttons with frantic desperation, yanking at the fabric as though tearing it away would somehow bring her closer to the pleasure that was already consuming her whole.

He chuckled again, a slow, indulgent sound, dragging his thrusts into something torturously deep, making her gasp as he lifted just enough to strip the tunic from his body. The firelight bathed his skin in flickering gold, highlighting every sculpted ridge, every chiseled muscle of his powerful form.

Her breath caught as her gaze devoured him, tracing over the sharp lines of his jaw, the broad expanse of his chest, the taut cut of his abdomen—and finally, lower.

Her mouth went dry at the sight of his thick, glistening length, wet with the evidence of her arousal, just before he buried it so deeply inside of her that she could *feel* every inch of him stretching her, claiming her.

He caught her staring.

His lips curled into a wicked smirk. "Like what you see?" he mocked, shifting his hips just enough to tease the sensitive, aching nerves at the base of her sex. The wet, slow drag of him sent uncontrollable bursts of pleasure shivering through her, arching her back, spilling moans into the air like a confession.

And gods, he seemed to *love* making her confess.

"Have you any more vicious little lies to tell me?" he taunted, his voice smooth as silk and sharp as a blade. "Any more defiant outbursts?"

He watched her with a dark, triumphant hunger, reveling in the way she struggled to hold onto any last fragment of composure.

But there was nothing left. Nothing but *him*. Nothing but this. Nothing but the shattering, inescapable grip of submission.

"Please," she moaned desperately, though she wasn't even sure what she was begging for. Surely it was *more*—more of him, more of this vile, beautiful thing that made her feel reckless and passionate and sinful.

As if answering her plea, he sank into her again, slow and deep, impossibly *full*. The stretch of him was exquisite torment, pressing into her so thoroughly she swore she could feel him in her very soul.

She couldn't breathe.

"Now that I have you," he murmured, each syllable a velvet promise laced with something dangerous, something unrelenting. "I will not relent. I will not yield. I will take you, all of you, over and over—until I am *sated*."

His lips captured hers in a slow, reverent kiss, his tongue caressing hers with a tenderness that contradicted the sheer possession of his words. It was devastating. It was *worship*. He was devouring her, *claiming* her, and she was melting, dissolving into his touch, his taste, the relentless pull of his body against hers.

And then—gods.

His pace shifted, his thrusts growing deeper, more intense, each stroke pulling more pleasure from her than she thought she could bear. His thickened length stretched her perfectly, pressing against something devastating inside her, something that sent helpless, gasping moans spilling from her lips.

The pleasure began to *build*. A slow, torturous ascent, coiling tighter, stronger, until the pressure inside her was unbearable. She arched beneath him, fingers curling against his shoulders, her body clenching around him in desperate anticipation.

And still, he didn't stop. Didn't slow.

He was going to *ruin* her.

Her body was trembling, coiled tight, every nerve frayed and burning with pleasure. The pressure inside her had become unbearable, a scorching need that threatened to consume her whole.

Zakar could no doubt feel it—*feel* her unraveling beneath

him, her slick heat gripping him with every stroke, pulling him deeper, *tighter*, dragging him toward the edge with her.

"That's it," he groaned, his voice thick with possession, his thrusts turning punishing, desperate. "You were starved for this, weren't you?" His hand slid between them, his fingers pressing against her aching, throbbing center, stroking her exactly where she needed.

She gasped—a broken, helpless sound—as her body seized around him, her muscles clamping down, gripping him like a vice. "*Zakar*—!" His name tore from her lips as the pleasure detonated, white-hot and overwhelming, her entire body shattering beneath him. She convulsed, her back arching, thighs quaking, her core pulsing around him as wave after wave of pleasure crashed through her.

He cursed, as if his control was splintering, snapping like a taut wire. A hoarse growl tore from his throat as he buried himself inside her, grinding deep while her release gripped him, pulled him under. His hands clamped around her hips, body locking tight as his release crashed through him.

He jerked deep inside her, thick ropes of his seed spilling into her, flooding her as his body convulsed above her. A strangled groan left him, his face buried in the crook of her neck, his breath ragged, his muscles locking as she squeezed him through every last pulse.

They stayed like that—panting, clinging, bodies still fused, their skin slick with sweat and pleasure.

Zakar let out a slow, shuddering breath, his lips brushing against her throat, his voice hoarse. "You're *mine* now, Myra," he murmured, pressing a final, languid thrust into her sensitive heat, relishing the way she whimpered. "Say it."

She could barely form words, still drowning in the aftershocks, but she knew—*gods* she knew—there was no denying it. No fighting it. Not anymore.

"...Yours," she breathed, spent and satisfied.

And *damn* him—he smiled, utterly victorious.

CHAPTER 55

Zakar

Morning light streamed through the tall windows, flooding the forgotten estate with warm golden hues. Dust motes drifted lazily in the beams, undisturbed by the quiet peace of dawn.

Soft silver strands tickled his cheek, shifting slightly with each slow, steady rise and fall of her breath. Zakar blinked, his vision sharpening on the delicate curve of Myrithia's body nestled against his bare chest.

A deep, satisfied breath left him, his arms tightening just slightly around her as if securing her in place—as if there were anywhere left for her to be except right here.

Last night.

The memory sent a shudder of pure satisfaction down his spine. She had taken him—*all* of him—with such pleasure and enthusiasm. Her body had welcomed him as if she had been made for no other purpose, every inch of her designed to unravel him, to drag him into a pleasure so deep he was certain he'd never recover.

Her moans, breathless and desperate, still echoed in his mind, a sound he was sure he could never hear enough of.

His hand moved instinctively, sliding over the soft curve of her breast, molding to its perfect weight. Desire surged through him, already hard, already pressing insistently against the heat of her backside. Gods.

THE ARCANE BARGAIN

He was ready for her again. Already needing her.

The rhythm of her breathing shifted, a slight hitch that sent fire through him.

She was waking.

A sleepy, heady moan spilled from her lips as she stirred against him, her body stretching ever so slightly, pressing back into him in a way that had his jaw tightening.

He bit his lip, grinding against her, unable to help himself—like some primal beast made only for this, made only for her.

The power she would hold over him after this was unthinkable.

There was nothing he would deny her, nothing he wouldn't surrender just to feel her again, just to have the sweet warmth of her body wrapped around him, pulling him under, dragging him to ruin.

"Zakar..."

Her voice was husky, a whisper of sound that nearly broke him.

He wanted her again.

Now.

Senseless. Breathless. Until the only word left on her lips was his name.

A soft, teasing giggle poured from her lips as she turned, tilting her head just enough to peer up at him beneath the thick sweep of her lashes. Her lips curled into a slow, knowing smirk.

"You're already so aroused, my prince?" she murmured, her voice a lilting taunt. Her fingers traced the hard lines of his stomach, nails dragging just faintly, just enough to make him shudder. "How desperate you are—"

He silenced her with a kiss—a deep, claiming, possessive kiss.

His tongue swept into her mouth, demanding, devouring, claiming her just as he had claimed every inch of her last night.

This was agony.

To love her. To obsess over her. To know that he could never have enough of her. He had never truly stopped being mad for her. It was foolish—laughable—to think he could ever keep her as a slave. He wasn't her master. He was her captive. A man driven to obsession, desperate for his next ruin.

She parted their lips gently, a soft sigh escaping as she turned fully to face him. Her delicate fingers traced over his jaw, featherlight—as if he were something to be cherished.

Something to be loved.

Her blue eyes locked onto his, brimming with something warm, something certain.

"I must say," she cooed, teasing, though her touch remained unbearably tender, "it is nice to see you so desperate. I feel I have been the desperate one for five years."

He huffed a laugh, rich, incredulous. "You?"

"Yes." She flashed him a radiant smile, a smile that reached all the way into his bones, threatening to upend everything he thought he knew. "Zakar, I have loved you from the moment I first kissed you."

He froze.

The words pierced through him like a blade, sharp and clean, severing doubt, unraveling his defenses. Was this real? Was he dreaming this?

His hands tightened over the delicate blades of her shoulders, his grip firm, grounding. If this was a dream, he refused to wake. Just like the memory of her pleading to Draevok that she loved him, he knew this was no lie. He knew that she loved him then. He was surprised that she loved him still.

"You asked me why I spared your life." She exhaled, and he felt it in his chest, like an invisible tether between them pulling tight. "I led you away from that ballroom so that you wouldn't have to die. So that I wouldn't have to live without you."

He knew that already. He knew it now. But, gods he loved to hear her say it.

Selfless. Selfish. A woman trapped in a fate not of her making, choosing him anyway.

"I did it because I loved you," she whispered, the words raw, stripped bare of every defense. "Because I still do. Because I never knew how to quit loving you."

The world tilted. Even that illusion cast by Nyxian, of her and the children in that small little cottage came to him in that moment. That future, that fantasy... he wanted it. Truly, deeply wanted it.

"I didn't want to tell you in Stonehollow," she admitted, her voice dipping into something almost ashamed. "I was too afraid of you laughing in my face. Of you taking the last of my spirit and crushing it, as if that was all you might need to finally destroy what little was left of me."

He swallowed hard. "And now?"

She smiled.

"And now, I can see," she whispered, pressing her forehead to his, binding herself to him in a way deeper than magic, deeper than fate.

"If this is what you call slavery, then I will accept my chains with pleasure."

He breathed her in, deeply, with quiet devotion, savoring the feel of her surrender. Her submission was not just to him—it was to this truth between them, to the love she had once denied.

She had always been his.

And gods, he had always been hers.

"I do not offer you slavery anymore, Myra," he whispered, his voice gentle, unwavering. "You are not a slave. And as long as I live, you will never serve another master."

A small breath escaped her, her lips parting slightly, her eyes shining with something unspoken, something fragile.

He was certain she had never heard words like these before. And he would spend every day of his life ensuring that she never felt like a slave again. Not to *him*. Not to *anyone*. She would be adored, worshiped in a way she had never been before. And gods help him—he would make sure she never doubted it.

Being with her like this, skin against skin, heart against heart, was sublime. It was everything. The thing he had needed for longer than he dared admit, the thing he could not—*would not*—live without.

But then his eyes snapped open.

A sharp tension coiled in his chest, his euphoria fracturing beneath cold reality. They were not done yet. She was still dying.

Worse, their connection had been severed.

Nyxian had ripped away his claim on her—the tether of power he had poured into her veins, the fragile thread that had been sustaining her life. She had only lasted this long because of him, because of his magic binding her to this world. And although the god had said she would live another week, he didn't have the luxury of trusting him.

"What's wrong?" Her voice was soft, worried, catching the sudden stiffness in the way he held her. "Did I say something wrong?"

"No," he murmured, pressing a tender kiss to her forehead, as if he could shield her from what was coming. "No, it's not that." He swallowed. "It's your curse."

Her entire body went rigid.

Like a spell breaking, she shot upright in the bed. Panic bled into her features, turning her into something wild and desperate.

"The tome!" she gasped, her breathing coming fast, erratic. "When my horse got scared last night, it ran off! The tome was in the pack—Zakar, it's gone!"

She was frantic, clutching the sheets, her delicate fingers trembling

He watched her in quiet pity. Nyxian had never given her the book. The replica, and perhaps the horse along with it, would evaporate into nothing more than the illusions that they were.

"Don't mind the book," Zakar said at last, his voice even, measured. "It cannot save you."

Her gasp was small, but the devastation in her eyes was not.

"It can't save me?" she repeated, shaking her head. "No, that's not possible! I need it!" She scrambled closer to him, reaching for him as if she could physically will him to understand. "I need the counter-curse. Without it, I will die! You know this."

He steadied his breathing, forcing himself back into the man he needed to be. The Arcane Master. Not a lover tangled in sheets, but a man with a singular purpose.

A man who needed to save her. A man who needed to kill Draevok.

"The god lied to you."

He watched as the truth hit her like a blow, the slow unraveling of it flashing across her face.

"No," she whispered, her voice barely a breath. "He wouldn't—"

"He would." Zakar met her gaze, unflinching. "And he did. He gave you a replica. But even if you had the real book, it still wouldn't save you. There is no counter-curse."

She stared at him, her mind warring against itself, trying to reconcile what he was saying.

"He could have lied to you," she murmured, almost pleading. "Couldn't he?"

Zakar nodded once. "He could have." A pause. "But I don't think he did."

She watched as he stood, the moment of indulgence between them fading, replaced by the cold, sharp edge of their reality.

He retrieved his tunic from the floor, pulling it over his head as if sealing himself away from her, from the night they had shared.

Then, as he fastened his belt, he unsheathed the dagger.

The blackened blade gleamed, dark and menacing, soaked in something ancient, something unnatural.

"He gave me this," he said, showing it to her.

She stared, wide-eyed, her breath shallow.

"He asked me to kill Draevok for him," Zakar continued, his tone cold, clinical. "And in his death, the curse on your life will be broken."

Silence.

She didn't move. Didn't speak.

Then, slowly, she gathered the sheets to her chest, the stark white fabric a fragile shield against the darkness of the weapon still resting in his hand.

Gods, she was beautiful.

Bathed in the soft glow of morning, she looked almost celestial — radiant in gold and ivory, with silver waves cascading over her bare shoulders, her eyes wide and uncertain but still so full of depth. The light made her glow, softening everything around her until she became the only thing in focus. Zakar stepped toward her, caught in the gravity of her presence.

He needed to protect her.

He needed Draevok dead — for all the torment, for all the stolen years, for what he had done to Zakar himself. But more than that, Zakar needed Myrithia to live. To be free. To never cower again.

"Myra," he said, his voice low and gentle, fingers brushing across her cheek. She leaned into the touch instinctively, and it nearly undid him.

THE ARCANE BARGAIN

"We need to join together again," he continued, "but not as slave and master. Never again like that."

He lifted a hand and made a swift motion through the air, tugging at invisible threads of power. A parchment burst to life before them in a swirl of green light, hovering between them. The words were etched in delicate silver script, the letters flickering and shifting like ripples on a lake. They reflected in her eyes—liquid light caught in a sea of blue.

"This is an Arcane Bargain," he murmured. "A true one. Typically formed between a Master and apprentice. But this time..." His gaze softened. "This time, I bind myself to you."

He unsheathed a small golden dagger from his belt and pricked his finger, pressing it to the contract. It pulsed once, waiting.

"Unlike before, this bond flows both ways. I can pull from you... but more importantly, you can pull from me. Freely. Without fear."

He reached for her hand, his touch reverent as he made the smallest prick at her fingertip and guided it to the parchment.

Her eyes widened as the silver script flared, then ignited in a rush of emerald fire, vanishing into the air like smoke on the wind. She looked back at him, lips parted, breath trembling—and he knew she understood.

This time, he trusted her.

This time, he would protect her not with force, but with faith.

And then she kissed him.

With no hesitation, no guarded pretense—just quiet, aching tenderness. Her mouth pressed against his in a slow, consuming kiss, one that stole his breath and gave him something far deeper in return. Her lips were soft, warm, and desperate in a way that matched his own heartache. He kissed her back hungrily, tasting not only her love, but her loyalty—earned now, not taken.

He had longed for this—for her—for so long.

To feel her like this, choosing him despite everything, was almost too much. Gratitude swelled inside his chest, fierce and raw. This was all he'd wanted. Not power. Not revenge. Just her. Just this.

When she finally drew back, her cheeks were flushed, her expression unguarded. He rested his forehead against hers, his hand sliding gently into her hair, threading through the silken silver strands.

"We should get moving," he murmured, his voice still low, still thick with everything he hadn't said. His thumb brushed along her jaw, lingering for a moment. "The road ahead won't wait for us."

She gave a soft nod, but didn't look away from him—her eyes searching his as though memorizing the shape of his soul.

He let his lips curve into something faintly amused. "Though... if we had the luxury, I wouldn't mind a few more hours of delay."

A blush rose to her cheeks, but she smiled—quiet and warm.

He leaned in, pressed a last kiss to her temple, then pulled away with a reluctant breath.

"Dress quickly," he said, rising to his feet. "Valthoria awaits us."

CHAPTER 56

Zakar

They were closer to Valthoria than Zakar had anticipated. Nyxian must have released them from the far edge of the Hollow Mist's reach—an unexpected mercy. The abandoned estate they'd found last night, little more than a crumbling relic, had been nestled near the outskirts of Wolfhaven. That meant the capital was perhaps a day's ride away.

He hadn't realized just how close they were. Myrithia was already beginning to falter. She didn't complain, but he noticed the way she shifted her weight, the occasional wince she tried to hide, the growing weariness in her steps. They'd been walking for hours. Her feet had to be blistered, her body aching.

They would need to stop soon. But if they could just push a few more hours—just enough to reach the Arcane Citadel—he could secure her safety before facing what lay ahead. There, she could rest. Bathe. Recover. He could leave her behind its fortified walls and go alone to Draevok.

She would protest, of course. Insist that it wasn't safe, and that she wouldn't be left behind again. But he still had the Nythera. With it, he could pierce through any barrier Draevok had erected, emerge right inside the heart of his defenses—his old chambers—and take the bastard by surprise. No more games. No more running. Just a final reckoning, on his terms.

But not yet. Not until Myrithia was safe. Not until they had rested. Resupplied. Rebuilt what little strength remained.

He took another step.

The earth trembled.

The air thinned around him just before the spectral forms of his Sentinels rose from the soil like wraiths, their misty bodies swirling and hissing with quiet urgency.

"Master," one intoned, its voice a layered ripple of whispers. "We are surrounded."

Zakar's pulse sharpened. "Surrounded?" he repeated, his stance tightening. Every muscle in his body coiled with sudden tension.

He turned toward Myrithia—just in time to see the color drain from her face.

"Draevok arranged a trap," the Sentinel rasped, its form rippling with flickers of pale magic. "One even we could not see. He approaches. We will stand guard until your command."

Zakar didn't hesitate.

Magic ignited along his forearms, searing through the air with lethal intensity. The forest felt like a drumbeat before thunder, the power building—waiting to strike. His aura flared outward like a warning bell.

The Sentinels shifted, reacting instantly, closing ranks in a tight, defensive circle around Zakar and Myrithia. They hovered like silent shadows, their bodies half-formed and flickering between planes. Protective. Menacing.

Zakar could feel the ground itself holding its breath.

And then the forest erupted.

Black-armored soldiers surged from the trees like a black tide, steel flashing, voices silent. They moved with brutal coordination, spreading around the clearing like ink spilled on parchment—encircling the Sentinels, boxing them in. There were too many of them. Dozens. No—at least a hundred.

Steel rang as they took position, blades angled inward.

At the center of it all, astride a black stallion draped in silver-threaded barding, rode General Garron. His smirk gleamed even beneath the shadow of his helm, his posture relaxed, but his hand never straying far from his weapon. He watched them from a distance, saying nothing. He was here to intimidate, not negotiate.

But it wasn't his presence that made the air feel like it had turned to ice.

The pressure shifted—suffocating, cold, as though the land itself braced for something unholy.

And then he arrived.

Draevok stepped through the mist like a crack torn into reality, space warping around his frame. He didn't walk—he emerged. One breath he wasn't there, and the next, he simply was. His boots met the ground without sound, robes trailing like a storm behind him. Smoky runes of emberlight crawled up his sleeves, whispering power into the wind.

Zakar's magic snarled in recognition.

It had been five years. And yet Draevok looked untouched by time. Not a day older. Not a line deeper. Still tall. Still broad-shouldered. Still emanating the unshakable poise of a man born to rule through domination. The gray streaks through his dark auburn hair only made him more imposing, like he'd aged not from wear, but from conquest.

He stopped just at the edge of the clearing, within striking distance—but drew no weapon.

Instead, he smiled.

It wasn't warm. It wasn't welcoming.

It was the smile of a man who believed he'd already won.

"Zakar," he said smoothly, his voice a rich baritone, polished and unhurried. "I see that my wayward little traitor is with you." He clicked his tongue, glancing over his shoulder. "General—she can ride back with you. No doubt you wish to collect your prize before her execution in the morning."

Garron gave a mocking salute. "With pleasure."

Zakar seethed. No one would touch her. Not Garron. Not Draevok. Not anyone.

But they were surrounded—boxed in by a hundred blades and a sadistic monster. Even with the Sentinels at his side, the risk was too great. He couldn't fight freely with her here. Not when every strike might cost her life.

She had to go.

His hand moved before the thought could finish, diving into

his coat and closing around the smooth, familiar weight of the golden medallion.

The Nythera.

His one way to guarantee her safety, even if it cost him everything else.

"Myrithia," he barked, whirling toward her.

She turned to him, startled—eyes wide, breath catching—but there was no time for questions.

He slammed the relic into her palm, muttered the activation phrase under his breath, and in a burst of brilliant green light—she vanished.

Gone.

Safe.

Or so he hoped.

A heartbeat of silence followed.

Then Draevok laughed, a cold, guttural sound. "I knew you had that little artifact on you," he said with a sigh, his tone casual. "Should've apprehended you first. Waste of a good tool, if you ask me."

He turned to Garron with a flick of his hand. "She's one mile north of here. Find her. I don't care what you do with her—but I need her alive by morning."

Zakar's body coiled behind the wall of his sentinels, every muscle drawn tight with murderous intent. He wanted to strike Garron down where he sat—cut him from his saddle before he ever reached the tree line. But the general would never make it in time to Myrithia. She was too far ahead.

Zakar would cut a path through every man in this clearing before he could catch her. If she was smart, she'd hide. If she was stubborn... His jaw tensed. He would end this quickly, then hunt Garron down and rip him apart.

The general only laughed, cruel and triumphant, as he spurred his horse into a gallop, vanishing into the trees.

Draevok stepped forward, his dark robes stirring like smoke as he lifted his hand. His eyes met Zakar's—cold, unreadable—then slid away, dismissive. "Kill him," he said softly, and a hundred blades rang free of their sheaths.

Zakar didn't flinch. His hand rose in answer, not in defense—

but in defiance. No words. No warning.

Only fire.

Magic burst from his fingertips like a thunderclap, and in the next breath, the forest plunged into chaos. Steel met spell. Shouts rose, clashing with the hiss of arcane power. The first wave of Draevok's soldiers surged forward—only to crash like waves against the unyielding wall of his sentinels.

They moved as one, shadows laced with light, their incorporeal forms sweeping through armored ranks and tearing away weapons, knocking men off their feet, leaving trails of frostbite and stunned cries in their wake.

Zakar followed, a tempest given form, his magic answering his every thought.

A soldier lunged. Zakar's hand snapped up. The man froze midair, his blade suspended inches from Zakar's chest, before he was flung backward into a tree, the wind knocked from his lungs. He didn't rise.

Another charged from the side— Zakar snapped his hand outward, and roots burst from the earth, wrapping the man in a tight cocoon of bark and vine, binding him to the ground.

Still more pressed in, but Zakar moved like a scythe through tall grass—elegant, brutal, efficient. He conjured sigils in the air, lashing out with invisible force that sent men flying into the dirt. One tried to flee—a flick of Zakar's wrist sent a wall of wind to flatten him to the ground, where glowing shackles wrapped around his limbs.

He had no intention to kill these men. They were soldiers, not enemies—bound by duty, by fear, by orders they had no power to refuse. This was never meant to be their war. The fight had always been between him and Draevok. The rest were just collateral the false king had thrown at his feet.

But he would not relent.

They would not win against him.

The sentinels mirrored his wrath. Smoke and steel, they blurred through the enemy ranks, disarming, disabling, dropping men with graceful brutality—like predators herding sheep. Every movement was a warning. Every spell, a reminder of who they served.

THE ARCANE BARGAIN

In minutes, the battlefield was no longer a charge—it was a rout.

Dozens of men writhed on the ground, groaning, their weapons torn from reach. Some clutched broken limbs. Others simply lay dazed, too winded to rise.

Those still standing hesitated. Shaken. Staggered.

The tide had shifted.

And still—Zakar stood at the center, untouched, his cloak drifting behind him, his eyes aglow with the full, merciless force of his power.

Across the battlefield, Draevok hadn't moved. But the smile was gone from his face now. His brow was faintly furrowed, his jaw set tight.

"I underestimated you, boy," Draevok said, his voice like ice. "A mistake I won't repeat." From within the folds of his sleeve, he drew a slender vial—glass catching the light with a sinister gleam.

Zakar's heart dropped.

He had his blood.

CHAPTER 57

Myrithia

Branches tore at her arms as she ran, breath ragged in her throat, the warm evening air smothering her lungs. Her boots struck the earth again and again, her pace uneven from fatigue and fury—but she didn't stop.

Zakar had used the Nythera on her.

She knew it the moment she landed hard in the mossy undergrowth, its magic fizzing faintly in the air like static. The flash of gold, the way the world folded in on itself for a heartbeat—there was no mistaking it. He had sent her away. Exactly one mile.

To save her life.

And she hated him for it.

Tears threatened the corners of her eyes, but she blinked them back. She wouldn't weep. Not while he was still out there. Not while Draevok was alive.

"I'm not leaving you," she whispered aloud, as if he might hear her.

The forest blurred around her as she gathered her magic, silvery sparks lighting her fingertips, and surged forward in a burst of speed. Fifty feet. Then another. And another. The magic pulled harder with each interval, sapping her strength in ways that left her bones aching.

She could pull from Zakar—she knew that now. Their new

bond would allow it.

But she wouldn't. Not when he needed every drop of his power to survive.

So she pushed forward on her own, each burst shorter than the last, her limbs growing heavier. Her final flash left her stumbling, catching herself on a tree trunk, her vision hazy and her body trembling.

Then, she saw something that made her heart stop in her chest. A glint through the trees, steel catching the sunlight. Hooves pounding like thunder through the forest floor.

It was Garron, and he was coming straight for her. Panic surged through her veins.

Myrithia spun on her heel and bolted in the opposite direction, heart thundering as the branches whipped at her face and arms. She tried again—desperately—to draw from her magic. Silver sparks flared in her palms, and she launched herself forward.

Only a few feet.

Her body trembled. She tried again, but the flare was even smaller. Her magic was weakening fast.

Her chest ached. Her vision blurred. She tripped over an exposed root and fell hard, scraping her knees and hands against the dirt. Still, she pushed up, staggering forward, refusing to stop.

Behind her, the sound of hoofbeats slowed.

A sickening voice cut through the trees. "I've waited a long time for this."

No.

She tried to crawl, her limbs trembling beneath her weight, fingers clawing at the dirt. Magic sparked again—faint, pitiful.

And then he was there.

Garron dismounted leisurely, his boots crunching on the earth as he approached, each step deliberate, confident. She tried to drag herself away, her palms slick with sweat and soil, her body betraying her.

He crouched beside her.

Myrithia collapsed fully, too weak to keep moving, the world spinning.

Garron reached out and flipped her onto her back with little effort. Her silver hair spilled around her like a halo as she blinked up at him in helpless dread.

"So lovely," he said with a smile, almost tender—*mockingly* so. His knuckles brushed her cheek, the back of his hand cold and condescending. "I want you awake for this."

Her lip trembled.

"I want you to remember it," he murmured, "as one of the last things you'll feel before your pretty little head goes on a spike come morning."

Her fingertips flickered with light. A pitiful, final effort.

He laughed. "Oh no, none of that."

The light died.

Her vision dimmed.

Everything went white, soft, and strangely still.

Myrithia's eyes fluttered open slowly. She lay on something impossibly gentle, as though the earth itself had become a bed of silk. The air smelled faintly of blooming petals, and all around her, tiny flowers swayed lazily in a breeze she couldn't feel. Above her, the sky stretched on forever, bluer than any sky she'd ever known, with white clouds like soft brushstrokes drifting slowly across the heavens.

Did I die? she thought.

She eased herself upright, her movements careful, driven by instinct more than thought. Her heart was calm. Her breath moved easily. Nothing ached. No fear pressed at the edges of her thoughts. For the first time in what felt like forever, there was only stillness.

Around her was an endless meadow, open and glowing with gentle golden light. Far in the distance, snowcapped mountains rose in a hazy line, like memories too far to reach. Birds chirped faintly overhead, flitting between invisible trees, their songs delicate and unbroken.

She stood, a little unsteady, her mind still wrapped in a veil of fog. Her hands smoothed over her stomach, her chest. She was whole. Unbruised. Clean.

Her gaze was drawn toward the brightest point on the horizon—a waterfall slowly coming into focus, pouring from nowhere into a sparkling stream that cut through the meadow. Light shimmered around it like a beacon, beckoning her forward.

She took a step, then another. She felt lighter. Each footfall was weightless, as if the world had forgotten to hold her down, until a sound broke her concentration.

"*Wait.*" The voice was ethereal and feminine, like the whispers of the Hollow Mist.

Myrithia froze. Her breath caught, the hairs on her arms lifting.

Slowly, she turned toward the voice.

Standing a few paces away was a figure bathed in light—so luminous, so radiant, that Myrithia couldn't discern the edges of her form. The woman's silhouette shimmered in gold and white, ethereal and shifting like morning fog in sunlight. She had the outline of a woman, yes, but beyond that, her features were impossible to discern—too divine, too otherworldly.

"I've waited a long time to finally meet you, Myrithia," the woman said. Her voice was serene, layered with both sorrow and reverence. "Though I do hate that it had to be like this."

"Like what?" Myrithia asked, though dread was already coiling inside her.

"In death," came the gentle reply.

The word echoed like a tolling bell.

And suddenly, it all returned to her—flashes, vivid and sharp. Draevok. His soldiers. Garron's sneer. The dirt beneath her fingertips. The crushing weight of defeat. She gasped and clutched her chest, as if she could physically smother the panic rising there.

"You're not dead yet," the woman soothed, her voice wrapping around her like silk. "You sleep now. We are in the Ether."

The space between. Neither here nor there. Not the living world—but not the afterlife either.

"I have to go back," Myrithia said, the words leaving her lips before she could think. They rose from something deeper than instinct—something rooted in love, in fury, in purpose. "Zakar will die if I do nothing. And I…" She faltered, her thoughts catching on Garron's cruel face. "I can't let myself be overtaken. I can't let him die."

"No," the woman agreed softly. "You must return. But not as you are. You are too close to the edge, and if I release you now, you'll shatter."

Myrithia's brow furrowed. "Who are you?" she whispered, her voice reverent.

There was a pause—a moment suspended in perfect stillness. Only the birdsong echoed faintly in the distance, as though the entire world waited on the answer.

"I am Sylara," she said at last.

The name hit like a thunderclap cloaked in velvet. Myrithia's breath caught.

Sylara.

The goddess.

The one Nyxian had mentioned—the one he claimed Myrithia reminded him of. And now here she stood, glorious and terrible and beautiful beyond comprehension.

It felt as though her entire life had curved toward this moment. That every decision, every wound, every breath had pulled her here.

"If you accept it," Sylara said, raising one hand, palm up, "I will grant you a gift. I will share my essence with you—just a fragment, but it will be enough to sustain you. Enough to burn through your curse. Enough to destroy the one who placed it upon you."

In her palm, light bloomed—pale, pure, and impossibly bright.

Myrithia's lips parted. The answer was already waiting, hovering on her tongue. A resounding yes. For Zakar. For herself. For every scar that Draevok had carved into her life.

But Sylara wasn't finished.

"There is a cost," she said softly. "Your bloodline."

Myrithia's inhale trembled, betraying her resolve.

The world held still once more.

"One day, I must return," Sylara continued. "And when I do, I will need a vessel. Not you—but your descendant. When the time comes, your line will carry my spark. It may not be for a century, or many. But it must begin with you."

Myrithia's heart twisted. A future she had only begun to imagine—one with Zakar, with peace, with a life that was hers—shivered under the weight of that cost. A child. A bloodline born of her. One day, a vessel for a goddess.

She closed her eyes.

THE ARCANE BARGAIN

The silence of the meadow pressed in on her, tender and eternal.

But then she saw Zakar—bloody, broken, fighting alone. She saw Garron's leering face. She felt the brand of Draevok's curse still clinging to her soul. There was no more time for what-ifs. The world would burn unless she acted.

She opened her eyes.

"I accept."

Sylara stepped forward. She raised her glowing hand and pressed it against Myrithia's stomach.

At once, warmth flooded her body—no, not warmth—*light*. Light that seared and healed, that devoured the remnants of weakness, that set every vein ablaze with power and divinity.

Myrithia arched with the force of it, her eyes going wide, a cry escaping her lips.

The world exploded into white.

And then—nothing.

***

She woke with a jolt. The world snapped into focus all at once—the cold press of the forest floor beneath her, the scent of pine and loam, and the feel of thick fingers tugging at the laces of her trousers.

Her eyes flew open in horror just as Garron's gloved hand slipped beneath the hem of her chemise. Her breath caught violently in her throat.

Before she could even think, her hand shot out and clamped around his wrist.

He didn't flinch.

Instead, he grinned—smug and vile—then twisted her hold with brutal efficiency, slamming her arm above her head and pinning it hard against the ground.

"No point in resisting," he murmured, his breath hot against her cheek as he leaned over her. He straddled her now, looming like a beast, his weight pressing her into the dirt, his other hand working the laces of his own trousers with terrifying intent. Her stomach turned.

"Try to stay awake for this," he mused, his tone laced with mockery. "I want to tell Zakar what I did to you, and how you whimpered beneath me like a broken thing." His teeth flashed. "Just before we both watch him die."

Rage.

It burst from her chest so fast she couldn't breathe around it. He would not take this from her. Not her dignity. Not her body. Not her power.

The words didn't leave her mouth—but something else did.

Light.

It blazed through her like wildfire, white-hot and absolute.

A scream tore through Garron's throat as he recoiled, his hand releasing her wrist in an instant, smoke rising from where their skin had touched. He staggered back, clawing at his chest.

She rose.

Not with trembling limbs.

Not with fear.

But with fire in her veins.

Her eyes gleamed, cerulean and brilliant, twin stars in a storm. The ground quaked beneath her feet as the meadow's light—the goddess's essence—surged to the surface. Her hair lifted on an unseen wind, and the trees around them trembled, leaves scattering like startled birds.

Garron barely had time to look up before she struck.

A blast of blinding power erupted from her palms, engulfing him in a radiant, howling torrent of light.

He didn't scream.

There wasn't time.

His body incinerated before it hit the ground, reduced to ash and scorched armor in an instant—no blood, no bones. Nothing but dust.

The forest fell still again.

Myrithia stood in the stillness, her breath unsteady, her body trembling with the aftershock of fury. Ash and embers clung to the wind as she looked down at the smoldering remnants of Garron, her gaze cold, unmoved. Then, without a word, she turned to the waiting horse. With a single, fluid motion, she mounted the saddle, cast one last glance toward the fading horizon—and rode toward the firelit edge of dusk.

CHAPTER 58
Zakar

Draevok stood proudly, a silhouette of malice against the darkening sky, his expression carved from smugness and cruelty. His eyes glinted with triumph, pale fingers toying absently with Zakar's vial of blood. It gleamed, familiar and unmistakable.

The very same blood he had traded to Calveren days ago in exchange for the Nythera. Panic twisted in his chest. Had Calveren betrayed him? Or—worse—had he been killed?

There was no time to know. No time to grieve, to rage, to question.

Because the pain came instantly.

A searing bolt of agony tore through Zakar's core. His breath hitched—cut off—as he dropped to one knee, the world careening sideways. The edges of his vision pulsed with darkness.

All around him, his sentinels shrieked in fractured unison, their spectral forms convulsing before evaporating into curling black smoke. The bond severed.

Above it all, Draevok raised the vial higher, its glow pulsing with cruel triumph.

Zakar's blood shimmered within—alive, writhing—magic coiled around it like a noose. And now, it was tightening.

"Coward!" he snarled, the words rasping through clenched teeth.

"Cowardice? No," Draevok mused darkly. "You're not a man,

Zakar—you're a beast. And beasts must be chained."

Draevok chuckled softly, and with a flex of his fingers around the glowing vial, another brutal jolt of pain wracked Zakar's body.

He arched violently, a raw, guttural sound ripping from his throat as the pain tore through him like molten chains.

"You'll be happy to know you weren't betrayed easily. Calveren clung to his loyalty, even when I offered him a very painful alternative." He tilted his head, a gleam of cruelty lighting his eyes. "At least until I had his granddaughter by the throat."

Zakar groaned, blood flecking the dirt as he writhed beneath the hex's grip. Rage swelled in his chest, helpless and boiling.

"He begged, you know. Hands shaking. Voice cracking. Begged me to spare her. It was all very touching." Draevok smiled. "So I did. For now. But we both know I can change my mind. Just because the man is old and retired doesn't excuse him from refusing to serve his king."

Zakar bared his teeth, struggling against the invisible chains pinning him down.

"Did you truly believe," Draevok began, his tone dripping with condescension, "that this would end any other way?" He paced leisurely around Zakar, savoring the moment, his boots crunching on dried earth as the army behind him stood still at his command.

Zakar's fingers twitched, nails digging into the soil, as the hex twisted deeper into his marrow.

"You were meant to die that night," Draevok said with an annoyed sigh of breath. "And it was my folly to have entrusted the task to her. Such a simple order—to end you—and yet, she faltered."

A fresh wave of torment wracked Zakar's frame, eliciting a guttural groan. He clenched his teeth, refusing to give Draevok the satisfaction of his suffering.

Draevok's eyes gleamed with cruel delight. "Your father met his end much the same way," he mused. "Gasping, pleading for mercy that would never come."

Summoning the remnants of his strength, Zakar spat a mixture of blood and defiance onto the ground. "My father was many things—a bastard, a coward, a tyrant. But he would never beg for his life. In that, we are the same."

Draevok's smile widened, a hunter reveling in the helplessness of its prey. "Oh, but you will learn to beg, boy. I will ensure it."

Zakar's voice was steel, even through the pain. "I would sooner die."

"Is that so?" Draevok asked with a delighted smile. "I wonder if you might consider begging for *her*?"

Zakar glared up at him, the hatred in his gaze unyielding.

Draevok crouched slightly, lowering his voice to a venomous murmur. "I could keep her alive, you know. Spare her. Let her live, even after I put your head on a spike."

Zakar's eyes flickered.

"Oh yes," Draevok went on, savoring the cruelty. "She doesn't have to die. Not yet, anyway. Garron seems quite taken with her. He'll enjoy breaking her." He leaned in, grinning as Zakar seethed through the pain. "I'd let him have her. Over and over. Every night until your name means nothing to her but pain."

Zakar shook, rage burning so fiercely within him it left no room to breathe.

"And maybe," Draevok mused, "if you beg nicely, I'll let her live out her days as his favorite toy. Wouldn't that be a mercy?" He leaned in closer, his voice a venomous whisper. "So tell me, Zakar, how much is her life worth to you?"

Zakar growled, a feral sound deep in his throat, hatred boiling in his blood. "If you touch her—"

"You'll what?" Draevok cut in, tilting his head mockingly. "Collapse harder?"

Another wave of agony surged through him, this one twisting sharp enough to make his vision splinter. Draevok laughed again, rising to his feet and spreading his arms as if presenting the finale of some grand performance.

Zakar's vision blurred with ire and pain, his heart pounding a furious rhythm against his ribs. The world narrowed to the face of the man who had taken everything from him.

The distant sound of galloping hooves broke the oppressive silence. Draevok straightened, a chuckle rumbling from his throat. "Ah, that must be Garron now, returning with his wayward prize." Zakar's heart dropped like a stone in his chest.

Both men turned their gazes toward the tree line, anticipation thick in the air. The horse emerged first, its powerful form illuminated by the full moon's glow. But it was the rider that drew a collective breath from the assembled soldiers.

Draevok tensed, his brows drawing low as the approaching figure sharpened into focus.

Zakar strained to lift his head, his body wracked with pain, his vision fogged—but then he saw her.

His heart stopped.

Myrithia.

Only... it couldn't be.

Silhouetted beneath the full moon, she gleamed like a specter of vengeance. She was a vision, a burning wraith astride Garron's horse, and the general nowhere in sight. Her skin shimmered faintly, kissed by a pearlescent hue that pulsed with something ancient and unknowable. Her eyes glowed, otherworldly—bright blue like the core of a dying star, and full of purpose. Her silver hair floated around her face as though she were suspended in water, strands shifting in slow motion. Her clothing, too, moved as if untouched by wind or weight—fluid and divine.

She dismounted slowly, gliding forward like a creature of myth—half flame, half mist—untouchable, undeniable.

Draevok took an instinctive step back.

Zakar wanted to speak, to call out, but he could only watch—enthralled and aching—as Myrithia's glowing gaze locked onto the man who had once owned her.

Draevok's lip curled. "Where is Garron?" he spat, though his voice had lost its usual certainty. His fingers reached into his coat and produced a small glass vial of blood, glinting in the low light.

He held it up like a threat. "Don't forget, girl. I still have your—"

"Dead," she said.

The word rang through the clearing like a tolling bell, her voice layered with something else ancient and resonant, like a whisper carved into time itself.

Draevok blinked. "What?"

Myrithia didn't flinch. "Garron is dead. And *you* are next."

THE ARCANE BARGAIN

Draevok's grip tightened on the vial, holding it higher. "You forget your place."

But the vial burst.

A sharp crack split the air, and Zakar watched as shards of glass and crimson splashed across Draevok's palm.

He recoiled, staring in disbelief at his bleeding hand.

"You *had* my blood," Myrithia said coldly, her palm still raised, silver light flickering in her fingers. That same haunting duality laced her voice—earthly and divine. "You have no power over me now."

The look on Draevok's face was pure disbelief. Not fear—*not yet*—but confusion. As if he couldn't comprehend what he was seeing.

Zakar, still collapsed and half-buried in pain, watched her with a heart that thundered in his chest.

She was stunning. A vision. A wrathful goddess cloaked in mortal skin.

And she had come back for him.

CHAPTER 59

Myrithia

She could still feel it—the goddess's essence burning steady in her veins. The world had sharpened, slowed. Every breath, every heartbeat, was laced with clarity. Her body moved as if it no longer obeyed the limitations of flesh and fatigue. She felt untouchable. Not immortal, not invincible. Just... free. For the first time in her life.

Draevok was looking at her differently now.

Not with disdain. Not even with disbelief.

But with something far more gratifying—fear.

It crept into the edges of his expression, unsettling the arrogance in his eyes. For the first time, she saw confusion flicker across his face, as if he was only just beginning to grasp the truth: that whatever stood before him was no longer the helpless girl he'd once commanded. This was something else. Something ancient. Something divine. And it terrified him.

Her gaze dropped to Zakar.

He was still pinned to the ground, body tense with the last remnants of agony, his breath shallow and ragged. Beneath him, blood had pooled—trickling from his lips, from the unseen wounds tearing through him from within. And there, in Draevok's hand, was the second vial.

She hadn't seen it until now.

Her fury answered before thought could. No words. No

gesture.

The glass exploded in Draevok's grasp, the sharp crack echoing across the clearing. Crimson scattered like dust, and Zakar exhaled—low and pained—as the crushing force binding him finally released. His limbs slackened, his breathing easing, though the injuries remained.

Myrithia's hands trembled at her sides.

He had used it. That same cruel hex. The one he had threatened her with her entire life. The one that had kept her leashed like an animal. And now he had dared use it on Zakar.

The man she loved.

She couldn't even look at him without her heart cracking—Zakar, strong and unyielding, brought to his knees by Draevok's vile magic. Blood had marked him inside and out, the toll of it written across every inch of his form. It was unspeakable.

Unforgivable.

A raw, primal heat surged through her chest.

When she looked back at Draevok, there was no humanity left in her expression.

She raised a single hand—and without a word, flung him upward into the air like he weighed nothing at all. His body snapped off the ground, suspended in a helpless arc before she hurled him across the clearing with terrifying speed.

The impact against the tree was deafening. Bark splintered, and Draevok crumpled to the earth in a heap of limbs and broken pride. A strangled cry tore from his throat, ragged and guttural.

And still, she didn't move. Her glowing eyes stayed fixed on him, unblinking.

This was only the beginning.

He groaned, struggling to rise, but she was already there.

A flick of her wrist—and the earth rose beneath him, slamming his body back against the trunk he'd just crumpled from. He choked on the impact, his limbs flailing uselessly. His eyes widened.

She walked toward him slowly, the weightless drift of her silver hair haloing around her, like mist on a breeze. Her feet didn't so much touch the ground as pass through it, and with every step, the power around her pulsed hotter, heavier.

THE ARCANE BARGAIN

Draevok staggered upright, dazed. He raised a hand as if to cast a spell—but it fizzled the moment it sparked. The pressure around him was too much.

She didn't stop.

Another wave of force slammed into his side. He hit the dirt again, harder this time, coughing and scrambling. He managed to push himself to his knees, face twisted in disbelief.

She waited. Let him try.

When he braced to stand, she sent a column of silver fire crashing into the earth beside him. The ground split at his feet, and he flinched backward in terror, tumbling into the dirt once more.

His chest heaved. Panic began to replace pride.

She lifted her hand again—this time slower. He rose with it, limbs dangling like a marionette on invisible strings. He thrashed, but he was weightless in her grasp.

And then she dropped him.

Hard.

He hit the ground with a grunt, left gasping and sprawled, one hand clawing at the dirt as though to dig his way out.

She stood above him now.

Silent.

Composed.

Power incarnate.

And in that stillness, in that terrible quiet, Draevok did not reach for another spell.

He only looked up at her—

—and finally understood.

"I think I was wrong, Draevok," Myrithia said, her voice smooth as water over glass—echoing with something far older, far deeper than herself. The divine undertone lingered beneath every word, as if two voices spoke in harmony: one mortal, one eternal. "I was wrong when I told you that Zakar wouldn't be a threat to you."

She turned from Draevok like he was nothing—an afterthought. With a casual flick of her fingers, his body rose, limp and weightless, then hurled across the clearing. He struck the ground with a crunch of shattered bone and scraped earth.

THE ARCANE BARGAIN

When she reappeared beside him in a shimmer of light, her bare feet hovering an inch above the blood-soaked grass, he didn't even try to move. A whimper slipped from his lips—pathetic, broken. The great Draevok, groveling in dirt.

But Myrithia wasn't looking at him anymore.

She turned to Zakar.

He was on his hands and knees, panting through clenched teeth, struggling to rise. His body trembled with pain, blood still dripping from wounds that hadn't yet sealed. His magic flickered uselessly around him, too fractured to mend what had been torn.

She dropped beside him, gentle now, kneeling as though time itself had slowed to allow her this one soft moment. Her hand cupped his jaw, smoothing away the blood streaking his mouth. Her thumb brushed his cheek with such reverence it nearly brought him to tears.

She smiled.

Then she kissed him—deep and steady, her mouth warm against his, her fingers trembling where they rested at his nape. And with the kiss came light.

Power.

It poured from her lips into his like breath, like life itself. The divine essence of Sylara—borrowed, burning—spilled through the cracks in his soul and filled every inch of him. Golden warmth surged through his veins, searing away the pain, the hex, the agony. His ribs knitted. His muscles reformed. His wounds closed with a soft hiss, vanishing beneath glowing skin. His lungs filled fully for the first time in hours, and his strength roared back into him like a dam breaking.

He opened his eyes—green and brilliant—and found her watching him.

The light was gone from her now.

Her divinity... spent.

She was mortal again.

But she was whole.

And so was he.

She smiled softly as she reached to his hip, fingers curling around the hilt of the black dagger he carried. She drew it, placed it in his palm with quiet finality.

Their eyes met.
And he understood.
He nodded and stood to his feet, his eyes already fixed on Draevok's trembling feeble body in the dirt.

CHAPTER 60
Zakar

As Zakar approached, each step across the scorched and bloodstained earth felt like crossing the final threshold of a war that had defined him.

Draevok lay at his feet, slumped and broken, the rise and fall of his chest shallow, uneven. Blood darkened his robes, matted his hair, and smeared across the cracked ground beneath him. The tyrant of Valthoria—the architect of Zakar's ruin—was no longer a figure of legend or fear. Just a man.

A ruined one.

Their eyes met—briefly.

There was no hatred left in Draevok's gaze. No last curse. No plea for mercy. Only the quiet, hollow awareness of what was coming.

Zakar said nothing.

He drew the dagger—Nyxian's gift, the emberstone still pulsing faintly in his hand—and knelt.

For a heartbeat, he hesitated. Not from doubt. Not from mercy. But from the strange emptiness that washed over him now that the end was finally here.

He drove the blade forward.

Quick. Clean. Final.

Draevok shuddered once, a soft, broken sound escaping him— then stilled.

Zakar stayed crouched there for a moment, listening to the silence settle in like dust.

It was done.

The monster was dead.

He rose slowly, the dagger still warm in his grip, but the weight in his chest was heavier. He had chased this moment for so long, shaped himself around it, let it become his purpose.

But now that it was over, there was no satisfaction. No relief.

Just the ache of something finished.

And the quiet that came with it.

Zakar lifted his gaze, eyes sweeping over the gathered soldiers. They stood frozen, their swords limp at their sides, their helms concealing the fear that clung to them like smoke. Still, they had not fled—not when Zakar had effortlessly incapacitated their ranks, nor when Myrithia had descended like a divine wraith to destroy their king. Their loyalty, or perhaps their terror, had rooted them in place.

He spoke, his voice low but steady, carrying across the silence like a bell.

"Men," he said, eyes sharp as blades, "your king is dead. Your cause is broken. And your fate, at this moment, rests with me."

He paused, letting the weight of his words sink in. "Lay down your weapons and walk away."

A long silence followed—tight, breathless. Then, a single voice broke through.

"We have a new king."

All eyes turned as one of the soldiers stepped forward and removed his helmet. The insignia on his chest marked him as a First Commander—and with Garron dead, that made him the highest-ranking officer still standing.

Zakar recognized him at once.

Brannock.

A man of discipline and quiet strength. Years ago, he had mentored Zakar in the art of war, before everything shattered. He'd had four young daughters back then, always with ribbons in their hair and joy in their laughter. Brannock had served because he had no choice. Because he'd had people to protect.

"We followed Draevok because we feared for our lives... and

for the lives of our wives and children," Brannock said, voice steady but full of old weight. "But you, Your Majesty, were always meant to lead the Valthorian army."

A chorus of agreement rippled through the ranks.

Then—a thunderous beat of spears to the earth, the sound unified, resounding like a drumroll of loyalty.

"We will serve you," Brannock said, his voice firm. "Gladly. If you would have us... if you would take back the throne that is rightfully yours."

Zakar stood still, quiet. He was moved, shocked by their readiness, their belief. Not just in his name, but in *him*.

He glanced over his shoulder—drawn to her like a tide pulled by the moon. Myrithia stood just behind him, her silver hair glowing in the twilight, her eyes bright with pride and something deeper... something that made his chest tighten.

"What are you waiting for, your highness?" she asked softly, a gentle smile tugging at her lips. "This is long overdue."

Then, without another word, she lowered herself to the ground.

The motion was simple, but it echoed like thunder.

Her head bowed, her posture reverent—but it was not submission. It was ceremony.

The signal rippled through the ranks like wind through tall grass. Zakar turned, and the sound of shifting metal filled the clearing. One by one, soldiers knelt. A hundred heads bowed beneath the moonlight, a single motion of loyalty and recognition.

His heart pounded as he took in the sight. Not a soul stood. Not one. They knelt not to a tyrant. Not to fear. But to him. And to the future he now held in his hands.

He turned back to Myrithia, his voice low and certain.

"You," he said, extending his hand to her, "will never kneel again."

He pulled her gently to her feet, lifting her with care—as if anything less would diminish what she had become. She rose, and when she stood beside him, it felt as though the world had aligned at last.

Zakar faced his men.

"This night," he said, his voice cutting through the silence, "you will have a new king. And you have a new queen."

He paused, letting the words settle, letting the truth of it fill the clearing.

"Together, we will build the kingdom Valthoria was always meant to be. I will not carry on the legacy of my father—the Butcher who called himself king. Nor will I rule with lies and chains like Draevok, who stole what was never his to claim."

His eyes swept over the soldiers. Over every face turned to him in hope.

"There will be balance. There will be peace. And never again will a mage be forced into servitude. From this day forward, you are free to choose your path. If you leave this army, you will go without fear or punishment."

He drew in a breath.

"But if you stay… if you choose to stand with me, you will be part of a kingdom worth fighting for. One forged not in cruelty— but in conviction."

A hush fell over the field, as if the wind itself was holding its breath.

Then—movement.

The First Commander, Brannock, rose first. He struck his fist to his chest in solemn salute.

"For Valthoria," he said, loud enough for all to hear.

One by one, the others followed. A wave of movement as soldiers stood and echoed the cry.

"For Valthoria!"

The words thundered through the clearing, striking like drums in Zakar's chest. It wasn't just a chant. It was a vow.

He felt Myrithia's fingers curl around his own, grounding him in the moment as the army gathered around them—not in ranks, but as people, men who had been made into weapons… and were now being offered something more.

Zakar turned, his gaze sweeping over the bloodstained field— over the wounded, the weary, and finally, the lifeless body crumpled in the dirt.

Draevok.

Nothing more than a remnant now. A ruin.

Zakar said nothing. He didn't look long.

The dead didn't matter.

THE ARCANE BARGAIN

He turned back to Myrithia—no longer the girl bound by curses and guilt, but the woman who had stood beside him through fire and ruin. The woman who had saved him just as much as he had saved her.

She met his eyes and smiled.

And for the first time in five long years, he let himself breathe.

The battle was over.

And the future had just begun.

CHAPTER 61

Myrithia

Myrithia flexed her soapy toes, stretching her legs beneath the surface of the wide marble bath, watching the lavender-hued water ripple in gentle waves. The scent of sandalwood and clove clung to the steam rising around her, mixing with the fragrant oils swirled into the bath. Her head rested back against the lip of the tub as she exhaled slowly, letting the heat soothe what little tension remained in her bones.

The bathing chamber had not changed. Towering black and white columns framed the domed ceiling above her, where colored glass panels scattered dappled light across the floors like spilled gemstones. Red velvet drapes hung against green-veined marble walls, and delicate gold trim lined the edges of the tall archways and polished fixtures. Everything about the room whispered of history, opulence, and memory.

Zakar's memory.

She had once been in this room when she was his lover—no, when she had been pretending to be. A weapon cloaked in silk and lies. But the truth was, even then, she'd felt a strange comfort here. Even now, after all that had passed between them, it still felt like his presence lingered in the very air. The warmth in the stones. The low, distant crackle of the hearth. The light from the high windows catching against the gold fixtures—everything felt like him.

And now... this was hers too.

The journey back to Valthoria had passed in a blur. Zakar had been pulled into a meeting with the council to begin the long process of restoring order to the fractured kingdom. And she—after so long—was finally whole.

She felt it in every limb, every breath. Sylara had undone the curse with nothing more than a touch, and though the goddess's power had faded, Myrithia felt stronger than she ever had. Alive, vibrant, *real*.

She rose from the water, droplets trailing down her skin like diamonds, and stepped across the glossy black marble floor. She reached for a soft white towel and wrapped it around her body, her movements unhurried, unafraid. It was a strange thing, to feel safe. Unthreatened. *Free.*

She moved toward the gilded mirror, her bare feet quiet on the tile. The reflection staring back at her seemed like someone new—someone she was still learning to recognize. And yet... there was something.

A glimmer. Low in her abdomen.

She parted the towel instinctively, eyes narrowing as she spotted the faint pulse of light beneath her skin—soft, golden, fleeting. A glow that faded before she could fully register its shape. But she knew what it meant.

Your bloodline, Sylara's voice echoed in her memory, serene and certain.

Her hand lowered to her womb, the towel clutched loosely at her chest Had it already begun? Had Sylara chosen her moment, taken root in the life within her before Myrithia even knew it existed?

The thought brought no fear. Only stillness.

She felt no regret. Not even a shadow of doubt. She would make the same choice again—again and again—if it meant Zakar lived. If it meant their lives could finally be their own. The bargain had been costly, yes. But it was not cruel. It had felt... right. A promise, not a punishment. A divine accord made not in desperation, but in trust. And if something stirred now within her—some flicker of godhood wrapped in flesh and future—then she would meet it with open arms. For her daughter. Or her daughter's daughter. Whoever it would be.

She would be ready.

The door creaked open.

Myrithia startled slightly, clutching the towel back to her chest, but the tension melted instantly when she saw him—Zakar, framed in the soft glow of candlelight pouring through the doorway. His expression eased when he saw her, his smile tugging with familiar fondness and something deeper. Something close to awe. His gaze swept over her, lingering without a word. Intent. Devouring. As if seeing something sacred.

"You're staring," she murmured, a touch of playfulness in her voice.

His smile deepened. "I've earned the right."

She rolled her eyes, but her cheeks flushed as he stepped inside.

"Have you now?" she asked coyly, brushing past him with a whisper of a smirk as she crossed the threshold into his bedchamber. Her bare feet padded across the smooth stone floor, her towel cinched around her as she made her way toward his bed—now theirs. She glanced over her shoulder as she reached the edge of the mattress, dark lashes low. "Bold of you, telling your soldiers I'll be your queen. I don't recall giving you any such confirmation."

Zakar chuckled as he closed the bathing room door behind him. His footsteps were smooth and sure as he approached her, his gaze burning with unspoken promises.

"You *will* be my queen, Myra," he said, voice like velvet and iron.

Something fluttered in her chest—treacherously soft, achingly sure. Because she knew he was right. She had no intention of ever escaping such a fate, nor did she want to.

"Whether I am king," he continued, reaching for her, "the Master of the Arcane... or a nameless man living in a nameless town." His smile tugged at memory, at the echo of all they had endured. "You will be my queen."

He cupped her face reverently, his thumbs brushing her cheeks before he pressed tender kisses to each one. Then her forehead. As though he could seal his vow into her skin.

She blushed. Her heart stretched with warmth, with the fullness of a love she had once thought she would never know again. She hardly had the audacity to speak—how could she, when every word he gave her was a tether, grounding her to him?

"In any life," he whispered, "in any role you or I play, I will be yours. And you will be mine."

He lowered her to the bed, the cool satin yielding beneath her bare skin. Her towel slipped from her shoulders and pooled to the floor, forgotten. His hands moved over her with reverence, his lips catching hers in a kiss that stole the breath from her lungs and replaced it with something holy.

She kissed him back, deeply, desperately—lips parting with a hunger that had nothing to do with lust and everything to do with longing, survival, *home*.

Then she broke away with a breathless laugh, her voice teasing, even as her fingers curled into his hair. "If you think for a moment I'm letting you into this bed, so filthy and unwashed, then you are *sorely* mistaken, your majesty." She arched a brow. "Just because you're king now doesn't mean you can barge in and dirty my linens. I won't have it."

He gave her an unimpressed smirk—one part amused, two parts aroused. "Oh, I'm going to make you filthy, my queen."

And then he kissed her again—*silenced* her with it. Raw. Primal. A possession claimed with lips and tongue and breath. She melted into it, her spine arching as his hands traveled down her waist, slipping past the curve of her hips.

She gasped against his mouth, flushed with heat. "Zakar—"

"I'll make you a mess," he growled into her ear, voice wicked with promise, "and then I'll grant you the honor of bathing me."

She laughed, startled and breathless, a giddy, full-bodied sound of disbelief. "You arrogant—"

Another kiss devoured her words, and this time, it wasn't gentle. His fingers found her—parted her—and slipped inside with practiced precision, coaxing a sharp inhale from her lungs.

"Zakar," she tried again, already unraveling, "shouldn't we… rest first? Just for a moment?"

He didn't stop. Didn't even slow.

"I'll rest," he murmured darkly, "after I've made both you and this bed thoroughly undone."

She gasped as Zakar's fingers curled inside her, slow and precise, the heel of his palm pressed against her with delicious pressure. Her thighs parted instinctively, back arching against the silk sheets as she clenched around him, breath catching in her throat.

"Zakar…" she moaned, one hand gripping the sheets while the other tangled in his dark hair. He was still fully clothed while she lay bare beneath him, flushed and trembling. She could feel the heat of his body between her legs, his magic like a second skin dancing along her nerves.

He watched her, green eyes smoldering, devouring every flicker of her pleasure. "You look ruined already," he murmured, voice thick with hunger. "And I've barely begun."

Her head tipped back as he withdrew his fingers and replaced them with the tip of his tongue, licking a slow, wicked path through her folds. She cried out, one leg thrown over his shoulder as he pinned her in place with the strength of his grip. His tongue worked her expertly, ravenous and reverent all at once, flicking, sucking, teasing until her thighs trembled and her hands fisted helplessly in the bedding.

"Zakar—please—"

He growled low in his throat, the sound vibrating through her as he pulled back, licking his lips with maddening satisfaction. "You'll beg properly before I'm done with you."

And then he was kissing his way up her body, mouth hot on her belly, her ribs, her breasts—sucking and biting until her skin bore his mark, until her body writhed beneath him.

When his mouth finally reached hers again, she could taste herself on his lips.

She was breathing hard, hands sliding under his tunic to feel the warmth of his skin, nails grazing down his abdomen. "Take this off," she ordered, tugging at the fabric. "Now."

But he only smirked, pinning her wrists above her head with one hand. "Oh no, little queen. You don't give the orders anymore."

She shivered as he shifted his hips between her legs, the hard, thick length of him pressing against her slick entrance. Not yet inside her, just poised there, teasing. Her entire body was strung tight, aching for him, needing him to fill her.

His mouth hovered just above hers, his voice a whisper of a promise:

"Beg for it, Myra."

CHAPTER 62
Zakar

She lay beneath him like a vision from a fevered dream—flushed and glistening, her silver hair spilled across the sheets like starlight, her lips parted and kiss-bruised, her chest rising and falling with rapid, eager breaths. Zakar hovered above her, soaking in the sight, the scent, the impossible beauty of her.

Her wrists were still pinned by his grip, her legs parted in welcome, hips shifting restlessly beneath him. She was soaked and trembling and burning for him—and yet she had the audacity to try and command him. His smile curled darkly.

"Beg," he repeated, voice low, dangerous, silk over steel.

A sharp breath slipped past her lips, and for a moment, pride flickered in her eyes. But he saw past it. He saw the need, the hunger, the desperate ache she tried so valiantly to hide.

And she whispered, "Please."

Gods, the sound of it. He nearly lost control then and there.

But not yet.

He released her wrists, only to slide both hands down her arms, savoring the feel of her skin, the way she shivered beneath his touch. He brushed his knuckles over her breasts, watching the way her nipples peaked at the featherlight touch. He leaned down to suck one into his mouth, slow and thorough, teasing her with his tongue until she whimpered.

She arched against him, hips rolling, seeking friction.

"Patience," he rasped, releasing her breast with a wet sound. "You'll get what you want. You'll get everything."

He reached down, guiding himself into place, and slid the tip of his length along her soaked heat, coating himself in her arousal. She gasped, her hands flying to his shoulders, nails digging in.

He didn't push in. Not yet.

Instead, he gripped her hips, held her still, and dragged himself along her entrance again, slow and tormenting.

"Zakar—" she choked out, her voice cracking under the strain.

"Yes, my queen?"

She whimpered, thighs trembling. "I need you."

He kissed her, slow and deep, his tongue claiming her mouth just as he was about to claim the rest of her. Then, in one smooth, relentless thrust, he sank inside her—inch by glorious inch—until he was fully sheathed in her heat.

She gasped against his mouth, breaking the kiss to cry out his name.

He stilled, savoring the feel of her wrapped around him—tight, perfect, pulsing with need.

"Gods, you feel like sin," he growled, pressing his forehead to hers. "Like you were made for me."

He began to move, slow at first, dragging each stroke to its fullest, pulling soft cries from her throat with every thrust. Her legs wrapped around him, her hips rising to meet each push, her hands exploring his back, his shoulders, his hair.

Zakar was relentless, consumed by the way she moved beneath him, by the sound of her moans in his ear. He drove into her with precision and hunger, each thrust coaxing her higher, until she broke—shattering with a cry that tore from her lips, her body tightening around him, pulling him closer to the edge with every trembling pulse.

But he wasn't done.

Not yet.

He slowed, letting her ride the wave, his hand slipping between them, working her with practiced ease. "Again," he commanded softly. "You can give me another, Myra. I want to feel you fall apart again."

She whimpered, overwhelmed, her body trembling beneath

his—but she nodded.

And he gave her exactly what she begged for.

She was still fluttering around him, her inner muscles pulsing with the aftershocks of release, but he didn't stop. Wouldn't let her drift down. Not yet.

Zakar's hand never left her, his fingers moving in slow, deliberate circles while he thrust back into her—deeper now, firmer. She gasped, her head tipping back, silver hair fanning across the pillows as her mouth parted on a soft moan.

"That's it," he whispered against her jaw, his voice thick with reverence and desire. "Feel me, Myra. Every inch."

She did.

He was relentless—each stroke made her thighs tremble, her hands fist in the sheets. Her body was flushed and gleaming, slick with sweat and lust, and still he worshiped her. His mouth moved down her neck, across her collarbone, over the swell of her breasts, pausing only to drag his tongue across her nipple before claiming it with his lips again.

Her moans rose into a crescendo, her body starting to tighten again beneath him.

"Zakar—" she gasped, her nails clawing at his back.

She was so close again—already spiraling. But this time, he wouldn't let her face it alone.

He shifted, lifting her leg higher, plunging deeper into her as he finally gave in to the full force of his need. He took her like a king seizing his throne—claiming, ruling, loving. Every thrust was a promise. Every kiss was an oath.

And then she shattered for him—again.

She cried out his name, her body arching, thighs trembling as another climax tore through her like lightning. Her walls clamped down around him, pulling him into her deeper still—and this time, Zakar followed her.

He groaned, deep and broken, burying himself to the hilt as his own release slammed into him. He poured into her with a shudder, clutching her like she was the only thing anchoring him to the world.

They stayed joined—locked together, panting, bodies tangled, hearts pounding in sync.

He nuzzled her cheek, brushing damp strands of hair from her face as her eyes slowly opened. Still dazed. Still glowing.

His queen.

He pulled out slowly, gently, and kissed her cheek tenderly. "You're already so filthy," he whispered, breathless, kissing her forehead.

She only hummed in response, her eyes softened with satisfaction. He smirked and ran a slow hand down her side. Her body was still trembling from aftershocks, soft and pliant in his arms.

Zakar's fingers trailed lower, tracing her hipbone, his touch feather-light—teasing. Myrithia shivered against him, eyes flashing, already knowing what that smirk meant.

She gave him a playful, exhausted groan. "You said you'd rest."

"I will," he murmured, voice velvet-smooth as he dipped his head to kiss the hollow of her throat. "I said I'd rest when I'd thoroughly undone you. And I'm not nearly finished."

He rolled her gently onto her back, nestling between her thighs again, already hard, already eager. She gasped as he pressed against her slick entrance, and he grinned into her skin.

"I want to see how many times I can make you fall apart," he whispered, lips brushing her ear. "Tonight, you don't beg for mercy. You beg for more."

Her breath hitched, a whimper escaping as he slowly entered her again—inch by inch—claiming her, consuming her all over again. Her fingers dug into his arms, legs wrapping around his waist like she couldn't bear to let him go.

He kissed her then—slow and deep and full of every burning thing he couldn't say aloud. And as the rhythm began again—hotter, deeper, slower—he held her gaze and vowed silently:

Forever.

And when her head tipped back, lips parting in another moan of his name...

The rest of the night faded into fire and shadow.

EPILOGUE
Myrithia

The scent of sweet pies and spiced cider wafted through the air, carried on a warm breeze that fluttered the ribbons strung along windows and railings. The sun hung low over the city of Valthoria, bathing everything in a soft golden haze as the horizon began to burn with orange and rose. Laughter spilled into the streets, mingling with the lively strum of lutes and the rhythmic beat of tambourines, as musicians performed on every corner and dancers twirled with carefree joy.

Colorful lanterns bobbed overhead, strung from one building to the next like stars caught in celebration. Banners in red and gold unfurled from balconies, catching the light and drawing cheers from below. Children with sugar-dusted faces darted between stalls, sticky pastries clutched in their hands, while their parents raised mugs of mead and offered toasts to strangers and friends alike. Joy bloomed in every smile, in every song, in every flicker of candlelight that lit the city anew.

It was the birthday celebration of their third child—their first son, Sorien—and all of Valthoria had turned out to welcome him into the world. A future king, born of peace and hard-won freedom, and the promise of a brighter age. There was a hopefulness in the air, a kind of magic that had nothing to do with spells or sorcery, and everything to do with joy and love and life.

THE ARCANE BARGAIN

Myrithia and Zakar had slipped away from the crowds into a quiet alley just off the main thoroughfare—narrow, cobbled, and shadowed by high stone walls draped in ivy and lantern light. Music from the square floated in soft and distant, the cheerful noise of the festival muffled here beneath the canopy of fading twilight. Guards stood at the mouth of the alley, no doubt red-faced and doing their best to pretend they couldn't hear a thing. It wasn't far from the celebration, but it felt like another world entirely—hidden, stolen, perfectly theirs.

Zakar's arms circled her waist, his lips brushing the curve of her neck before trailing upward to find her mouth. She kissed him back with a smile, sinking into the familiarity of him—his scent, his warmth, the way his hands never seemed content unless they were holding some part of her.

She pulled back with a soft breath. "As much as I'm enjoying this," she said, amused, "I'm not quite ready to start working on our next child just yet."

He chuckled low in his throat, his nose nuzzling the hollow of her cheek. "You'll give in eventually," he murmured. "The healer says you're finally cleared for... everything." He lifted his brows suggestively, smirking. "And I want a big family."

She laughed, swatting lightly at his chest. "Three children are not large enough a family for you?"

"We shall have a hundred," he teased, kissing her neck tenderly.

She balked, shoving at him, but he held her firm.

"Zakar, be serious! We really should be getting back to Sorien."

She had left her infant son in the care of Calveren Wren—who had, by his own stubborn insistence, declared himself the grandfather to their children the moment he had learned of her first pregnancy. Despite his former skepticism toward her, something had shifted after Draevok's defeat. Not immediately. But enough.

Over the past few years, their relationship had softened—melted, even—from something brittle and begrudging into a quiet camaraderie that skirted the edges of friendship. She supposed that counted for something. Calveren was no longer just Zakar's cantankerous old mentor. He had become her mentor too—a guide, a reluctant confidant, and a keeper of truths she didn't always want to hear but often needed to.

When Zakar had taken the throne, he hadn't wanted to relinquish his role as Arcane Master—refused, in fact. So, instead, he named Calveren his second: co-warden of magic, steward of balance within the Arcane Citadel. And when Zakar offered Myrithia a position beside him—something official, something with weight—she had refused.

Not because she didn't want it.

But because she wanted to earn it.

And, after her years of training, she *had*.

"Calveren is happy as a lark," Zakar said with a wave of his hand. "You saw his face when we handed Sorien over. He'll be clutching that baby like a holy relic until someone pries him away." His lips found hers again in a lingering kiss. "We'd be monsters to deprive the old man of such joy."

Myrithia chuckled, shaking her head. "He's probably juggling Sorien with Juliana and Brienne hanging off his sleeves. We should go rescue him."

"They're off playing with his granddaughter, not tormenting him."

"Then they're tormenting the guests," she countered. "You know how our daughters cause trouble."

"They take after their father," he said smugly. "Unstoppable."

She laughed, pushing gently at his chest. "Zakar, come on. The people are waiting. We really should start the festival before someone starts setting off fireworks without us."

He kissed her again, slower this time. "You'll dance until your legs give out," he whispered against her lips, "and then I'll take you upstairs and make you scream until there's not a sound left in your throat."

Her laugh rang like music in the breeze. "I was hoping for a relaxing evening."

"Oh, I'll make it very relaxing," he promised, eyes gleaming wickedly.

She kissed him one last time before slipping from his grasp, her fingers lacing with his as she tugged him toward the palace steps. "Start the celebration, your majesty."

THE ARCANE BARGAIN

He followed, his smile full of affection and amusement. "As you command, my queen."

The cobbled alley gave way to golden light and laughter as Zakar and Myrithia stepped back into the heart of the square. The festival had come alive in full—their two young daughters darting between vendors with sugar-dusted cheeks, laughter trailing behind them like music. Calveren's granddaughter raced alongside them, her curls bouncing as the three girls wove through the crowd in a blur of silk and giggles. A pair of guards kept a steady, discreet distance, their eyes sharp despite the festive air—watchful, yet accustomed to the girls' mischief, and clearly well-practiced in letting them roam without ever letting them out of sight.

Music played from every corner, tambourines clinking, fiddles weaving lively tunes that mingled with the scent of roasted almonds, honey-glazed pastries, and spiced meats.

Zakar's hand rested lightly on her lower back as they approached the raised dais in the center of the square, where the crowd eagerly gathered. The cheer that greeted them was thunderous. Myrithia lingered behind him as he took the steps, standing tall in his black and gold regalia, trimmed with the crimson crest of Valthoria's new dawn.

"My friends," he called out, his voice warm and strong, "tonight, we do not gather to honor a king or a crown—but a child. My son. And more than that, your future king. Let him be born into a world we are all building together—a kingdom of balance, of peace, and of power used for good."

The applause swelled, loud and joyful.

Myrithia remained near the edge of the dais, her eyes quietly studying him. The way he addressed his people—unpretentious, grounded, fiercely determined—made her chest swell with pride. In just a few short years, she'd watched him reshape the kingdom alongside his council, undoing years of cruelty against mages. And it was only the beginning.

Her gaze drifted to the edge of the crowd, where Calveren stood under a lantern post, cradling baby Sorien with surprising grace for a man of his stiffness. The infant cooed, eyes wide and bright. The sight brought a soft smile to her lips.

THE ARCANE BARGAIN

Yes, they were building something new. Something tender and fierce and wholly theirs.

And in the quiet edges of her heart, a memory stirred—of a goddess wreathed in golden light, of a promise made not in fear, but in faith. She hadn't known the full shape of what she was giving then, only that Zakar would live, and so would she. That had been enough. It still was.

Not because the cost had vanished, but because the gift had bloomed into something far greater than she could have imagined. Love. Life. A future that belonged to them.

She no longer wondered when Sylara might return, or what she might ask in the end. The bargain had not been a trap, but a bridge—a way forward when all paths had seemed closed.

And should another moment come, another choice, another turning—Myrithia would meet it with open hands and a steady gaze. Not to undo what had been done, but to shape what came next. Because this life, this joy, was hers.

She had found her freedom.

She had found her love.

And at long last, with Zakar—and the children they had made together, she had a home.

Thank you for reading!

Please enjoy some artwork in the next pages. I just though everyone might enjoy a little bonus art for fun. If you like it (and all things pertaining to more of my novels), feel free to join my patreon for more content.
Patreon.com/lifelight

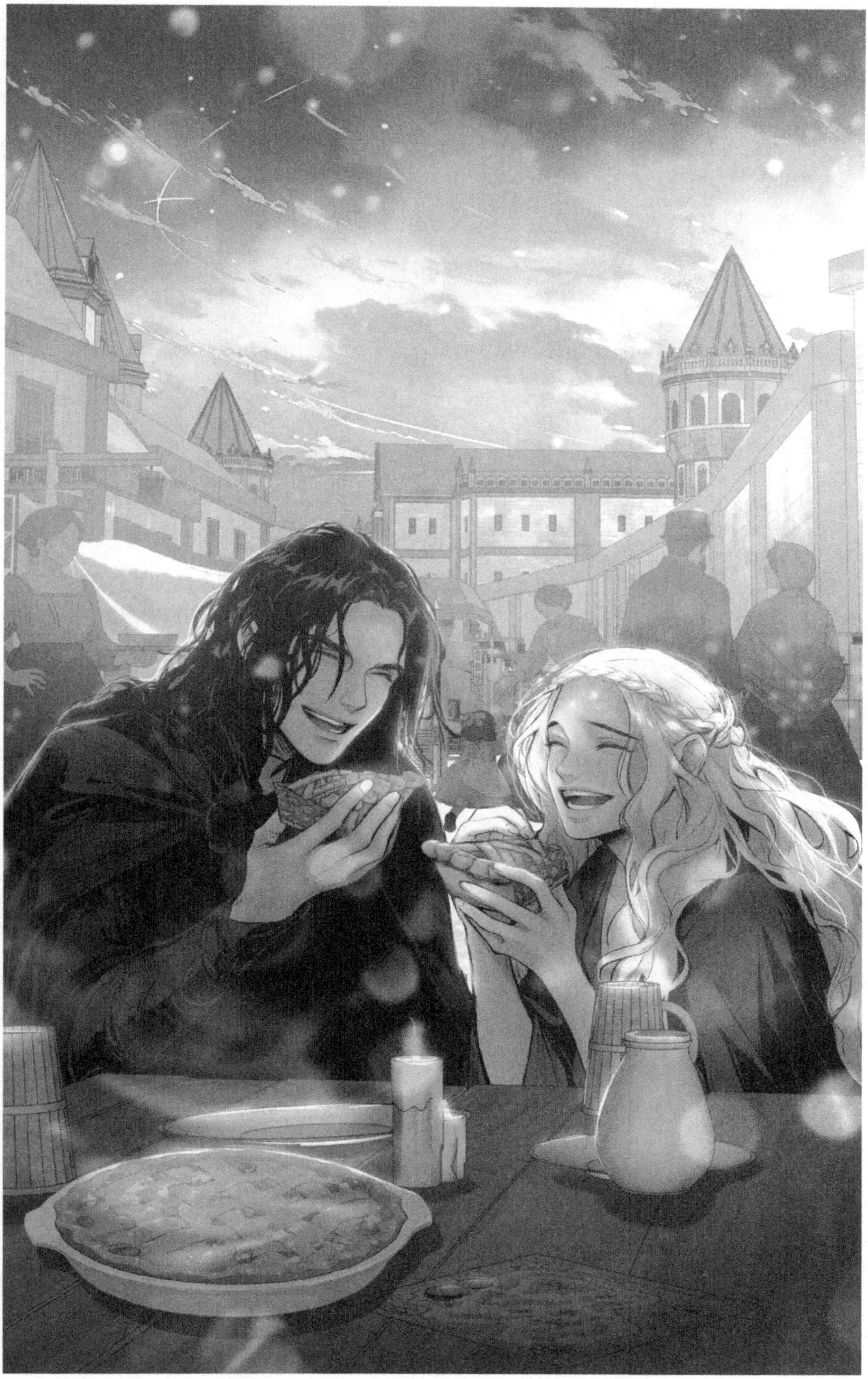

UMBERKERN PIE
(A beloved treat of both hearth and palace)

Ingredients:

1 9-inch pastry crust (prepared or homemade)
1 cup umberkern seeds (or substitute: whole pecans)
½ cup moonfruit syrup (or substitute: light corn syrup mixed with a spoonful of honey)
½ cup packed brown sugar
3 large eggs
3 tablespoons melted butter
1 teaspoon silverleaf extract (or substitute: pure vanilla extract)
½ teaspoon ground cinnamon
A pinch of fine salt
(Optional) ¼ cup chopped gilded dates (or substitute: regular dates tossed with a sprinkle of edible gold dust or just plain dates)

Instructions:

Preheat your oven to 350°F (175°C). Arrange your umberkern seeds (or pecans) in the bottom of your pastry shell. Scatter in the chopped gilded dates if using for an extra pop of sweetness.

In a mixing bowl, whisk together the moonfruit syrup, brown sugar, eggs, melted butter, silverleaf extract, cinnamon, and salt until smooth and glistening. Pour the mixture over the seeds in the pie shell, letting it seep into all the nooks and crannies. Bake for 50–55 minutes, or until the center is set and the top is a rich, toasty brown.

Cool completely before serving to allow the filling to set up properly — though few in the kingdom can resist stealing a warm slice right out of the pan.

Serving Suggestion:
Best enjoyed under the stars, with a dollop of snowberry cream (or regular whipped cream for the less adventurous).

The Legend of Umberkern Pie

They say Umberkern Pie was first baked by the forest dwarves — the Grimbroots, if you believe the old songs. They lived beneath the roots of the Fogwillow trees, soot-smudged and fussy.

One bitter winter, a lost child stumbled into their woods, nearly frozen to death. A soft-hearted Grimbroot grandmother wrapped him in a mossblanket, fed him a warm slice of pie, and tucked him beside the hearth. The boy survived — and he carried the story back with him.

The following spring, a curious village baker wandered into the forest, bearing a tart of his own as a gift. He and the dwarves traded recipes, argued about butter ratios, and eventually laughed over shared crumbs and secrets. From that unlikely meeting, the pie began its journey beyond the woods.

These days, Umberkern Pie graces royal banquets and village feasts alike. But between you and me? The dwarves still make it better.

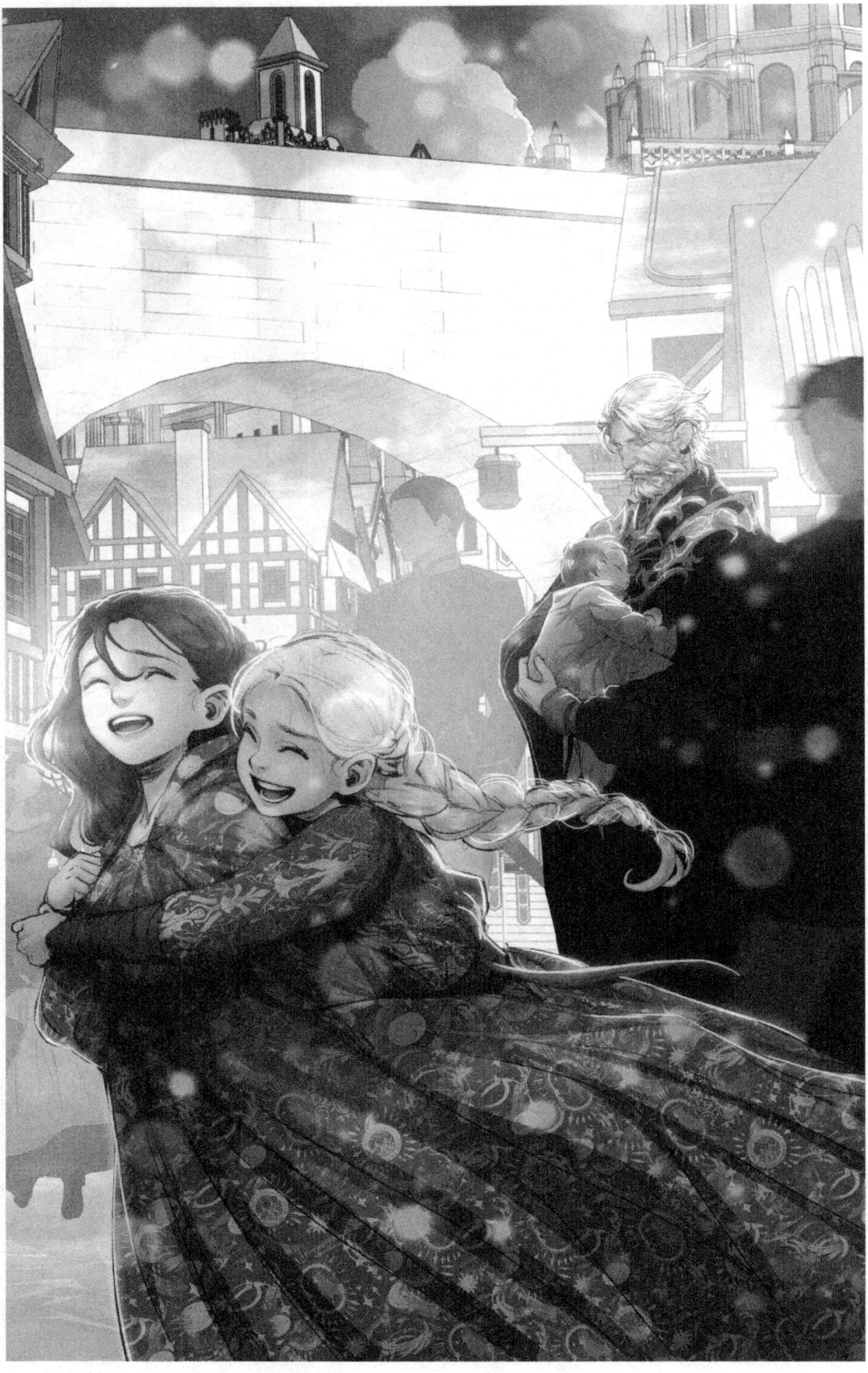

THE ARCANE BARGAIN
MINI COMIC

DO YOU TRULY UNDERSTAND WHAT YOU'RE AGREEING TO?

...YES.

GOOD.

THEN YOU UNDERSTAND THAT I EXPECT YOU TO SATISFY ME, TO GIVE YOURSELF TO ME WHENEVER I WANT YOU.

"YOUR BODY NOW BELONGS TO ME."

GODS. WHY DOES THE SOUND OF THAT... MAKE ME FEEL SO—

NO. THIS ISN'T ABOUT THAT. THIS ISN'T ABOUT WHATEVER PART OF ME STILL REMEMBERS THE WAY HE USED TO TOUCH ME...

...THE WAY HE USED TO LOOK AT ME BEFORE I RUINED EVERYTHING.

...I UNDERSTAND.

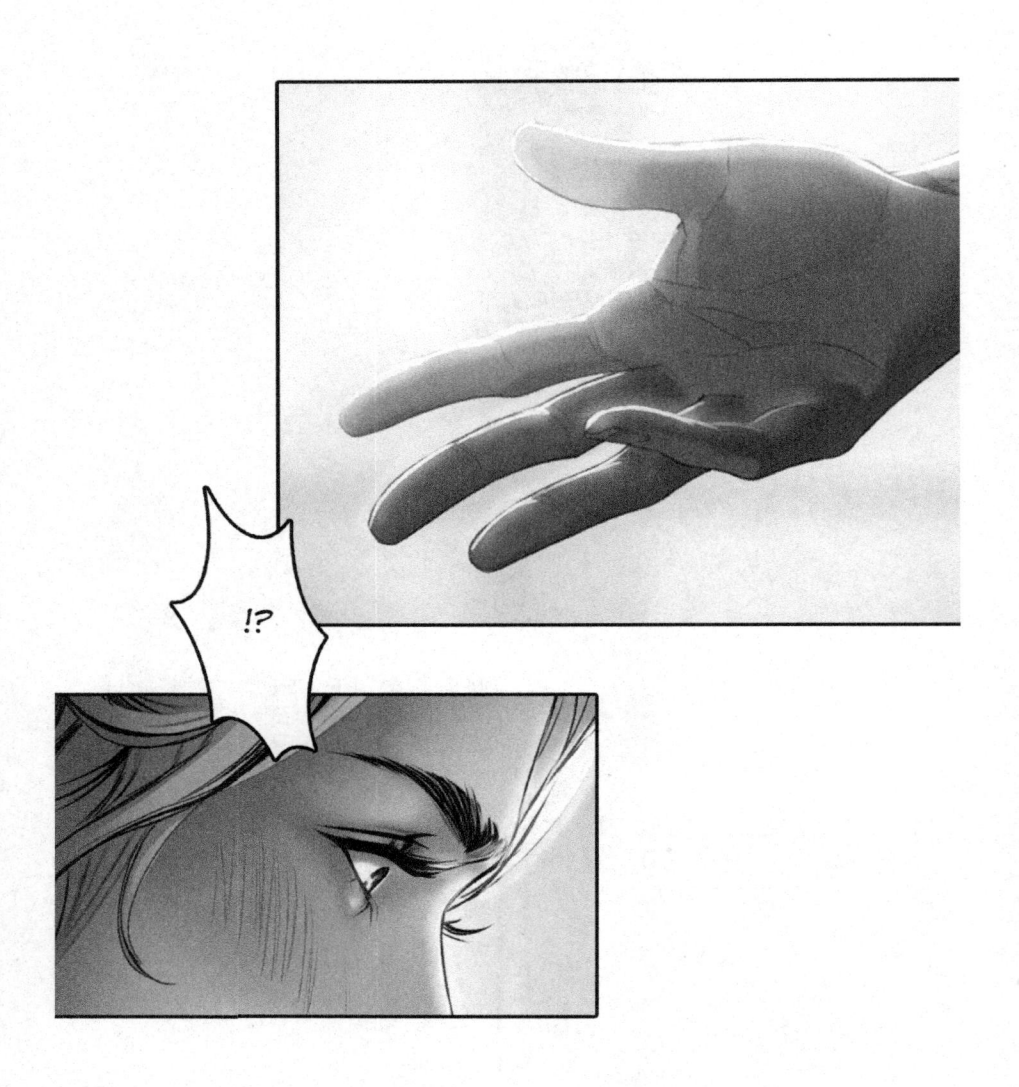

!?

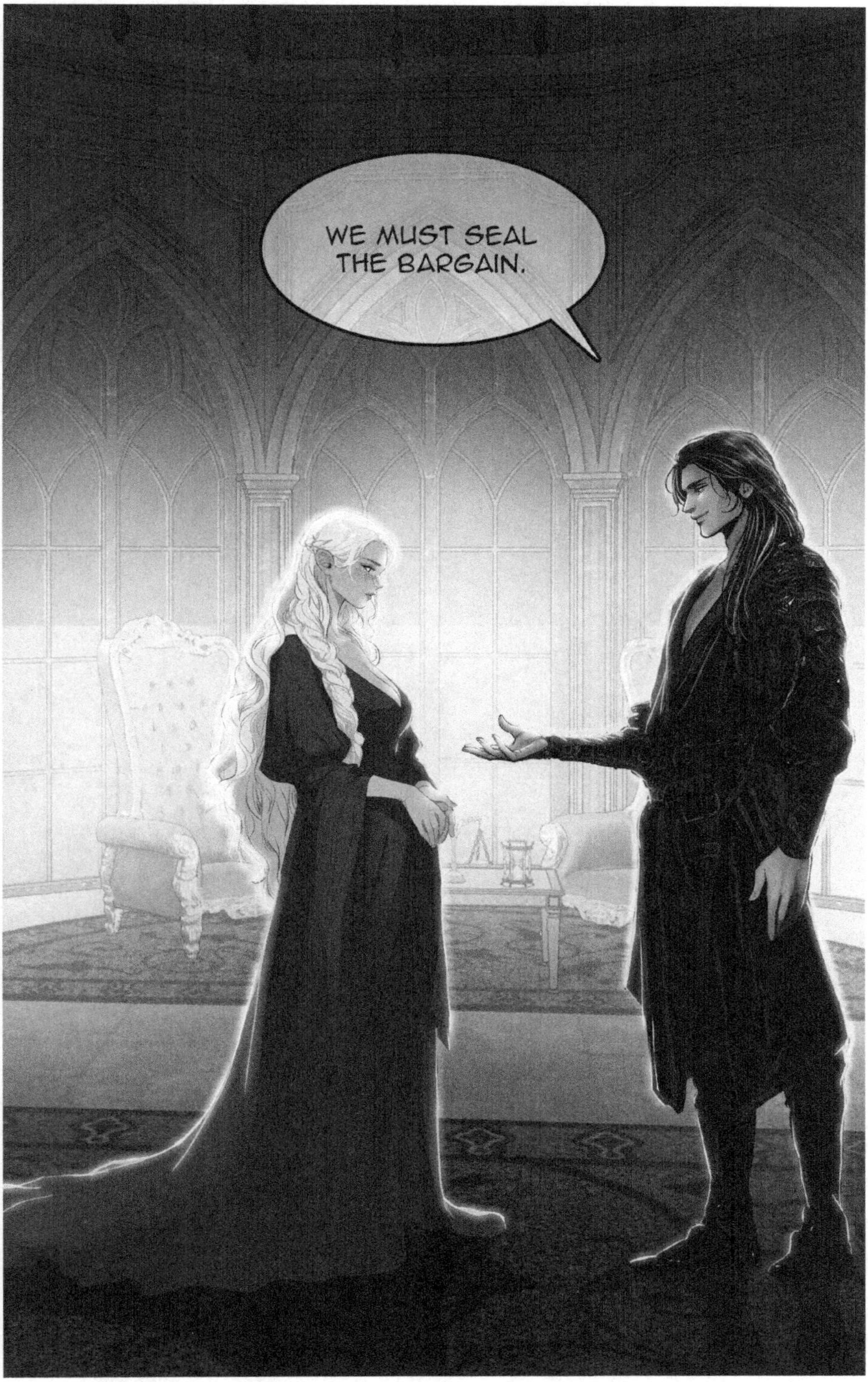
WE MUST SEAL THE BARGAIN.

HOW? A SPELL? A CONTRACT? A BLOOD DRAW?

GRAB

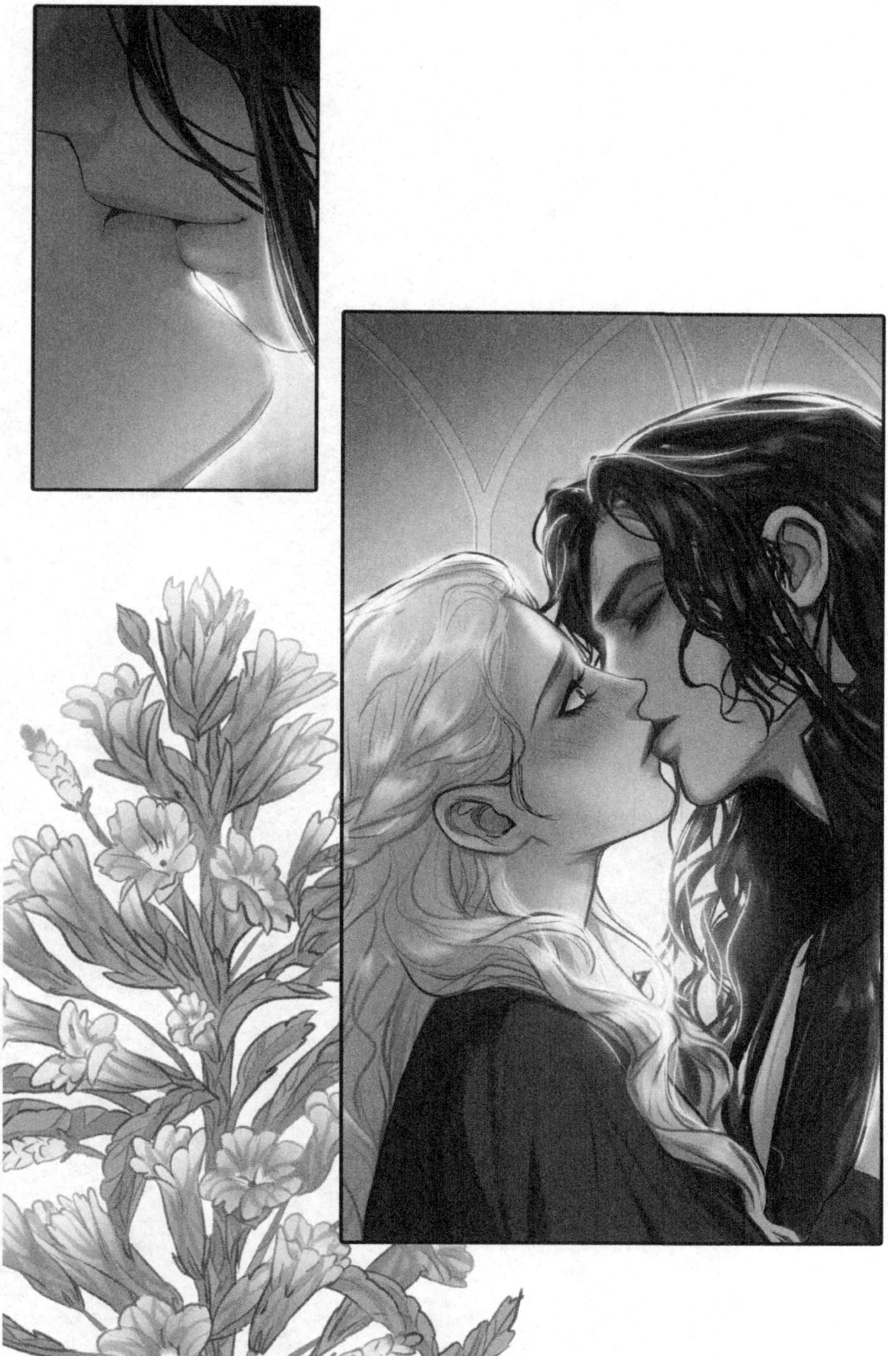

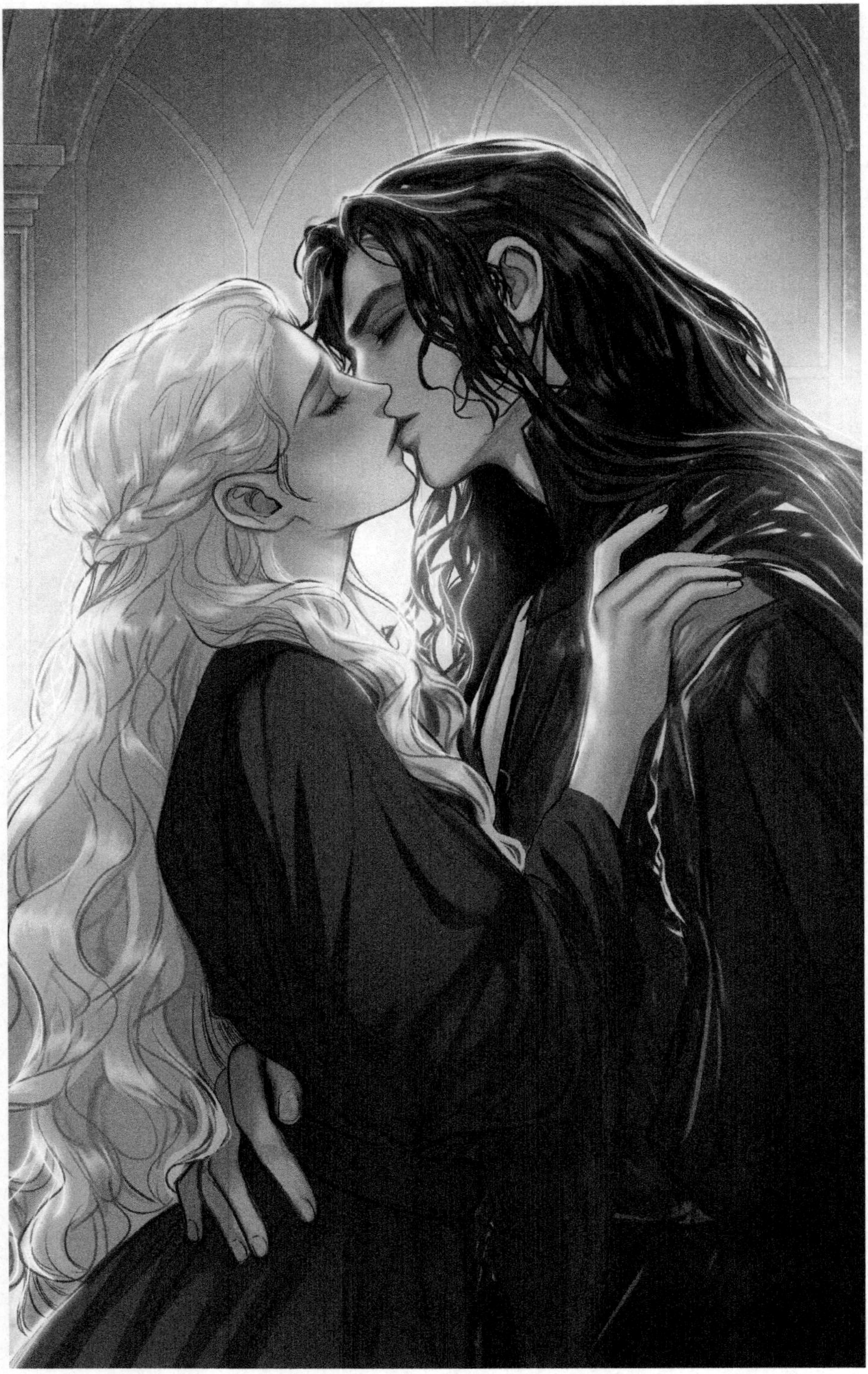

IS THAT...

...HOW YOU SEAL *ALL* YOUR BARGAINS?

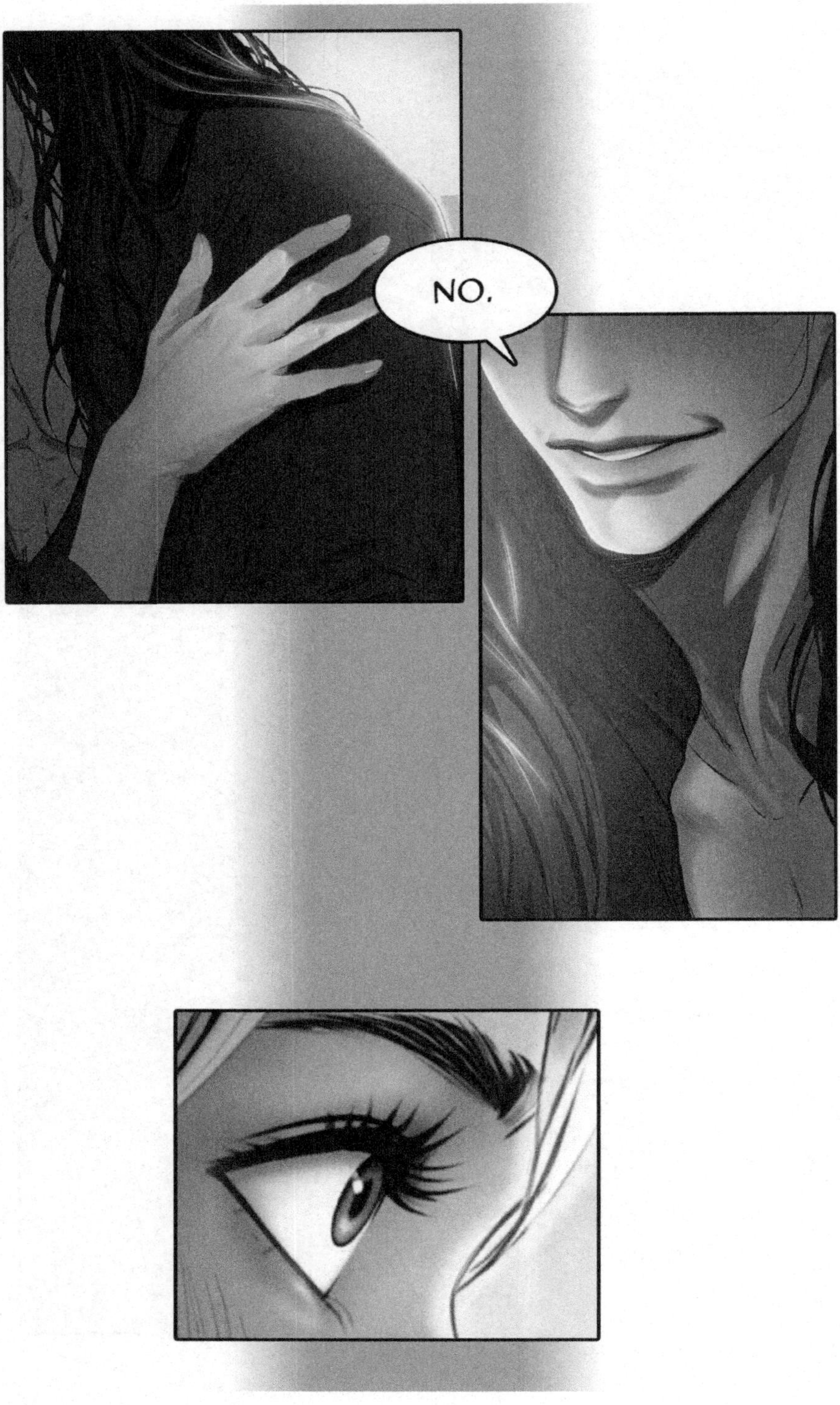
NO.

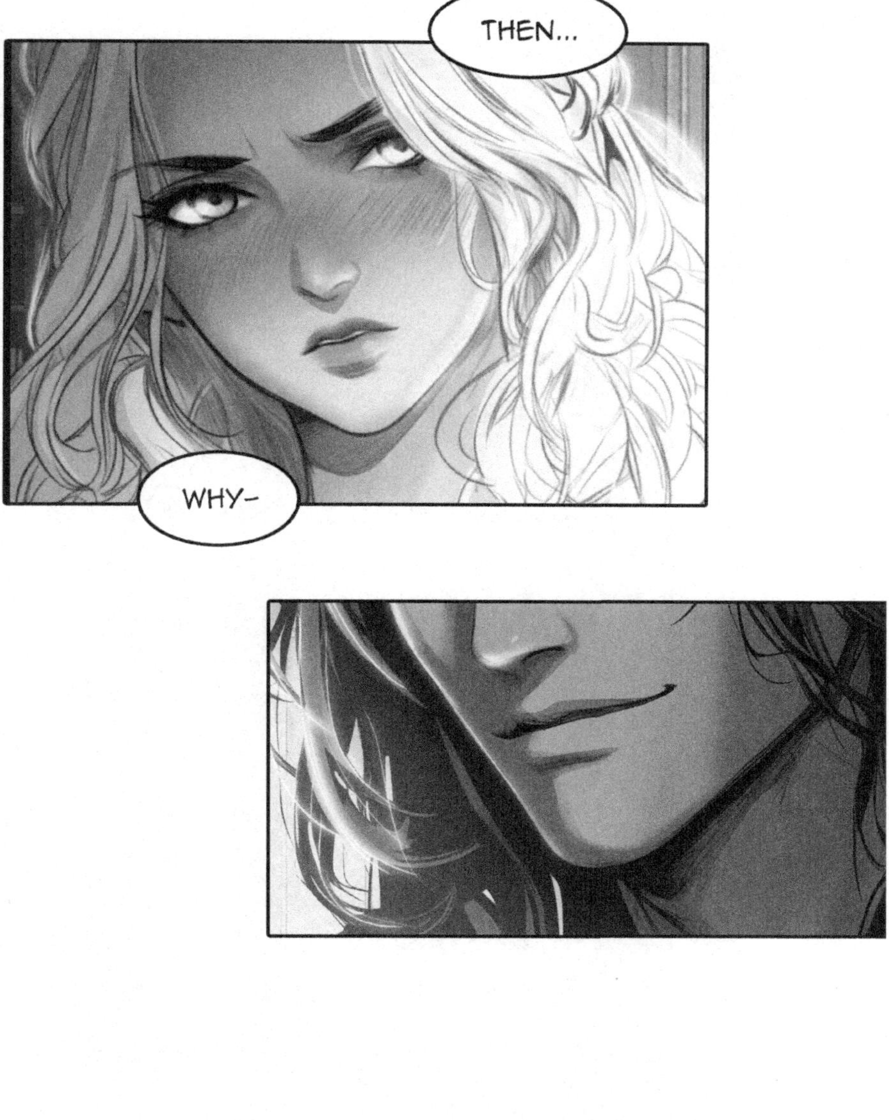
THEN...
WHY-
....

BECAUSE HE *COULD*.

BECAUSE HE *WANTED* TO.

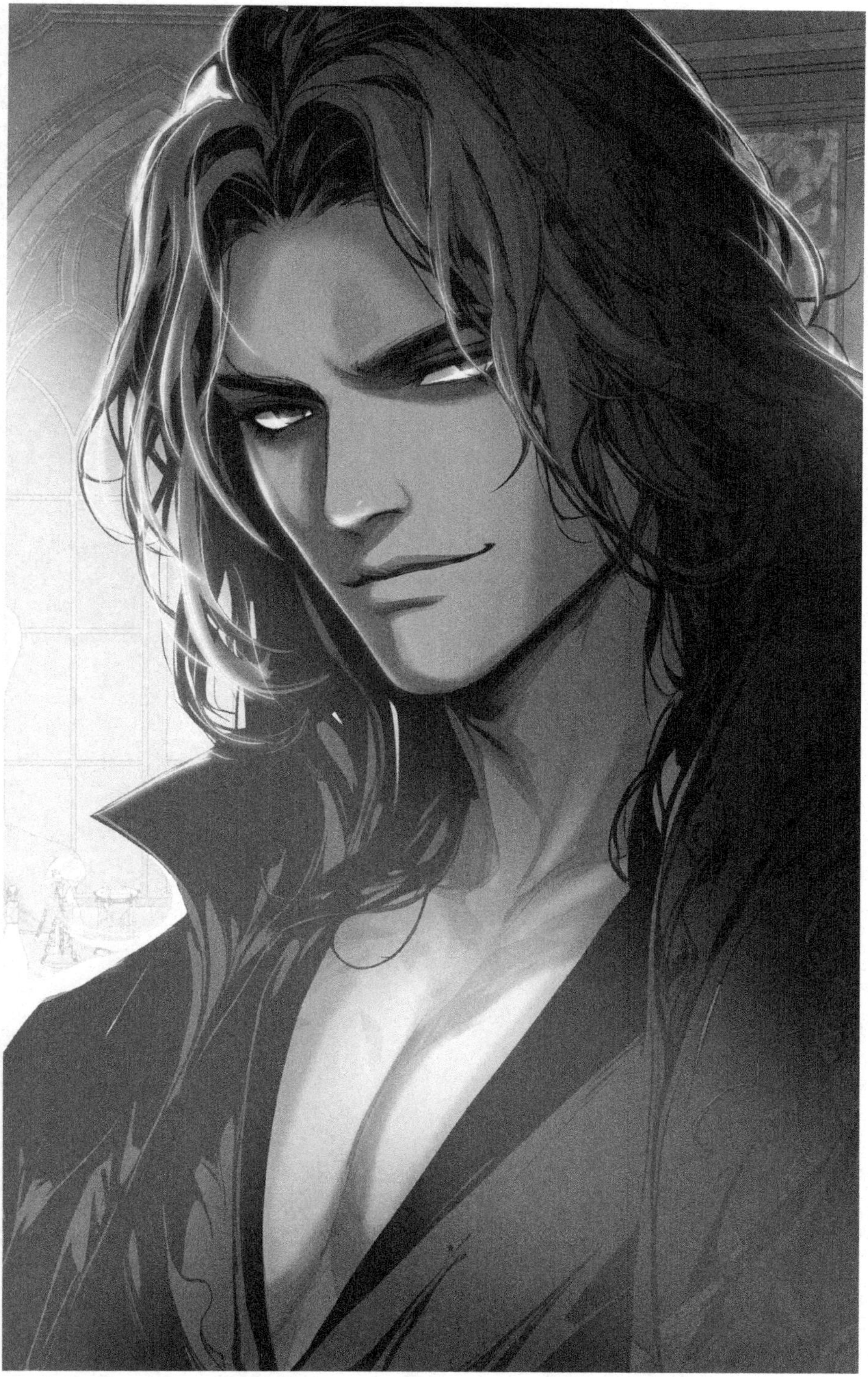

This story may be over... but the debt remains.

The oath Myrithia swore to the goddess Sylara was meant to save a life — but divine bargains are never without consequence. Somewhere in the Hollow Mist, that promise has stirred something ancient.

And now, a new story begins.

One where a goddess reborn meets the god who was never meant to be freed.
A god of chaos. A god of mischief. A god who remembers every sin against him... and plans to collect.

He has a score to settle.
She has everything to lose.
And there is nothing he won't demand from her.

NYXIAN

SYLARA

BONUS CONTENT

Need more content pertaining to The Arcane Bargain?

Please visit patreon.com/lifelight

For bonus scenes, artwork, trailers and more!

Printed in Dunstable, United Kingdom